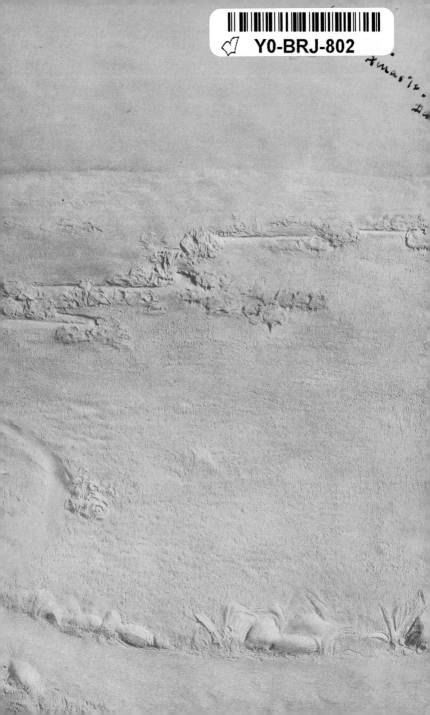

CORPORAL CAMERON

RALPH CONNOR

RALPH CONNOR'S NOVELS

CORPORAL CAMERON

THE FOREIGNER

BLACK ROCK

THE SKY PILOT

THE PROSPECTOR

THE DOCTOR

THE MAN FROM GLENGARRY

GLENGARRY SCHOOL DAYS

CORPORAL CAMERON

OF THE NORTH WEST MOUNTED POLICE

A TALE OF THE MACLEOD TRAIL

BY

RALPH CONNOR

AUTHOR OF "THE SKY PILOT," "THE FOREIGNER,"
"THE MAN FROM GLENGARRY," ETC.

HODDER & STOUGHTON
NEW YORK
GEORGE H. DORAN COMPANY

CONTENTS

BOOK I

CHAPTER   PAGE

   I THE QUITTER, ... 1

  II THE GLEN OF THE CUP OF GOLD, . . 14

III THE FAMILY SOLICITOR, ... 22

 IV A QUESTION OF HONOUR, ... 43

   V A LADY AND THE LAW, ... 55

 VI THE WASTER'S REFUGE, ... 82

VII FAREWELL TO CUAGH OIR, ... 105

VIII WILL HE COME BACK? 120

BOOK II

   I HO FOR THE OPEN! 135

  II A MAN'S JOB, ... 158

III A DAY'S WORK, ... 173

 IV A RAINY DAY, ... 199

   V HOW THEY SAVED THE DAY, . . . 226

 VI A SABBATH DAY IN LATE AUGUST, . . 258

VII THE CHIVAREE, ... 276

VIII IN APPLE TIME, ... 293

CONTENTS

BOOK III

CHAPTER   PAGE

    I THE CAMP BY THE GAP, ... 305

   II ON THE WINGS OF THE STORM, . . . 321

  III THE STONIES, ... 332

  IV THE DULL RED STAIN, ... 347

   V SERGEANT CRISP, ... 364

  VI A DAY IN THE MACLEOD BARRACKS, . . 375

 VII THE MAKING OF BRAVES, ... 399

VIII NURSE HALEY, ... 421

  IX "CORPORAL" CAMERON 434

BOOK ONE

CORPORAL CAMERON

CHAPTER I

THE QUITTER

"OH-H-H-H, Cam-er-on!" Agony, reproach, entreaty, vibrated in the clear young voice that rang out over the Inverleith grounds. The Scottish line was sagging!—that line invincible in two years of International conflict, the line upon which Ireland and England had broken their pride. Sagging! And because Cameron was weakening! Cameron, the brilliant half-back, the fierce-fighting, erratic young Highlander, disciplined, steadied by the great Dunn into an instrument of Scotland's glory! Cameron going back! A hush fell on the thronged seats and packed inner-circle,—a breathless, dreadful hush of foreboding. High over the hushed silence that vibrant cry rang; and Cameron heard it. The voice he knew. It was young Rob Dunn's, the captain's young brother, whose soul knew but two passions, one for the captain and one for the half-back of the Scottish International.

And Cameron responded. The enemy's next high punt found him rock-like in steadiness. And rock-like he tossed high over his shoulders the tow-headed Welshman rushing joyously at him, and delivered his ball far down the line safe into touch. But after his kick he was observed to limp back into his place. The fierce pace of the Welsh forwards was drinking the life of the Scottish backline.

An hour; then a half; then another half, without a score. And now the final quarter was searching, searching the weak spots in their line. The final quarter it is that finds a man's history and habits; the clean of blood and of life defy its pitiless probe, but the rotten fibre yields and snaps. That momentary weakness of Cameron's like a subtle poison runs through the Scottish line; and like fluid lightning through the Welsh. It is the touch upon the trembling balance. With cries exultant with triumph, the Welsh forwards fling themselves upon the steady Scots now fighting for life rather than for victory. And under their captain's directions these fierce, victory-sniffing Welsh are delivering their attack upon the spot where he fancies he has found a yielding. In vain Cameron rallies his powers; his nerve is failing him, his strength is done. Only five minutes to play, but one minute is enough. Down upon him through a broken field, dribbling the ball and following hard like hounds on a hare, come the Welsh, the tow-head raging in front, bloody and fearsome. There is but one thing for Cameron to do; grip that tumbling ball, and, committing body and soul to fate, plunge into that line. Alas, his doom is upon him! He grips the ball, pauses a moment—only a fatal moment,—but it is enough. His plunge is too late. He loses the ball. A surge of Welshmen overwhelm him in the mud and carry the ball across. The game is won—and lost. What though the Scots, like demons suddenly released from hell, the half-back Cameron most demon-like of all, rage over the field, driving the Welshmen hither and thither at will, the gods deny them victory; it is for Wales that day!

In the retreat of their rubbing-room the gay, gallant humour which the Scots have carried with them off the field of their defeat, vanishes into gloom. Through the steaming silence a groan breaks now and then. At length a voice:

"Oh, wasn't it rotten! The rank quitter that he is!"

"Quitter? Who is? Who says so?" It was the captain's voice, sharp with passion.

"I do, Dunn. It was Cameron lost us the game. You know it, too. I know it's rotten to say this, but I can't help it. Cameron lost the game, and I say he's a rank 'quitter,' as Martin would say."

"Look here, Nesbitt," the captain's voice was quiet, but every man paused in his rubbing. "I know how sore you are and I forgive you that; but I don't want to hear from you or from any man on the team that word again. Cameron is no quitter; he made—he made an error,—he wasn't fit,—but I say to you Cameron is no quitter."

While he was speaking the door opened and into the room came a player, tall, lanky, with a pale, gaunt face, plastered over the forehead with damp wisps of straight, black hair. His deep-set, blue-grey eyes swept the room.

"Thanks, Dunn," he said hoarsely. "Let them curse me! I deserve it all. It's tough for them, but God knows I've got the worst of it. I've played my last game." His voice broke huskily.

"Oh, rot it, Cameron," cried Dunn. "Don't be an ass! Your first big game—every fellow makes his mistake—"

"Mistake! Mistake! You can't lie easily, Dunn. I was a fool and worse than a fool. I let myself down and I wasn't fit. Anyway, I'm through with it." His voice was wild and punctuated with unaccustomed oaths; his breath came in great sobs.

"Oh, rot it, Cameron!" again cried Dunn. "Next year you'll be twice the man. You're just getting into your game."

Right loyally his men rallied to their captain:

"Right you are!"

"Why, certainly; no man gets into the game first year!"

"We'll give 'em beans next year, Cameron, old man!"

They were all eager to atone for the criticism which all had held in their hearts and which one of them had spoken. But this business was serious. To lose a game was bad enough, but to round on a comrade was unpardonable; while to lose from the game a half-back of Cameron's calibre was unthinkable.

Meanwhile Cameron was tearing off his football togs and hustling on his clothes with fierce haste. Dunn kept his eye on him, hurrying his own dressing and chatting quietly the while. But long before he was ready for the street, Cameron had crushed his things into a bag and was looking for his hat.

"Hold on! I'm with you; I'm with you in a jiffy," said Dunn.

"My hat," muttered Cameron, searching wildly among the jumble.

"Oh, hang the hat; let it go! Wait for me, Cameron. Where are you going?" cried Dunn.

"To the devil," cried the lad, slamming the door behind him.

"And, by Jove, he'll go, too!" said Nesbitt. "Say, I'm awfully sorry I made that break, Dunn. It was beastly low-down to round on a chap like that. I'll go after him."

"Do, old chap! He's frightfully cut up. And get him for to-night. He may fight shy of the dinner. But he's down for the pipes, you know, and—well, he's just got to be there. Good-bye, you chaps; I'm off! And—I say, men!" When Dunn said "men" they all knew it was their captain that was speaking. Everybody stood listening. Dunn hesitated a moment or two, as if searching for words. "About the dinner to-night: I'd like you to remember—I mean—I don't want any man to—oh, hang it, you know what I mean! There will be lots of fellows there who will want to fill you up. I'd hate to see any of our team—" The captain paused embarrassed.

"We tumble, Captain," said Martin, a medical student from Canada, who played quarter. "I'll keep an eye on 'em, you bet!"

Everybody roared; for not only on the quarter-line but also at the dinner table the little quarter-back was a marvel of endurance.

"Hear the blooming Colonist!" said Linklater, Martin's comrade on the quarter-line, and his greatest friend. "We know who'll want the watching, but we'll see to him, Captain."

"All right, old chap! Sorry I'll have to cut the van. I'm afraid my governor's got the carriage here for me."

But the men all made outcry. There were other plans for him.

"But, Captain; hold on!"

"Aw, now, Captain! Don't forsake us!"

"But I say, Dunn, see us through; we're shy!"

"Don't leave us, Captain, or you'll be sorry," sang out Martin. "Come on, fellows, let's keep next him! We'll give him 'Old Grimes!'"

Already a mighty roar was heard outside. The green, the drive, the gateways, and the street were blocked with the wildest football fanatics that Edinburgh, and all Scotland could produce. They were waiting for the International players, and were bent on carrying their great captain down the street, shoulder high; for the enthusiasm of the Scot reaches the point of madness only in the hour of glorious defeat. But before they were aware, Dunn had shouldered his mighty form through the opposing crowds and had got safely into the carriage beside his father and his young brother. But the crowd were bound to have him.

"We want him, Docthor," said a young giant in a tam-o'-shanter. "In fac', Docthor," he argued with a humourous smile, "we maun hae him."

"Ye'll no' get him, Jock Murchison," shouted young Rob, standing in front of his big brother. "We want him wi' us."

The crowd laughed gleefully.

"Go for him, Jock! You can easy lick him," said a voice encouragingly.

"Pit him oot, Docthor," said Jock, who was a great friend of the family, and who had a profound respect for the doctor.

"It's beyond me, Jock, I fear. See yon bantam cock! I doubt ye'll hae to be content," said the doctor, dropping into Jock's kindly Doric.

"Oh, get on there, Murchison," said Dunn impatiently. "You're not going to make an ass of me; make up your mind to that!"

Jock hesitated, meditating a sudden charge, but checked by his respect for Doctor Dunn.

"Here, you fellows!" shouted a voice. "Fall in; the band is going to play! Get into line there, you Tam-o'-shanter; you're stopping the procesh! Now then, wait for the line, everybody!" It was Little Martin on top of the van in which were the Scottish players. "Tune, 'Old Grimes'; words as follows. Catch on, everybody!"

"Old Dunn, old Dunn, old Dunn, old Dunn,
Old Dunn, old Dunn, old Dunn,
Old Dunn, old Dunn, old Dunn, old Dunn,
Old Dunn, old Dunn, old Dunn."

With a delighted cheer the crowd formed in line, and,

led by the little quarter-back on top of the van, they set off down the street, two men at the heads of the doctor's carriage horses, holding them in place behind the van. On went the swaying crowd and on went the swaying chant, with Martin director of ceremonies and Dunn hurling unavailing objurgations and entreaties at Jock's head.

Through the uproar a girl's voice reached the doctor's ear:

"Aren't they lovely, Sir?"

The doctor turned to greet a young lady, tall, strong, and with the beauty of perfect health rather than of classic feature in her face. There was withal a careless disregard of the feminine niceties of dress.

"Oh, Miss Brodie! Will you not come up? We can easily make room."

"I'd just love to," cried the girl, "but I'm only a humble member of the procession, following the band and the chariot wheels of the conqueror." Her strong brown face was all aglow with ardour.

"Conqueror!" growled Dunn. "Not much of a conqueror!"

"Why not? Oh fudge! The game? What matters the game? It's the play we care about."

"Well spoken, lassie," said the doctor. "That's the true sport."

"Aren't they awful?" cried Dunn. "Look at that young Canadian idiot up there."

"Well, if you ask me, I think he's a perfect dear," said Miss Brodie, deliberately. "I'm sure I know him; anyway I'm going to encourage him with my approval." And she waved her hand at Martin.

The master of ceremonies responded by taking off his hat and making a sweeping bow, still keeping up the beat. The crowd, following his eyes, turned their attention to the young lady, much to Dunn's delight.

"Oh," she gasped, "they'll be chanting me next! Good-bye! I'm off!" And she darted back to the company of her friends marching on the pavement.

At this point Martin held up both arms and called for silence.

"Second verse," he shouted, "second verse! Get the words now!"

> "Old Dunn ain't done, old Dunn ain't done,
>   Old Dunn, old Dunn ain't done,
> Old Dunn ain't done, old Dunn ain't done,
>   Old Dunn, old Dunn ain't done."

But the crowd rejected the Colonial version, and rendered in their own good Doric:

> "Old Dunn's no' done, old Dunn's no' done,
>   Old Dunn, old Dunn's no' done,
> Old Dunn's no' done, old Dunn's no' done,
>   Old Dunn, old Dunn's no' done."

And so they sang and swayed, following the van till they neared Queen Street, down which lay the doctor's course.

"For heaven's sake, can't they be choked off?" groaned Dunn.

The doctor signalled Jock to him.

"Jock," he said, "we'll just slip through at Queen Street."

"We'd like awfully to do Princes Street, Sir," pleaded Jock.

"Princes Street, you born ass!" cried Dunn wrathfully.

"Oh, yes, let them!" cried young Rob, whose delight in the glory of his hero had been beyond all measure. "Let them do Princes Street, just once!"

But the doctor would not have it. "Jock," he said quietly, "just get us through at Queen Street."

"All right, Sir," replied Jock with great regret. "It will be as you say."

Under Jock's orders, when Queen Street was reached, the men at the horses' heads suddenly swung the pair from the crowd, and after some struggling, got them safely into the clear space, leaving the procession to follow the van, loudly cheering their great International captain, whose prowess on the field was equalled only by his modesty and his hatred of a demonstration.

"Listen to the idiots," said Dunn in disgust, as the carriage bore them away from the cheering crowd.

"Man, they're just fine! Aren't they, Father?" said young Rob in an ecstasy of joy.

"They're generous lads, generous lads, boy," said Doctor Dunn, his old eyes shining, for his son's triumph touched him deeply. "That's the only way to take defeat."

"That's all right, Sir," said Dunn quickly, "but it's rather embarrassing, though it's awfully decent of them."

The doctor's words suggested fresh thoughts to young Rob. "But it was terrible; and you were just on the win, too, I know."

"I'm not so sure at all," said his brother.

"Oh, it is terrible," said Rob again.

"Tut, tut, lad! What's so terrible?" said his father. "One side has to lose."

"Oh, it's not that," said Rob, his lip trembling. "I don't care a sniff for the game."

"What, then?" said his big brother in a voice sharpened by his own thoughts.

"Oh, Jack," said Rob, nervously wreathing his hands,

"he—it looked as if he—" the lad could not bring himself to say the awful word. Nor was there need to ask who it was the boy had in mind.

"What do you mean, Rob?" the captain's voice was impatient, almost angry.

Then Rob lost his control. "Oh, Jack, I can't help it; I saw it. Do you think—did he really *funk* it?" His voice broke. He clutched his brother's knee and stood with face white and quivering. He had given utterance to the terrible suspicion that was torturing his heroic young soul. Of his two household gods one was tottering on its pedestal. That a football man should *funk*— the suspicion was too dreadful.

The captain glanced at his father's face. There was gloom there, too, and the same terrible suspicion. "No, Sir," said Dunn, with impressive deliberation, answering the look on his father's face, "Cameron is no quitter. He didn't *funk*. I think," he continued, while Rob's tear-stained face lifted eagerly, "I know he was out of condition; he had let himself run down last week, since the last match, indeed, got out of hand a bit, you know, and that last quarter—you know, Sir, that last quarter was pretty stiff—his nerve gave just for a moment."

"Oh," said the doctor in a voice of relief, "that explains it. But," he added quickly in a severe tone, "it was very reprehensible for a man on the International to let himself get out of shape, very reprehensible indeed. An International, mind you!"

"It was my fault, Sir," I'm afraid," said Dunn, regretfully. "I ought to have—"

"Nonsense! A man must be responsible for himself. Control, to be of any value, must be ultroneous, as our old professor used to say."

"That's true, Sir, but I had kept pretty close to him up to the last week, you see, and—"

"Bad training, bad training. A trainer's business is to school his men to do without him."

"That is quite right, Sir. I believe I've been making a mistake," said Dunn thoughtfully. "Poor chap, he's awfully cut up!"

"So he should be," said the doctor sternly. "He had no business to get out of condition. The International, mind you!"

"Oh, Father, perhaps he couldn't help it," cried Rob, whose loyal, tender heart was beating hard against his little ribs, "and he looks awful. I saw him come out and when I called to him he never looked at me once."

There is no finer loyalty in this world than that of a boy below his teens. It is so without calculation, without qualification, and without reserve. Dr. Dunn let his eyes rest kindly upon his little flushed face.

"Perhaps so, perhaps so, my boy," he said, "and I have no doubt he regrets it now more than any of us. Where has he gone?"

"Nesbitt's after him, Sir. He'll get him for to-night."

But as Dunn, fresh from his bath, but still sore and stiff, was indulging in a long-banished pipe, Nesbitt came in to say that Cameron could not be found.

"And have you not had your tub yet?" said his captain.

"Oh, that's all right! You know I feel awfully about that beastly remark of mine."

"Oh, let it go," said Dunn. "That'll be all right. You get right away home for your tub and get freshened up for to-night. I'll look after Cameron. You know he is down for the pipes. He's simply got to be there, and

I'll get him if I have to bring him in a crate, pipes, kilt and all."

And Nesbitt, knowing that Dunn never promised what he could not fulfil, went off to his tub in fair content. He knew his captain.

As Dunn was putting on his coat Rob came in, distress written on his face.

"Are you going to get Cameron, Jack?" he asked timidly. "I asked Nesbitt, and he said—"

"Now look here, youngster," said his big brother, then paused. The distress in the lad's face checked his words. "Now, Rob," he said kindly, "you needn't fret about this. Cameron is all right.

The kind tone broke down the lad's control. He caught his brother's arm. "Say, Jack, are you sure—he didn't—*funk?*" His voice dropped to a whisper.

Then his big brother sat down and drew the lad to his side. "Now listen, Rob; I'm going to tell you the exact truth. *Cameron did not funk.* The truth is, he wasn't fit,—he ought to have been, but he wasn't,—and because he wasn't fit he came mighty near quitting—for a moment, I'm sure, he felt like it, because his nerve was gone,—but he didn't. Remember, he felt like quitting and didn't. And that's the finest thing a chap can do,— never to quit, even when he feels like it. Do you see?"

The lad's head went up. "I see," he said, his eyes glowing. "It was fine! I'm awfully glad he didn't quit, 'specially when he felt like it. You tell him for me." His idol was firm again on his pedestal.

"All right, old chap," said his big brother. "You'll never quit, I bet!"

"Not if I'm fit, will I?"

"Right you are! Keep fit—that's the word!"

And with that the big brother passed out to find the

man who was writhing in an agony of self-contempt; for in the face of all Scotland and in the hour of her need he had failed because he wasn't fit.

After an hour Dunn found his man, fixed in the resolve to there and then abandon the game with all the appurtenances thereof, and among these the dinner. Mightily his captain laboured with him, plying him with varying motives,—the honour of the team was at stake; the honour of the country was at stake; his own honour, for was he not down on the programme for the pipes? It was all in vain. In dogged gloom the half-back listened unmoved.

At length Dunn, knowing well the Highlander's tender heart, cunningly touched another string and told of Rob's distress and subsequent relief, and then gave his half-back the boy's message. "I promised to tell you, and I almost forgot. The little beggar was terribly worked up, and as I remember it, this is what he said: 'I'm awfully glad he didn't quit, 'specially when he felt like it.' Those were his very words."

Then Cameron buried his face in his hands and groaned aloud, while Dunn, knowing that he had reached his utmost, stood silent, waiting. Suddenly Cameron flung up his head:

"Did he say I didn't quit? Good little soul! I'll go; I'd go through hell for that!"

And so it came that not in a crate, but in the gallant garb of a Highland gentleman, pipes and all, Cameron was that night in his place, fighting out through the long hilarious night the fiercest fight of his life, chiefly because of the words that lay like a balm to his lacerated heart:

"He didn't quit, 'specially when he felt like it."

CHAPTER II

THE GLEN OF THE CUP OF GOLD

JUST over the line of the Grampians, near the head-waters of the Spey, a glen, small and secluded, lies bedded deep among the hills,—a glen that when filled with sunlight on a summer day lies like a cup of gold; the gold all liquid and flowing over the cup's rim. And hence they call the glen "The Cuagh Oir," The Glen of the Cup of Gold.

At the bottom of the Cuagh, far down, a little loch gleams, an oval of emerald or of sapphire, according to the sky above that smiles into its depths. On dark days the loch can gloom, and in storm it can rage, white-lipped, just like the people of the Glen.

Around the emerald or sapphire loch farmlands lie sunny and warm, set about their steadings, and are on this spring day vivid with green, or rich in their red-browns where the soil lies waiting for the seed. Beyond the sunny fields the muirs of brown heather and bracken climb abruptly up to the dark-massed firs, and they to the Cuagh's rim. But from loch to rim, over field and muir and forest, the golden, liquid light ever flows on a sunny day and fills the Cuagh Oir till it runs over.

On the east side of the loch, among some ragged firs, a rambling Manor House, ivy-covered and ancient, stood; and behind it, some distance away, the red tiling of a farm-cottage, with its steading clustering near, could be seen. About the old Manor House the lawn and garden told of neglect and decay, but at the farmhouse order reigned. The trim little garden plot, the trim lawn, the trim walks and hedges, the trim thatch of the roof, the trim do'-cote above it, the trim stables, byres, barns and yard of the steading, proclaimed the prudent, thrifty care of a prudent, thrifty soul.

And there in the steading quadrangle, amidst the feathered creatures, hens, cocks and chicks, ducks, geese, turkeys and bubbly-jocks, stood the mistress of the Manor and prudent, thrifty manager of the farm,—a girl of nineteen, small, well-made, and trim as the farmhouse and its surroundings, with sunny locks and sunny face and sunny brown eyes. Her shapely hands were tanned and coarsened by the weather; her little feet were laced in stout country-made brogues; her dress was a plain brown winsey, kilted and belted open at the full round neck; the kerchief that had fallen from her sunny, tangled hair was of simple lawn, spotless and fresh; among her fowls she stood, a country lass in habit and occupation, but in face and form, in look and poise, a lady every inch of her. Dainty and daunty, sweet and strong, she stood, "the bonny like o' her bonny mither," as said the South Country nurse, Nannie, who had always lived at the Glen Cuagh House from the time that that mother was a baby; "but no' sae fine like," the nurse would add with a sigh. For she remembered ever the gentle airs and the high-bred, stately grace of Mary Robertson,—for though married to Captain Cameron of Erracht, Mary Robertson she continued to be to the Glen folk,—the lady of her ancestral manor, now for five years lain under the birch trees yonder by the church tower that looked out from its clustering firs and birches on the slope beyond the loch. Five years ago the gentle lady had passed from them, but like the liquid, golden sunlight, and like the perfume of the heather and the firs, the aroma of her saintly life still filled the Glen.

A year after that grief had fallen, Moira, her one daughter, "the bonny like o' her bonny mither, though no' sae fine," had somehow slipped into command of the House Farm, the only remaining portion of the wide demesne of farmlands once tributary to the House. And by the thrift which she learned from her South Country nurse in the care of her poultry and her pigs, and by her shrewd oversight of the thriftless, doddling Highland farmer and his more thriftless and more doddling womenfolk, she brought the farm to order and to a basis of profitable returns. And this, too, with so little "clash and claver" that her father only knew that somehow things were more comfortable about the place, and that there were fewer calls than formerly upon his purse for the upkeep of the House and home. Indeed, the less appeared Moira's management, both in the routine of the House and in the care of the farm, the more peacefully flowed the current of their life. It seriously annoyed the Captain at intervals when he came upon his daughter directing operations in barnyard or byre. That her directing meant anything more than a girlish meddling in matters that were his entire concern and about which he had already given or was about to give orders, the Captain never dreamed. That things about the House were somehow prospering in late years he set down to his own skill and management and his own knowledge of scientific farming; a knowledge which, moreover, he delighted to display at the annual dinners of the Society for the Improvement of Agriculture in the Glen, of which he was honourary secretary; a knowledge which he aired in lengthy articles in local agricultural and other periodicals; a knowledge which, however, at times became the occasion of dismay to his thrifty daughter and her Highland farmer, and not seldom the occasion of much useless expenditure of guineas hard won from pigs and poultry. True, more serious loss was often averted by the facility with which the Captain turned from one scheme to another, happily forgetful of orders he had given and which were never carried out; and by the invincible fabianism of the Highland farmer, who, listening with gravest attention to the Captain's orders delivered in the most definite and impressive terms, would make reply, "Yess, yess indeed, I know; she will be attending to it immediately—to-morrow, or fery soon whateffer." It cannot be said that this capacity for indefinite procrastination rendered the Highlander any less valuable to his "tear young leddy."

The days on which Postie appeared with a large bundle of mail were accounted good days by the young mistress, for on these and succeeding days her father would be "busy with his correspondence." And these days were not few, for the Captain held many honourary offices in county and other associations for the promotion and encouragement of various activities, industrial, social, and philanthropic. Of the importance of these activities to the county and national welfare, the Captain had no manner of doubt, as his voluminous correspondence testified. As to the worth of his correspondence his daughter, too, held the highest opinion, estimating her father, as do all dutiful daughters, at his own valuation. For the Captain held himself in high esteem; not simply for his breeding, which was of the Camerons of Erracht; nor for his manners, which were of the most courtly, if occasionally marred by fretfulness; nor for his dress, which was that of a Highland gentleman, perfect in detail and immaculate, but for his many and public services rendered to the people, the county, and the nation. Indeed his mere membership dues to the various associations, societies and committees with which he was connected, and his dining expenses contingent upon their annual meetings, together with the amounts expended upon the equipment and adornment of his person proper to such festive occasions, cut so deep into the slender resources of the family as to give his prudent daughter some considerable concern; though it is safe to say that such concern her father would have regarded not only as unnecessary but almost as impertinent.

The Captain's correspondence, however extensive, was on the whole regarded by his daughter as a good rather than an evil, in that it secured her domestic and farm activities from disturbing incursions. This spring morning Moira's apprehensions awakened by an extremely light mail, were realized, as she beheld her father bearing down upon her with an open letter in his hand. His handsome face was set in a fretful frown.

"Moira, my daughter!" he exclaimed, "how often have I spoke to you about this—this—unseemly—ah—mussing and meddling in the servants' duties!"

"But, Papa," cried his daughter, "look at these dear things! I love them and they all know me, and they behave so much better when I feed them myself. Do they not, Janet?" she added, turning to the stout and sonsy farmer's daughter standing by.

"Indeed, then, they are clever at knowing you," replied the maid, whose particular duty was to hold a reserve supply of food for the fowls that clamoured and scrambled about her young mistress.

"Look at that vain bubbly-jock there, Papa," cried Moira, "he loves to have me notice him. Conceited creature! Look out, Papa, he does not like your kilts!" The bubbly-jock, drumming and scraping and sidling ever nearer to the Captain's naked knees, finally with great outcry flew straight at the affronting kilts.

"Get off with you, you beast!" cried the Captain, kicking vainly at the wrathful bird, and at the same time beating a wise retreat before his onset.

Moira rushed to his rescue. "Hoot, Jock! Shame on ye!" she cried. "There now, you proud thing, be off! He's just jealous of your fine appearance, Papa." With her kerchief she flipped into submission the haughty bubbly-jock and drew her father out of the steading. "Come away, Papa, and see my pigs."

But the Captain was in no humour for pigs. "Nonsense, child," he cried, "let us get out of this mess! Besides, I wish to speak to you on a matter of importance." They passed through the gate. "It is about Allan," he continued, "and I'm really vexed. Something terrible has happened."

"Allan!" the girl's voice was faint and her sunny cheek grew white. "About Allan!" she said again. "And what is wrong with Allan, Papa?"

"That's what I do not know," replied her father fretfully; "but I must away to Edinburgh this very day, so you'll need to hasten with my packing. And bid Donald bring round the cart at once."

But Moira stood dazed. "But, Papa, you have not told me what is wrong with Allan." Her voice was quiet, but with a certain insistence in it that at once irritated her father and compelled his attention.

"Tut, tut, Moira, I have just said I do not know."

"Is he ill, Papa?" Again the girl's voice grew faint.

"No, no, not ill. I wish he were! I mean it is some business matter you cannot understand. But it must be serious if Mr. Rae asks my presence immediately. So you must hasten, child."

In less than half an hour Donald and the cart were waiting at the door, and Moira stood in the hall with her father's bag ready packed. "Oh, I am glad," she said, as she helped her father with his coat, "that Allan is not ill. There can't be much wrong."

"Wrong! Read that, child!" cried the father impatiently.

She took the letter and read, her face reflecting her changing emotions, perplexity, surprise, finally indignation. "'A matter for the police,'" she quoted, scornfully, handing her father the letter. "'A matter for the police' indeed! My but that Mr. Rae is the clever man! The police! Does he think my brother Allan would cheat?—or steal, perhaps!" she panted, in her indignant scorn.

"Mr. Rae is a careful man and a very able lawyer," replied her father.

"Able! Careful! He's an auld wife, and that's what he is! You can tell him so for me." She was trembling and white with a wrath her father had never before seen in her. He stood gazing at her in silent surprise.

"Papa," cried Moira passionately, answering his look, "do you think what he is saying? I know my brother Allan clean through to the heart. He is wild at times, and might rage perhaps and—and—break things, but he will not lie nor cheat. He will die first, and that I warrant you."

Still her father stood gazing upon her as she stood proudly erect, her pale face alight with lofty faith in her brother and scorn of his traducer. "My child, my child," he said, huskily, "how like you are to your mother! Thank God! Indeed it may be you're right! God grant it!" He drew her closely to him.

"Papa, Papa," she whispered, clinging to him, while her voice broke in a sob, "you know Allan will not lie. You know it, don't you, Papa?"

"I hope not, dear child, I hope not," he replied, still holding her to him.

"Papa," she cried wildly, "say you believe me."

"Yes, yes, I do believe you. Thank God, I do believe you. The boy is straight."

At that word she let him go. That her father should not believe in Allan was to her loyal heart an intolerable pain. Now Allan would have someone to stand for him against "that lawyer" and all others who might seek to do him harm. At the House door she stood watching her father drive down through the ragged firs to the highroad, and long after he had passed out of sight she still stood gazing. Upon the church tower rising out of its birches and its firs her eyes were resting, but her heart was with the little mound at the tower's foot, and as she gazed, the tears gathered and fell.

"Oh, Mother!" she whispered. "Mother, Mother! You know Allan would not lie!"

A sudden storm was gathering. In a brief moment the world and the Glen had changed. But half an hour ago and the Cuagh Oir was lying glorious with its flowing gold. Now, from the Cuagh as from her world, the flowing gold was gone.

CHAPTER III

THE FAMILY SOLICITOR

THE senior member of the legal firm of Rae & Macpherson was perplexed and annoyed, indeed angry, and angry chiefly because he was perplexed. He resented such a condition of mind as reflecting upon his legal and other acumen. Angry, too, he was because he had been forced to accept, the previous day, a favour from a firm—Mr. Rae would not condescend to say a rival firm—with which he for thirty years had maintained only the most distant and formal relations, to wit, the firm of Thomlinson & Shields. Messrs. Rae & Macpherson were family solicitors and for three generations had been such; hence there gathered about the firm a fine flavour of assured respectability which only the combination of solid integrity and undoubted antiquity can give. Messrs. Rae & Macpherson had not yielded in the slightest degree to that commercialising spirit which would transform a respectable and self-respecting firm of family solicitors into a mere financial agency; a transformation which Mr. Rae would consider a degradation of an ancient and honourable profession. This uncompromising attitude toward the commercialising spirit of the age had doubtless something to do with their losing the solicitorship for the Bank of Scotland, which went to the firm of Thomlinson & Shields, to Mr. Rae's keen, though unacknowledged, disappointment; a disappointment that arose not so much from the loss of the very honourable and lucrative appointment, and more from the fact that the appointment should go to such a firm as that of Thomlinson

& Shields. For the firm of Thomlinson & Shields were of recent origin, without ancestry, boasting an existence of only some thirty-five years, and, as one might expect of a firm of such recent origin, characterised by the commercialising modern spirit in its most pronounced and objectionable form. Mr. Rae, of course, would never condescend to hostile criticism, dismissing Messrs. Thomlinson & Shields from the conversation with the single remark, "Pushing, Sir, very pushing, indeed."

It was, then, no small humiliation for Mr. Rae to be forced to accept a favour from Mr. Thomlinson. "Had it been any other than Cameron," he said to himself, as he sat in his somewhat dingy and dusty office, "I would let him swither. But Cameron! I must see to it and at once." Behind the name there rose before Mr. Rae's imagination a long line of brave men and fair women for whose name and fame and for whose good estate it had been his duty and the duty of those who had preceded him in office to assume responsibility.

"Young fool! Much he cares for the honour of his family! I wonder what's at the bottom of this business! Looks ugly! Decidedly ugly! The first thing is to find him." A messenger had failed to discover young Cameron at his lodgings, and had brought back the word that for a week he had not been seen there. "He must be found. They have given me till to-morrow. I cannot ask a further stay of proceedings; I cannot and I will not." It made Mr. Rae more deeply angry that he knew quite well if necessity arose he would do just that very thing. "Then there's his father coming in this evening. We simply must find him. But how and where?"

Mr. Rae was not unskilled in such a matter. "Find a man, find his friends," he muttered. "Let's see. What does the young fool do? What are his games? Ah! Football! I have it! Young Dunn is my man." Hence to young Dunn forthwith Mr. Rae betook himself.

It was still early in the day when Mr. Rae's mild, round, jolly, clean-shaven face beamed in upon Mr. Dunn, who sat with dictionaries, texts, and class note-books piled high about him, burrowing in that mound of hidden treasure which it behooves all prudent aspirants for university honours to diligently mine as the fateful day approaches. With Mr. Dunn time had now come to be measured by moments, and every moment golden. But the wrathful impatience that had gathered in his face at the approach of an intruder was over-whelmed in astonishment at recognising so distinguished a visitor as Mr. Rae the Writer.

"Ah, Mr. Dunn," said Mr. Rae briskly, "a moment only, one moment, I assure you. Well do I know the rage which boils behind that genial smile of yours. Don't deny it, Sir. Have I not suffered all the pangs, with just a week before the final ordeal? This is your final, I believe?"

"I hope so," said Mr. Dunn somewhat ruefully.

"Yes, yes, and a very fine career, a career befitting your father's son. And I sincerely trust, Sir, that as your career has been marked by honour, your exit shall be with distinction; and all the more that I am not un-aware of your achievements in another department of— ah—shall I say endeavour. I have seen your name, Sir, mentioned more than once, to the honour of our university, in athletic events." At this point Mr. Rae's face broke into a smile.

An amazing smile was Mr. Rae's; amazing both in the suddenness of its appearing and in the suddenness of its vanishing. Upon a face of supernatural gravity, without warning, without beginning, the smile, broad, full and effulgent, was instantaneously present. Then equally without warning and without fading the smile ceased to be. Under its effulgence the observer unfamiliar with Mr. Rae's smile was moved to a responsive geniality of expression, but in the full tide of this emotion he found himself suddenly regarding a face of such preternatural gravity as rebuked the very possibility or suggestion of geniality. Before the smile Mr. Rae's face was like a house, with the shutters up and the family plunged in gloom. When the smile broke forth every shutter was flung wide to the pouring sunlight, and every window full of flowers and laughing children. Then instantly and without warning the house was blank, lifeless, and shuttered once more, leaving you helplessly apologetic that you had ever been guilty of the fatuity of associating anything but death and gloom with its appearance.

To young Mr. Dunn it was extremely disconcerting to discover himself smiling genially into a face of the severest gravity, and eyes that rebuked him for his untimely levity. "Oh, I beg pardon," exclaimed Mr. Dunn hastily, "I thought—"

"Not at all, Sir," replied Mr. Rae. "As I was saying, I have observed from time to time the distinctions you have achieved in the realm of athletics. And that reminds me of my business with you to-day,—a sad business, a serious business, I fear." The solemn impressiveness of Mr. Rae's manner awakened in Mr. Dunn an awe amounting to dread. "It is young Cameron- a friend of yours, I believe, Sir."

"Cameron, Sir!" echoed Dunn.

"Yes, Cameron. Does he, or did he not have a place on your team?"

Dunn sat upright and alert. "Yes, Sir. What's the matter, Sir?"

"First of all, do you know where he is? I have tried his lodgings. He is not there. It is important that I find him to-day, extremely important; in fact, it is necessary; in short, Mr. Dunn,—I believe I can confide in your discretion,—if I do not find him to-day, the police will to-morrow."

"The police, Sir!" Dunn's face expressed an awful fear. In the heart of the respectable Briton the very mention of the police in connection with the private life of any of his friends awakens a feeling of gravest apprehension. No wonder Mr. Dunn's face went pale! "The police!" he said a second time. "What for?"

Mr. Rae remained silent.

"If it is a case of debts, Sir," suggested Mr. Dunn, "why, I would gladly—"

Mr. Rae waved him aside. "It is sufficient to say, Mr. Dunn, that we are the family solicitors, as we have been for his father, his grandfather and great-grandfather before him."

"Oh, certainly, Sir. I beg pardon," said Mr. Dunn hastily.

"Not at all; quite proper; does you credit. But it is not a case of debts, though it is a case of money; in fact, Sir,—I feel sure I may venture to confide in you,—he is in trouble with his bank, the Bank of Scotland. The young man, or someone using his name, has been guilty of—ah—well, an irregularity, a decided irregularity, an irregularity which the bank seems inclined to—to—follow up; indeed, I may say, instructions have been issued through their solicitors to that effect. Mr. Thomlinson was good enough to bring this to my attention, and to offer a stay of proceedings for a day."

"Can I do anything, Sir?" said Dunn. "I'm afraid I've neglected him. The truth is, I've been in an awful funk about my exams. and I haven't kept in touch as I should."

"Find him, Mr. Dunn, find him. His father is coming to town this evening, which makes it doubly imperative. Find him; that is, if you can spare the time."

"Of course I can. I'm awfully sorry I've lost touch with him. He's been rather down all this winter; in fact, ever since the International he seems to have lost his grip of himself."

"Ah, indeed!" said Mr. Rae. "I remember that occasion; in fact, I was present myself," he admitted. "I occasionally seek to renew my youth." Mr. Rae's smile broke forth, but anxiety for his friend saved Mr. Dunn from being caught again in any responsive smile. "Bring him to my office, if you can, any time to-day. Good-bye, Sir. Your spirit does you credit. But it is the spirit which I should expect in a man who plays the forward line as you play it."

Mr. Dunn blushed crimson. "Is there anything else I could do? Anyone I could see? I mean, for instance, could my father serve in any way?"

"Ah, a good suggestion!" Mr. Rae seized his right ear,—a characteristic action of his when in deep thought,—twisted it into a horn, and pulled it quite severely as if to assure himself that that important feature of his face was firmly fixed in its place. "A very good suggestion! Your father knows Mr. Sheratt, the manager of the bank, I believe."

"Very well, Sir, I think," answered Mr. Dunn. "I am sure he would see him. Shall I call him in, Sir?"

"Nothing of the sort, nothing of the sort; don't think of it! I mean, let there be nothing formal in this matter. If Mr. Dunn should chance to meet Mr. Sheratt, that is, casually, so to speak, and if young Cameron's name should come up, and if Mr. Dunn should use his influence, his very great influence, with Mr. Sheratt, the bank might be induced to take a more lenient view of the case. I think I can trust you with this." Mr. Rae shook the young man warmly by the hand, beamed on him for one brief moment with his amazing smile, presented to his answering smile a face of unspeakable gravity, and left him extremely uncertain as to the proper appearance for his face, under the circumstances.

Before Mr. Rae had gained the street Dunn was planning his campaign; for no matter what business he had in hand, Dunn always worked by plan. By the time he himself had reached the street his plan was formed. "No use trying his digs. Shouldn't be surprised if that beast Potts has got him. Rotten bounder, Potts, and worse! Better go round his way." And oscillating in his emotions between disgust and rage at Cameron for his weakness and his folly, and disgust and rage at himself for his neglect of his friend, Dunn took his way to the office of the Insurance Company which was honoured by the services of Mr. Potts.

The Insurance Company knew nothing of the whereabouts of Mr. Potts. Indeed, the young man who assumed responsibility for the information appeared to treat the very existence of Mr. Potts as a matter of slight importance to his company; so slight, indeed, that the company had not found it necessary either to the stability of its business or to the protection of its policyholders—a prime consideration with Insurance Companies—to keep in touch with Mr. Potts. That gentleman had left for the East coast a week ago, and that was the end of the matter as far as the clerk of the Insurance Company was concerned.

At his lodgings Mr. Dunn discovered an even more callous indifference to Mr. Potts and his interests. The landlady, under the impression that in Mr. Dunn she beheld a prospective lodger, at first received him with that deferential reserve which is the characteristic of respectable lodging-house keepers in that city of respectable lodgers and respectable lodging-house keepers. When, however, she learned the real nature of Mr. Dunn's errand, she became immediately transformed. In a voice shrill with indignation she repudiated Mr. Potts and his affairs, and seemed chiefly concerned to re-establish her own reputation for respectability, which she seemed to consider as being somewhat shattered by that of her lodger. Mr. Dunn was embarrassed both by her volubility and by her obvious determination to fasten upon him a certain amount of responsibility for the character and conduct of Mr. Potts.

"Do you know where Mr. Potts is now, and have you any idea when he may return?" inquired Mr. Dunn, seizing a fortunate pause.

"Am I no' juist tellin' ye," cried the landlady, in her excitement reverting to her native South Country dialect, "that I keep nae coont o' Mr. Potts' stravagins? An' as to his return, I ken naething aboot that an' care less. He's paid what he's been owing me these three months an' that's all I care aboot him."

"I am glad to hear that," said Mr. Dunn heartily.

"An' glad I am tae, for it's feared I was for my pay a month back."

"When did he pay up?" inquired Mr. Dunn, scenting a clue.

"A week come Saturday,—or was it Friday?—the

day he came in with a young man, a friend of his. And a night they made of it, I remember," replied the landlady, recovering command of herself and of her speech under the influence of Mr. Dunn's quiet courtesy.

"Did you know the young man that was with him?"

"Yes, it was young Cameron. He had been coming about a good deal."

"Oh, indeed! And have you seen Mr. Cameron since?"

"No; he never came except in company with Mr. Potts."

And with this faint clue Mr. Dunn was forced to content himself, and to begin a systematic search of Cameron's haunts in the various parts of the town. It was Martin, his little quarter-back, that finally put him on the right track. He had heard Cameron's pipes not more than an hour ago at his lodgings in Morningside Road.

"But what do you want of Cameron these days?" inquired the young Canadian. "There's nothing on just now, is there, except this infernal grind?"

Dunn hesitated. "Oh, I just want him. In fact, he has got into some trouble."

"There you are!" exclaimed Martin in disgust. "Why in thunder should you waste time on him? You've taken enough trouble with him this winter already. It's his own funeral, ain't it?"

Dunn looked at him a half moment in surprise. "Well, you can't go back on a fellow when he's down, can you?"

"Look here, Dunn, I've often thought I'd give you a little wise advice. This sounds bad, I know, but there's a lot of blamed rot going around this old town just on this point. When a fellow gets on the bum and gets into a hole he knows well that there'll be a lot of people tumbling over each other to get him out, hence he deliberately and cheerfully slides in. If he knew he'd have to scramble out himself he wouldn't be so blamed keen to get in. If he's in a hole let him frog it for awhile, by Jingo! He's hitting the pace, let him take his bumps! He's got to take 'em sooner or later, and better sooner than later, for the sooner he takes 'em the quicker he'll learn. Bye-bye! I know you think I'm a semi-civilised Colonial. I ain't; I'm giving you some wisdom gained from experience. You can't swim by hanging on to a root, you bet!"

Dunn listened in silence, then replied slowly, "I say, old chap, there's something in that. My governor said something like that some time ago: 'A trainer's business is to train his men to do without him.'"

"There you are!" cried Martin. "That's philosophy! Mine's just horse sense."

"Still," said Dunn thoughtfully, "when a chap's in you've got to lend a hand; you simply can't stand and look on." Dunn's words, tone, and manner revealed the great, honest heart of human sympathy which he carried in his big frame.

"Oh, hang it," cried Martin, "I suppose so! Guess I'll go along with you. I can't forget you pulled me out, too."

"Thanks, old chap," cried Dunn, brightening up, "but you're busy, and—"

"Busy! By Jingo, you'd think so if you'd watch me over night and hear my brain sizzle. But come along, I'm going to stay with you!"

But Dunn's business was private, and could be shared with no one. It was difficult to check his friend's newly-aroused ardour. "I say, old chap," he said, "you really don't need to come along. I can do—"

"Oh, go to blazes! I know you too well! Don't you worry about me! You've got me going, and I'm in on this thing; so come along!"

Then Dunn grew firm. "Thanks, awfully, old man," he said, "but it's a thing I'd rather do alone, if you don't mind."

"Oh!" said Martin. "All right! But say, if you need me I'm on. You're a great old brick, though! Tra-la!"

As Martin had surmised, Dunn found Cameron in his rooms. He was lying upon his bed enjoying the luxury of a cigarette. "Hello! Come right in, old chap!" he cried, in gay welcome. "Have a—no, you won't have a cigarette—have a pipe?"

Dunn gazed at him, conscious of a rising tide of mingled emotions, relief, wrath, pity, disgust. "Well, I'll be hanged!" at last he said slowly. "But you've given us a chase! Where in the world have you been?"

"Been? Oh, here and there, enjoying my emancipation from the thralldom in which doubtless you are still sweating."

"And what does that mean exactly?"

"Mean? It means that I've cut the thing,—note-books, lectures, professors, exams., 'the hale hypothick,' as our Nannie would say at home."

"Oh rot, Cameron! You don't mean it?"

"*Circumspice.* Do you behold any suggestion of knotted towels and the midnight oil?"

Dunn gazed about the room. It was in a whirl of confusion. Pipes and pouches, a large box of cigarettes, a glass and a half-empty decanter, were upon the table; boots, caps, golf-clubs, coats, lay piled in various corners. "Pardon the confusion, dear sir," cried Cameron cheerfully, "and lay it not to the charge of my landlady. That estimable woman was determined to make entry this afternoon, but was denied." Cameron's manner was one of gay and nervous bravado.

"Come, Cameron," said Dunn sadly, "what does this mean? You're not serious; you're not chucking your year?"

"Just that, dear fellow, and nothing less. Might as well as be ploughed."

"And what then are you going to do?" Dunn's voice was full of a great pity. "What about your people? What about your father? And, by Jove, that reminds me, he's coming to town this evening. You know they've been trying to find you everywhere this last day or two."

"And who are 'they,' pray?"

"Who? The police," said Dunn bluntly, determined to shock his friend into seriousness.

Cameron sat up quickly. "The police? What do you mean, Dunn?"

"What it means I do not know, Cameron, I assure you. Don't you?"

"The police!" said Cameron again. "It's a joke, Dunn."

"I wish to Heaven it were, Cameron, old man! But I have it straight from Mr. Rae, your family solicitor. They want you."

"Old Rae?" exclaimed Cameron. "Now what the deuce does this all mean?"

"Don't you really know, old chap?" said Dunn kindly, anxiety and relief struggling in his face.

"No more than you. What did the old chap say, anyway?"

"Something about a Bank; an irregularity, he called it, a serious irregularity. He's had it staved off for a day."

"The Bank? What in Heaven's name have I got to

do with the Bank? Let's see; I was there a week or ten days ago with—" he paused. "Hang it, I can't remember!" He ran his hands through his long black locks, and began to pace the room.

Dunn sat watching him, hope and fear, doubt and faith filling his heart in succession.

Cameron sat down with his face in his hands. "What is it, old man? Can't I help you?" said Dunn, putting his hand on his shoulder.

"I can't remember," muttered Cameron. "I've been going it some, you know. I had been falling behind and getting money off Potts. Two weeks ago I got my monthly five-pound cheque, and about ten days ago the usual fifty-pound cheque to square things up for the year, fees, etc. Seems to me I cashed those. Or did Potts? Anyway I paid Potts. The deuce take it, I can't remember! You know I can carry a lot of Scotch and never show it, but it plays the devil with my memory." Cameron was growing more and more excited.

"Well, old chap, we must go right along to Mr. Rae's office. You don't mind?"

"Mind? Not a bit. Old Rae has no love for me,— I get him into too much trouble,—but he's a straight old boy. Just wait till I brush up a bit." He poured out from a decanter half a glass of whiskey.

"I'd cut that out if I were you," said Dunn.

"Later, perhaps," replied Cameron, "but not to-day."

Within twenty minutes they were ushered into Mr. Rae's private office. That gentleman received them with a gravity that was portentous in its solemnity. "Well, Sir, you have succeeded in your task," he said to Mr. Dunn. "I wish to thank you for this service, a most valuable service to me, to this young gentleman, and to his family; though whether much may come of it remains to be seen."

"Oh, thanks," said Dunn hurriedly. "I hope everything will be all right." He rose to go. Cameron looked at him quickly. There was no mistaking the entreaty in his face.

Mr. Rae spoke somewhat more hurriedly than his wont. "If it is not asking too much, and if you can still spare time, your presence might be helpful, Mr. Dunn."

"Stay if you can, old chap," said Cameron. "I don't know what this thing is, but I'll do better if you're in the game, too." It was an appeal to his captain, and after that nothing on earth could have driven Dunn from his side.

At this point the door opened and the clerk announced, "Captain Cameron, Sir."

Mr. Rae rose hastily. "Tell him," he said quickly, "to wait—"

He was too late. The Captain had followed close upon the heels of the clerk, and came in with a rush. "Now, what does all this mean?" he cried, hardly waiting to shake hands with his solicitor. "What mischief—?"

"I beg your pardon, Captain," said Mr. Rae calmly, "let me present Mr. Dunn, Captain Dunn, I might say, of International fame." The solicitor's smile broke forth with its accustomed unexpectedness, but had vanished long before Mr. Dunn in his embarrassment had finished shaking hands with Captain Cameron.

The Captain then turned to his son. "Well, Sir, and what is this affair of yours that calls me to town at a most inconvenient time?" His tone was cold, fretful, and suspicious.

Young Cameron's face, which had lighted up with a

certain eagerness and appeal as he had turned toward
his father, as if in expectation of sympathy and help,
froze at this greeting into sullen reserve. "I don't know
any more than yourself, Sir," he answered. "I have
just come into this office this minute."

"Well, then, what is it, Mr. Rae?" The Captain's
voice and manner were distinctly imperious, if not over-
bearing.

Mr. Rae, however, was king of his own castle. "Will
you not be seated, Sir?" he said, pointing to a chair.
"Sit down, young gentlemen."

His quiet dignity, his perfect courtesy, recalled the
Captain to himself. "I beg your pardon, Mr. Rae, but
I am really much disturbed. Can we begin at once?"
He glanced as he spoke at Mr. Dunn, who immediately
rose.

"Sit down, Mr. Dunn," said Mr. Rae quietly. "I
have asked this young gentleman," he continued, turning to the Captain, "to remain. He has already given
me valuable assistance. I fancy he may be able to serve
us still further, if he will be so good."

Mr. Dunn bowed in silence.

"Now let us proceed with what must be an exceedingly painful matter for us all, and out of which nothing
but extreme candour on the part of Mr. Allan here, and
great wisdom on the part of us all, can possibly extract
us." Mr. Rae's glance rested upon the Captain, who
bowed, and upon his son, who made no sign whatever,
but remained with his face set in the same sullen gloom
with which he had greeted his father.

Mr. Rae opened a drawer and brought forth a slip of
paper. "Mr. Allan," he said, with a certain sharpness
in his tone, "please look at this."

Cameron came to the desk, picked up the paper,

glanced at it. "It is my father's cheque," he said, "which I received about a week ago."

"Look at the endorsement, please," said Mr. Rae.

Cameron turned it over. A slight flush came to his pale face. "It is mine to—" he hesitated, "Mr. Potts."

"Mr. Potts cashed it then?"

"I suppose so. I believe so. I owed him money, and he gave me back some."

"How much did you owe him?"

"A considerable amount. I had been borrowing of him for some time."

"As much as fifty pounds?"

"I cannot tell. I did not keep count, particularly; Potts did that."

The Captain snorted contemptuously. "Do you mean to say—?" he began.

"Pardon me, Captain Cameron. Allow me," said Mr. Rae.

"Now, Mr. Allan, do you think you owed him as much as the amount of that cheque?"

"I do not know, but I think so."

"Had you any other money?"

"No," said Allan shortly; "at least I may have had a little remaining from the five pounds I had received from my father a few days before."

"You are quite sure you had no other money?"

"Quite certain," replied Allan.

Again Mr. Rae opened his desk and drew forth a slip and handed it to young Cameron. "What is that?" he said.

Cameron glanced at it hurriedly, and turned it over. "That is my father's cheque for five pounds, which I cashed."

Mr. Rae stretched out his hand and took the cheque. "Mr. Allan," he said, "I want you to consider most carefully your answer." He leaned across the desk and for some moments—they seemed like minutes to Dunn—his eyes searched young Cameron's face. "Mr. Allan," he said, with a swift change of tone, his voice trembling slightly, "will you look at the amount of that cheque again?"

Cameron once more took the cheque, glanced at it. "Good Lord!" he cried. "It is fifty!" His face showed blank amazement.

Quick, low, and stern came Mr. Rae's voice. "Yes," he said, "it is for fifty pounds. Do you know that that is a forgery, the punishment for which is penal servitude, and that the order for your arrest is already given?"

The Captain sprang to his feet. Young Cameron's face became ghastly pale. His hand clutched the top of Mr. Rae's desk. Twice or thrice he moistened his lips preparing to speak, but uttered not a word. "Good God, my boy!" said the Captain hoarsely. "Don't stand like that. Tell him you are innocent."

"One moment, Sir," said Mr. Rae to the Captain. "Permit me." Mr. Rae's voice, while perfectly courteous, was calmly authoritative.

"Mr. Allan," he continued, turning to the wretched young man, "what money have you at present in your pockets?"

With shaking hands young Cameron emptied upon the desk the contents of his pocketbook, from which the lawyer counted out ten one-pound notes, a half-sovereign and some silver. "Where did you get this money, Mr. Allan?"

The young man, still silent, drew his handkerchief

from his pocket, touched his lips, and wiped the sweat from his white face.

"Mr. Allan," continued the lawyer, dropping again into a kindly voice, "a frank explanation will help us all."

"Mr. Rae," said Cameron, his words coming with painful indistinctness, "I don't understand this. I can't think clearly. I can't remember. That money I got from Potts; at least I must have—I have had money from no one else."

"My God!" cried the Captain again. "To think that a son of mine should—!"

"Pardon me, Captain Cameron," interrupted Mr. Rae quickly and somewhat sharply. "We must not prejudge this case. We must first understand it."

At this point Dunn stepped swiftly to Cameron's side. "Brace up, old chap," he said in a low tone. Then turning towards the Captain he said, "I beg your pardon, Sir, but I do think it's only fair to give a man a chance to explain."

"Allow me, gentlemen," said Mr. Rae in a firm, quiet voice, as the Captain was about to break forth. "Allow me to conduct this examination."

Cameron turned his face toward Dunn. "Thank you, old man," he said, his white lips quivering. "I will do my best, but before God, I don't understand this."

"Now, Mr. Allan," continued the lawyer, tapping the desk sharply, "here are two cheques for fifty pounds, both drawn by your father, both endorsed by you, one apparently cashed by Mr. Potts, one by yourself. What do you know about this?"

"Mr. Rae," replied the young man, his voice trembling and husky, "I tell you I can't understand this. I ought to say that for the last two weeks I haven't been quite myself, and whiskey always makes me forget. I can walk around steadily enough, but I don't always know what I am doing—"

"That's so, Sir," said Dunn quickly, "I've seen him."

"—And just what happened with these cheques I do not know. This cheque," picking up the one endorsed to Potts, "I remember giving to Potts. The only other cheque I remember is a five-pound one."

"Do you remember cashing that five-pound cheque?" inquired Mr. Rae.

"I carried it about for some days. I remember that, because I once offered it to Potts in part payment, and he said—" the white face suddenly flushed a deep red.

"Well, Mr. Allan, what did he say?"

"It doesn't matter," said Cameron.

"It may and it may not," said Mr. Rae sharply. "It is your duty to tell us."

"Out with it," said his father angrily. "You surely owe it to me, to us all, to let us have every assistance."

Cameron paid no attention to his father's words. "It has really no bearing, Sir, but I remember saying as I offered a five-pound cheque, 'I wish it was fifty.'"

"And what reply did Mr. Potts make?" said Mr. Rae, with quiet indifference, as if he had lost interest in this particular feature of the case.

Again Cameron hesitated.

"Come, out with it!" said his father impatiently.

His son closed his lips as if in a firm resolve. "It really has nothing whatever to do with the case."

"Play the game, old man," said Dunn quietly.

"Oh, all right!" said Cameron. "It makes no difference anyway. He said in a joke, 'You could easily make this fifty; it is such mighty poor writing.'"

Still Mr. Rae showed no sign of interest. "He suggested in a joke, I understand, that the five-pound cheque could easily be changed into fifty pounds. That was a mere pleasantry of Mr. Potts', doubtless. How did the suggestion strike you, Mr. Allan?"

Allan looked at him in silence.

"I mean, did the suggestion strike you unpleasantly, or how?"

"I don't think it made any impression, Sir. I knew it was a joke."

"A joke!" groaned his father. "Good Heavens! What do you think—?"

"Once more permit me," said Mr. Rae quietly, with a wave of his hand toward the Captain. "This cheque of five pounds has evidently been altered to fifty pounds. The question is, by whom, Mr. Allan? Can you answer that?" Again Mr. Rae's eyes were searching the young man's face.

"I have told you I remember nothing about this cheque."

"Is it possible, Mr. Allan, that you could have raised this cheque yourself without your knowing—?"

"Oh, nonsense!" said his father hotly, "why make the boy lie?"

His son started as if his father had struck him. "I tell you once more, Mr. Rae, and I tell you all, I know nothing about this cheque, and that is my last word." And from that position nothing could move him.

"Well," said Mr. Rae, closing the interview, "we have done our best. The law must take its course."

"Great Heavens!" cried the Captain, springing to his feet. "Do you mean to tell me, Allan, that you persist in this cursed folly and will give us no further light? Have you no regard for my name, if not for your own?" He grasped his son fiercely by the arm.

But his son angrily shook off his grasp. "You," he said, looking his father full in the face, "you condemned me before you heard a word from me, and now for my name or for yours I care not a tinker's curse." And with this he flung himself from the room.

"Follow him," said Mr. Rae to Dunn, quietly; "he will need you. And keep him in sight; it is important."

"All right, Sir!" said Dunn. "I'll stay with him." And he did.

CHAPTER IV

A QUESTION OF HONOUR

MR. RAE in forty years' experience had never been so seriously disturbed. To his intense humiliation he found himself abjectly appealing to the senior member of the firm of Thomlinson & Shields. Not that Mr. Thomlinson was obdurate; in the presence of mere obduracy Mr. Rae might have found relief in the conscious possession of more generous and humane instincts than those supposed to be characteristic of the members of his profession. Mr. Thomlinson, however, was anything but obdurate. He was eager to oblige, but he was helpless. The instructions he had received were simple but imperative, and he had gone to unusual lengths in suggesting to Mr. Sheratt, the manager of the Bank, a course of greater leniency. That gentleman's only reply was a brief order to proceed with the case.

With Mr. Sheratt, therefore, Mr. Rae proceeded to deal. His first move was to invite the Bank manager to lunch, in order to discuss some rather important matters relative to one of the great estates of which Mr. Rae was supposed to be the guardian. Some fifty years' experience of Mr. Sheratt as boy and man had let Mr. Rae into a somewhat intimate knowledge of the workings of that gentleman's mind. Under the mollifying influences of the finest of old port, Mr. Rae made the discovery that as with Mr. Thomlinson, so with Mr. Sheratt there was every disposition to oblige, and indeed an eagerness to yield to the lawyer's desires; it was not Mr. Sheratt, but the Bank that was immovable. Firm-fixed it stood upon its bedrock of tradition that in matters of fraud, crime should be punished to the full limit of the law.

"The estate of the criminal, high or low," said Mr. Sheratt impressively, "matters not. The Bank stands upon the principle, and from this it cannot be moved." Mr. Sheratt began to wax eloquent. "Fidelity to its constituency, its shareholders, its depositors, indeed to the general public, is the corner-stone of its policy. The Bank of Scotland is a National Institution, with a certain National obligation."

Mr. Rae quietly drew from his pocket a pamphlet, opened it slowly, and glanced at the page. "Ay, it's as I thought, Mr. Sheratt," he said dryly. "At times I wondered where Sir Archibald got his style."

Mr. Sheratt blushed like a boy caught copying.

"But now since I know who it is that writes the speech of the Chairman of the Board of Directors, tell me, Sheratt, as man to man, is it you or is it Sir Archibald that's at the back of this prosecution? For if it is you, I've something to say to you; if not, I'll just say it where it's most needed. In some way or other I'm bound to see this thing through. That boy can't go to prison. Now tell me, Tom? It's for auld sake's sake."

"As sure as death, Rae, it's the Chairman, and it's God's truth I'm telling ye, though I should not." They were back again into the speech and spirit of their boyhood days.

"Then I must see Sir Archibald. Give me time to see him, Tom."

"It's a waste of time, I'm tellin' ye, but two days I'll give ye, Sandy, for auld sake's sake, as you say. A friendship of half a hundred years should mean something to us. For your sake I'd let the lad go, God knows, and there's my han' upon it, but as I said, that lies with Sir Archibald."

The old friends shook hands in silence.

"Thank ye, Tom, thank ye," said Mr. Rae; "I knew it."

"But harken to me, ye'll no' move Sir Archibald, for on this particular point he's quite mad. He'd prosecute the Duke of Argyll, he would. But two days are yours, Sandy. And mind with Sir Archibald ye treat his Bank with reverence! It's a National Institution, with National obligations, ye ken?" Mr. Sheratt's wink conveyed a volume of meaning. "And mind you, Rae," here Mr. Sheratt grew grave, "I am trusting you to produce that lad when wanted."

"I have him in safe keeping, Tom, and shall produce him, no fear."

And with that the two old gentlemen parted, loyal to a lifelong friendship, but loyal first to the trust of those they stood pledged to serve; for the friendship that gives first place to honour is the only friendship that honourable men can hold.

Mr. Rae set off for his office through the drizzling rain. "Now then, for the Captain," he said to himself; "and a state he will be in! Why did I ever summon him to town? Then for Mr. Dunn, who must keep his eye upon the young man."

In his office he found Captain Cameron in a state of distraction that rendered him incapable of either coherent thought or speech. "What now, Rae? Where have you been? What news have you? My God, this thing is driving me mad! Penal servitude! Think of it, man, for my son! Oh, the scandal of it! It will kill me and kill his sister. What's your report? Come, out with it! Have you seen Mr. Sheratt?" He was pacing up and down the office like a beast in a cage.

"Tut, tut, Captain Cameron," said Mr. Rae lightly, "this is no way for a soldier to face the enemy. Sit down and we will just lay out our campaign."

But the Captain's soldiering, which was of the lightest, had taught him little either of the spirit or of the tactics of warfare. "Campaign!" he exclaimed. "There's no campaign about it. It's a complete smash, horse, foot, and artillery."

"Nonsense, Captain Cameron!" exclaimed Mr. Rae more briskly than his wont, for the Captain irritated him. "We have still fighting to do, and hence we must plan our campaign. But first let us get comfortable. Here Davie," he called, opening the office door, "here, mend this fire. It's a winter's day this," he continued to the Captain, "and goes to the marrow."

Davie, a wizened, clean-shaven, dark-visaged little man, appeared with a scuttle of coal. "Ay, Davie; that's it! Is that cannel?"

"Ay, Sir, it is. What else? I aye get the cannel."

"That's right, Davie. It's a gran' coal."

"Gran' it's no'," said Davie shortly, who was a fierce radical in politics, and who strove to preserve his sense of independence of all semblance of authority by cultivating a habit of disagreement. "Gran' it's no'," he repeated, "but it's the best the Farquhars hae, though that's no' saying much. It's no' what I call cannel."

"Well, well, Davie, it blazes finely at any rate," said Mr. Rae, determined to be cheerful, and rubbing his hands before the blazing coal.

"Ay, it bleezes," grumbled Davie, "when it's no' smootherin'."

"Come then, Davie, that will do. Clear out," said Mr. Rae to the old servant, who was cleaning up the hearth with great diligence and care.

But Davie was not to be hurried. He had his regular routine in fire-mending, from which no power could move him. "Ay, Sir," he muttered, brushing away with his feather besom. "I'll clear oot when I clear up. When a thing's no' dune richt it's no dune ava."

"True, Davie, true enough; that's a noble sentiment. But will that no' do now?" Mr. Rae knew himself to be helpless in Davie's hands, and he knew also that nothing short of violence would hasten Davie from his "usual."

"Ay, that'll dae, because it's richt dune. But that's no' what I call cannel," grumbled Davie, glowering fiercely at the burning coal, as if meditating a fresh attack.

"Well, well," said Mr. Rae, "tell the Farquhars about it."

"Ay, Sir, I will that," said Davie, as he reluctantly took himself off with his scuttle and besom.

The Captain was bursting with fretful impatience. "Impudent old rascal!" he exclaimed. "Why don't you dismiss him?"

"Dismiss him!" echoed Mr. Rae in consternation. "Dismiss him!" he repeated, as if pondering an entirely new idea. "I doubt if Davie would consider that. But now let us to work." He set two arm-chairs before the fire, and placed a box of cigars by the Captain's elbow. "I have seen Sheratt," he began. "I'm quite clear it is not in his hands."

"In whose then?" burst forth the Captain.

Mr. Rae lit his cigar carefully. "The whole matter, I believe, lies now with the Chairman of the Board of Directors, Sir Archibald Brodie."

"Brodie!" cried the Captain. "I know him. Pompous little fool!"

"Fool, Captain Cameron! Make no mistake. Sir Archibald may have—ah—the self-importance of a self-made man somewhat under the average height, but he is, without doubt, the best financier that stands at this moment in Scotland, and during the last fifteen years he has brought up the Bank of Scotland to its present position. Fool! He's anything but that. But he has his weak spots—I wish I knew what they were!—and these we must seek to find out. Do you know him well?"

"Oh, yes, quite well," said the Captain; "that is, I've met him at various functions, where he always makes speeches. Very common, I call him. I know his father; a mere cottar. I mean," added the Captain hurriedly, for he remembered that Mr. Rae was of the same humble origin, "you know, he is thoroughly respectable and all that, but of no—ah—social or family standing; that is—oh, you understand."

"Quite," said Mr. Rae drily.

"Yes, I shall see him," continued the Captain briskly. "I shall certainly see him. It is a good suggestion. Sir Archibald knows my family; indeed, his father was from the Erracht region. I shall see him personally. I am glad you thought of that, Mr. Rae. These smaller men, Sheratt and the rest, I do not know—in fact, I do not seem to be able to manage them,—but with Sir Archibald there will be no difficulty, I feel quite confident. When can you arrange the interview?"

Mr. Rae sat gazing thoughtfully into the fire, more and more convinced every moment that he had made a false move in suggesting a meeting between the Captain and Sir Archibald Brodie. But labour as he might he could not turn the Captain from his purpose. He was resolved to see Sir Archibald at the earliest moment, and of the result of the meeting he had no manner of doubt.

"He knew my family, Sir," insisted the Captain. "Sir Archibald will undoubtedly accede to my suggestion —ah—request to withdraw his action. Arrange it, Mr. Rae, arrange it at once."

And ruefully enough Mr. Rae was compelled to yield against his better judgment.

It was discovered upon inquiry that Sir Archibald had gone for a day or two to his country estate. "Ah, much better," said the Captain, "away from his office and away from the—ah—commercial surroundings of the city. Much better, much better! We shall proceed to his country home."

Of the wisdom of this proposal Mr. Rae was doubtful. There seemed, however, no other way open. Hence, the following morning found them on their way to Sir Archibald's country seat. Mr. Rae felt that it was an unusual course to pursue, but the time was short, the occasion was gravely critical, and demanded extreme measures.

During their railway journey Mr. Rae strove to impress upon the Captain's mind the need of diplomacy. "Sir Archibald is a man of strong prejudices," he urged; "for instance, his Bank he regards with an affection and respect amounting to veneration. He is a bachelor, you understand, and his Bank is to him wife and bairns. On no account must you treat his Bank lightly."

"Oh, certainly not," replied the Captain, who was inclined to resent Mr. Rae's attempts to school him in diplomacy.

"He is a great financier," continued Mr. Rae, "and with him finance is a high art, and financial integrity a sacred obligation."

"Oh, certainly, certainly," again replied the Captain, quite unimpressed by this aspect of the matter, for while he considered himself distinctly a man of affairs, yet his interests lay more in matters of great public moment. Commercial enterprises he regarded with a feeling akin to contempt. Money was an extremely desirable, and indeed necessary, appendage to a gentleman's position, but how any man of fine feeling could come to regard a financial institution with affection or veneration he was incapable of conceiving. However, he was prepared to deal considerately with Sir Archibald's peculiar prejudices in this matter.

Mr. Rae's forebodings as to the outcome of the approaching interview were of the most gloomy nature as they drove through the finely appointed and beautifully kept grounds of Sir Archibald Brodie's estate. The interview began inauspiciously. Sir Archibald received them with stiff courtesy. He hated to be pursued to his country home with business matters. Besides, at this particular moment he was deeply engrossed in the inspection of his pigs, for which animals he cherished what might almost be called an absorbing affection. Mr. Rae, who was proceeding with diplomatic caution and skill to approach the matter in hand by way of Sir Archibald's Wiltshires, was somewhat brusquely interrupted by the Captain, who, in the firm conviction that he knew much better than did the lawyer how to deal with a man of his own class, plunged at once into the subject.

"Awfully sorry to introduce business matters, Sir Archibald, to the attention of a gentleman in the privacy of his own home, but there is a little matter in connection with the Bank in which I am somewhat deeply interested."

Sir Archibald bowed in silence.

"Rather, I should say, it concerns my son, and therefore, Sir Archibald, myself and my family."

Again Sir Archibald bowed.

"It is, after all, a trivial matter, which I have no doubt can be easily arranged between us. The truth is, Sir Archibald—," here the Captain hesitated, as if experiencing some difficulty in stating the case.

"Perhaps Captain Cameron will allow me to place the matter before you, Sir Archibald," suggested Mr. Rae, "as it has a legal aspect of some gravity, indeed of very considerable gravity. It is the case of young Mr. Cameron."

"Ah," said Sir Archibald shortly. "Forgery case, I believe."

"Well," said Mr. Rae, "we have not been able as yet to get at the bottom of it. I confess that the case has certainly very grave features connected with it, but it is by no means clear that—"

"There is no need for further statement, Mr. Rae," said Sir Archibald. "I know all about it. It is a clear case of forgery. The facts have all been laid before me, and I have given my instructions."

"And what may these be, may I inquire?" said the Captain somewhat haughtily.

"The usual instructions, Sir, where the Bank of Scotland is concerned,—instructions to prosecute." Sir Archibald's lips shut in a firm, thin line. As far as he was concerned the matter was closed.

"But, Sir," exclaimed the Captain, "this young man is my son."

"I deeply regret it," replied Sir Archibald.

"Yes, Sir, he is my son, and the honour of my family is involved."

Sir Archibald bowed.

"I am here prepared to offer the fullest reparation, to offer the most generous terms of settlement; in short, I am willing to do anything in reason to have this matter—this unfortunate matter—hushed up."

"Hushed up!" exclaimed Sir Archibald. "Captain Cameron, it is impossible. I am grieved for you, but I have a duty to the Bank in this matter."

"Do you mean to say, Sir," cried the Captain, "that you refuse to consider any arrangement or compromise or settlement of any kind whatever? I am willing to pay the amount ten times over, rather than have my name dragged through legal proceedings."

"It is quite impossible," said Sir Archibald.

"Come, come, Sir Archibald," said the Captain, exercising an unusual self-control; "let us look at this thing as two gentlemen should who respect each other, and who know what is due to our—ah—class."

It was an unfortunate remark of the Captain's.

"Our class, Sir? I presume you mean the class of gentlemen. All that is due to our class or any other class is strict justice, and that you, Sir, or any other gentleman, shall receive to the very fullest in this matter. The honour of the Bank, which I regard as a great National Institution charged with National responsibilities, is involved, as is also my own personal honour. I sincerely trust your son may be cleared of every charge of crime, but this case must be prosecuted to the very fullest degree."

"And do you mean to tell me, Sir Archibald," exclaimed the Captain, now in a furious passion, "that for the sake of a few paltry pounds you will blast my name and my family name in this country?—a name, I venture to say, not unknown in the history of this nation.

The Camerons, Sir, have fought and bled for King and country on many a battlefield. What matters the question of a few pounds in comparison with the honour of an ancient and honourable name? You cannot persist in this attitude, Sir Archibald!"

"Pounds, Sir!" cried Sir Archibald, now thoroughly aroused by the contemptuous reference to what to him was dearer than anything in life. "Pounds, Sir! It is no question of pounds, but a question of the honour of a National Institution, a question of the lives and happiness of hundreds of widows and orphans, a question of the honour of a name which I hold as dear as you hold yours."

Mr. Rae was in despair. He laid a restraining hand upon the Captain, and with difficulty obtained permission to speak. "Sir Archibald, I crave your indulgence while I put this matter to you as to a business man. In the first place, there is no evidence that fraud has been committed by young Mr. Cameron, absolutely none.— Pardon me a moment, Sir Archibald.—The fraud has been committed, I grant, by someone, but by whom is as yet unknown. The young man for some weeks has been in a state of incapacity; a most blameworthy and indeed shameful condition, it is true, but in a state of incapacity to transact business. He declares that he has no knowledge of this act of forgery. He will swear this. I am prepared to defend him."

"Very well, Sir," interrupted Sir Archibald, "and I hope, I sincerely hope, successfully."

"But while it may be difficult to establish innocence, it will be equally difficult to establish guilt. Meantime, the young man's life is blighted, his name dishonoured, his family plunged into unspeakable grief. I venture to say that it is a case in which the young man might be given, without injury to the Bank, or without breaking through its traditional policy, the benefit of the doubt."

But Sir Archibald had been too deeply stirred by Captain Cameron's unfortunate remarks to calmly weigh Mr. Rae's presentation of the case. "It is quite useless, Mr. Rae," he declared firmly. "The case is out of my hands, and must be proceeded with. I sincerely trust you may be able to establish the young man's innocence. I have nothing more to say."

And from this position neither Mr. Rae's arguments nor the Captain's passionate pleadings could move him.

Throughout the return journey the Captain raged and swore. "A contemptible cad, Sir! a base-born, low-bred cad, Sir! What else could you expect from a fellow of his breeding? The insolence of these lower orders is becoming insupportable. The idea! the very idea! His bank against my family name, my family honour! Preposterous!"

"Honour is honour, Captain Cameron," replied Mr. Rae firmly, "and it might have been better if you had remembered that the honour of a cottar's son is as dear to him as yours is to you."

And such was Mr. Rae's manner that the Captain appeared to consider it wise to curb his rage, or at least suppress all reference to questions of honour in as far as they might be related to the question of birth and breeding.

CHAPTER V

A LADY AND THE LAW

MR. RAE'S first care was to see Mr. Dunn. This case was getting rather more trying to Mr. Rae's nerves than he cared to acknowledge. For a second time he had been humiliated, and humiliation was an experience to which Mr. Rae was not accustomed. It was in a distinctly wrathful frame of mind that he called upon Mr. Dunn, and the first quarter of an hour of his interview he spent in dilating upon his own folly in having allowed Captain Cameron to accompany him on his visit to Sir Archibald.

"In forty years I never remember having made such an error, Sir. This was an occasion for diplomacy. We should have taken time. We should have discovered his weak spots; every man has them. Now it is too late. The only thing left for us is fight, and the best we can hope for is a verdict of *not proven,* and that leaves a stigma."

"It is terrible," said Mr. Dunn, "and I believe he is innocent. Have you thought of Potts, Sir?"

"I have had Potts before me," said Mr. Rae, "and I may safely say that though he strikes me as being a man of unusual cleverness, we can do nothing with Mr. Potts. Of course," added Mr. Rae hastily, "this is not to say we shall not make use of Mr. Potts in the trial, but Mr. Potts can show from his books debts amounting to nearly sixty pounds. He frankly acknowledges the pleasantry in suggesting the raising of the five-pound cheque to fifty pounds, but of the act itself he professes entire ignorance. I frankly own to you, Sir," continued Mr. Rae, folding his ear into a horn after his manner when in perplexity, "that this case puzzles me. I must not take your time," he said, shaking Mr. Dunn warmly by the hand. "One thing more I must ask you, however, and that is, keep in touch with young Cameron. I have pledged my honour to produce him when wanted. Furthermore, keep him—ah—in good condition; cheer him up; nerve him up; much depends upon his manner."

Gravely Mr. Dunn accepted the trust, though whether he could fulfil it he doubted. "Keep him cheerful," said Mr. Dunn to himself, as the door closed upon Mr. Rae. "Nice easy job, too, under the circumstances. Let's see, what is there on? By Jove, if I could only bring him!" There flashed into Mr. Dunn's mind the fact that he was due that evening at a party for students, given by one of the professors, belated beyond the period proper to such functions by one of those domestic felicities which claim right of way over all other human events. At this party Cameron was also due. It was hardly likely, however, that he would attend. But to Dunn's amazement he found Cameron, with a desperate jollity such as a man might feel the night before his execution, eager to go.

"I'm going," he cried, in answer to Dunn's somewhat timid suggestion. "They'll all be there, old man, and I shall make my exit with much éclat, with pipe and dance and all the rest of it."

"Exit, be blowed!" said Dunn impatiently. "Let's cut all this nonsense out. We're going into a fight for all there's in us. Why should a fellow throw up the sponge after the first round?"

"Fight!" said Cameron gloomily. "Did old Rae say so?"

"Most decidedly."

"And what defence does he suggest?"

"Defence? Innocence, of course."

"Would to God I could back him up!" groaned Cameron.

Dunn gazed at him in dismay. "And can you not? You do not mean to tell me you are guilty?"

"Oh, I wish to heaven I knew!" cried Cameron wildly. "But there, let it go. Let the lawyers and the judge puzzle it out. 'Guilty or not guilty?' 'Hanged if I know, my lord. Looks like guilty, but don't see very well how I can be.' That will bother old Rae some; it would bother Old Nick himself. 'Did you forge this note?' 'My lord, my present ego recognizes no intent to forge; my alter ego *in vino* may have done so. Of that, however, I know nothing; it lies in that mysterious region of the subconscious.' 'Are you, then, guilty?' 'Guilt, my lord, lies in intent. Intent is the soul of crime.' It will be an interesting point for Mr. Rae and his lordship."

"Look here, old chap," asked Dunn suddenly, "what of Potts in this business?"

"Potts! Oh, hang it, Dunn, I can't drag Potts into this. It would be altogether too low-down to throw suspicion upon a man without the slightest ground. Potts is not exactly a lofty-souled creature. In fact, he is pronouncedly a bounder, though I confess I did borrow money of him; but I'd borrow money of the devil when I'm in certain moods. A man may be a bounder, however, without being a criminal. No, I have thought this thing out as far as I can, and I've made my mind up that I've got to face it myself. I've been a fool, ah, such a fool!" A shudder shook his frame. "Oh, Dunn, old man, I don't mind for myself, I can go out easily enough, but it's my little sister! It will break her heart, and she has no one else; she will have to bear it all alone."

"What do you mean, Cameron?" asked Dunn sharply.

Cameron sprang to his feet. "Let it go," he cried. "Let it go for to-night, anyway." He seized a decanter which stood all too ready to his hand, but Dunn interposed.

"Listen to me, old man," he said, in a voice of grave and earnest sadness, while he pushed Cameron back into a chair. "We have a desperately hard game before us, you and I,—this is my game, too,—and we must be fit; so, Cameron, I want your word that you will play up for all that's in you; that you will cut this thing out," pointing to the decanter, "and will keep fit to the last fighting minute. I am asking you this, Cameron. You owe it to yourself, you owe it to me, you owe it to your sister."

For some moments Cameron sat gazing straight before him, his face showing the agony in his soul. "As God's above, I do! I owe it to you, Dunn, and to her, and to the memory of my—" But his quivering lips could not utter the word; and there was no need, for they both knew that his heart was far away in the little mound that lay in the shadow of the church tower in the Cuagh Oir. The lad rose to his feet, and stretching out his hand to Dunn cried, "There's my hand and my honour as a Highlander, and until the last fighting moment I'll be fit."

At the party that night none was gayer than young Cameron. The shy reserve that usually marked him was thrust aside. His fine, lithe figure, set off by his Highland costume, drew all eyes in admiration, and whether in the proud march of the piper, or in the wild abandon of the Highland Fling, he seemed to all the very beau ideal of a gallant Highland gentleman.

Dunn stood in the circle gathered to admire, watching Cameron's performance of that graceful and intricate Highland dance, all unconscious of a pair of bright blue eyes fastened on his face that reflected so manifestly the grief and pain in his heart.

"And wherefore this gloom?" said a gay voice at his side. It was Miss Bessie Brodie.

Poor Dunn! He was not skilled in the fine art of social deception. He could only gaze stupidly and with blinking eyes upon his questioner, devoutly hoping meanwhile that the tears would not fall.

"Splendid Highlander, isn't he?" exclaimed Miss Bessie, hastily withdrawing her eyes from his face, for she was much too fine a lady to let him see her surprise.

"What?" exclaimed Dunn. "I don't know. I mean —yes, awfully—oh, confound the thing, it's a beastly shame!"

Thereupon Miss Bessie turned her big blue eyes slowly upon him. "Meaning what?" she said quietly.

"Oh, I beg pardon. I'm just a fool. Oh, hang it all!" Dunn could not recover his composure. He backed out of the circle of admirers into a darker corner.

"Fool?" said Miss Brodie, stepping back with him. "And why, pray? Can I know? I suppose it's Cameron again," she continued. "Oh, I know all about you and your mothering of him."

"Mothering!" said Dunn bitterly. "That is just what he needs, by Jove. His mother has been dead these five years, and that's been the ruin of him."

The cheers from Cameron's admirers broke in upon Dunn's speech. "Oh, it's too ghastly," he muttered.

"Is it really so bad? Can't I help?" cried Miss Brodie. "You know I've had some experience with boys."

As Dunn looked into her honest, kindly eyes he hesitated. Should he tell her? He was in sore need of counsel, and besides he was at the limit of his self-control. "I say," he said, staring at her, while his lips quivered, "I'd like awfully to tell you, but I know if I ever begin I shall just burst into tears before this gaping crowd."

"Tears!" exclaimed Miss Bessie. "Not you! And if you did it wouldn't hurt either them or you. An International captain possesses this advantage over other mortals: that he may burst into tears or anything else without losing caste, whereas if I should do any such thing— But come, let's get somewhere and talk it over. Now, then," said Miss Brodie as they found a quiet corner, "first of all, ought I to know?"

"You'll know, all Edinburgh will know the day after to-morrow," said Dunn.

"All right, then, it can't do any harm for me to know to-night. It possibly may do good."

"It will do me good, anyway," said Dunn, "for I have reached my limit."

Then Dunn told her, and while she listened she grew grave and anxious. "But surely it can be arranged!" she exclaimed, after he had finished.

"No, Mr. Rae has tried everything. The Bank is bound to pursue it to the bitter end. It is apparently a part of its policy."

"What Bank?"

"The Bank of Scotland."

"Why, that's my uncle's Bank! I mean, he is the Chairman of the Board of Directors, and the Bank is the apple of his eye; or one of them, I mean—I'm the other."

"Oh, both, I fancy," said Dunn, rather pleased with his own courage.

"But come, this is serious," said Miss Brodie. "The Bank, you know, or you don't know, is my uncle's weak spot."

Mr. Rae's words flashed across Dunn's mind: "We ought to have found his weak spots."

"He says," continued Miss Brodie with a smile—"you know he's an old dear!—I divide his heart with the Bank, that I have the left lobe. Isn't that the bigger one? So the Bank and I are his weak spots; unless it is his Wiltshires—he is devoted to Wiltshires."

"Wiltshires?"

"Pigs. There are times when I feel myself distinctly second to them. Are you sure my uncle knows all about Cameron?"

"Well, Mr. Rae and Captain Cameron—that's young Cameron's father—went out to his place—"

"Ah, that was a mistake," said Miss Brodie. "He hates people following him to the country. Well, what happened?"

"Mr. Rae feels that it was rather a mistake that Captain Cameron went along."

"Why so? He is his father, isn't he?"

"Yes, he is, though I'm bound to say he's rather queer for a father." Whereupon Dunn gave her an account of his interview in Mr. Rae's office.

Miss Brodie was indignant. "What a shame! And what a fool! Why, he is ten times more fool than his son; for mark you, his son is undoubtedly a fool, and a selfish fool at that. I can't bear a young fool who sacrifices not simply his own life, but the interests of all who care for him, for some little pet selfishness of his own. But this father of his seems to be even worse than the son. Family name indeed! And I venture to say he expatiated upon the glory of his family name to my uncle. If there's one thing that my uncle goes quite mad about it is this affectation of superiority on the ground of the colour of a man's blood! No wonder he refused to withdraw the prosecution! What could Mr. Rae have been thinking about? What fools men are!"

"Quite true," murmured Mr. Dunn.

"Some men, I mean," cried Miss Brodie hastily. "I wish to heaven I had seen my uncle first!"

"I suppose it's too late now," said Dunn, with a kind of gloomy wistfulness.

"Yes, I fear so," said Miss Brodie. "You see when my uncle makes up his mind he appears to have some religious scruples against changing it."

"It was a ghastly mistake," said Dunn bitterly.

"Look here, Mr. Dunn," said Miss Brodie, turning upon him suddenly, "I want your straight opinion. Do you think this young man guilty?"

They were both looking at Cameron, at that moment the centre of a group of open admirers, his boyish face all aglow with animation. For the time being it seemed as if he had forgotten the terrible catastrophe overhanging him.

"If I hadn't known Cameron for three years," replied Dunn slowly, "I would say offhand that this thing would be impossible to him; but you see you never know what a man in drink will do. Cameron can carry a bottle of Scotch without a stagger, but of course it knocks his head all to pieces. I mean, he is quite incapable of anything like clear thought."

"It is truly terrible," said Miss Brodie. "I wish I had known yesterday, but those men have spoilt it all. But here's 'Lily' Laughton," she continued hurriedly, "coming for his dance." As she spoke a youth of willowy figure, languishing dark eyes and ladylike manner drew near.

"Well, here you are at last! What a hunt I have had! I am quite exhausted, I assure you," cried the youth, fanning himself with his handkerchief. "And though you have quite forgotten it, this is our dance. What can you two have been talking about? But why ask? There is only one theme upon which you could become so terrifically serious."

"And what is that, pray? Browning?" inquired Miss Brodie sweetly.

"Dear Miss Brodie, if you only would, but—ugh!—" here "Lily" shuddered, "I can in fancy picture the gory scene in which you have been revelling for the last hour!" And "Lily's" handsome face and languid, liquid eyes indicated his horror. It was "Lily's" constant declaration that he "positively loathed" football, although his persistent attendance at all the great matches rather belied this declaration. "It is the one thing in you, Miss Bessie, that I deplore, 'the fly in the pot—' no, 'the flaw—' ah, that's better—'the flaw in the matchless pearl.'"

"How sweet of you," murmured Miss Brodie.

"Yes, indeed," continued "Lily," wreathing his tapering fingers, "it is your devotion to those so-called athletic games,—games! ye gods!—the chief qualifications for excellence in which appear to be brute strength and a blood-thirsty disposition; as witness Dunn there. I was positively horrified last International. There he was, our own quiet, domestic, gentle Dunn, raging through that howling mob of savages like a bloody Bengal tiger. —Rather apt, that!— A truly awful and degrading exhibition!"

"Ah, perfectly lovely!" murmured Miss Brodie ecstatically. "I can see him yet."

"Miss Brodie, how can you!" exclaimed "Lily," casting up his eyes in horror towards heaven. "But it was ever thus! In ancient days upon the bloody sands of the arena, fair ladies were wont to gaze with unrelenting eyes and thumbs turned down—or up, was it—?"

"Excellent! But how clever of them to gaze with their thumbs in that way!"

"Please don't interrupt," said "Lily" severely; "I have just 'struck my gait,' as that barbaric young Colonial, Martin, another of your bloody, brawny band, would say. And here you sit, unblushing, glorying in their disgusting deeds and making love open and unabashed to their captain!"

"Go away, 'Lily' or I'll hurt you," cried Dunn, his face a brilliant crimson. "Come, get out!"

"But don't be uplifted," continued "Lily," ignoring him, "you are not the first. By no means! It is always the last International captain, and has been to my certain knowledge for the last ten years."

"Ten years!" exclaimed Miss Brodie in horrified accents. "You monster! If you have no regard for my character you might at least respect my age."

"Age! Dear Miss Brodie," ejaculated "Lily," "who could ever associate age with your perennial youth?"

"Perennial! Wretch! If there is anything I am sensitive about, really sensitive about, it is my age! Mr. Dunn, I beseech you, save me from further insult! Dear 'Lily,' run away now. You are much too tired to dance, and besides there is Mrs. Craig-Urquhart waiting to talk your beloved Wagner-Tennyson theory; or what is the exact combination? Mendelssohn-Browning, is it?"

"Oh, Miss Bessie!" cried "Lily" in a shocked voice. "How can you? Mendelssohn-Browning! How awful! Do have some regard for the affinities."

"Mr. Dunn, I implore you, save me! I can bear no more. There! A merciful providence has accomplished

my deliverance. They are going. Good-night, 'Lily.'
Run away now. I want a word with Mr. Dunn."

"Oh, heartless cruelty!" exclaimed "Lily," in an agonised voice. "But what can you expect from such associations?" And he hastened away to have a last word with
Mrs. Craig-Urquhart, who was swimming languidly by.

Miss Brodie turned eagerly to Dunn. "I'd like to
help you awfully," she said; "indeed I must try. I have
very little hope. My uncle is so strong when he is once
set, and he is so funny about that Bank. But a boy is
worth more than a Bank, if he *is* a fool; besides, there is
his sister. Good-night. Thanks for letting me help. I
have little hope, but to-morrow I shall see Sir Archibald,
and—and his pigs."

It was still in the early forenoon of the following day
when Miss Brodie greeted her uncle as he was about to
start upon his round of the pastures and pens where the
Wiltshires of various ages and sizes and sexes were kept.
With the utmost enthusiasm Miss Brodie entered into
his admiration of them all, from the lordly prize tusker
to the great mother lying broadside on in grunting and
supreme content, every grunt eloquent of happiness and
maternal love and pride, to allow her week-old brood to
prod and punch her luxuriant dugs for their breakfast.

By the time they had made their rounds Sir Archibald had arrived at his most comfortable and complac-
ent mood. He loved his niece. He loved her for the
sake of his dead brother, and as she grew in years, he
came to love her for herself. Her sturdy independent
fearlessness, her sound sense, her honest heart, and
chiefly, if it must be told, her whole-souled devotion to
himself, made for her a great space in his heart. And
besides all this, they were both interested to the point of
devotion in pigs. As he watched his niece handling the

little sucklings with tender care, and listened to her appraising their varying merits with a discriminating judgment, his heart filled up with pride in her many accomplishments and capabilities.

"Isn't she happy, Uncle?" she exclaimed, lifting her brown, sunny face to him.

"Ay, lassie," replied Sir Archibald, lapsing into the kindly "braid Scots," "I ken fine how she feels."

"She's just perfectly happy," said his niece, "and awfully useful and good. She is just like you, Uncle."

"What? Oh, thank you, I'm extremely flattered, I assure you."

"Uncle, you know what I mean! Useful and good. Here you are in this lovely home—how lovely it is on a warm, shiny day like this!—safe from cares and worries, where people can't get at you, and making—"

"Ah, I don't know about that," replied her uncle, shaking his head with a frown. "Some people have neither sense nor manners. Only yesterday I was pestered by a fellow who annoyed me, seriously annoyed me, interfering in affairs which he knew nothing of,— actually the affairs of the Bank!—prating about his family name, and all the rest of it. Family name!" Here, it must be confessed, Sir Archibald distinctly snorted, quite in a manner calculated to excite the envy of any of his Wiltshires.

"I know, Uncle. He is a fool, a conceited fool, and a selfish fool."

"You know him?" inquired her uncle in a tone of surprise.

"No, I have no personal acquaintance with him, I'm glad to say, but I know about him, and I know that he came with Mr. Rae, the Writer."

"Ah, yes! Thoroughly respectable man, Mr. Rae."

"Yes, Mr. Rae is all right; but Captain Cameron—oh, I can't bear him! He came to talk to you about his son, and I venture to say he took most of the time in talking about himself."

"Exactly so! But how—?"

"And, Uncle, I want to talk to you about that matter, about young Cameron." For just a moment Miss Brodie's courage faltered as she observed her uncle's figure stiffen. "I want you to know the rights of the case."

"Now, now, my dear, don't you go—ah—"

"I know, Uncle, you were going to say 'interfering,' only you remember in time that your niece never interferes. Isn't that true, Sir?"

"Yes, yes! I suppose so; that is, certainly."

"Now I am interested in this young Cameron, and I want you to get the right view of his case, which neither your lawyer nor your manager nor that fool father of his can give you. I know that if you see this case as I see it you will do—ah—exactly what is right; you always do."

Miss Brodie's voice had assumed its most reasonable and business-like tone. Sir Archibald was impressed, and annoyed because he was impressed.

"Look here, Bessie," he said, in as impatient a tone as he ever adopted with his niece, "you know how I hate being pestered with business affairs out here."

"I know quite well, Uncle, and I regret it awfully, but I know, too, that you are a man of honour, and that you stand for fair play. But that young man is to be arrested to-day, and you know what that will mean for a young fellow with his way to make."

Her appeal was not without its effect. Sir Archibald set himself to give her serious attention. "Let us have

it, then," he said briefly. "What do you know of the
young man?"

"This first of all: that he has a selfish, conceited prig
for a father."

With which beginning Sir Archibald most heartily
agreed. "But how do you know?"

"Now, let me tell you about him." And Miss Brodie
proceeded to describe the scene between father and son
in Mr. Rae's office, with vigorous and illuminating comments. "And just think, the man in the company who
was first to condemn the young chap was his own father.
Would you do that? You'd stand for him against the
whole world, even if he were wrong."

"Steady, steady, lass!"

"You would," repeated Miss Bessie, with indignant
emphasis. "Would you chuck me over if I were dis-
graced and all the world hounding me? Would you?"

"No, by God!" said Sir Archibald in a sudden tempest
of emotion, and Miss Bessie smiled lovingly upon him.

"Well, that's the kind of a father he has. Now about
the young fellow himself: He's just a first-class fool, like
most young fellows. You know how they are, Uncle."

Sir Archibald held up his hand. "Don't make any
such assumptions."

"Oh, I know you, and when you were a boy you were
just as gay and foolish as the rest of them."

Her arch, accusing smile suddenly cast a rich glow of
warm colour over the long, grey road of Sir Archibald's
youth of self-denial and struggle. The mild indulgences
of his early years, under the transforming influence of
that same arch and accusing smile, took on for Sir Archibald such an aspect of wild and hilarious gaiety as to
impart a tone of hesitation to his voice while he deprecated his niece's charge.

"What, I? Nonsense! What do you know about it? Well, well, we have all had our day, I suppose!"

"Aha! I know you, and I should love to have known you when you were young Cameron's age. Though I'm quite sure you were never such a fool as he. You always knew how to take care of yourself."

Her uncle shook his head as if to indicate that the less said about those gay young days the better.

"Now what do you think this young fool does? Gets drinking, and gets so muddled up in all his money matters—he's a Highlander, you know, and Dunn, Mr. Dunn says—"

"Dunn!"

"Yes, Mr. Dunn, the great International captain, you know! Mr. Dunn says he can take a whole bottle of Scotch—"

"What, Dunn?"

"No, no; you know perfectly well, Uncle! This young Cameron can take a whole bottle of Scotch and walk a crack, but his head gets awfully muddled."

"Shouldn't be surprised!"

"And Mr. Dunn had a terrible time keeping him fit for the International. You know he was Dunn's half-back. Yes," cried his niece with enthusiasm, suddenly remembering a tradition that in his youth Sir Archibald had been a famous quarter, his one indulgence, "a glorious half-back, too! You must remember in the match with England last fall the brilliant work of the half-back. Everybody went mad about him. That was young Cameron!"

"You don't tell me! The left-half in the English International last fall?"

"Yes, indeed! Oh, he's wonderful! But he has to be watched, you know, and the young fool lost us the last—" Miss Bessie abruptly checked herself. "But never mind! Well, after the season, you know, he got going loose, and this is the result. Owed money everywhere, and with the true Highland incapacity for business, and the true Highland capacity for trusting people—"

"Huh!" grunted Sir Archibald in disapproval.

"—When his head is in a muddled condition he does something or other to a cheque—or doesn't do it, nobody knows—and there he is in this awful fix. Personally, I don't believe he is guilty of the crime."

"And why, pray?"

"Why? Well, Mr. Dunn, his captain, who has known him for years, says it is quite impossible; and then the young man himself doesn't deny it."

"What? Does *not* deny it?"

"Exactly! Like a perfectly straightforward gentleman,—and I think it's awfully fine of him,—though he has a perfectly good chance to put the thing on a—a fellow Potts, quite a doubtful character, he simply says, 'I know nothing about it. That looks like my signature. I can't remember doing this, don't know how I could have, but don't know a thing about it.' There you are, Uncle! And Mr. Dunn says he is quite incapable of it."

"Mr. Dunn, eh? It seems you build somewhat broadly upon Mr. Dunn."

The brown on Miss Bessie's cheek deepened slightly. "Well, Mr. Dunn is a splendid judge of men."

"Ah; and of young ladies, also, I imagine," said Sir Archibald, pinching her cheek.

It may have been the pinch, but the flush on her cheek grew distinctly brighter. "Don't be ridiculous, Uncle! He's just a boy, a perfectly splendid boy, and glorious in his game, but a mere boy, and—well, you know, I've arrived at the age of discretion."

"Quite true!" mused her uncle. "Thirty last birthday, was it? How time does—!"

"Oh, you perfectly horrid uncle! Thirty indeed! Are you not ashamed to add to the already intolerable burden of my years? Thirty! No, Sir, not by five good years at least! There now, you've made me tell my age! You ought to blush for shame."

Her uncle patted her firm, round cheek. "Never a blush, my dear! You bear even your advanced age with quite sufficient ease and grace. But now about this young Cameron," he continued, assuming a sternly judicial tone.

"All I ask for him is a chance," said his niece earnestly.

"A chance? Why he will get every chance the law allows to clear himself."

"There you are!" exclaimed Miss Bessie, in a despairing tone. "That's the way the lawyers and your manager talk. They coolly and without a qualm get him arrested, this young boy who has never in all his life shown any sign of criminal tendency. These horrid lawyers display their dreadful astuteness and ability in catching a lad who never tries to run away, and your manager pleads the rules of the Bank. The rules! Fancy rules against a young boy's whole life!"

Her uncle rather winced at this.

"And like a lot of sheep they follow each other in a circle; there is absolutely no independence, no initiative. Why, they even went so far as to suggest that you could do nothing, that you were bound by rules and must follow like the rest of them; but I told them I knew better."

"Ah!" said Sir Archibald in his most dignified manner. "I trust I have a mind of my own, but—"

"Exactly! So I said to Mr. Dunn. 'Rules or no rules,' I said, 'my uncle will do the fair thing.' And I know you will," cried Miss Brodie triumphantly. "And if you look at it, there's a very big chance that the boy never did the thing, and certainly if he did it at all it was when he was quite incapable. Oh, I know quite well what the lawyers say. They go by the law,—they've got to,—but you—and—and—I go by the—the real facts of the case." Sir Archibald coughed gently. "I mean to say—well you know, Uncle, quite well, you can tell what a man is by—well, by his game."

"His game!"

"And by his eye."

"His eye! And his eye is—?"

"Now, Uncle, be sensible! I mean to say, if you could only see him. Oh, I shall bring him to see you!" she cried, with a sudden inspiration.

Sir Archibald held up a deprecating hand. "Do not, I beg."

"Well, Uncle, you can trust my judgment, you know you can. You would trust me in—in—" For a moment Miss Brodie was at a loss; then her eyes fell upon the grunting, comfortable old mother pig with her industrious litter. "Well, don't I know good Wiltshires when I see them?"

"Quite true," replied her uncle solemnly; "and therefore, men."

"Uncle, you're very nearly rude."

"I apologise," replied her uncle hastily. "But now, Bessie, my dear girl, seriously, as to this case, you must understand that I cannot interfere. The Bank—hem —the Bank is a great National—"

Miss Bessie saw that the Guards were being called upon. She hastened to bring up her reserves. "I know, Uncle, I know! I wouldn't for the world say a word against the Bank, but you see the case against the lad is at least doubtful."

"I was going on to observe," resumed her uncle, judicially, "that the Bank—"

"Don't misunderstand me, Uncle," cried his niece, realising that she had reached a moment of crisis. "You know I would not for a moment presume to interfere with the Bank, but"—here she deployed her whole force, —"the lad's youth and folly; his previous good character, guaranteed by Dunn, who knows men; his glorious game—no man who wasn't straight could play such a game!—the large chance of his innocence, the small chance of his guilt; the hide-bound rigidity of lawyers and bank managers, dominated by mere rules and routine, in contrast with the open-minded independence of her uncle; the boy's utter helplessness; his own father having been ready to believe the worst,—just think of it, Uncle, his own father thinking of himself and of his family name—much he has ever done for his family name!—and not of his own boy, and"— here Miss Brodie's voice took a lower key—"and his mother died some five or six years ago, when he was thirteen or fourteen, and I know, you know, that is hard on a boy." In spite of herself, and to her disgust, a tremor came into her voice and a rush of tears to her eyes.

Her uncle was smitten with dismay. Only on one terrible occasion since she had emerged from her teens had he seen his niece in tears. The memory of that terrible day swept over his soul. Something desperate was doing. Hard as the little man was to the world against which he had fought his way to his present position of distinction, to his niece he was soft-hearted as a mother. "There, there!" he exclaimed hastily. "We'll give the boy a chance. No mother, eh? And a confounded prig for a father! No wonder the boy goes all wrong!" Then with a sudden vehemence he cried, striking one hand into the other, "No, by—! that is, we will certainly give the lad the benefit of the doubt. Cheer up, lassie! You've no need to look ashamed," for his niece was wiping her eyes in manifest disgust; "indeed," he said, with a heavy attempt at playfulness, "you are a most excellent diplomat."

"Diplomat, Uncle!" cried the girl, vehement indignation in her voice and face. "Diplomat!" she cried again. "You don't mean that I've not been quite sincere?"

"No, no, no; not in the least, my dear! But that you have put your case with admirable force."

"Oh," said the girl with a breath of relief, "I just put it as I feel it. And it is not a bit my putting it, Uncle, but it is just that you are a dear and—well, a real sport; you love fair play." The girl suddenly threw her strong, young arms about her uncle's neck, drew him close to her, and kissed him almost as if she had been his mother.

The little man was deeply touched, but with true Scotch horror of a demonstration he cried, "Tut, tut, lassie, ye're makin' an auld fule o' your uncle. Come now, be sensible!"

"Sensible!" echoed his niece, kissing him again. "That's my living description among all my acquaintance. It is their gentle way of reminding me that the ordinary feminine graces of sweetness and general loveliness are denied me."

"And more fools they!" grunted her uncle. "You're worth the hale caboodle o' them."

That same evening there were others who shared this

opinion, and none more enthusiastically than did Mr. Dunn, whom Miss Brodie chanced to meet just as she turned out of the Waverly Station.

"Oh, Mr. Dunn," she cried, "how very fortunate!" Her face glowed with excitement.

"For me; yes, indeed!" said Mr. Dunn, warmly greeting her.

"For me, for young Cameron, for us all," said Miss Brodie. "Oh, Rob, is that you?" she continued, as her eye fell upon the youngster standing with cap off waiting her recognition. "Look at this!" she flashed a letter before Dunn's face. "What do you think of that?"

Dunn took the letter. "It's to Sheratt," he said, with a puzzled air.

"Yes," cried Miss Brodie, mimicking his tone, "it's to Sheratt, from Sir Archibald, and it means that Cameron is safe. The police will never—"

"The police," cried Dunn, hastily, getting between young Rob and her and glancing at his brother, who stood looking from one to the other with a startled face.

"How stupid! The police are a truly wonderful body of men," she went on with enthusiasm. "They look so splendid. I saw some of them as I came along. But never mind them now. About this letter. What's to do?"

Dunn glanced at his watch. "We need every minute." He stood a moment or two thinking deeply while Miss Brodie chatted eagerly with Rob, whose face retained its startled and anxious look. "First to Mr. Rae's office. Come!" cried Mr. Dunn.

"But this letter ought to go."

"Yes, but first Mr. Rae's office." Mr. Dunn had assumed command. His words shot out like bullets.

Miss Brodie glanced at him with a new admiration in her face. As a rule she objected to being ordered about, but somehow it seemed good to accept commands from this young man, whose usually genial face was now set in such resolute lines.

"Here, Rob, you cut home and tell them not to wait dinner for me."

"All right, Jack!" But instead of tearing off as was his wont whenever his brother gave command, Rob lingered. "Can't I wait a bit, Jack, to see—to see if anything—?" Rob was striving hard to keep his voice in command and his face steady. "It's Cameron, Jack. I know!" He turned his back on Miss Brodie, unwilling that she should see his lips quiver.

"What are you talking about?" said his brother sharply.

"Oh, it is all my stupid fault, Mr. Dunn," said Miss Brodie. "Let him come along a bit with us. I say, youngster, you are much too acute," she continued, as they went striding along together toward Mr. Rae's office. "But will you believe me if I tell you something? Will you? Straight now?"

The boy glanced up into her honest blue eyes, and nodded his head.

"Your friend Cameron is quite all right. He was in some difficulty, but now he's quite all right. Do you believe me?"

The boy looked again steadily into her eyes. The anxious fear passed out of his face, and once more he nodded; he knew he could not keep his voice quite steady. But after a few paces he said to his brother, "I think I'll go now, Jack." His mind was at rest; his idol was safe.

"Oh, come along and protect me," cried Miss Brodie. "These lawyer people terrify me."

The boy smiled a happy smile. "I'll go," he said resolutely.

"Thanks, awfully," said Miss Brodie. "I shall feel so much safer with you in the waiting room."

It was a difficult matter to surprise Mr. Rae, and even more difficult to extract from him any sign of surprise, but when Dunn, leaving Miss Brodie and his brother in the anteroom, entered Mr. Rae's private office and laid the letter for Mr. Sheratt before him, remarking, "This letter is from Sir Archibald, and withdraws the prosecution," Mr. Rae stood speechless, gazing now at the letter in his hand, and now at Mr. Dunn's face.

"God bless my soul! This is unheard of. How came you by this, Sir?"

"Miss Brodie—" began Dunn.

"Miss Brodie?"

"She is in the waiting room, Sir."

"Then, for heaven's sake, bring her in! Davie, Davie! Where is that man now? Here, Davie, a message to Mr. Thomlinson."

Davie entered with deliberate composure.

"My compliments to Mr. Thomlinson, and ask if he would step over at once. It is a matter of extreme urgency. Be quick!"

But Davie had his own mind as to the fitness of things. "Wad a note no' be better, Sir? Wull not—?"

"Go, will you!" almost shouted Mr. Rae.

Davie was so startled at Mr. Rae's unusual vehemence that he seized his cap and made for the door. "He'll no' come for the like o' me," he said, pausing with the door-knob in his hand. "It's no' respectable like tae—"

"Man, will ye no' be gone?" cried Mr. Rae, rising from his chair.

"I will that!" exclaimed Davie, banging the door after

him. "But," he cried furiously, thrusting his head once more into the room, "if he'll no' come it's no' faut o' mine." His voice rose higher and higher, and ended in a wrathful scream as Mr. Rae, driven to desperation, hurled a law book of some weight at his vanishing head.

"The de'il take ye! Ye'll be my deith yet."

The book went crashing against the door-frame just as Miss Brodie was about to enter. "I say," she cried, darting back. "Heaven protect me! Rob, save me!"

Rob sprang to her side. She stood for a moment gazing aghast at Mr. Dunn, who gazed back at her in equal surprise. "Is this his 'usual'?" she inquired.

At that the door opened. "Ah, Mr. Dunn, this is Miss Brodie, I suppose. Come in, come in!" Mr. Rae's manner was most bland.

Miss Brodie gave him her hand with some hesitation. "I'm very glad to meet you, Mr. Rae, but is this quite the usual method? I mean to say, I've heard of having advice hurled at one's head, but I can't say that I ever was present at a demonstration of the method."

"Oh," said Mr. Rae, with bland and gallant courtesy, "the method, my dear young lady, varies with the subject in hand."

"Ah, the subject!"

"And with the object in view."

"Oh, I see."

"But pray be seated. And now explain this most wonderful phenomenon." He tapped the letter.

"Oh, that is quite simple," said Miss Brodie. "I set the case of young Mr. Cameron before my uncle, and of course he at once saw that the only thing to do was withdraw the prosecution."

Mr. Rae stood gazing steadily at her as if striving to take in the meaning of her words, the while screwing up his ear most violently till it stuck out like a horn upon the side of his shiny, bald head. "Permit me to say, Miss Brodie," he said, with a deliberate and measured emphasis, "that you must be a most extraordinary young lady." At this point Mr. Rae's smile broke forth in all its glory.

"Oh, thank you, Mr. Rae," replied Miss Brodie, smiling responsively at him. "You are most—" But Mr. Rae's smile had vanished. "What! I beg your pardon!" Miss Brodie's smiling response was abruptly arrested by finding herself gazing at a face whose grave solemnity rebuked her smile as unwarranted levity.

"Not at all, not at all!" said Mr. Rae. "But now, there are matters demanding immediate action. First, Mr. Sheratt must receive and act upon this letter without delay." As he spoke he was scribbling hastily a note. "Mr. Dunn, my young men have gone for the day. Might I trouble you?"

"Most certainly," cried Mr. Dunn. "Is an answer wanted?"

"Bring him with you, if possible; indeed, bring him whether it is possible or not. But wait, it is past the hour appointed. Already the officer has gone for young Cameron. We must save him the humiliation of arrest."

"Oh, could I not warn him?" cried Miss Brodie eagerly. "No," she added, "Rob will go. He is in the waiting room now, poor little chap. It will be a joy to him."

"It is just as well Rob should know nothing. He is awfully fond of Cameron. It would break his heart," said Mr. Dunn.

"Oh, of course! Quite unnecessary that he should know anything. We simply wish Cameron here at the earliest possible moment."

Dunn went with his young brother down the stairs and out to the street. "Now, Rob, you are to go to Cameron's lodgings and tell him that Mr. Rae wants him, and that I want him. Hold on, youngster!" he cried, grabbing Rob by the collar, "do you understand? It is very important that Cameron should get here as quick as he possibly can, and—I say, Rob," the big brother's eyes traveled over the darkening streets that led up into the old town, "you're not afraid?"

"A wee bit," said Rob, tugging at the grasp on his collar; "but I don't care if I am."

"Good boy!" cried his brother. "Good little brick! I wouldn't let you go, but it's simply got to be done, old chap. Now fly!" He held him just a moment longer to slap him on the back, then released his hold. Dunn stood watching the little figure tearing up the North Bridge. "Great little soul!" he muttered. "Now for old Sheratt!"

He put his head down and began to bore through the crowd toward Mr. Sheratt's house. When he had gone but a little distance he was brought up short by a bang full in the stomach. "Why, what the deuce!"

"Dod gast ye! Whaur are ye're een?" It was Davie, breathless and furious from the impact. "Wad ye walk ower me, dang ye?" cried the little man again. Davie was Free Kirk, and therefore limited in the range of his vocabulary.

"Oh! That you, Davie? I'm sorry I didn't see you."

"A'm no' as big as a hoose, but a'm veesible." And Davie walked wrathfully about his business.

"Oh, quite," acknowledged Dunn cheerfully, hurrying on; "and tangible, as well."

"He's comin'," cried Davie over his shoulder; "but

gar it had been masel'," he added grudgingly, "catch me!"

But Dunn was too far on his way to make reply. Already his mind was on the meeting of the lawyers in Mr. Rae's office, and wondering what would come of it. On this subject he meditated until he reached Mr. Sheratt's home. Twice he rang the bell, still meditating.

"By Jove, she is stunning! She's a wonder!" he exclaimed to himself as he stood in Mr. Sheratt's drawing-room. "She's got 'em all skinned a mile, as Martin would say." It is safe to affirm that Mr. Dunn was not referring to the middle-aged and highly respectable maid who had opened the door to him. It is equally safe to affirm that this was the unanimous verdict of the three men who, half an hour later, brought their deliberations to a conclusion, frankly acknowledging to each other that what they had one and all failed to achieve, the lady had accomplished.

CHAPTER VI

THE WASTER'S REFUGE

"I SAY, you blessed Colonial, what's come over you?" Linklater was obviously disturbed. He had just returned from a summer's yachting through the Norway fjords, brown and bursting with life. The last half-hour he had been pouring forth his experiences to his friend Martin. These experiences were some of them exciting, some of them of doubtful ethical quality, but all of them to Linklater at least interesting. During the recital it was gradually borne in upon him that his friend Martin was changed. Linklater, as the consciousness of the change in his friend grew upon him, was prepared to resent it. "What the deuce is the matter with you?" he enquired. "Are you ill?"

"Never better. I could at this present moment sit upon your fat and florid carcass."

"Well, what then is wrong? I say, you haven't—it isn't a girl, is it?"

"Nothing so lucky for a bloomin' Colonial in this land of wealth and culture. If I only dared!"

"There's something," insisted Linklater; "but I've no doubt it will develop. Meantime let us go out, and, in your own picturesque vocabulary, let us 'hit the flowing bowl.'"

"No, Sir!" cried Martin emphatically. "No more! I am on the water wagon, and have been all summer."

"I knew it was something," replied Linklater gloomily, "but I didn't think it was quite so bad as that. No wonder you've had a hard summer!"

"Best summer ever!" cried Martin. "I only wish I had started two years ago when I came to this bibulous burgh."

"How came it? Religion?"

"No; just horse sense, and the old chief."

"Dunn!" exclaimed Linklater. "I always knew he was against that sort of thing in training, but I didn't think he would carry it to this length."

"Yes, Dunn! I say, old boy, I've no doubt you think you know him, I thought so, too, but I've learned some this summer. Here's a yarn, and it is impressive. Dunn had planned an extensive walking tour in the Highlands; you know he came out of his exams. awfully fagged. Well, at this particular moment it happened that Balfour Murray—you know the chap that has been running that settlement joint in the Canongate for the last two years—proposes to Dunn that he should spend a few weeks in leading the young hopefuls in that interesting and uncleanly neighbourhood into paths of virtue and higher citizenship by way of soccer and kindred athletic stunts. Dunn in his innocence agrees, whereupon Balfour Murray promptly develops a sharp attack of pneumonia, necessitating rest and change of air, leaving the poor old chief in the deadly breach. Of course, everybody knows what the chief would do in any deadly breach affair. He gave up his Highland tour, shouldered the whole Canongate business, organised the thing as never before, inveigled all his friends into the same deadly breach, among the number your humble servant, who at the time was fiercely endeavouring in the last lap of the course to atone for a two years' loaf, organised a champion team which has licked the spots off everything in sight, and in short, has made the whole business a howling success; at the cost, however, of all worldly delights, including his Highland tour and the International."

"Oh, I say!" moaned Linklater. "It makes me quite ill to think of the old chief going off this way."

Martin nodded sympathetically. "Kind of 'Days that are no more,' 'Lost leader' feeling, eh?"

"Exactly, exactly! Oh, it's rotten! And you, too! He's got you on this same pious line."

"Look here," shouted Martin, with menace in his voice, "are you classifying me with the old chief? Don't be a derned fool."

Linklater brightened perceptibly. "Now you're getting a little natural," he said in a hopeful tone.

"Oh, I suppose you'd like to hear me string out a lot of damns."

"Well, it might help. I wouldn't feel quite so lonely. But don't violate——"

"I'd do it if I thought it would really increase your comfort, though I know I'd feel like an infernal ass. I've got new light upon this 'damning' business. I've come to regard it as the refuge of the mentally inert, not to say imbecile, who have lost the capacity for originality and force in speech. For me, I am cured."

"Ah!" said Linklater. "Dunn again, I suppose."

"Not a bit! Clear case of psychological reaction. After listening to the Canongate experts I was immediately conscious of an overwhelming and mortifying sense of inadequacy, of amateurishness; hence I quit. Besides, of course, the chief is making rather a point of uplifting the Canongate forms of speech."

Linklater gazed steadily at this friend, then said with mournful deliberation, "You don't drink, you don't swear, you don't smoke——"

"Oh, that's your grouch, is it?" cried Martin. "Forgive me; here's my pouch, old chap; or wait, here's something altogether finer than anything you've been accustomed to. I was at old Kingston's last night, and the old boy would have me load up with his finest. You know I've been working with him this summer. Awfully fine for me! Dunn got me on; or rather, his governor. There you are now! Smoke that with reverence."

"Ah," sighed Linklater, as he drew in his first whiff, "there is still something left to live for. Now tell me, what about Cameron?"

"Oh, Cameron! Cameron's all up a tree. The last time I saw him, by Jove, I was glad it was in the open daylight and on a frequented street. His face and manner suggested Roderick Dhu, The Black Douglas, and all the rest of that interesting gang of cutthroats. I can't bring myself to talk of Cameron. He's been the old chief's relaxation during dog-days. It makes me hot to see Dunn with that chap."

"Why, what's the trouble?"

"He tried him out in half a dozen positions, in every one of which he proved a dead failure. The last was in Mr. Rae's office, a lawyer, you know, Writer, to use your lucid and luminous speech. That experiment proved the climax." At the memory of that experience Martin laughed loud and long. "It was funny! Mr. Rae, the cool, dignified, methodical, exact man of the law, struggling to lick into shape this haughty Highland chieftain, who in his heart scorned the whole silly business. The result, the complete disorganisation of Mr. Rae's business, and total demoralisation of Mr. Rae's office staff, who one and all swore allegiance to the young chief. Finally, when Mr. Rae had reached the depths of desperation, Cameron graciously deigned to inform his boss that he found the office and its claims quite insupportable."

"Oh, it must have been funny. What happened?"

"What happened? You bet old Rae fell on his neck with tears of joy, and sent him off with a handsome *honorarium,* as your gentle speech has it. That was a fortnight ago. Then Dunn, in despair, took Cameron off to his native haunts, and there he is to this day. By the same token, this is the very afternoon that Dunn returns. Let us go to meet him with cornets and cymbals! The unexpected pleasure of your return made me quite forget. But won't he revel in you, old boy!"

"I don't know about that," said Linklater gloomily. "I've a kind of feeling that I've dropped out of this combination."

"What?" Then Martin fell upon him.

But if Martin's attempts to relieve his friend of melancholy forebodings were not wholly successful, Dunn's shout of joy and his double-handed shake as he grappled Linklater to him, drove from that young man's heart the last lingering shade of doubt as to his standing with his friends.

On his way home Dunn dropped into Martin's diggings for a "crack," and for an hour the three friends reviewed the summer's happenings, each finding in the experience of the others as keen a joy as in his own.

Linklater's holiday had been the most fruitful in exciting incident. For two months he and his crew had dodged about among quaint Norwegian harbours and in and out of fjords of wonderful beauty. Storms they had weathered and calms they had endured; lazy days they had spent, swimming, fishing, loafing; and wild days in fighting gales and high-running seas that threatened to bury them and their crew beneath their white-topped mountainous peaks.

"I say, that must have been great," cried Dunn with enthusiastic delight in his friend's experiences.

"It sounds good, even in the telling," cried Martin, who had been listening with envious ears. "Now my experiences are quite other. One word describes them, grind, grind, grind, day in and day out, in a gallant but futile attempt to justify the wisdom of my late examiners in granting me my Triple."

"Don't listen to him, Linklater," said Dunn. "I happen to know that he came through with banners flying and drums beating; and he has turned into no end of a surgeon. I've heard old Kingston on him."

"But what about you, Dunn?" asked Linklater, with a kind of curious uncertainty in his voice, as if dreading a tale of calamity.

"Oh, I've loafed about town a little, golfing a bit and slumming a bit for a chap that got ill, and in spare moments looking after Martin here."

"And the International?"

Dunn hesitated.

"Come on, old chap," said Martin, "take your medicine."

"Well," admitted Dunn, "I had to chuck it. But," he hastened to add, "Nesbitt has got the thing in fine shape, though of course lacking the two brilliant quarters of last year and the half—for Cameron's out of it—it's rather rough on Nesbitt."

"Oh, I say! It's rotten, it's really ghastly! How could you do it, Dunn?" said Linklater. "I could weep tears of blood."

To this Dunn made no reply. His disappointment was even yet too keen for him to treat it lightly. "Anything else seemed quite impossible," at length he said; "I had to chuck it."

"By the way," said Martin, "how's Cameron?"

Again Dunn paused. "I wish I could tell you. He's had hard luck this summer. He somehow can't get hold of himself. In fact, I'm quite worried about Cameron. I can't tell you chaps the whole story, but last spring he had a really bad jolt."

"Well, what's he going to do?" Martin asked, somewhat impatiently.

"I wish I knew," replied Dunn gloomily. "There seems nothing he can get here that's suitable. I'm afraid he will have to try the Colonies; Canada for preference."

"Oh, I say, Dunn," exclaimed Martin, "it can't really be as bad as all that?"

Dunn laughed. "I apologise, old chap. That was rather a bad break, wasn't it? But all the same, to a Scotchman, and especially to a Highlander, to leave home and friends and all that sort of thing, you know—"

"No, he doesn't know," cried Linklater. "The barbarian! How could he?"

"No, thank God," replied Martin fervently, "I don't know! To my mind any man that has a chance to go to Canada on a good job ought to call in his friends and neighbours to rejoice with him."

"But I say, that reminds me," said Dunn. "Mr. Rae is coming to have a talk with my governor and me about this very thing to-morrow night. I'd like awfully if you could drop in, Martin; and you, too, Linklater."

Linklater declined. "My folks have something on, I fear."

Martin hesitated, protesting that there was "altogether too much of this coddling business" in the matter of Cameron's future. "Besides, my work is rather crowding me."

"Oh, my pious ancestors! Work!" exclaimed Linklater in disgust. "At this season of the year! Come, Martin, this pose is unworthy of you."

"If you could, old man," said Dunn earnestly, "we won't keep you long. It would be a great help to us all."

"All right, I'll come," said Martin.

"There'll be no one there but Mr. Rae. We'll just have a smoke and a chat."

But in this expectation Dunn was reckoning without his young brother, Rob, who, ever since a certain momentous evening, had entered into a covenant of comradeship with the young lady who had figured so prominently in the deliverance of his beloved Cameron from pending evil, and who during the summer had allowed no week to pass without spending at least a part of a day with her. On this particular evening, having obtained leave from his mother, the young gentleman had succeeded in persuading his friend to accept an invitation to dinner, assuring her that no one would be there except Jack, who was to arrive home the day before.

The conclave of Cameron's friends found themselves, therefore, unexpectedly reinforced by the presence of Miss Brodie, to the unmingled joy of all of them, although in Martin's case his joy was tinged with a certain fear, for he stood in awe of the young lady, both because of her reputation for cleverness, and because of the grand air which, when it pleased her, she could assume. Martin, too, stood in wholesome awe of Doctor Dunn, whose quiet dignity and old-time courtesy exercised a chastening influence upon the young man's somewhat picturesque style of language and exuberance of metaphor. But with Mrs. Dunn he felt quite at ease, for with that gentle, kindly soul, her boys' friends were her friends and without question she took them to her motherly heart.

Immediately upon Mr. Rae's arrival Cameron's future became the subject of conversation, and it required only the briefest discussion to arrive at the melancholy, inevitable conclusion that, as Mr. Rae put it, "for a young man of his peculiar temperament, training, and habits, Scotland was clearly impossible."

"But I have no doubt," continued that excellent adviser, "that in Canada, where the demand for a high standard of efficiency is less exacting, and where openings are more plentiful, the young man will do very well indeed."

Martin took the lawyer up somewhat sharply. "In other words, I understand you to mean that the man who is a failure in Scotland may become a success in Canada."

"Exactly so. Would you not say so, Mr. Martin?"

"It depends entirely upon the cause of failure. If failure arises from unfitness, his chances in Canada are infinitely less than in Scotland."

"And why?" inquired Miss Brodie somewhat impatiently.

Martin hesitated. It was extremely difficult in the atmosphere of that home to criticise one whom he knew to be considered as a friend of the family.

"Why, pray?" repeated Miss Brodie.

"Well, of course," began Martin hesitatingly, "comparisons are always odious."

"Oh, we can bear them." Miss Brodie's smile was slightly sarcastic.

"Well, then, speaking generally," said Martin, somewhat nettled by her smile, "in this country there are heaps of chaps that simply can't fall down because of the supports that surround them, supports of custom, tradition, not to speak of their countless friends, sisters, cousins, and aunts; if they're anyways half decent they're kept a going; whereas if they are in a new country and with few friends, they must stand alone or fall. Here the crowd support them; there the crowd, eager to get on, shove them aside or trample them down."

"Rather a ghastly picture that," said Miss Brodie.

"But true; that is, of the unfit. People haven't time to bother with them; the game is too keen."

"Surely the picture is overdrawn," said Doctor Dunn.

"It may be, Sir," replied Martin, "but I have seen so many young fellows who had been shipped out to Canada because they were failures at home. I have seen them in very hard luck."

"And what about the fit?" inquired Miss Brodie.

"They get credit for every ounce that's in them."

"But that is so in Scotland as well."

"Pardon me, Miss Brodie, hardly. Here even strong men and fit men have to wait half a lifetime for the chance that calls for all that's in them. They must march in the procession and the pace is leisurely. In Canada the chances come every day, and the man that's ready jumps in and wins."

"Ah, I see!" exclaimed Miss Brodie. "There are more ladders by which to climb."

"Yes," cried Martin, "and fewer men on them."

"But," argued Dunn, "there are other causes of failure in this country. Many a young fellow, for instance, cannot get a congenial position."

"Yes," replied Martin quickly, "because you won't

let him; your caste law forbids. With us a man can do anything decent and no one thinks the less of him."

"Ah, I see!" again cried Miss Brodie, more eagerly than before. "Not only more ladders, but more kinds of ladders."

"Exactly," said Martin with an approving glance. "And he must not be too long in the choosing."

"Then, Mr. Martin," said Mr. Rae, "what would you suggest for our young friend?"

But this Martin refused to answer.

"Surely there are openings for a young fellow in Canada," said Dunn. "Take a fellow like myself. What could I do?"

"You?" cried Martin, his eyes shining with loving enthusiasm. "There are doors open on every business street in every town and city in Canada for you, or for any fellow who has brain or brawn to sell and who will take any kind of a job and stay with it."

"Well, what job, for instance?"

"What job?" cried Martin. "Heaps of them."

At this point a diversion was created by the entrance of "Lily" Laughton. Both Martin and Dunn envied the easy grace of his manner, his perfect self-possession, as he greeted each member of the company. For each he had exactly the right word. Miss Brodie he greeted with an exaggerated devotion, but when he shook hands with Dunn there was no mistaking the genuine warmth of his affection.

"Heard you were home, old chap, so I couldn't help dropping in. Of course I knew that Mrs. Dunn would be sure to be here, and I more than suspected that my dear Miss Brodie," here he swept her an elaborate bow, "whom I discovered to be away from her own home, might be found in this pleasant company."

"Yes, I fear that my devotion to her youngest boy is leading me to overstep the bounds of even Mrs. Dunn's vast and generous hospitality."

"Not a bit, my dear," replied Mrs. Dunn kindly. "You bring sunshine with you, and you do us all good."

"Exactly my sentiments!" exclaimed "Lily" with enthusiasm. "But what are you all doing? Just having a 'collyshog'?"

For a moment no one replied; then Dunn said, "We were just talking about Cameron, who is thinking of going to Canada."

"To Canada of all places!" exclaimed "Lily" in tones of horrified surprise. "How truly dreadful! But why should Cameron of all beings exile himself in those remote and barbarous regions?"

"And why should he not?" cried Miss Brodie. "What is there for a young man of spirit in Mr. Cameron's position in this country?"

"Why, my dear Miss Brodie, how can you ask? Just think of the heaps of things, of perfectly delicious things, Cameron can do,—the Highlands in summer, Edinburgh, London, in the season, a run to the Continent! Just think of the wild possibility of a life of unalloyed bliss!"

"Don't be silly!" said Miss Brodie. "We are talking seriously."

"Seriously! Why, my dear Miss Brodie, do you imagine—?"

"But what could he do for a life-work?" said Dunn. "A fellow must have something to do."

"Oh, dear, I suppose so," said "Lily" with a sigh. "But surely he could have some position in an office or something!"

"Exactly!" replied Miss Brodie. "How beautifully

you put it! Now Mr. Martin was just about to tell us of the things a man could do in Canada when you interrupted."

"Awfully sorry, Martin. I apologise. Please go on. What do the natives do in Canada?"

"Please don't pay any attention to him, Mr. Martin. I am extremely interested. Now tell me, what are the openings for a young fellow in Canada? You said the professions are all wide open."

It took a little persuasion to get Martin started again, so disgusted was he with Laughton's references to his native country. "Yes, Miss Brodie, the professions are all wide open, but of course men must enter as they do here, but with a difference. Take law, for instance: Knew a chap—went into an office at ten dollars a month —didn't know a thing about it. In three months he was raised to twenty dollars, and within a year to forty dollars. In three or four years he had passed his exams., got a junior partnership worth easily two thousand dollars a year. They wanted that chap, and wanted him badly. But take business: That chap goes into a store and—"

"A store?" inquired "Lily."

"Yes, a shop you call it here; say a drygoods—"

"Drygoods? What extraordinary terms these Colonials use!"

"Oh, draper's shop," said Dunn impatiently. "Go on, Martin; don't mind him."

"A draper's clerk!" echoed "Lily." "To sell tapes and things?"

"Yes," replied Martin stoutly; "or groceries."

"Do you by any chance mean that a University man, a gentleman, takes a position in a grocer's shop to sell butter and cheese?"

"I mean just that," said Martin firmly.

"Oh, please!" said "Lily" with a violent shudder. "It is too awful!"

"There you are! You wouldn't demean yourself."

"Not I!" said "Lily" fervently.

"Or disgrace your friends. You want a gentleman's job. There are not enough to go round in Canada."

"Oh, go on," said Miss Brodie impatiently. " 'Lily,' we must ask you to not interrupt. What happens? Does he stay there?"

"Not he!" said Martin. "From the small business he goes to bigger business. First thing you know a man wants him for a big job and off he goes. Meantime he saves his money, invests wisely. Soon he is his own boss."

"That's fine!" cried Miss Brodie. "Go on, Mr. Martin. Start him lower down."

"All right," said Martin, directing his attention solely to the young lady. "Here's an actual case. A young fellow from Scotland found himself strapped—"

"Strapped? What *does* he mean?" said "Lily" in an appealing voice.

"On the rocks."

"Rocks?"

"Dear me!" cried Miss Brodie impatiently. "You are terribly lacking in imagination. Broke, he means."

"Oh, thanks!"

"Well, finds himself broke," said Martin; "gets a shovel, jumps into a cellar—"

"And why a cellar, pray?" inquires "Lily" mildly. "To hide himself from the public?"

"Not at all; they were digging a cellar preparatory to building a house."

"Oh!"

"He jumps in, blisters his hands, breaks his back—but he stays with the job. In a week the boss makes him timekeeper; in three months he himself is boss of a small gang; the next year he is made foreman at a hundred a month or so."

"A hundred a month?" cries "Lily" in astonishment. "Oh, Martin, please! We are green, but a hundred pounds a month—!"

"Dollars," said Martin shortly. "Don't be an ass! I beg pardon," he added, turning to Mrs. Dunn, who was meantime greatly amused.

"A hundred dollars a month; that is—I am so weak in arithmetic—twenty pounds, I understand. Go on, Martin; I'm waiting for the carriage and pair."

"That's where you get left," said Martin. "No carriage and pair for this chap yet awhile; overalls and slouch hat for the next five years for him. Then he begins contracting on his own."

"I beg your pardon," says "Lily."

"I mean he begins taking jobs on his own."

"Great!" cried Miss Brodie.

"Or," continued Martin, now fairly started on a favourite theme, "there are the railroads all shouting for men of experience, whether in the construction department or in the operating department."

"Does anyone here happen to understand him?" inquires "Lily" faintly.

"Certainly," cried Miss Brodie; "all the intelligent people do. At least, I've a kind of notion there are big things doing. I only wish I were a man!"

"Oh, Miss Brodie, how can you?" cried "Lily." "Think of us in such a contingency!"

"But," said Mr. Rae, "all of this is most interesting,

extremely interesting, Mr. Martin. Still, they cannot all arrive at these exalted positions."

"No, Mr. Rae. I may have given that impression. I confess to a little madness when I begin talking Canada."

"Ah!" exclaimed "Lily."

"But I said men of brawn and brains, you remember."

"And bounce, to perfect the alliteration," murmured "Lily."

"Yes, bounce, too," said Martin; "at least, he must never take back-water; he must be ready to attempt anything, even the impossible."

"That's the splendid thing about it!" cried Miss Brodie. "You're entirely on your own and you never say die!"

"Oh, my dear Miss Brodie," moaned "Lily" in piteous accents, "you are so fearfully energetic! And then, it's all very splendid, but just think of a—of a gentleman having to potter around among butter and cheese, or mess about in muddy cellars! Ugh! Positively *ghawstly!* I would simply die."

"Oh, no, you wouldn't, 'Lily,'" said Martin kindly. "We have afternoon teas and Browning Clubs, too, you must remember, and some 'cultchaw' and that sort of thing."

There was a joyous shout from Dunn.

"But, Mr. Martin," persisted Mr. Rae, whose mind was set in arriving at a solution of the problem in hand, "I have understood that agriculture was the chief pursuit in Canada."

"Farming! Yes, it is, but of course that means capital. Good land in Ontario means seventy-five to a hundred dollars per acre, and a man can't do with less than a hundred acres; besides, farming is getting to be a science now-a-days, Sir."

"Ah, quite true! But to a young man bred on a farm in this country—"

"Excuse me, Mr. Rae," replied Martin quickly, "there is no such thing in Canada as a gentleman farmer. The farmer works with his men."

"Do you mean that he actually works?" inquired "Lily." "With the plough and hoe, and that sort of thing?"

"Works all day long, as long as any of his men, and indeed longer."

"And does he actually live—? of course he doesn't eat with his servants?" said "Lily" in a tone that deprecated the preposterous proposition.

"They all eat together in the big kitchen," replied Martin.

"How awful!" gasped "Lily."

"My father does," replied Martin, a little colour rising in his cheek, "and my mother, and my brothers. They all eat with the men; my sister, too, except when she waits on table."

"Fine!" exclaimed Miss Brodie. "And why not? 'Lily,' I'm afraid you're horribly snobbish."

"Thank the Lord," said "Lily" devoutly, "I live in this beloved Scotland!"

"But, Mr. Martin, forgive my persistence, I understand there is cheaper land in certain parts of Canada; in, say, Manito*baw*."

"Ah, yes, Sir, of course, lots of it; square miles of it!" cried Martin with enthusiasm. "The very best out of doors, and cheap, but I fancy there are some hardships in Manitoba."

"But I see by the public newspapers," continued Mr.

Rae, "that there is a very large movement in the way of emigration toward that country."

"Yes, there's a great boom on in Manitoba just now."

"Boom?" said "Lily." "And what exactly may that be in the vernacular?"

"I take it," said Mr. Rae, evidently determined not to allow the conversation to get out of his hands, "you mean a great excitement consequent upon the emigration and the natural rise in land values?"

"Yes, Sir," cried Martin, "you've hit it exactly."

"Then would there not be opportunity to secure a considerable amount of land at a low figure in that country?"

"Most certainly! But it's fair to say that success there means work and hardship and privation. Of course it is always so in a new country; it was so in Ontario. Why, the new settlers in Manitoba don't know what hardships mean in comparison with those that faced the early settlers in Ontario. My father, when a little boy of ten years, went with his father into the solid forest; you don't know what that means in this country, and no one can who has not seen a solid mass of green reaching from the ground a hundred feet high without a break in it except where the trail enters. Into that solid forest in single file went my grandfather, his two little boys, and one ox carrying a bag of flour, some pork and stuff. By a mark on a tree they found the corner of their farm." Martin paused.

"Do go on," said Miss Brodie. "Tell me the very first thing he did."

But Martin seemed to hesitate. "Well," he began slowly, "I've often heard my father tell it. When they came to that tree with the mark on it, grandfather said, 'Boys, we have reached our home. Let us thank God.'

He went up to a big spruce tree, drove his ax in to the butt, then kneeled down with the two litle boys beside him, and I have heard my father say that when he looked away up between the big trees and saw the bit of blue sky there, he thought God was listening at that blue hole between the tree-tops." Martin paused abruptly, and for a few moments silence held the group. Then Doctor Dunn, clearing his throat, said with quiet emphasis:

"And he was right, my boy; make no doubt of that."

"Then?" inquired Miss Brodie softly. "If you don't mind."

Martin laughed. "Then they had grub, and that afternoon grandfather cut the trees and the boys limbed them off, clearing the ground where the first house stood. That night they slept in a little brush hut that did them for a house until grandmother came two weeks later."

"What?" said Doctor Dunn. "Your grandmother went into the forest?"

"Yes, Sir," said Martin; "and two miles of solid black bush stretched between her and the next woman."

"Why, of course, my dear," said Mrs. Dunn, taking part for the first time in the conversation. "What else?"

They all laughed.

"Of course, Mother," said her eldest son, "that's what you would do."

"So would I, Mamma, wouldn't I?" whispered Rob, leaning towards her.

"Certainly, my dear," replied his mother; "I haven't the slightest doubt."

"And so would any woman worth her salt if she loved her husband," cried Miss Brodie with great emphasis.

"Why, why," cried Doctor Dunn, "it's the same old breed, Mother."

"But in Manitoba—?" began Mr. Rae, still clinging to the subject.

"Oh, in Manitoba there is no forest to cut. However, there are other difficulties. Still, hundreds are crowding in, and any man who has the courage and the nerve to stay with it can get on."

"And what did they do for schools?" said Mrs. Dunn, returning to the theme that had so greatly interested her.

"There were no schools until father was too big to be spared to go except for a few weeks in the winter."

"How big do you mean?"

"Say fifteen."

"Fifteen!" exclaimed Miss Brodie. "A mere infant!"

"Infant!" said Martin. "Not much! At fifteen my father was doing a man's full work in the bush and on the farm, and when he grew to be a man he cleared most of his own land, too. Why, when I was eleven I drove my team all day on the farm."

"And how did you get your education, Mr. Martin?"

"Oh, they kept me at school pretty steadily, except in harvest and hay time, until I was fourteen, and after that in the winter months. When I was sixteen I got a teacher's certificate, and then it was easy enough."

"And did you put yourself through college?" inquired Mr. Rae, both interest and admiration in his voice, for now they were on ground familiar in his own experience.

"Why, yes, mostly. Father helped, I suspect more than he ought to, but he was anxious for me to get through."

"Rob," cried Miss Brodie suddenly, "let's go! What do you say? We'll get a big bit of that land in the West, and won't it be splendid to build up our own estate and all that?"

Rob glanced from her into his mother's face. "I'd

like it fine, Mamma," he said in a low voice, slipping his hand into hers.

"But what about me, Rob?" said his mother, smiling tenderly down into the eager face.

"Oh, I'd come back for you, Mamma."

"Hold on there, youngster," said his elder brother, "there are others that might have something to say about that. But I say, Martin," continued Dunn, "we hear a lot about the big ranches further West."

"Yes, in Alberta, but I confess I don't know much about them. The railways are just building and people are beginning to go in. But ranching needs capital, too. It must be a great life! They practically live in the saddle. It's a glorious country!"

"On the whole, then," said Mr. Rae, as if summing up the discussion, "a young man has better opportunities of making his fortune, so to speak, in the far West rather than in, say, Ontario."

"I didn't speak of fortune, Mr. Rae,—fortune is a chance thing, more or less,—but what I say is this, that any young man not afraid of work, of any kind of work, and willing to stay with his job, can make a living and get a home in any part of Canada, with a bigger chance of fortune in the West."

"All I say, Mr. Rae, is this," said Miss Brodie emphatically, "that I only wish I were a man with just such a chance as young Cameron!"

"Ah, my dear young lady, if all the young men were possessed of your spirit, it would matter little where they went, for they would achieve distinct success." As he spoke Mr. Rae's smile burst forth in all its effulgent glory.

"Dear Mr. Rae, how very clever of you to discover that!" replied Miss Brodie, smiling sweetly into Mr.

Rae's radiant face. "And how very sweet of you—ah, I beg your pardon; that is—" The disconcerting rapidity with which Mr. Rae's smile gave place to an appearance of grave, of even severe solemnity, threw Miss Brodie quite "out of her stride," as Martin said afterward, and left her floundering in a hopeless attempt to complete her compliment.

Her confusion was the occasion of unlimited joy to "Lily," who was not unfamiliar with this facial phenomenon on the part of Mr. Rae. "Oh, I say!" he cried to Dunn in a gale of smothered laughter, "how does the dear man do it? It is really too lovely! I must learn the trick of that. I have never seen anything quite so appallingly flabbergasting."

Meantime Mr. Rae was blandly assisting Miss Brodie out of her dilemma. "Not at all, Miss Brodie, not at all! But," he continued, throwing his smile about the room, "I think, Doctor Dunn, we have reason to congratulate ourselves upon not only a pleasant but an extremely profitable evening—ah—as far as the matter in hand is concerned. I hope to have further speech with our young friend," bowing to Mr. Martin and bringing his smile to bear upon that young gentleman.

"Oh, certainly," began Martin with ready geniality, "whenever you—eh? What did you say, Sir? I didn't quite—"

But Mr. Rae was already bidding Mrs. Dunn goodnight, with a face of preternatural gravity.

"What the deuce!" said Martin, turning to his friend Dunn. "Does the old boy often go off at half-cock that way? He'll hurt himself some time, sure."

"Isn't it awful?" said Dunn. "He's got me a few times that way, too. But I say, old boy, we're awfully grateful to you for coming."

"I feel like a fool," said Martin; "as if I'd been delivering a lecture."

"Don't think it," cried Miss Brodie, who had drawn near. "You've been perfectly lovely, and I am so glad to have got to know you better. For me, I am quite resolved to go to Canada."

"But do you think they can really spare us all, Miss Brodie?" exclaimed "Lily" in an anxious voice. "For, of course, if you go we must."

"No, 'Lily,' I'm quite sure they can't spare you. Just think, what could the Browning-Wagner circle do? Besides, what could we do with you when we were all working, for I can quite see that there is no use going to Canada unless you mean to work?"

"You've got it, Miss Brodie," said Martin. "My lecture is not in vain. There is no use going to Canada unless you mean to work and to stay with the job till the cows come home."

"Till the cows come—?" gasped "Lily."

"Oh, never mind him, Mr. Martin! Come, 'Lily' dear, I'll explain it to you on the way home. Good-night, Mr. Dunn; we've had a jolly evening. And as for our friend Cameron, I've ceased to pity him; on the contrary, I envy him his luck."

CHAPTER VII

FAREWELL TO CUAGH OIR

ONCE more the golden light of a sunny spring day was shining on the sapphire loch at the bottom, and overflowing at the rim of the Cuagh Oir. But for all its flowing gold, there was grief in the Glen —grief deep and silent, like the quiet waters of the little loch. It was seen in the grave faces of the men who gathered at the "smiddy." It was heard in the cadence of the voices of the women as they gathered to "kalie" (Ceilidh) in the little cottages that fringed the loch's side, or dotted the heather-clad slopes. It even checked the boisterous play of the bairns as they came in from school. It lay like a cloud on the Cuagh, and heavy on the hearts that made up the little hill-girt community of one hundred souls, or more.

And the grief was this, that on the "morrow's morn" Mary Robertson's son was departing from the Glen "neffer to return for effermore," as Donald of the House farm put it, with a face gloomy as the loch on a dark winter's day.

"A leaving" was ever an occasion of wailing to the Glen, and many a leaving had the Glen known during the last fifty years. For wherever the tartan waved, and the bonnie feathers danced for the glory of the Empire, sons of the Glen were ever to be found; but not for fifty years had the heart of the Glen known the luxury of a single rallying centre for their pride and their love till the "young chentleman," young Mr. Allan, began to go in and out among them. And as he grew into manhood so grew their pride in him. And as, from time to time, at the Great Games he began to win glory for the

Glen with his feats of skill and strength, and upon the pipes, and in the dances, their pride in him grew until it passed all limits. Had he not, the very year before he went to the college, cut the comb of the "Cock of the North" from Glen Urquhart, in running and jumping; and the very same year had he not wrested from Callum Bheg, the pride of Athole, the coveted badge of Special Distinction in Highland Dancing? Then later, when the schoolmaster would read from the Inverness *Courier* to one group after another at the post office and at the "smiddy" (it was only fear of the elder MacPherson, that kept the master from reading it aloud at the kirk door before the service) accounts of the "remarkable playing" of Cameron, the brilliant young "half-back" of the Academy in Edinburgh, the Glen settled down into an assured conviction that it had reached the pinnacle of vicarious glory, and that in all Scotland there was none to compare with their young "chieftain" as, quite ignoring the Captain, they loved to call him.

And there was more than pride in him, for on his holidays he came back to the Glen unspoiled by all his honours and achievements, and went about among them "jist like ain o' their ain sels," accepting their homage as his right, but giving them in return, according to their various stations, due respect and honour, and their love grew greater than their pride.

But the "morrow's morn" he was leaving the Glen, and, worse than all, no one knew for why. A mystery hung over the cause of his going, a mystery deepened by his own bearing during the past twelve months, for all these months a heavy gloom had shrouded him, and from all that had once been his delight and their glory he had withdrawn. The challenge, indeed, from the men of Glen Urquhart which he had accepted long ago, he refused not, but even the overwhelming defeat which he had administered to his haughty challengers, had apparently brought him no more than a passing gleam of joy. The gloom remained unlifted and the cause the Glen knew not, and no man of them would seek to know. Hence the grief of the Glen was no common grief when the son of Mary Robertson, the son of the House, the pride of the Glen, and the comrade and friend of them all, was about to depart and never to return.

His last day in the Glen Allan spent making his painful way through the cottages, leaving his farewell, and with each some slight gift of remembrance. It was for him, indeed, a pilgrimage of woe. It was not only that his heart roots were in the Glen and knit round every stick and stone of it; it was not that he felt he was leaving behind him a love and loyalty as deep and lasting as life itself. It was that in tearing himself from them he could make no response to the dumb appeal in the eyes that followed him with adoration and fidelity: "Wherefore do you leave us at all?" and "Why do you make no promise of return?" To that dumb appeal there was no answer possible from one who carried on his heart for himself, and on his life for some few others, and among these his own father, the terrible brand of the criminal. It was this grim fact that stained black the whole landscape of his consciousness, and that hung like a pall of death over every living and delightsome thing in the garden of his soul. While none could, without challenge, condemn him, yet his own tongue refused to proclaim his innocence. Every face he loved drove deeper into his heart his pain. The deathless loyalty and unbounded pride of the Glen folk rebuked him, without their knowing, for the dishonour

he had done them. The Glen itself, the hills, the purpling heather, the gleaming loch, how dear to him he
had never known till now, threw in his face a sad and
silent reproach. Small wonder that the Glen, that Scotland had become intolerable to him. With this bitter
burden on his heart it was that young Mr. Allan went
his way through the Glen making his farewells, not
daring to indulge the luxury of his grief, and with never
a word of return.

His sister, who knew all, and who would have carried
—oh! how gladly!—on her own heart, and for all her
life long, that bitter burden, pleaded to be allowed to go
with him on what she knew full well was a journey of
sorrow and sore pain, but this he would not permit.
This sorrow and pain which were his own, he would
share with no one, and least of all with her upon whose
life he had already cast so dark a shadow. Hence she
was at the house alone, her father not having yet returned from an important meeting at a neighbouring
village, when a young man came to the door asking for
young Mr. Cameron.

"Who is it, Kirsty?" she inquired anxiously, a new
fear at her heart for her brother.

"I know not, but he has neffer been in this Glen before
whateffer," replied Kirsty, with an ominous shake of the
head, her primitive instincts leading her to view the
stranger with suspicion. "But!" she added, with a
glance at her young mistress' face, "he iss no man to
be afraid of, at any rate. He is just a laddie."

"Oh, he is a *young* man, Kirsty?" replied her mistress, glancing at her blue serge gown, her second best,
and with her hands striving to tuck in some of her way-
ward curls.

"Och, yess, and not much at that!" replied Kirsty,

with the idea of relieving her young mistress of unnecessary fears.

Then Moira, putting on her grand air, stepped into the parlour, and saw standing there and awaiting her, a young man with a thin and somewhat hard face, a firm mouth, and extraordinarily keen, grey eyes. Upon her appearing the young man stood looking upon her without a word. As a matter of fact, he was struggling with a problem; a problem that was quite bewildering; the problem, namely, "How could hair ever manage to get itself into such an arrangement of waves and curls, and golden gleams and twinkles?" Struggling with this problem, he became conscious of her voice gravely questioning him. "You were wishing to see my brother?" The young man came back part way, and replied, "Oh! how does it—? That is—. I beg your pardon." The surprise in her face brought him quite to the ground, and he came at once to his business. "I am Mr. Martin," he said in a quick, sharp voice. "I know your brother and Mr. Dunn." He noted a light dawn in her eyes. "In fact, I played with them on the same team—at football, you know."

"Oh!" cried the girl, relief and welcome in her voice, "I know you, Mr. Martin, quite well. I know all about you, and what a splendid quarter-back you are." Here she gave him both her hands, which Mr. Martin took in a kind of dream, once more plunged into the mazes of another and more perplexing problem, viz., Was it her lips with that delicious curve to them? or her eyes so sunny and brown (or were they brown?) with that alluring, bewitching twinkle? or was it both lips and eyes that gave to the smile with which she welcomed him its subtle power to make his heart rise and choke him as it never had been known to do in the most strenuous of his matches? "I'm awfully glad," he heard himself say, and her voice replying, "Oh, yes! Allan has often and often spoken of you, Mr. Martin." Mr. Martin immediately became conscious of a profound and grateful affection to Allan, still struggling, however, with the problem which had been complicated still further by the charm of her soft, Highland voice. He was on the point of deciding in favour of her voice, when on her face he noted a swift change from glad welcome to suspicion and fear, and then into her sunny eyes a sudden leaping of fierce wrath, as in those of a lioness defending her young.

"Why do you look so?" she cried in a voice sharp and imperious. "Is it my brother—? Is anything wrong?"

The shock of the change in eyes and voice brought Martin quite to himself.

"Wrong? Not a bit," he hastened to say, "but just the finest thing in the world. It is all here in this letter. Dunn could not come himself, and there was no one else, and he thought Cameron ought to have it to-day, so here I am, and here is the letter. Where is he?"

"Oh!" cried the girl, clasping her hands upon her heart, her voice growing soft, and her eyes dim with a sudden mist. "I am so thankful! I am so glad!" The change in her voice and in her eyes so affected Mr. Martin that he put his hands resolutely behind his back lest they should play him tricks, and should, without his will, get themselves round her and draw her close to his heart.

"So am I," he said, "awfully glad! Never was so glad in all my life!" He was more conscious than ever of bewilderment and perplexity in the midst of increasing problems that complicated themselves with mist brown eyes, trembling lips, and a voice of such pathetic cadences as aroused in him an almost uncontrollable desire to exercise his utmost powers of comfort. And all the while there was growing in his heart a desperate anxiety as to what would be the final issue of these bewildering desires and perplexities; when at the extremity of his self-control he was saved by the girl's suggestion.

"Let us go and find my brother."

"Oh, yes!" cried Martin, "for heaven's sake let us."

"Wait until I get my hat."

"Oh! I wouldn't put on a hat," cried he in dismay.

"Why?" enquired the girl, looking at him with surprised curiosity.

"Oh! because—because you don't need one; it's so beautiful and sunny, you know." In spite of what he could do Mr. Martin's eyes kept wandering to her hair.

"Oh, well!" cried Moira, in increasing surprise at this strange young man, "the sun won't hurt me, so come, let us go."

Together they went down the avenue of rugged firs. At the highway she paused. Before them lay the Glen in all the splendid sweep of its beauty.

"Isn't it lovely!" she breathed.

"Lovely!" echoed Martin, his eyes not on the Glen. "It is so sunny, you know."

"Yes," she answered quickly, "you notice that?"

"How could I help it?" said Martin, his eyes still resting upon her. "How could I?"

"Of course," she replied, "and so we call it the Glen Cuagh Oir, that is the 'Glen of the Cup of Gold.' And to think he has to leave it all to-morrow!" she added.

The pathetic cadences in her voice again drove Martin to despair. He recovered himself, however, to say, "But he is going to Canada!"

"Yes, to Canada. And we all feel it so dreadfully for him, and," she added in a lower voice. "for ourselves."

Had it been yesterday Martin would have been ready with scorn for any such feeling, and with congratulations to Cameron upon his exceptionally good luck in the expectation of going to Canada; but to-day, somehow it was different. He found the splendid lure of his native land availed not to break the spell of the Glen, and as he followed the girl in and out of the little cottages, seeking her brother, and as he noted the perfect courtesy and respect which marked her manner with the people, and their unstudied and respectful devotion to their "tear young leddy," this spell deepened upon him. Unconsciously and dimly he became aware of a mysterious and mighty power somehow and somewhere in the Glen straining at the heart-strings of its children. Of the nature and origin of this mysterious and mighty power, the young Canadian knew little. His country was of too recent an origin for mystery, and its people too heterogeneous in their ethnic characteristics to furnish a soil for tribal instincts and passions. The passionate loves and hatreds of the clans, their pride of race, their deathless lealty; and more than all, and better than all, their religious instincts, faiths and prejudices; these, with the mystic, wild loveliness of heather-clad hill and rock-rimmed loch, of roaring torrent and jagged crags, of lonely muir and sunny pasture nuiks; all these, and ten thousand nameless and unnamable things united in the weaving of the spell of the Glen upon the hearts of its people. Of how it all came to be, Martin knew nothing, but like an atmosphere it stole in upon him, and he came to vaguely understand something of what it meant to be a Highlander, and to bid farewell to the land into whose

grim soil his life roots had struck deep, and to tear himself from hearts whose life stream and his had flowed
as one for a score of generations. So from cot to cot
Martin followed and observed, until they came to the
crossing where the broad path led up from the highroad
to the kirkyard and the kirk. Here they were halted
by a young man somewhat older than Martin. Tall and
gaunt he stood. His face, pale and pock-marked and lit
by light blue eyes, and crowned by brilliant red hair,
was, with all its unloveliness, a face of a certain rugged
beauty; while his manner and bearing showed the native
courtesy of a Highland gentleman.

"You are seeking Mr. Allan?" he said, taking off his
bonnet to the girl. "He is in yonder," waving his hand
towards the kirkyard.

"In yonder? You are sure, Mr. Maclise?" She might
well ask, for never but on Sabbath days, since the day
they had laid his mother away under the birch trees,
had Allan put foot inside the kirkyard.

"Half an hour ago he went in," replied the young
Highlander, "and he has not returned."

"I will go in, then," said the girl, and hesitated, unwilling that a stranger's eyes should witness what she
knew was waiting her there.

"You, Sir, will perhaps abide with me," suggested Mr.
Maclise to Martin, with a quick understanding of her
hesitation.

"Oh, thank you," cried Moira. "This is Mr. Martin
from Canada, Mr. Maclise—my brother's great friend.
Mr. Maclise is our schoolmaster here," she added, turning to Martin, "and we are very proud of him." The
Highlander's pale face became the colour of his brilliant
hair as he remarked, "You are very good indeed, Miss
Cameron, and I am glad to make the acquaintance of

Mr. Martin. It will give me great pleasure to show Mr. Martin the little falls at the loch's end, if he cares to step that far." If Mr. Martin was conscious of any great desire to view the little falls at the loch's end, his face most successfully dissembled any such feeling, but to the little falls he must go as the schoolmaster quietly possessed himself of him and led him away, while Miss Cameron, with never a thought of either of them, passed up the broad path into the kirkyard. There, at the tower's foot, she came upon her brother, prone upon the little grassy mound, with arms outspread, as if to hold it in embrace. At the sound of his sister's tread upon the gravel, he raised himself to his knees swiftly, and with a fierce gesture, as if resenting intrusion.

"Oh, it is you, Moira," he said quietly, sinking down upon the grass. At the sight of his tear-stained, haggard face, the girl ran to him with a cry, and throwing herself down beside him put her arms about him with inarticulate sounds of pity. At length her brother raised himself from the ground.

"Oh, it is terrible to leave it all," he groaned; "yet I am glad to leave, for it is more terrible to stay; the very Glen I cannot look at; and the people, I cannot bear their eyes. Oh," he groaned, wringing his hands, "if she were here she would understand, but there is nobody."

"Oh, Allan," cried his sister in reproach.

"Oh, yes, I know! I know! You believe in me, Moira, but you are just a lassie, and you cannot understand."

"Yes, you know well I believe in you, Allan, and others, too, believe in you. There is Mr. Dunn, and—"

"Oh, I don't know," said her brother bitterly, "he wants to believe it."

"Yes, and there is Mr. Martin," she continued, "and

—Oh, I forgot! here is a letter Mr. Martin brought you."

"Martin?"

"Yes, your Martin, a strange little man; your quarter-back, you know. He brought this, and he says it is good news." But already Allan was into his letter. As he read his face grew white, his hand began to shake, his eyes to stare as if they would devour the very paper. The second time he read the letter his whole body trembled, and his breath came in gasps, as if he were in a physical struggle. Then lifting arms and voice towards the sky, he cried in a long, low wail, "Oh God, it is good, it is good!"

With that he laid himself down prone upon the mound again, his face in the grass, sobbing brokenly, "Oh, mother, mother dear, I have got you once more; I have got you once more!"

His sister stood, her hands clasped upon her heart—a manner she had—her tears, unnoted, flowing down her cheeks, waiting till her brother should let her into his joy, as she had waited for entrance into his grief. His griefs and his joys were hers, and though he still held her a mere child, it was with a woman's self-forgetting love she ministered to him, gladly accepting whatever confidence he would give, but content to wait until he should give more. So she stood waiting, with her tears flowing quietly, and her face alight with wonder and joy for him. But as her brother's sobbing continued, this terrible display of emotion amazed her, startled her, for since their mother's death none of them had seen Allan weep. At length he raised himself from the ground and stood beside her.

"Oh, Moira, lassie, I never knew how terrible it was till now. I had lost everything, my friends, you, and," he added in a low voice, "my mother. This cursed thing shut me out from all; it got between me and all I ever loved. I have not for these months been able to see her face clear, but do you know, Moira," here his voice fell and the mystic light grew in his eyes, "I saw her again just now as clear as clear, and I know I have got her again; and you, too, Moira, darling," here he gathered his sister to him, "and the people! and the Glen! Oh! is it not terrible what a crime can do? How it separates you from your folk, and from all the world, for, mind you, I have felt myself a criminal; but I am not! I am not!" His voice rose into an exultant shout, "I am clear of it, I am a man again! Oh, it is good! it is good! Here, read the letter, it will prove to you."

"Oh, what does it matter at all, Allan," she cried, still clinging to him, "as if it made any difference to me. I always knew it."

Her brother lifted her face from his breast and looked into her eyes. "Do you tell me you don't want to know the proof of it?" he asked in wonder. "No," she said simply. "Why should I need any proof? I always knew it."

For a moment longer he gazed upon her, then said, "Moira, you are a wonder, lassie. No, you are a lassie no longer, you are a woman, and, do you know, you are like mother to me now, and I never saw it."

She smiled up at him through her tears. "I should like to be," she said softly. Then, because she was truly Scotch, she added, "for your sake, for I love you terribly much; and I am going to lose you."

A quiver passed through her frame, and her arms gripped him tight. In the self-absorption in his grief and pain he had not thought of hers, nor considered how with his going her whole life would be changed.

"I have been a selfish brute," he muttered. "I have

only thought of my own suffering; but, listen Moira, it is all past; thank God, it is all past. This letter from Mr. Rae holds a confession from Potts (poor Potts! I am glad that Rae let him off): it was Potts who committed the forgery. Now I feel myself clean again; you can't know what that is; to be yourself again, and to be able to look all men in the face without fear or shame. Come, we must go; I must see them all again. Let us to the burn first, and put my face right."

A moment he stood looking down upon his mother's grave. The hideous thing that had put her far from him, and that had blurred the clear vision of her face, was gone. A smile soft and tender as a child's stole over his face, and with that smile he turned away. As they were coming back from the burn, Martin and the schoolmaster saw them in the distance.

"Bless me, man, will you look at him?" said the master in an awestruck tone, clutching Martin's arm. "What ever is come to him?"

"What's up," cried Martin. "By Jove! you're right! the Roderick Dhu and Black Douglas business is gone, sure!"

"God bless my soul!" said Maclise in an undertone. "He is himself once more."

He might well exclaim, for it was a new Allan that came striding up the high road, with head lifted, and with the proud swing of a Highland chieftain.

"Hello, old man!" he shouted, catching sight of Martin and running towards him with hands outstretched, "You are welcome"—he grasped his hands and held them fast—"you are welcome to this Glen, and to me welcome as Heaven to a Hell-bound soul."

"Maclise," he cried, turning to the master, "this letter," waving it in his hand, "is like a reprieve to a man on the scaffold." Maclise stood gazing in amazement at him.

"They accused me of crime!"

"Of crime, Mr. Allan?" Maclise stiffened in haughty surprise.

"Yes, of base crime!"

"But this letter completely clears him," cried Martin eagerly.

Maclise turned upon him with swift scorn, "There was no need, for anyone in this Glen whatever." The Highlander's face was pale, and in his light blue eyes gleamed a fierce light.

Martin flashed a look upon the girl standing so proudly erect beside her brother, and reflecting in her face and eyes the sentiments of the schoolmaster.

"By Jove! I believe you," cried Martin with conviction, "it is not needed here, but—but there are others, you know."

"Others?" said the Highlander with fine scorn, "and what difference?"

The Glen folk needed no clearing of their chief, and the rest of the world mattered not.

"But there was myself," said Allan. "Now it is gone, Maclise, and I can give my hand once more without fear or shame."

Maclise took the offered hand almost with reverence, and, removing his bonnet from his head, said in a voice, deep and vibrating with emotion,

"Neffer will a man of the Glen count it anything but honour to take thiss hand."

"Thank you, Maclise," cried Allan, keeping his grip of the master's hand. "Now you can tell the Glen."

"You will not be going to leave us now?" said Maclise eagerly.

"Yes, I shall go, Maclise, but," with a proud lift of his head, "tell them I am coming back again."

And with that message Maclise went to the Glen. From cot to cot and from lip to lip the message sped, that Mr. Allan was himself again, and that, though on the morrow's morn he was leaving the Glen, he himself had promised that he would return.

That evening, as the gloaming deepened, the people of the Glen gathered, as was their wont, at their cottage doors to listen to old piper Macpherson as he marched up and down the highroad. This night, it was observed, he no longer played that most heart-breaking of all Scottish laments, "Lochaber No More." He had passed up to the no less heart-thrilling, but less heart-breaking, "Macrimmon's Lament." In a pause in Macpherson's wailing notes there floated down over the Glen the sound of the pipes up at the big House.

"Bless my soul! whisht, man!" cried Betsy Macpherson to her spouse. "Listen yonder!" For the first time in months they heard the sound of Allan's pipes.

"It is himself," whispered the women to each other, and waited. Down the long avenue of ragged firs, and down the highroad, came young Mr. Allan, in all the gallant splendour of his piper's garb, and the tune he played was no lament, but the blood-stirring "Gathering of the Gordons." As he came opposite to Macpherson's cottage he gave the signal for the old piper, and down the highroad stepped the two of them together, till they passed beyond the farthest cottage. Then back again they swung, and this time it was to the "Cock of the North," that their tartans swayed and their bonnets nodded. Thus, not with woe and lamentation, but with good hope and gallant cheer, young Mr. Allan took his leave of the Glen Cuagh Oir.

CHAPTER VIII

WILL HE COME BACK?

IT was the custom in Doctor Dunn's household that, immediately after dinner, his youngest son would spend half an hour in the study with his father. It was a time for confidences. During this half hour father and son met as nearly as possible on equal terms, discussing, as friends might, the events of the day or the plans for the morrow, school work or athletics, the latest book or the newest joke; and sometimes the talk turned upon the reading at evening prayers. This night the story had been one of rare beauty and of absorbing interest, the story, viz., of that idyllic scene on the shore of Tiberias where the erring disciple was fully restored to his place in the ranks of the faithful, as he had been restored, some weeks before, to his place in the confidence of his Master.

"That was a fine story, Rob?" began Doctor Dunn.

"That it was," said Rob gravely. "It was fine for Peter to get back again."

"Just so," replied his father. "You see, when a man once turns his back on his best Friend, he is never right till he gets back again."

"Yes, I know," said Rob gravely. For a time he sat with a shadow of sadness and anxiety on his young face. "It is terrible!" he exclaimed.

"Terrible?" inquired the Doctor. "Oh, yes, you mean Peter's fall? Yes, that was a terrible thing—to be untrue to our Master and faithless to our best Friend."

"But he did not mean to, Dad," said Rob quickly, as if springing to the fallen disciple's defence. "He forgot,

just for a moment, and was awfully sorry afterwards."

"Yes, truly," said his father, "and that was the first
step back."

For a few moments Rob remained silent, his face sad
and troubled.

"Man! It must be terrible!" at length he said, more
to himself than to his father. The Doctor looked closely
at the little lad. The eager, sensitive face, usually so
radiant, was now clouded and sad.

"What is it, Rob? Is it something you can tell me?"
asked his father in a tone of friendly kindness.

Rob moved closer to him. The father waited in silence.
He knew better than to force an unwilling confidence.
At length the lad, with an obvious effort at self-com-
mand, said:

"It is to-morrow, Daddy, that Cameron—that Mr.
Cameron is going away."

"To-morrow? So it is. And you will be very sorry,
Rob. But, of course, he will come back."

"Oh, Dad," cried Rob, coming quite close to his father,
"it isn't that! It isn't that!"

His father waited. He did not understand his boy's
trouble, and so he wisely refrained from uttering words
that might hinder rather than help. At length, with a
sudden effort, Rob asked in a low, hurried voice:

"Do you think, Dad, he has—got—back?"

"Got back?" said his father. "Oh, I see. Why, my
boy? What do you know of it? Did you know there
was a letter from a man named Potts, that completely
clears your friend of all crime?"

"Is there?" asked the boy quickly. "Man! That is
fine! But I always knew he could not do anything
really bad—I mean, anything that the police could

touch him for. But it is not that, Dad. I have heard Jack say he used to be different when he came down first, and now sometimes he—" The lad's voice fell silent. He could not bring himself to accuse his hero of any evil. His father drew him close to his side.

"You mean that he has fallen into bad ways—drink, and things like that?"

The boy hung his head; he was keenly ashamed for his friend. After a few moments' silence he said:

"And he is going away to Canada to-morrow, and I wonder, Dad, if he has—got—back? It would be terrible— Oh, Dad, all alone and away from—!"

The boy's voice sank to a whisper, and a rush of tears filled his eyes.

"I see what you mean, my boy. You mean it would be terrible for him to be in that far land, and away from that Friend we know and love best."

The lad looked at his father through his tears, and nodded his head, and for some moments there was silence between them. If the truth must be told, Doctor Dunn felt himself keenly rebuked by his little son's words. Amid the multitude of his responsibilities, the responsibility for his sons' best friend he had hardly realised.

"I am glad that you spoke of it, Rob; I am glad that you spoke of it. Something will be done. It is not, after all, in our hands. Still, we must stand ready to help. Good-night, my boy. And remember, it is always good to hurry back to our best Friend, if ever we get away from Him."

The boy put his arms around his father's neck and kissed him good-night; then, kissing him again, he whispered: "Thank you, Daddy."

And from the relief in his tone the father recognised

that upon him the lad had laid all the burden of his solicitude for his friend.

Later in the evening, when his elder son came home, the father called him in, and frankly gave him the substance of the conversation of the earlier part of the evening.

Jack laughed somewhat uneasily. "Oh, Rob is an awfully religious little beggar; painfully so, I think, sometimes—you know what I mean, Sir," he added, noticing the look on his father's face.

"I am not sure that I do, Jack," said his father, "but I want to tell you that as far as I am concerned, I felt distinctly rebuked at the little chap's anxiety for his friend in a matter of such vital import. His is a truly religious little soul, as you say, but I wonder if his type is not more nearly like the normal than is ours. Certainly, if reality, simplicity, sincerity are the qualities of true religious feeling—and these, I believe, are the qualities emphasised by the Master Himself—then it may indeed be that the boy's type is nearer the ideal than ours."

At this point Mrs. Dunn entered the room.

"Anything private?" she enquired with a bright smile at her husband.

"Not at all! Come in!" said Doctor Dunn, and he proceeded to repeat the conversation with his younger son, and his own recent comment thereupon.

"I am convinced," he added, "that there is a profundity of meaning in those words, 'Whosoever shall not receive the kingdom of God as a little child, he shall not enter therein,' that we have not yet fathomed. I suspect Wordsworth is not far astray when he suggests that with the passing years we grow away from the simplicity of our faith and the clearness of our vision.

There is no doubt that to Rob, Jesus is as real as I am."

"There is no doubt of that," said his wife quickly. "Not only as real, but quite as dear; indeed, dearer. I shall never forget the shock I received when I heard him one day, as a wee, wee boy, classifying the objects of his affection. I remember the ascending scale was: 'I love Jack and Daddy just the same, then mother, then Jesus.' It was always in the highest place, Jesus; and I believe that the scale is the same to-day, unless Jack," she added, with a smile at her son, "has moved to his mother's place."

"Not much fear of that, mother," said Jack, "but I should not be surprised if you are quite right about the little chap. He is a queer little beggar!"

"There you are again, Jack," said his father, "and it is upon that point I was inclined to take issue with you when your mother entered."

"I think I shall leave you," said the mother. "I am rather tired, and so I shall bid you good-night."

"Yes," said the father, when they had seated themselves again, "the very fact that to you, and to me for that matter, Rob's attitude of mind should seem peculiar raises the issue. What is the normal type of Christian faith? Is it not marked by the simplicity and completeness of the child's?"

"And yet, Sir," replied Jack, "that simplicity and completeness is the result of inexperience. Surely the ideal faith is not that which ignores the facts and experiences of life?"

"Not exactly," replied his father, "yet I am not sure but after all, 'the perfect love which casteth out fear' is one which ignores the experiences of life, or, rather, classifies them in a larger category. That is, it refuses to be disturbed by life's experiences, because among those experiences there is a place for the enlarged horizon, the clearer vision. But I am not arguing about this matter; I rather wish to make a confession and enlist your aid. Frankly, the boy's words gave me an uneasy sense of failure in my duty to this young man; or, perhaps I should say, my privilege. And really, it is no wonder! Here is this little chap actually carrying every day a load of intense concern for our friend, as to whether, as he puts it himself, 'he has come back.' And, after all, Jack, I wonder if this should not have been more upon our minds? The young man, I take it, since his mother's death has little in his home life to inspire him with religious faith and feeling. If she had been alive, one would not feel the same responsibility; she was a singularly saintly woman."

"You are quite right, Sir," said Jack quickly, "and I suspect you rather mean that I am the one that should feel condemned."

"Not at all! Not at all, Jack! I am thinking, as every man must, of my own responsibility, though, doubtless, you have yours as well. Of course I know quite well you have stuck by him splendidly in his fight for a clean and self-controlled life, but one wonders whether there is not something more."

"There is, Sir!" replied his son quickly. "There undoubtedly is! But though I have no hesitation in speaking to men down in the Settlement about these things, you know, still, somehow, to a man of your own class, and to a personal friend, one hesitates. One shrinks from what seems like assuming an attitude of superiority."

"I appreciate that," said his father, "but yet one wonders to what extent this shrinking is due to a real sense of one's own imperfections, and to what extent it is due to an unwillingness to risk criticism, even from ourselves, in a loyal attempt to serve the Master and His cause. And, besides that, one wonders whether from any cause one should hesitate to do the truly kind and Christian thing to one's friend. I mean, you value your religion; or, to put it personally, as Rob would, you would esteem as your chief possession your knowledge of the Christ, as Friend and Saviour. Do not loyalty to Him and friendship require that you share that possession with your dearest friend?"

"I know what you mean, Sir," said Jack earnestly. "I shall think it over. But don't you think a word from you, Sir—"

His father looked at his son with a curious smile.

"Oh, I know what you are thinking," said his son, "but I assure you it is not quite a case of funk."

"Do you know, Jack," said his father earnestly, "we make our religion far too unreal; a thing either of forms remote from life, or a thing of individualistic emotion divorced from responsibility. One thing history reveals, that the early propagandum for the faith was entirely unprofessional. It was from friend to friend, from man to man. It was horizontal rather than perpendicular."

"Well, I shall think it over," said Jack.

"Do you know," said his father, "that I have the feeling of having accepted from Rob responsibility for our utmost endeavour to bring it about that, as Rob puts it, 'somehow he shall get back'?"

It was full twenty minutes before train time when Rob, torn with anxiety lest they should be late, marched his brother on to the railway platform to wait for the Camerons, who were to arrive from the North. Up and down they paraded, Dunn turning over in his mind the conversation of the night before, Rob breaking away every three minutes to consult the clock and the booking clerk at the wicket.

"Will he come to us this afternoon, Jack, do you think?" enquired the boy.

"Don't know! He turned down a football lunch! He has his sister and his father with him."

"His sister could come with him!" argued the boy.

"What about his father?"

Rob had been close enough to events to know that the Captain constituted something of a difficulty in the situation.

"Well, won't he have business to attend to?"

His brother laughed. "Good idea, Rob, let us hope so! At any rate we will do our best to get Cameron and his sister to come to us. We want them, don't we?"

"We do that!" said the boy fervently; "only I'm sure something will happen! There," he exclaimed a moment later, in a tone of disappointment and disgust, "I just knew it! There is Miss Brodie and some one else; they will get after him, I know!"

"So it is," said Dunn, with a not altogether successful attempt at surprise.

"Aw! you knew!" said Rob reproachfully.

"Well! I kind of thought she might turn up!" said his brother, with an air of a convicted criminal. "You know she is quite a friend of Cameron's. But what is Sir Archibald here for?"

"They will just get him, I know," said Rob gloomily, as he followed his brother to meet Miss Brodie and her uncle.

"We're here!" cried that young lady, "to join in the

demonstration to the hero! And, my uncle being some-what conscience-stricken over his tardy and unwilling acceptance of our superior judgment in the recent famous case, has come to make such reparation as he can."

"What a piece of impertinence! Don't listen to her, Sir!" cried Sir Archibald, greeting Dunn warmly and with the respect due an International captain. "The truth is I have a letter here for him to a business friend in Montreal, which may be of service. Of course, I may say to you that I am more than delighted that this letter of Potts has quite cleared the young man, and that he goes to the new country with reputation unstained. I am greatly delighted! greatly delighted! and I wish the opportunity to say so."

"Indeed, we are all delighted," replied Dunn cordially, "though, of course, I never could bring myself to believe him guilty of crime."

"Well, on the strength of the judgment of yourself and, I must confess, of this young person here, I made my decision."

"Well," cried Miss Brodie, "I gave you my opinion because it was my opinion, but I confess at times I had my own doubts—"

Here she paused abruptly, arrested by the look on young Rob's face; it was a look of surprise, grief, and horror.

"That is to say," continued Miss Brodie hastily, an-swering the look, and recognising that her high place in Rob's regard was in peril, "the whole thing was a mystery—was impossible to solve—I mean," she con-tinued, stumbling along, "his own attitude was so very uncertain and so unsatisfactory—if he had only been able to say clearly 'I am not guilty' it would have been different—I mean—of course, I don't believe him guilty. Don't look at me like that, Rob! I won't have it! But was it not clever of that dear Mr. Rae to extract that letter from the wretched Potts?"

"There's the train!" cried Dunn. "Here, Rob, you stay here with me! Where has the young rascal gone!"

"Look! Oh, look!" cried Miss Brodie, clutching at Dunn's arm, her eyes wide with terror. There before their horrified eyes was young Rob, hanging on to the window, out of which his friend Cameron was leaning, and racing madly with the swiftly moving train, in momentary danger of being dragged under its wheels. With a cry, Dunn rushed forward.

"Merciful heavens!" cried Miss Brodie. "Oh! he is gone!"

A porter, standing with his back towards the racing boy, had knocked his feet from under him. But as he fell, a strong hand grabbed him, and dragged him to safety through the window.

Pale and shaking, the three friends waited for the car door to be opened, and as Rob issued in triumphant possession of his friend, Miss Brodie rushed at him and, seizing him in her strong grasp, cried:

"You heartless young rascal! You nearly killed me —not to speak of yourself! Here," she continued, throwing her arms about him, and giving him a loud smack, "take that for your punishment! Do you hear, you nearly killed me! I had a vision of your mangled form ground up between the wheels and the platform. Hold on, you can't get away from me! I have a mind to give you another!"

"Oh, Miss Brodie, please," pleaded Cameron, coming forward to Rob's rescue, "I assure you I was partly to blame; it is only fair I should share his punishment."

"Indeed," cried Miss Brodie, the blood coming back into her cheeks that had been white enough a moment before, "if it were not for your size, and your—looks, I should treat you exactly the same, though not with the same intent, as our friend Mr. Rae would say. You did that splendidly!"

"Alas! for my size," groaned Cameron—he was in great spirits—"and alas! for my ugly phiz!"

"Who said 'ugly'?" replied Miss Brodie. "But I won't rise to your bait. May I introduce you to my uncle, Sir Archibald Brodie, who has a little business with you?"

"Ah! Mr. Cameron," said that gentleman, "that was extremely well done. Indeed, I can hardly get back my nerve—might have been an ugly accident. By the way, Sir," taking Cameron aside, "just a moment. You are on your way to Canada? I have a letter which I thought might be of service to you. It is to a business friend of mine, a banker, in Montreal, Mr. James Ritchie. You will find him a good man to know, and I fancy glad to serve any—ah—friend of mine."

On hearing Sir Archibald's name, Cameron's manner became distinctly haughty, and he was on the point of declining the letter, when Sir Archibald, who was quick to observe his manner, took him by the arm and led him somewhat further away.

"Now, Sir, there is a little matter I wish to speak of, if you will permit. Indeed, I came specially to say how delighted I am that the—ah—recent little unpleasantness has been removed. Of course you understand my responsibility to the Bank rendered a certain course of action imperative, however repugnant. But, believe me, I am truly delighted to find that my decision to withdraw the—ah—action has been entirely justified by events. Delighted, Sir! Delighted! And much more since I have seen you."

Before the overflowing kindliness of Sir Archibald's voice and manner, Cameron's hauteur vanished like morning mist before the rising sun.

"I thank you, Sir Archibald," he said, with dignity, "not only for this letter, but especially for your good opinion."

"Very good! Very good! The letter will, I hope, be useful," replied Sir Archibald, "and as for my opinion, I am glad to find not only that it is well founded, but that it appears to be shared by most of this company here. Now we must get back to your party. But let me say again, I am truly glad to have come to know you."

BOOK TWO

CHAPTER I

HO FOR THE OPEN!

MR. JAMES RITCHIE, manager of the Bank of Montreal, glanced from the letter in his hand to the young man who had just given it to him. "Ah! you have just arrived from the old land," he said, a smile of genial welcome illuminating his handsome face. "I am pleased to hear from my old friend, Sir Archibald Brodie, and pleased to welcome any friend of his to Canada."

So saying, with fine old-time courtesy, the banker rose to his splendid height of six feet two, and shook his visitor warmly by the hand.

"Your name is—?"

"Cameron, Sir," said the young man.

"Yes, I see! Mr. Allan Cameron—um, um," with his eyes on the letter. "Old and distinguished family— exactly so! Now, then, Mr. Cameron, I hope we shall be able to do something for you, both for the sake of my old friend, Sir Archibald, and, indeed, for your own sake," said the banker, with a glance of approval at Cameron's upright form.

"Sit down, Sir! Sit down! Now, business first is my motto. What can I do for you?"

"Well, first of all," said Cameron with a laugh, "I wish to make a deposit. I have a draft of one hundred pounds here which I should like to place in your care."

"Very well, Sir," said the banker, touching a button, "my young man will attend to that."

"Now, then," when the business had been transacted, "what are your plans, Mr. Cameron? Thirty-five years ago I came to Montreal a young man, from Scotland, like yourself, and it was a lonely day for me when I reached this city, the loneliest in my life, and so my heart warms to the stranger from the old land. Yes," continued Mr. Ritchie, in a reminiscent tone, "I remember well! I hired as errand boy and general factotum to a small grocer down near the market. Montreal was a small city then, with wretched streets—they're bad enough yet—and poor buildings; everything was slow and backward; there have been mighty changes since. But here we are! Now, what are your plans?"

"I am afraid they are of the vaguest kind," said Cameron. "I want something to do."

"What sort of thing? I mean, what has been the line of your training?"

"I am afraid my training has been defective. I have passed through Edinburgh Academy, also the University, with the exception of my last year. But I am willing to take anything."

"Ah!" said the banker thoughtfully. "No office training, eh?"

"No, Sir. That is, if you except a brief period of three or four months in the law office of our family solicitor."

"Law, eh?—I have it! Denman's your man! I shall give you a letter to Mr. Denman—a lawyer friend of mine. I shall see him personally to-day, and if you call to-morrow at ten I hope to have news for you. Meantime, I shall be pleased to have you lunch with me to-day at the club. One o'clock is the hour. If you would kindly call at the bank, we shall go down together."

Cameron expressed his gratitude.

"By the way!" said Mr. Ritchie, "where have you put up?"

"At the Royal," said Cameron.

"Ah! That will do for the present," said Mr. Ritchie.

I am sorry our circumstances do not permit of my inviting you to our home. The truth is, Mrs. Ritchie is at present out of the city. But we shall find some suitable lodging for you. The Royal is far too expensive a place for a young man with his fortune to make."

Cameron spent the day making the acquaintance of the beautiful, quaint, if somewhat squalid, old city of Montreal; and next morning, with a letter of introduction from Mr. Ritchie, presented himself at Mr. Denman's office. Mr. Denman was a man in young middle life, athletic of frame, keen of eye, and energetic of manner; his voice was loud and sharp. He welcomed Cameron with brisk heartiness, and immediately proceeded to business.

"Let me see," he began, "what is your idea? What kind of a job are you after?"

"Indeed," replied Cameron, "that is just what I hardly know."

"Well, what has been your experience? You are a University man, I believe? But have you had any practical training ? Do you know office work?"

"No, I've had little training for an office. I was in a law office for part of a year."

"Ah! Familiar with bookkeeping, or accounting? I suppose you can't run one of these typewriting machines?"

In regard to each of these lines of effort Cameron was forced to confess ignorance.

"I say!" cried Mr. Denman, "those old country people seriously annoy me with their inadequate system of education!"

"I am afraid," replied Cameron, "the fault is more mine than the system's."

"Don't know about that! Don't know about that!"

replied Mr. Denman quickly; "I have had scores of young men, fine young men, too, come to me; public school men, university men, but quite unfit for any practical line of work."

Mr. Denman considered for some moments. "Let us see. You have done some work in a law office. Now," Mr. Denman spoke with some hesitation; "I have a place in my own office here—not much in it for the present, but—"

"To tell the truth," interrupted Cameron, "I did not make much of the law; in fact, I do not think I am suited for office work. I would prefer something in the open. I had thought of the land."

"Farming," exclaimed Mr. Denman. "Ah!—you would, I suppose, be able to invest something?"

"No," said Cameron, "nothing."

Denman shook his head. "Nothing in it! You would not earn enough to buy a farm about here in fifteen years."

"But I understood," replied Cameron, "that further west was cheaper land."

"Oh! In the far west, yes! But it is a God-forsaken country! I don't know much about it, I confess. I know they are booming town lots all over the land. I believe they have gone quite mad in the business, but from what I hear, the main work in the west just now is jaw work; the only thing they raise is corner lots."

On Cameron's face there fell the gloom of discouragement. One of his fondest dreams was being dispelled—his vision of himself as a wealthy rancher, ranging over square miles of his estate upon a "bucking broncho," garbed in the picturesque cowboy dress, began to fade.

"But there is ranching, I believe?" he ventured.

"Ranching? Oh yes! There is, up near the Rockies, but that is out of civilization; out of reach of everything and everybody."

"That is what I want, Sir!" exclaimed Cameron, his face once more aglow with eager hope. "I want to get away into the open."

Mr. Denman did not, or could not, recognise this as the instinctive cry of the primitive man for a closer fellowship with Mother Nature. He was keenly practical, and impatient with everything that appeared to him to be purely visionary and unbusiness-like.

"But, my dear fellow," he said, "a ranch means cattle and horses; and cattle and horses means money, unless of course, you mean to be simply a cowboy—cowpuncher, I believe, is the correct term—but there is nothing in that; no future, I mean. It is all very well for a little fun, if you have a bank account to stand it, although some fellows stand it on someone's else bank account— not much to their credit, however. There is a young friend of mine out there at present, but from what I can gather his home correspondence is mainly confined to appeals for remittances from his governor, and his chief occupation spending these remittances as speedily as possible. All very well, as I have said, for fun, if you can pay the shot. But to play the role of gentleman cowboy, while somebody else pays for it, is the sort of thing I despise."

"And so do I, Sir!" said Cameron. "There will be no remittance in my case."

Denman glanced at the firm, closed lips and the stiffening figure.

"That is the talk!" he exclaimed. "No, there is no chance in ranching unless you have capital."

"As far as I can see," replied Cameron gloomily, "everything seems closed up except to the capitalist, and yet from what I heard at home situations were open on every hand in this country."

"Come here!" cried Denman, drawing Cameron to the office window. "See those doors!" pointing to a long line of shops. "Every last one is opened to a man who knows his business. See those smokestacks! Every last wheel in those factories is howling for a man who is on to his job. But don't look blue, there is a place for you, too; the thing is to find it."

"What are those long buildings?" inquired Cameron, pointing towards the water front.

"Those are railroad sheds; or, rather, Transportation Company's sheds; they are practically the same thing. I say! What is the matter with trying the Transportation Company? I know the manager well. The very thing! Try the Transportation Company!"

"How should I go about it?" said Cameron. "I mean to say just what position should I apply for?"

"Position!" shouted Denman. "Why, general manager would be good!"

Then, noting the flush in Cameron's face, he added quickly, "Pardon me! The thing is to get your foot in somehow, and then wire in till you are general manager, by Jove! It can be done! Fleming has done it! Went in as messenger boy, but—" Denman paused. There flashed through his mind the story of Fleming's career; a vision of the half-starved ragged waif who started as messenger boy in the company's offices, and who, by dint of invincible determination and resolute self-denial, fought his way step by step to his present position of control. In contrast, he looked at the young man, born and bred in circles where work is regarded as a calamity, and service wears the badge of social disfranchisement. Fleming had done it under compulsion of the inexorable mistress "Necessity." But what of this young man?

"Will we try?" he said at length. "I shall give you a letter to Mr. Fleming."

He sat down to his desk and wrote vigourously.

"Take this, and see what happens."

Cameron took the letter, and, glancing at the address, read, Wm. Fleming, Esquire, General Manager, Metropolitan Transportation & Cartage Company.

"Is this a railroad?" asked Cameron.

"No, but next thing to it. The companies are practically one. The transition from one to the other is easy enough. Let me know how you get on. Good-by! And—I say!" cried Mr. Denman, calling Cameron back again from the door, "see Mr. Fleming himself. Remember that! And remember," he added, with a smile, "the position of manager is not vacant just yet, but it will be. I give you my word for it when you are ready to take it. Good-by! Buck up! Take what he offers you! Get your teeth in, and never let go!"

"By George!" said Denman to himself as the door closed on Cameron, "these chaps are the limit. He's got lots of stuff in him, but he has been rendered helpless by their fool system—God save us from it! That chap has had things done for him ever since he was first bathed; they have washed 'em, dressed 'em, fed 'em, schooled 'em, found 'em positions, stuck 'em in, and watched that they didn't fall out. And yet, by George!" he added, after a pause, "they are running the world to-day—that is, some of them." Facing which somewhat puzzling phenomenon, Denman plunged into his work again.

Meantime Cameron was making his way towards the offices of the Metropolitan Transportation & Cartage Company, oppressed with an unacknowledged but none the less real sense of unfitness, and haunted by a depressing sense of the deficiency of his own training, and of the training afforded the young men of his class at home. As he started along he battled with his depression. True enough, he had no skill in the various accomplishments that Mr. Denman seemed to consider essential; he had no experience in business, he was not fit for office work—office work he loathed; but surely there was some position where his talents would bring him recognition and fortune at last. After all, Mr. Denman was only a Colonial, and with a Colonial's somewhat narrow view of life. Who was he to criticise the system of training that for generations had been in vogue at home? Had not Wellington said "that England's battles were first won on the football fields of Eton and Rugby," or something like that? Of course, the training that might fit for a distinguished career in the British army might not necessarily insure success on the battle fields of industry and commerce. Yet surely, an International player should be able to get somewhere!

At this point in his cogitations Cameron was arrested by a memory that stabbed him like a knife-thrust; the awful moment when upon the Inverleith grounds, in the face of the Welsh forward-line, he had faltered and lost the International. Should he ever be able to forget the agony of that moment and of the day that followed? And yet, he need not have failed. He knew he could play his position with any man in Scotland; he had failed because he was not fit. He set his teeth hard. He would show these bally Colonials! He would make good! And with his head high, he walked into the somewhat dingy offices of the Metropolitan Transportation & Cartage Company, of which William Fleming, Esquire, was manager.

Opening the door, Cameron found himself confronted by a short counter that blocked the way for the general public into the long room, filled with desks and chairs and clicking typewriting machines. Cameron had never seen so many of these machines during the whole period of his life. The typewriter began to assume an altogether new importance in his mind. Hitherto it had appeared to him more or less of a Yankee fad, unworthy of the attention of an able-bodied man of average intelligence. In Edinburgh a "writing machine" was still something of a new-fangled luxury, to be apologised for. Mr. Rae would allow no such finicky instrument in his office. Here, however, there were a dozen, more or less, manipulated for the most part by young ladies, and some of them actually by men; on every side they clicked and banged. It may have been the clicking and banging of these machines that gave to Cameron the sense of rush and hurry so different from the calm quiet and dignified repose of the only office he had ever known. For some moments he stood at the counter, waiting attention from one of the many clerks sitting before him, but though one and another occasionally glanced in his direction, his presence seemed to awaken not even a passing curiosity in their minds, much less to suggest the propriety of their inquiring his business.

As the moments passed Cameron became conscious of a feeling of affront. How differently a gentleman was treated by the clerks in the office of Messrs. Rae & Macpherson, where prompt attention and deferential courtesy in a clerk were as essential as a suit of clothes. Gradually Cameron's head went up, and with it his choler. At length, in his haughtiest tone, he hailed a passing youth:

"I say, boy, is this Mr. Fleming's office?"

The clicking and banging of the typewriters, and the hum of voices ceased. Everywhere heads were raised and eyes turned curiously upon the haughty stranger.

"Eh?" No letters can represent the nasal intonation of this syllabic inquiry, and no words the supreme indifference of the boy's tone.

"Is Mr. Fleming in? I wish to see him!" Cameron's voice was loud and imperious.

"Say, boys," said a lanky youth, with a long, cadaverous countenance and sallow, unhealthy complexion, illumined, however, and redeemed to a certain extent by black eyes of extraordinary brilliance, "it is the Prince of Wales!" The drawling, awe-struck tones, in the silence that had fallen, were audible to all in the immediate neighbourhood.

The titter that swept over the listeners brought the hot blood to Cameron's face. A deliberate insult a Highlander takes with calm. He is prepared to deal with it in a manner affording him entire satisfaction. Ridicule rouses him to fury, for, while it touches his pride, it leaves him no opportunity of vengeance.

"Can you tell me if Mr. Fleming is in?" he enquired again of the boy that stood scanning him with calm indifference. The rage that possessed him so vibrated in his tone that the lanky lad drawled again in a warning voice:

"Slide, Jimmy, slide!"

Jimmy "slid," but towards the counter.

"Want to see him?" he enquired in a tone of brisk impertinence, as if suddenly roused from a reverie.

"I have a letter for him."

"All right! Hand it over," said Jimmy, fully conscious that he was the hero of more than usual interest.

Cameron hesitated, then passed his letter over to Jimmy, who, reading the address with deliberate care, winked at the lanky boy, and with a jaunty step made towards a door at the farther end of the room. As he passed a desk that stood nearest the door, a man who during the last few minutes had remained with his head down, apparently so immersed in the papers before him as to be quite unconscious of his surroundings, suddenly called out, "Here, boy!"

Jimmy instantly assumed an air of respectful attention.

"A letter for Mr. Fleming," he said.

"Here!" replied the man, stretching out his hand.

He hurriedly glanced through the letter.

"Tell him there is no vacancy at present," he said shortly.

The boy came back to Cameron with cheerful politeness. The "old man's" eye was upon him.

"There is no vacancy at present," he said briefly, and turned away as if his attention were immediately demanded elsewhere by pressing business of the Metropolitan Transportation & Cartage Company.

For answer, Cameron threw back the leaf of the counter that barred his way, and started up the long room, past the staring clerks, to the desk next the door.

"I wish to see Mr. Fleming, Sir," he said, his voice trembling slightly, his face pale, his blue-gray eyes ablaze.

The man at the desk looked up from his work.

"I have just informed you there is no vacancy at present," he said testily, and turned to his papers again, as if dismissing the incident.

"Will you kindly tell me if Mr. Fleming is in?" said Cameron in a voice that had grown quite steady; "I wish to see him personally."

"Mr. Fleming cannot see you, I tell you!" almost shouted the man, rising from his desk and revealing himself a short, pudgy figure, with flabby face and shining bald head. "Can't you understand English?—I can't be bothered—!"

"What is it, Bates? Someone to see me?"

Cameron turned quickly towards the speaker, who had come from the inner room.

"I have brought you a letter, Sir, from Mr. Denman," he said quietly; "it is there," pointing to Bates' desk.

"A letter? Let me have it! Why was not this brought to me at once, Mr. Bates?"

"It was an open letter, Sir," replied Bates, "and I thought there was no need of troubling you, Sir. I told the young man we had no vacancy at present."

"This is a personal letter, Mr. Bates, and should have been brought to me at once. Why was Mr.—ah—Mr. Cameron not brought in to me?"

Mr. Bates murmured something about not wishing to disturb the manager on trivial business.

"I am the judge of that, Mr. Bates. In future, when any man asks to see me, I desire him to be shown in at once."

Mr. Bates began to apologise.

"That is all that is necessary, Mr. Bates," said the manager, in a voice at once quiet and decisive.

"Come in, Mr. Cameron. I am very sorry this has happened!"

Cameron followed him into his office, noting, as he passed, the red patches of rage on Mr. Bates' pudgy face, and catching a look of fierce hate from his small piggy eyes. It flashed through his mind that in Mr. Bates, at any rate, he had found no friend.

The result of the interview with Mr. Fleming was an intimation to Mr. Bates that Mr. Cameron was to have a position in the office of the Metropolitan Transportation & Cartage Company, and to begin work the following morning.

"Very well, Sir," replied Mr. Bates—he had apparently quite recovered his equanimity—"we shall find Mr. Cameron a desk."

"We begin work at eight o'clock exactly," he added, turning to Cameron with a pleasant smile.

Mr. Fleming accompanied Cameron to the door.

"Now, a word with you, Mr. Cameron. You may find Mr. Bates a little difficult—he is something of a driver —but, remember, he is in charge of this office; I never interfere with his orders."

"I understand, Sir," said Cameron, resolving that, at all costs, he should obey Mr. Bates' orders, if only to show the general manager he could recognise and appreciate a gentleman when he saw one.

Mr. Fleming was putting it mildly when he described Mr. Bates as "something of a driver." The whole office staff, from Jimmy, the office boy, to Jacobs, the gentle, white-haired clerk, whose desk was in the farthest corner of the room, felt the drive. He was not only office manager, but office master as well. His rule was absolute, and from his decisions there was no appeal. The general manager went on the theory that it was waste of energy to keep a dog and bark himself. In the policy that governed the office there were two rules which Mr. Bates enforced with the utmost rigidity—the first, namely, that every member of the staff must be in his or her place and ready for work when the clock struck eight; the other, that each member of the staff must work independently of every other member. A man must know his business, and go through with it; if he required instructions, he must apply to the office manager. But, as a rule, one experience of such application sufficed for the whole period of a clerk's service in the office of the Metropolitan Transportation & Cartage Company, for Mr. Bates was gifted with such an exquisiteness of ironical speech that the whole staff were wont to pause in the rush of their work to listen and to admire when a new member was unhappy enough to require instructions, their silent admiration acting as a spur to Mr. Bates' ingenuity in the invention of ironical discourse.

Of the peculiarities and idiosyncrasies of Mr. Bates' system, however, Cameron was quite ignorant; nor had his experience in the office of Messrs. Rae & Macpherson been such as to impress upon him the necessity of a close observation of the flight of time. It did not disturb him, therefore, to notice as he strolled into the offices of the Metropolitan Transportation & Cartage Company the next morning that the hands of the clock showed six minutes past the hour fixed for the beginning of the day's work. The office staff shivered in an ecstasy of expectant delight. Cameron walked nonchalantly to Mr. Bates' desk, his overcoat on his arm, his cap in his hand.

"Good morning, Sir," he said.

Mr. Bates finished writing a sentence, looked up, and nodded a brief good morning.

"We deposit our street attire on the hooks behind the door, yonder!" he said with emphatic politeness, pointing across the room.

Cameron flushed, as in passing his desk he observed the pleased smile on the lanky boy's sallow face.

"You evidently were not aware of the hours of this office," continued Mr. Bates when Cameron had returned. "We open at eight o'clock."

"Oh!" said Cameron, carelessly. "Eight? Yes, I thought it was eight! Ah! I see! I believe I am five minutes late! But I suppose I shall catch up before the day is over!"

"Mr. Cameron," replied Mr. Bates earnestly, "if you should work for twenty years for the Metropolitan Transportation & Cartage Company, never will you catch up those five minutes; every minute of your office hours is pledged to the company, and every minute has its own proper work. Your desk is the one next Mr. Jacobs, yonder. Your work is waiting you there. It is quite simple, the entry of freight receipts upon the ledger. If you wish further instructions, apply to me here—you understand?"

"I think so!" replied Cameron. "I shall do my best to—"

"Very well! That is all!" replied Mr. Bates, plunging his head again into his papers.

The office staff sank back to work with every expression of disappointment. A moment later, however, their hopes revived.

"Oh! Mr. Cameron!" called out Mr. Bates. Mr. Cameran returned to his desk. "If you should chance to be late again, never mind going to your desk; just come here for your cheque."

Mr. Bates' tone was kindly, even considerate, as if he were anxious to save his clerk unnecessary inconvenience.

"I beg your pardon!" stammered Cameron, astonished.

"That is all!" replied Mr. Bates, his nose once more in his papers.

Cameron stood hesitating. His eye fell upon the boy, Jimmy, whose face expressed keenest joy.

"Do you mean, Sir, that if I am late you dismiss me forthwith?"

"What?" Mr. Bates' tone was so fiercely explosive that it appeared to throw up his head with a violent motion.

Cameron repeated his question.

"Mr. Cameron, my time is valuable; so is yours. I thought that I spoke quite distinctly. Apparently I did not. Let me repeat: In case you should inadvertently be late again, you need not take the trouble to go to your desk; just come here. Your cheque will be immediately made out. Saves time, you know—your time and mine—and time, you perceive, in this office represents money."

Mr. Bates' voice lost none of its kindly interest, but it had grown somewhat in intensity; the last sentence was uttered with his face close to his desk.

Cameron stood a moment in uncertainty, gazing at the bald head before him; then, finding nothing to reply, he turned about to behold Jimmy and his lanky friend executing an animated war pantomime which they apparently deemed appropriate to the occasion.

With face ablaze and teeth set Cameron went to his desk, to the extreme disappointment of Jimmy and the lanky youth, who fell into each other's arms, apparently overcome with grief.

For half an hour the office hummed with the noise of subdued voices and clicked with the rapid fire of the typewriters. Suddenly through the hum Mr. Bates' voice was heard, clear, calm, and coldly penetrating:

"Mr. Jacobs!"

The old, white-haired clerk started up from Cameron's desk, and began in a confused and gentle voice to explain that he was merely giving some hints to the new clerk.

"Mr. Jacobs," said Mr. Bates, "I cannot hear you, and you are wasting my time!"

"He was merely showing me how to make these entries!" said Cameron.

"Ah! Indeed! Thank you, Mr. Cameron! Though I believe Mr. Jacobs has not yet lost the power of lucid speech. Mr. Jacobs, I believe you know the rules of this office; your fine will be one-quarter of a day."

"Thank you!" said Mr. Jacobs, hurriedly resuming his desk.

"And, Mr. Cameron, if you will kindly bring your work to me, I shall do my best to enlighten you in regard to the complex duty of entering your freight receipts."

An audible snicker ran through the delighted staff. Cameron seized his ledger and the pile of freight bills, and started for Mr. Bates' desk, catching out of the corner of his eye the pantomime of Jimmy and the lanky one, which was being rendered with vigor and due caution.

For a few moments Cameron stood at the manager's desk till that gentleman should be disengaged, but Mr. Bates was skilled in the fine art of reducing to abject humility an employé who might give indications of insubordination. Cameron's rage grew with every passing moment.

"Here is the ledger, Sir!" he said at length.

But Mr. Bates was so completely absorbed in the business of saving time that he made not the slightest pause in his writing, while the redoubled vigor and caution of the pantomime seemed to indicate the approach of a crisis. At length Mr. Bates raised his head. Jimmy and the lanky clerk became at once engrossed in their duties.

"You have had no experience of this kind of work, Mr. Cameron?" inquired Mr. Bates kindly.

"No, Sir. But if you will just explain one or two matters, I think I can—"

"Exactly! This is not, however, a business college! But we shall do our best!"

A rapturous smile pervaded the office. Mr. Bates was in excellent form.

"By the way, Mr. Cameron—pardon my neglect—but may I inquire just what department of this work you are familiar with?"

"Oh, general—"

"Ah! The position of general manager, however, is filled at present!" replied Mr. Bates kindly.

Cameron's flush grew deeper, while Jimmy and his friend resigned themselves to an ecstasy of delight.

"I was going to say," said Cameron in a tone loud and deliberate, "that I had been employed with the general copying work in a writer's office."

"Writing? Fancy! Writing, eh? No use here!" said Mr. Bates shortly, for time was passing.

"A writer with us means a lawyer!" replied Cameron.

"Why the deuce don't they say so?" answered Mr. Bates impatiently. "Well! Well!" getting hold of himself again. "Here we allow our solicitors to look after our legal work. Typewrite?" he inquired suddenly.

"I beg your pardon!" replied Cameron. "Typewrite? Do you mean, can I use a typewriting machine?"

"Yes! Yes! For heaven's sake, yes!"

"No, I cannot!"

"Bookkeep?"

"No."

"Good Lord! What have I got?" inquired Mr. Bates of himself, in a tone, however, perfectly audible to those in the immediate neighbourhood.

"Try him licking stamps!" suggested the lanky youth in a voice that, while it reached the ears of Jimmy and others near by, including Cameron, was inaudible to the manager. Mr. Bates caught the sound, however, and glared about him through his spectacles. Time was being wasted—the supreme offense in that office—and Mr. Bates was fast losing his self-command.

"Here!" he cried suddenly, seizing a sheaf of letters. "File these letters. You will be able to do that, I guess! File's in the vault over there!"

Cameron took the letters and stood looking helplessly from them to Mr. Bates' bald head, that gentleman's face being already in close proximity to the papers on his desk.

"Just how do I go about this?—I mean, what system do you—"

"Jim!" roared Mr. Bates, throwing down his pen, "show this con—show Mr. Cameron how to file these letters! Just like these blank old-country chumps!" added Mr. Bates, in a lower voice, but loud enough to be distinctly heard.

Jim came up with a smile of patronising pity on his face. It was the smile that touched to life the mass of combustible material that had been accumulating for the last hour in Cameron's soul. Instead of following the boy, he turned with a swift movement back to the manager's desk, laid his sheaf of letters down on Mr. Bates' papers, and, leaning over the desk, towards that gentleman, said:

"Did you mean that remark to apply to me?" His voice was very quiet. But Mr. Bates started back with a quick movement from the white face and burning eyes.

"Here, you get out of this!" he cried.

"Because," continued Cameron, "if you did, I must ask you to apologise at once."

All smiles vanished from the office staff, even Jimmy's face assumed a serious aspect. Mr. Bates pushed back his chair.

"A-po-pologise!" he sputtered. "Get out of this office, d'ye hear?"

"Be quick!" said Cameron, his hands gripping Mr. Bates' desk till it shook.

"Jimmy! Call a policeman!" cried Mr. Bates, rising from his chair.

He was too slow. Cameron reached swiftly for his collar, and with one fierce wrench swept Mr. Bates clear over the top of his desk, shook him till his head wobbled dangerously, and flung him crashing across the desk and upon the prostrate form of the lanky youth sitting behind it.

"Call a policeman! Call a policeman!" shouted Mr. Bates, who was struggling meantime with the lanky youth to regain an upright position.

Cameron, meanwhile, walked quietly to where his coat and cap hung.

"Hold him, somebody! Hold him!" shouted Mr. Bates, hurrying towards him.

Cameron turned fiercely upon him.

"Did you want me, Sir?" he inquired.

Mr. Bates arrested himself with such violence that his feet slid from under him, and once more he came sitting upon the floor.

"Get up!" said Cameron, "and listen to me!"

Mr. Bates rose, and stood, white and trembling.

"I may not know much about your Canadian ways of business, but I believe I can teach you some old-country manners. You have treated me this morning like the despicable bully that you are. Perhaps you will treat the next old-country man with the decency that is coming to him, even if he has the misfortune to be your clerk."

With these words Cameron turned upon his heel and walked deliberately towards the door. Immediately Jimmy sprang before him, and, throwing the door wide open, bowed him out as if he were indeed the Prince of Wales. Thus abruptly ended Cameron's connection with the Metropolitan Transportation & Cartage Company. Before the day was done the whole city had heard the tale, which lost nothing in the telling.

Next morning Mr. Denman was surprised to have Cameron walk in upon him.

"Hullo, young man!" shouted the lawyer, "this is a pretty business! Upon my soul! Your manner of entry into our commercial life is somewhat forceful! What the deuce do you mean by all this?"

Cameron stood, much abashed. His passion was all gone; in the calm light of after-thought his action of yesterday seemed boyish.

"I'm awfully sorry, Mr. Denman," he replied, "and I came to apologise to you."

"To me?" cried Denman. "Why to me? I expect, if you wish to get a job anywhere in this town, you will need to apologise to the chap you knocked down—what's his name?"

"Mr. Bates, I think his name is, Sir; but, of course, I cannot apologise to him."

"By Jove!" roared Mr. Denman, "he ought to have

thrown you out of his office! That is what I would have done!"

Cameron glanced up and down Mr. Denman's well-knit figure.

"I don't think so, Sir," he said, with a smile.

"Why not?" said Mr. Denman, grasping the arms of his office chair.

"Because you would not have insulted a stranger in your office who was trying his best to understand his work. And then, I should not have tried it on you."

"And why?"

"Well, I think I know a gentleman when I see one."

Mr. Denman was not to be appeased.

"Well, let me tell you, young man, it would have been a mighty unhealthy thing for you to have cut up any such shine in this office. I have done some Rugby in my day, my boy, if you know what that means."

"I have done a little, too," said Cameron, with slightly heightened colour.

"You have, eh! Where?"

"The Scottish International, Sir."

"By Jove! You don't tell me!" replied Mr. Denman, his tone expressing a new admiration and respect. "When? This year?"

"No, last year, Sir—against Wales!"

"By Jove!" cried Mr. Denman again; "give me your hand, boy! Any man who has made the Scottish Internationals is not called to stand any cheek from a cad like Bates."

Mr. Denman shook Cameron warmly by the hand.

"Tell us about it!" he cried. "It must have been rare sport. If Bates only knew it, he ought to count it an honour to have been knocked down by a Scottish International."

"I didn't knock him down, Sir!" said Cameron, apologetically; "he is only a little chap; I just gave him a bit of a shake," and Cameron proceeded to recount the proceedings of the previous morning.

Mr. Denman was hugely delighted.

"Serves the little beast bloody well right!" he cried enthusiastically. "But what's to do now? They will be afraid to let you into their offices in this city."

"I think, Sir, I am done with offices; I mean to try the land."

"Farm, eh?" mused Mr. Denman. "Well, so be it! It will probably be safer for you there—possibly for some others as well."

CHAPTER II

A MAN'S JOB

CAMERON siept heavily and long into the day, but as he awoke he was conscious of a delightful exhilaration possessing him. For the first time in his life he was a free man, ungoverned and unguided. For four dreary weeks he had waited in Montreal for answers to his enquiries concerning positions with farmers, but apparently the Canadian farmers were not attracted by the qualifications and experience Cameron had to offer. At length he had accepted the advice of Martin's uncle in Montreal, who assured him with local pride that, if he desired a position on a farm, the district of which the little city of London was the centre was the very garden of Canada. He was glad now to remember that he had declined a letter of introduction. He was now entirely on his own. Neither in this city nor in the country round about was there a soul with whom he had the remotest acquaintance. The ways of life led out from his feet, all untried, all unknown. Which he should choose he knew not, but with a thrill of exultation he thanked his stars the choosing was his own concern. A feeling of adventure was upon him, a new courage was rising in his heart. The failure that had hitherto dogged his past essays in life did not dampen his confidence, for they had been made under other auspices than his own. He had not fitted into his former positions, but they had not been of his own choosing. He would now find a place for himself and if he failed again he was prepared to accept the responsibility. One bit of philosophy he carried with him from Mr. Denman's farewell interview—"Now, young man, remember," that gentleman had said after he had bidden him farewell, "this world is pretty much made already; success consists in adjustment. Don't try to make your world, adjust yourself to it. Don't fight the world, serve it till you master it." Cameron determined he would study adjustments; his fighting tendency, which had brought him little success in the past, he would control.

At this point the throb of a band broke in upon his meditations and summoned him from his bed. He sprang to the window. It was circus day and the morning parade, in all its mingled and cosmopolitan glory, was slowly evolving its animated length to the strains of bands of music. There were bands on horses and bands on chariots, and at the tail of the procession a fearful and wonderful instrument bearing the euphonious and classic name of the "calliope," whose chief function seemed to be that of terrifying the farmers' horses into frantic and determined attempts to escape from these horrid alarms of the city to the peaceful haunts of their rural solitudes.

Cameron was still boy enough to hurry through his morning duties in order that he might mix with the crowd and share the perennial delights which a circus affords. The stable yard attached to his hotel was lined three deep with buggies, carriages, and lumber waggons, which had borne in the crowds of farmers from the country. The hotel was thronged with sturdy red-faced farm lads, looking hot and uncomfortable in their unaccustomed Sunday suits, gorgeous in their rainbow ties, and rakish with their hats set at all angles upon their elaborately brushed heads. Older men, too, bearded and staid, moved with silent and self-respecting dignity through the crowds, gazing with quiet and observant eyes upon the shifting phantasmagoria that filled the circus grounds and the streets nearby. With these, too, there mingled a few of both old and young who, with bacchanalian enthusiasm, were swaggering their way through the crowds, each followed by a company of friends good-naturedly tolerant or solicitously careful.

Cameron's eyes, roving over the multitude, fell upon a little group that held his attention, the principal figure of which was a tall middle aged man with a good-natured face, adorned with a rugged grey chin whisker, who was loudly declaiming to a younger companion with a hard face and very wide awake, "My name's Tom Haley; ye can't come over me."

"Ye bet yer life they can't. Ye ain't no chicken!" exclaimed his hard-faced friend. "Say, let's liquor up once more before we go to see the elephant."

With these two followed a boy of some thirteen years, freckled faced and solemn, slim and wiry of body, who was anxiously striving to drag his father away from one of the drinking booths that dotted the circus grounds, and towards the big tent; but the father had been already a too frequent visitor at the booth to be quite amenable to his son's pleading. He, in a glorious mood of self-appreciation, kept announcing to the public generally and to his hard-faced friend in particular—

"My name's Tom Haley; ye can't come over me!"

"Come on, father," pleaded Tim.

"No hurry, Timmy, me boy," said his father. "The elephants won't run away with the monkeys and the clowns can't git out of the ring."

"Oh, come on, dad, I'm sure the show's begun."

"Cheese it, young feller," said the young man, "yer dad's able to take care of himself."

"Aw, you shut yer mouth!" replied Tim fiercely. "I know what you're suckin' round for."

"Good boy, Tim," laughed his father; "ye giv' 'im one that time. Guess we'll go. So long, Sam, if that's yer name. Ye see I've jist got ter take in this 'ere show this morning with Tim 'ere, and then we have got some groceries to git for the old woman. See there," he drew a paper from his pocket, "wouldn't dare show up without 'em, ye bet, eh, Tim! Why, it's her egg and butter money and she wants value fer it, she does. Well, so long, Sam, see ye later," and with the triumphant Tim he made for the big tent, leaving a wrathful and disappointed man behind him.

Cameron spent the rest of the day partly in "taking in" the circus and partly in conversing with the farmers who seemed to have taken possession of the town; but in answer to his most diligent and careful enquiries he could hear of no position on a farm for which he could honestly offer himself. The farmers wanted mowers, or cradlers, or good smart turnip hands, and Cameron sorrowfully had to confess he was none of these. There apparently was no single bit of work in the farmer's life that Cameron felt himself qualified to perform.

It was wearing towards evening when Cameron once more came across Tim. He was standing outside the bar room door, big tears silently coursing down his pale and freckled cheeks.

"Hello!" cried Cameron, "what's up, old chap? Where's your dad, and has he got his groceries yet?"

"No," said Tim, hastily wiping away his tears and looking up somewhat shyly and sullenly into Cameron's face. What he saw there apparently won his confidence.

"He's in yonder," he continued, "and I can't git him

out. They won't let him come. They're jist making 'im full so he can't do anything, and we ought to be startin' fer home right away, too!"

"Well, let's go in anyway and see what they are doing," said Cameron cheerfully, to whom the pale tear-stained face made strong appeal.

"They won't let us," said Tim. "There's a feller there that chucks me out."

"Won't, eh? We'll see about that! Come along!"

Cameron entered the bar room, with Tim following, and looked about him. The room was crowded to the door with noisy excited men, many of whom were partially intoxicated. At the bar, two deep, stood a line of men with glasses in their hands, or waiting to be served. In the farthest corner of the room stood Tim's father, considerably the worse of his day's experiences, and lovingly embracing the hard-faced young man, to whom he was at intervals announcing, "My name's Tom Haley! Ye can't git over me!"

As Cameron began to push through the crowd, a man with a very red face, obviously on the watch for Tim, cried out—

"Say, sonny, git out of here! This is no place fer you!"

Tim drew back, but Cameron, turning to him, said,

"Come along, Tim. He's with me," he added, addressing the man. "He wants his father."

"His father's not here. He left half an hour ago. I told him so."

"You were evidently mistaken, for I see him just across the room there," said Cameron quietly.

"Oh! is he a friend of yours?" enquired the red-faced man.

"No, I don't know him at all, but Tim does, and Tim

wants him," said Cameron, beginning to push his way through the crowd towards the vociferating Haley, who appeared to be on the point of backing up some of his statements with money, for he was flourishing a handful of bills in the face of the young man Sam, who apparently was quite willing to accommodate him with the wager.

Before Cameron could make his way through the swaying, roaring crowd, the red-faced man slipped from his side, and in a very few moments appeared at a side door near Tom Haley's corner. Almost immediately there was a shuffle and Haley and his friends disappeared through the side door.

"Hello!" cried Cameron, "there's something doing! We'll just slip around there, my boy." So saying, he drew Tim back from the crowd and out of the front door, and, hurrying around the house, came upon Sam, the red-faced man, and Haley in a lane leading past the stable yard. The red-faced man was affectionately urging a bottle upon Haley.

"There they are!" said Tim in an undertone, clutching Cameron's arm. "You get him away and I'll hitch up."

"All right, Tim," said Cameron, "I'll get him. They are evidently up to no good."

"What's yer name?" said Tim hurriedly.

"Cameron!"

"Come on, then!" he cried, dragging Cameron at a run towards his father. "Here, Dad!" he cried, "this is my friend, Mr. Cameron! Come on home. I'm going to hitch up. We'll be awful late for the chores and we got them groceries to git. Come on, Dad!"

"Aw, gwan! yer a cheeky kid anyway," said Sam, giving Tim a shove that nearly sent him on his head.

"Hold on there, my man, you leave the boy alone," said Cameron.

"What's your business in this, young feller?"

"Never mind!" said Cameron. "Tim is a friend of mine and no one is going to hurt him. Run along, Tim, and get your horses."

"Friend o' Tim's, eh!" said Haley, in half drunken good nature. "Friend o' Tim's, friend o' mine," he added, gravely shaking Cameron by the hand. "Have a drink, young man. You look a' right!"

Cameron took the bottle, put it to his lips. The liquor burned like fire.

"Great Cæsar!" he gasped, contriving to let the bottle drop upon a stone. "What do you call that?"

"Pretty hot stuff!" cried Haley, with a shout of laughter.

But Sam, unable to see the humour of the situation, exclaimed in a rage, "Here, you cursed fool! That is my bottle!"

"Sorry to be so clumsy," said Cameron apologetically, "but it surely wasn't anything to drink, was it?"

"Yes, it jest was something to drink, was it?" mocked Sam, approaching Cameron with menace in his eye and attitude. "I have a blanked good notion to punch your head, too!"

"Oh! I wouldn't do that if I were you," said Cameron, smiling pleasantly.

"Say, Sam, don't get mad, Sam," interposed Haley. "This young feller's a friend o' Tim's. I'll git another bottle a' right. I've got the stuff right here." He pulled out his roll of bills. "And lots more where this comes from."

"Let me have that, Mr. Haley, I'll get the bottle for you," said Cameron, reaching out for the bills.

"A' right," said Haley. "Friend o' Tim's, friend o' mine."

"Here, young feller, you're too fresh!" cried the red-faced man, "buttin' in here! You make tracks, git out! Come, git out, I tell yeh!"

"Give it to him quick," said Sam in a low voice.

The red-faced man, without the slightest warning, swiftly stepped towards Cameron and, before the latter could defend himself, struck him a heavy blow. Cameron staggered, fell, and struggled again to his knees. The red-faced man sprang forward to kick him in the face, when Haley interposed—

"Hold up there, now! Friend o' Tim's, friend o' mine, ye know!"

"Hurry up," said Sam, closing in on Haley. "Quit fooling. Give 'im the billy and let's get away!"

But Haley, though unskilled with his hands, was a man of more than ordinary strength, and he swung his long arms about with such vigour that neither Sam, who was savagely striking at his head, nor the red-faced man, who was dancing about waiting for a chance to get in with the "billy," which he held in his hand, was able to bring the affair to a finish. It could be a matter of only a few moments, however, for both Sam and his friend were evidently skilled in the arts of the thug, while Haley, though powerful enough, was chiefly occupying himself in beating the air. A blow from the billy dropped one of Haley's arms helpless. The red-faced man, following up his advantage, ran in to finish, but Haley gripped him by the wrist and, exerting all his strength, gave a mighty heave and threw him heavily against Sam, who was running in upon the other side. At the same time Cameron, who was rapidly recovering, clutched Sam by a leg and brought him heavily to earth.

Reaching down, Haley gripped Cameron by the collar and hauled him to his feet just as Sam, who had sprung up, ran to the attack. Steadied by Haley, Cameron braced himself, and, at exactly the right moment, stiffened his left arm with the whole weight of his body behind it. The result was a most unhappy one for Sam, who, expecting no such reception, was lifted clear off his feet and hurled to the ground some distance away. The exhilaration of his achievement brought Cameron's blood back again to his brain. Swiftly he turned upon the red-faced man just as that worthy had brought Haley to his knees with a cruel blow and was preparing to finish off his victim. With a shout Cameron sprang at him, the man turned quickly, warded off Cameron's blow, and then, seeing Sam lying helpless upon the ground, turned and fled down the lane.

"Say, young feller!" panted Haley, staggering to his feet, "yeh came in mighty slick that time. Yeh ain't got a bottle on ye, hev yeh?"

"No!" said Cameron, "but there's a pump near by."

"Jest as good and a little better," said Haley, staggering towards the pump. "Say," he continued, with a humourous twinkle in his eye, and glancing at the man lying on the ground, "Sam's kinder quiet, ain't he? Run agin something hard like, I guess."

Cameron filled a bucket with water and into its icy depths Haley plunged his head.

"Ow! that's good," he sputtered, plunging his head in again and again. "Fill 'er up once more!" he said, wiping off his face with a big red handkerchief. "Now, I shouldn't wonder if it would help Sam a bit."

He picked up the bucket of water and approached Sam, who meantime had got to a sitting position and was blinking stupidly around.

"Here, ye blamed hog, hev a wash, ye need it bad!" So saying, Haley flung the whole bucket of water over Sam's head and shoulders. "Fill 'er up again," he said, but Sam had had enough, and, swearing wildly, gasping and sputtering, he made off down the lane.

"I've heard o' them circus toughs," said Haley in a meditative tone, "but never jest seen 'em before. Say, young feller, yeh came in mighty handy fer me a' right, and seeing as yer Tim's friend put it there." He gripped Cameron's hand and shook it heartily. "Here's Tim with the team, and, say, there's no need to mention anything about them fellers. Tim's real tender hearted. Well, I'm glad to hev met yeh. Good-bye! Living here?"

"No!"

"Travellin', eh?"

"Not exactly," replied Cameron. "The truth is I'm looking for a position."

"A position? School teachin', mebbe?"

"No, a position on a farm."

"On a farm? Ha! ha! good! Position on a farm," repeated Haley.

"Yes," replied Cameron. "Do you know of any?"

"Position on a farm!" said Haley again, as if trying to grasp the meaning of this extraordinary quest. "There ain't any."

"No positions?" enquired Cameron.

"Nary one! Say, young man, where do you come from?"

"Scotland," replied Cameron.

"Scotland! yeh don't say, now. Jest out, eh?"

"Yes, about a month or so."

"Well, well! Yeh don't say so!"

"Yes," replied Cameron, "and I am surprised to hear that there is no work."

"Oh! hold on there now!" interposed Haley gravely. "If it's work you want there are stacks of it lying round, but there ain't no positions. Positions!" ejaculated Haley, who seemed to be fascinated by the word, "there ain't none on my farm except one and I hold that myself; but there's lots o' work, and—why! I want a man right now. What say? Come along, stay 's long's yeh like. I like yeh fine."

"All right," said Cameron. "Wait till I get my bag, but I ought to tell you I have had no experience."

"No experience, eh!" Haley pondered. "Well, we'll give it to you, and anyway you saved me some experience to-day and you come home with me."

When he returned he found Haley sitting on the bottom of the wagon rapidly sinking into slumber. The effects of the bucket were passing off.

"What about the groceries, Tim?" enquired Cameron.

"We've got to git 'em," said Tim, "or we'll catch it sure."

Leaving Cameron to wonder what it might be that they were sure to catch, Tim extracted from his father's pocket the paper on which were listed the groceries to be purchased, and the roll of bills, and handed both to Cameron.

"You best git 'em," he said, and, mounting to the high spring seat, turned the team out of the yard. The groceries secured with Cameron's help, they set off for home as the long June evening was darkening into night.

"My! it's awful late," said Tim in a voice full of foreboding. "And Perkins ain't no good at chores."

"How far is it to your home?" enquired Cameron.

"Nine miles out this road and three off to the east."

"And who's Perkins?"

"Perkins! Joe Perkins! He's our hired man. He's a terror to work at plowin', cradlin', and bindin', but he ain't no good at chores. I bet yeh he'll leave Mandy to do the milkin', ten cows, and some's awful bad."

"And who's Mandy?" enquired Cameron.

"Mandy! She's my sister. She's an awful quick milker. She can beat Dad, or Perkins, or any of 'em, but ten cows is a lot, and then there's the pigs and the calves to feed, and the wood, too. I bet Perkins won't cut a stick. He's good enough in the field," continued Tim, with an obvious desire to do Perkins full justice, "but he ain't no good around the house. He says he ain't hired to do women's chores, and Ma she won't ask 'im. She says if he don't do what he sees to be done she'd see 'im far enough before she'd ask 'im." And so Timothy went on with a monologue replete with information, his high thin voice rising clear above the roar and rattle of the lumber wagon as it rumbled and jolted over the rutty gravel road. Those who knew the boy would have been amazed at his loquacity, but something in Cameron had won his confidence and opened his heart. Hence his monologue, in which the qualities, good and bad, of the members of the family, of their own hired man and of other hired men were fully discussed. The standard of excellence for work in the neighbourhood, however, appeared to be Perkins, whose abilities Tim appeared greatly to admire, but for whose person he appeared to have little regard.

"He's mighty good at turnip hoeing, too," he said. "I could pretty near keep up to him last year and I believe I could do it this year. Some day soon I'm going to git after 'im. My! I'd like to trim 'im to a fine point."

The live stock on the farm in general, and the young

colts in particular, among which a certain two-year-old was showing signs of marvellous speed, these and cognate subjects relating to the farm, its dwellers and its activities, Tim passed in review, with his own shrewd comments thereon.

"And what do you play, Tim?" asked Cameron, seeking a point of contact with the boy.

"Nothin'," said Tim shortly. "No time."

"Don't you go to school?"

"Yes, in fall and winter. Then we play ball and shinny some, but there ain't much time."

"But you can't work all the time, Tim? What work can you do?"

"Oh!" replied Tim carelessly, "I run a team."

"Run a team? What do you mean?"

Tim glanced up at him and, perceiving that he was quite serious, proceeded to explain that during the spring's work he had taken his place in the plowing and harrowing with the "other" men, that he expected to drive the mower and reaper in haying and harvest, that, in short, in almost all kinds of farm work he was ready to take the place of a grown man; and all this without any sign of boasting.

Cameron thought over his own life, in which sport had filled up so large a place and work so little, and in which he had developed so little power of initiative and such meagre self-dependence, and he envied the solemn-faced boy at his side, handling his team and wagon with the skill of a grown man.

"I say, Tim!" he exclaimed in admiration, "you're great. I wish I could do half as much."

"Oh, pshaw!" exclaimed Tim in modest self-disdain, "that ain't nothin', but I wish I could git off a bit."

"Get off? What do you mean?"

The boy was silent for some moments, then asked shyly:

"Say! Is there big cities in Scotland, an' crowds of people, an' trains, an' engines, an' factories, an' things? My! I wish I could git away!"

Then Cameron understood dimly something of the wander-lust in the boy's soul, of the hunger for adventure, for the colour and movement of life in the great world "away" from the farm, that thrilled in the boy's voice. So for the next half hour he told Tim tales of his own life, the chief glory of which had been his achievements in the realm of sport, and, before he was aware, he was describing to the boy the great International with Wales, till, remembering the disastrous finish, he brought his narrative to an abrupt close.

"And did yeh lick 'em?" demanded Tim in a voice of intense excitement.

"No," said Cameron shortly.

"Oh, hedges! I wisht ye had!" exclaimed Tim in deep disappointment.

"It was my fault," replied Cameron bitterly, for the eager wish in the boy's heart had stirred a similar yearning in his own and had opened an old sore.

"I was a fool," he said, more to himself than to Tim. "I let myself get out of condition and so I lost them the match."

"Aw, git out!" said Tim, with unbelieving scorn. "I bet yeh didn't! My! I wisht I could see them games!"

"Oh, pshaw! Tim, they are not half so worth while as plowing, harrowing, and running your team. Why, here you are, a boy of—how old?"

"Thirteen," said Tim.

"A boy of thirteen able to do a man's work, and here am I, a man of twenty-one, only able to do a boy's work, and not even that. But I'm going to learn, Tim," added Cameron. "You hear me, I am going to learn to do a man's work. If I can," he added doubtfully.

"Oh, shucks!" replied Tim, "you bet yeh can, and I'll show yeh," with which mutual determination they turned in at the gate of the Haley farm, which was to be the scene of Cameron's first attempt to do a man's work and to fill a man's place in the world.

CHAPTER III

A DAY'S WORK

THE Haley farm was a survival of an ambitious past. Once the property of a rich English gentleman, it had been laid out with an eye to appearance rather than to profit and, though the soil was good enough, it had never been worked to profit. Consequently, when its owner had tired of Colonial life, he had at first rented the farm, but, finding this unsatisfactory, he, in a moment of disgust, advertised it for sale. Pretentious in its plan and in its appointments, its neglected and run down condition gave it an air of decayed gentility, depressing alike to the eye of the beholder and to the selling price of the owner. Haley bought it and bought it cheap. From the high road a magnificent avenue of maples led to a house of fine proportions, though sadly needing repair. The wide verandahs, the ample steps were unpainted and falling into ruin; the lawn reaching from the front door to the orchard was spacious, but overgrown with burdocks, nettles and other noxious weeds; the orchard, which stretched from the lawn to the road on both sides of the lane, had been allowed to run sadly to wood. At the side of the house the door-yard was littered with abandoned farm implements, piles of old fence rails and lumber and other impedimenta, which, though kindly Nature, abhorring the unsightly rubbish, was doing her utmost to hide it all beneath a luxuriant growth of docks, milkweed, and nettles, lent an air of disorder and neglect to the whole surroundings. The porch, or "stoop," about the summer kitchen was set out with an assortment of tubs and pails, pots and pans, partially

filled with various evil looking and more evil smelling
messes, which afforded an excellent breeding and feeding place for flies, mosquitoes, and other unpleasant
insects. Adjoining the door yard, and separated from
it by a fence, was the barn yard, a spacious quadrangle
flanked on three sides by barns, stables, and sheds, which
were large and finely planned, but which now shared
the general appearance of decrepitude. The fence,
which separated one yard from the other, was broken
down, so that the barn yard dwellers, calves, pigs, and
poultry, wandered at will in search of amusement or
fodder to the very door of the kitchen, and so materially
contributed to the general disorder, discomfort, and dirt.

Away from the house, however, where Nature had her
own way, the farm stretched field after field on each
side of the snake fenced lane to the line of woods in the
distance, a picture of rich and varied beauty. From the
rising ground on which the house was situated a lovely
vista swept right from the kitchen door away to the remnant of the forest primeval at the horizon. On every
field the signs of coming harvest were luxuriantly visible, the hay fields, grey-green with blooming "Timothy"
and purple with the deep nestling clover, the fall wheat
green and yellowing into gold, the spring wheat a lighter
green and bursting into head, the oats with their graceful tasselated stalks, the turnip field ribboned with its
lines of delicate green on the dark soil drills, back of
all, the "slashing" where stumps, blackened with fire,
and trunks of trees piled here and there in confusion,
all overgrown with weeds, represented the transition
stage between forest and harvest field, and beyond the
slashing the dark cool masses of maple, birch, and elm;
all these made a scene of such varied loveliness as to
delight the soul attuned to nature.

Upon this scene of vivid contrasts, on one side house and barn and yard, and on the other the rolling fields and massive forest, Cameron stood looking in the early light of his first morning on the farm, with mingled feelings of disgust and pleasure. In a few moments, however, the loveliness of the far view caught and held his eye and he stood as in a dream. The gentle rolling landscape, with its rich variety of greens and yellows and greys, that swept away from his feet to the dark masses of woods, with their suggestions of cool and shady depth, filled his soul with a deep joy and brought him memory of how the "Glen of the Cup of Gold" would look that morning in the dear home-land so far away. True, there were neither mountains nor moors, neither lochs nor birch-clad cliffs here. Nature, in her quieter mood, looked up at him from these sloping fields and bosky woods and smiled with kindly face, and that smile of hers it was that brought to Cameron's mind the sunny Glen of the Cup of Gold. It was the sweetest, kindliest thing his eye had looked on since he had left the Glen.

A harsh and fretful voice broke in upon his dreaming. "Pa-a-w, there ain't a stick of wood for breakfast! There was none last night! If you want any breakfast you'd best git some wood!"

"All right, Mother!" called Haley from the barn yard, where he was assisting in the milking. "I'm a comin'."

Cameron walked to meet him.

"Can I help?" he enquired.

"Why, of course!" shouted Haley. "Here, Ma, here's our new hand, the very man for you."

Mrs. Haley, who had retired to the kitchen, appeared at the door. She was a woman past middle age, unduly stout, her face deep lined with the fret of a multitude

of cares, and hung with flabby folds of skin, browned
with the sun and wind, though it must be confessed its
color was determined more by the grease and grime than
by the tan upon it. Yet, in spite of the flabby folds of
flesh, in spite of the grime and grease, there was still
a reminiscence of a one-time comeliness, all the more
pathetic by reason of its all too obvious desecration.
Her voice was harsh, her tone fretful, which indeed was
hardly to be wondered at, for the burden of her life was
by no means light, and the cares of the household, within
and without, were neither few nor trivial.

For a moment or two Mrs. Haley stood in silence
studying and appraising the new man. The result did
not apparently inspire her with hope.

"Come on now, Pa," she said, "stop yer foolin' and
git me that wood. I want it right now. You're keepin'
me back and there's an awful lot to do."

"But I ain't foolin', Ma. Mr. Cameron is our new
hand. He'll knock yeh off a few sticks in no time." So
saying, Haley walked off with his pails to the milking,
leaving his wife and the new hand facing each other,
each uncertain as to the next move.

"What can I do, Mrs. Haley?" enquired Cameron
politely.

"Oh, I don't know," said Mrs. Haley wearily. "I
want a few sticks for the breakfast, but perhaps I can
get along with chips, but chips don't give no steady fire."

"If you would show me just what to do," said Cameron with some hesitation, "I mean, where is the wood
to be got?"

"There," she said, in a surprised tone, pointing to a
pile of long logs of ash and maple. "I don't want much."
She gathered her apron full of chips and turned away,
all too obviously refusing to place her hope of wood for

the breakfast fire upon the efforts of the new man. Cameron stood looking alternately at the long, hard, dry logs and at the axe which he had picked up from the bed of chips. The problem of how to produce the sticks necessary to breakfast by the application of the one to the other was one for which he could see no solution. He lifted his axe and brought it down hard upon a maple log. The result was a slight indentation upon the log and a sharp jar from the axe handle that ran up his arm unpleasantly. A series of heavy blows produced nothing more than a corresponding series of indentations in the tough maple log and of jars more or less sharp and painful shooting up his arms. The result was not encouraging, but it flashed upon him that this was his first attempt to make good at his job on the farm. He threw off his coat and went at his work with energy; but the probability of breakfast, so far as it depended upon the result of his efforts, seemed to be growing more and more remote.

"Guess ye ain't got the knack of it," said a voice, deep, full, and mellow, behind him. "That axe ain't no good for choppin', it's a splittin' axe."

Turning, he saw a girl of about seventeen, with little grace and less beauty, but strongly and stoutly built, and with a good-natured, if somewhat stupid and heavy face. Her hair was dun in colour, coarse in texture, and done up loosely and carelessly in two heavy braids, arranged about her head in such a manner as to permit stray wisps of hair to escape about her face and neck. She was dressed in a loose pink wrapper, all too plainly of home manufacture, gathered in at the waist, and successfully obliterating any lines that might indicate the existence of any grace of form, and sadly spotted and stained with grease and dirt. Her red stout arms

ended in thick and redder hands, decked with an array
of black-rimmed nails. At his first glance, sweeping
her "tout ensemble," Cameron was conscious of a feeling of repulsion, but in a moment this feeling passed
and he was surprised to find himself looking into two
eyes of surprising loveliness, dark blue, well shaped,
and of such liquid depths as to suggest pools of water
under forest trees.

"They use the saw mostly," said the girl.

"The saw?" echoed Cameron.

"Yes," she said. "They saw 'em through and then
split 'em with the axe."

Cameron picked up the buck-saw which lay against
a rickety saw horse. Never in his life had he used
such an instrument. He gazed helplessly at his companion.

"How do you use this thing?" he enquired.

"Say! are you funny," replied the girl, flashing a
keen glance upon him, "or don't ye know?"

"Never saw it done in my life," said Cameron
solemnly.

"Here!" she cried, "let me show you."

She seized the end of a maple log, dragged it forward
to the rickety saw horse, set it in position, took the saw
from his hands, and went at her work with such vigour
that in less than a minute as it seemed to Cameron she
had made the cut.

"Give me that axe!" she said impatiently to Cameron,
who was preparing to split the block.

With a few strong and skillful blows she split the
straight-grained block of wood into firewood, gathered
up the sticks in her arms, and, with a giggle, turned
toward the house.

"I won't charge you anything for that lesson," she

said, "but you'll have to hustle if you git that wood split 'fore breakfast."

"Thank you," said Cameron, grateful that none of the men had witnessed the instruction, "I shall do my best," and for the next half hour, with little skill, but by main strength, he cut off a number of blocks from the maple log and proceeded to split them. But in this he made slow progress. From the kitchen came cheerful sounds and scents of cooking, and ever and anon from the door waddled, with quite surprising celerity, the unwieldy bulk of the mistress of the house.

"Now, that's jest like yer Pa," Cameron heard her grumbling to her daughter, "bringin' a man here jest at the busy season who don't know nothin'. He's peckin' away at 'em blocks like a rooster peckin' grain."

"He's willin' enough, Ma," replied the girl, "and I guess he'll learn."

"Learn!" puffed Mrs. Haley contemptuously. "Did ye ever see an old-country man learn to handle an axe or a scythe after he was growed up? Jest look at 'im. Thank goodness! there's Tim."

"Here, Tim!" she called from the door, "best split some o' that wood 'fore breakfast."

Tim approached Cameron with a look of pity on his face.

"Let me have a try," he said. Cameron yielded him the axe. The boy set on end the block at which Cameron had been laboring and, with a swift glancing blow of the axe, knocked off a slab.

"By Jove!" exclaimed Cameron admiringly, "how did you do that?"

For answer the boy struck again the same glancing blow, a slab started and, at a second light blow, fell to the ground.

"I say!" exclaimed Cameron again, "I must learn that trick."

"Oh, that's easy!" said Tim, knocking the slabs off from the outside of the block. "This heart's goin' to be tough, though; got a knot in it," and tough it proved, resisting all his blows.

"You're a tough sucker, now, ain't yeh?" said Tim, through his shut teeth, addressing the block. We'll try yeh this way." He laid the end of the block upon a log and plied the axe with the full strength of his slight body, but the block danced upon the log and resisted all his blows.

"Say! you're a tough one now!" he said, pausing for breath.

"Let me try that," said Cameron, and, putting forth his strength, he brought the axe down fairly upon the stick with such force that the instrument shore clean through the knot and sank into the log below.

"Huh! that's a cracker," said Tim with ungrudging admiration. "All you want is knack. I'll slab it off and you can do the knots," he added with a grin.

As the result of this somewhat unequal division of labor, there lay in half an hour a goodly pile of fire wood ready for the cooking. It caught Haley's eye as he came in to breakfast.

"I say, Missus, that's a bigger pile than you've had for some time. Guess my new man ain't so slow after all."

"Huh!" puffed his wife, waddling about with great agility, "it was Tim that done it."

"Now, Ma, ye know well enough he helped Tim, and right smart too," said the daughter, but her mother was too busy getting breakfast ready for the hungry men who were now performing their morning ablutions with the help of a very small basin set upon a block of wood outside the kitchen door to answer.

There were two men employed by Haley, one the son of a Scotch-Canadian farmer, Webster by name, a stout young fellow, but slow in his movements, both physical and mental, and with no further ambition than to do a fair day's work for a fair day's pay. He was employed by the month during the busier seasons of the year. The other, Perkins, was Haley's "steady" man, which means that he was employed by the year and was regarded almost as a member of the family. Perkins was an Englishman with fair hair and blue eyes, of fresh complexion, burned to a clear red, clean-cut features, and a well knit, athletic frame. He was, as Tim declared, a terror to work; indeed, his fame as a worker was well established throughout the country side. To these men Cameron was introduced as being from Scotland and as being anxious to be initiated into the mysteries of Canadian farm life.

"Glad to see you!" said Perkins, shaking him heartily by the hand. "We'll make a farmer of you, won't we, Tim? From Scotland, eh? Pretty fine country, I hear --to leave," he added, with a grin at his own humour. Though his manner was pleasant enough, Cameron became conscious of a feeling of aversion, which he recognised at once as being as unreasonable as it was inexplicable. He set it down as a reflection of Tim's mental attitude toward the hired man. Perkins seized the tin basin, dipped some water from the rain barrel standing near, and, setting it down before Cameron, said:

"Here, pile in, Scotty. Do they wash in your country?"

"Yes," replied Cameron, "they are rather strong on that," wondering at the same time how the operation

could be performed successfully with such a moderate
supply of water.   After using a second and third supply,
however, he turned, with hands and face dripping, and
looked about for a towel.   Perkins handed him a long
roller towel, black with dirt and stiff with grease.   Had
his life depended upon it Cameron could not have avoided
a shuddering hesitation as he took the filthy cloth preparatory to applying it to his face.

"'Twon't hurt you," laughed Perkins.   "Wash day
ain't till next week, you know, and this is only Wednes-
day."   Suddenly the towel was snatched from Cameron's
hands.

"Gimme that towel!"   It was the girl, with face
aflame and eyes emitting blue fire.   "Here, Mr. Cameron,
take this," she said.

"Great Jerusalem, Mandy!   You ain't goin' to bring
on a clean towel the middle of the week?" said Perkins
in mock dismay.   "Guess it's for Mr. Cameron," he continued with another laugh.

"We give clean towels to them that knows how to use
'em," said Mandy, whisking wrathfully into the house.

"Say, Scotty!" said Perkins, in a loud bantering tone,
"guess you're makin' a mash on Mandy all right."

"I don't know exactly what you mean," said Cameron
with a quick rising of wrath, "but I do know that you
are making a beastly cad of yourself."

"Oh, don't get wrathy, Scotty!" laughed Perkins,
"we're just having a little fun.   Here's the comb!"   But
Cameron declined the article, which, from its appearance, seemed to be intended for family use, and, proceeding to his room, completed his toilet there.

The breakfast was laid in the kitchen proper, a
spacious and comfortable room, which served as living
room for the household.   The table was laden with a

variety and abundance of food that worthily sustained
the reputation of the Haleys of being "good feeders."
At one end of the table a large plate was heaped high
with slices of fat pork, and here and there disposed
along its length were dishes of fried potatoes, huge
piles of bread, hot biscuits, plates of butter, pies of different kinds, maple syrup, and apple sauce. It was a
breakfast fit for a lord, and Cameron sat down with
a pleasurable anticipation induced by his early rising
and his half hour's experience in the fresh morning air
with the wood pile. A closer inspection, however, of
the dishes somewhat damped the pleasure of his anticipation. The food was good, abundant, and well cooked,
but everywhere there was an utter absence of cleanli-
ness. The plates were greasy, the forks and knives bore
the all too evident remains of former meals, and everywhere were flies. In hundreds they swarmed upon the
food, while drowned in the gravy, cooked in the potatoes, overwhelmed in the maple syrup, buried in the
butter, their ghastly carcasses were to be seen. With
apparent unconcern the men brushed aside the living
and picked out and set aside the remains of the dead,
the unhappy victims of their own greed or temerity,
and went on calmly and swiftly with their business.
Not a word was spoken except by Cameron himself, who,
constrained by what he considered to be the ordinary
decencies of society, made an effort to keep up a conversation with Mr. Haley at the head of the table and
occasionally ventured a remark to his wife, who, with
Mandy, was acting as a waiter upon the hungry men.
But conversation is a social exercise, and Cameron found
himself compelled to abandon his well meant but soli-
tary efforts at maintaining the conventions of the breakfast table. There was neither time nor occasion for

conversation. The business of the hour was something quite other, namely, that of devouring as large a portion of the food set before them as was possible within the limits of time assigned for the meal. Indeed, the element of time seemed to be one of very considerable importance, as Cameron discovered, for he was still picking his way gingerly and carefully through his pork and potatoes by the time that Perkins, having completed a second course consisting of pie and maple syrup, had arrived at the final course of bread and butter and apple sauce.

"Circulate the butter!" he demanded of the table in general. He took the plate from Cameron's hand, looked at it narrowly for a moment, then with thumb and forefinger drew from the butter with great deliberation a long dun-coloured hair.

"Say!" he said in a low voice, but perfectly audible, "they forgot to comb it this morning."

Cameron was filled with unspeakable disgust, but, glancing at Mrs. Haley's face, he saw to his relief that both the action and the remark had been unnoticed by her. But on Mandy's face he saw the red ensign of shame and wrath, and in spite of himself he felt his aversion towards the ever-smiling hired man deepen into rage.

Finding himself distanced in his progress through the various courses at breakfast, Cameron determined to miss the intermediate course of pie and maple syrup and, that he might finish on more even terms with the others, proceeded with bread and butter and apple sauce.

"Don't yeh hurry," said Mrs. Haley with hearty hospitality. "Eat plenty, there's lots to spare. Here, have some apple sauce." She caught up the bowl which held this most delicious article of food.

"Where's the spoon?" she said, glancing round the table. There was none immediately available. "Here!" she cried, "this'll do." She snatched a large spoon from the pitcher of thick cream, held it dripping for a moment in obvious uncertainty, then with sudden decision she cried "Never mind," and with swift but effective application of lip and tongue she cleansed the spoon of the dripping cream, and, stirring the apple sauce vigourously, passed the bowl to Cameron. For a single moment Cameron held the bowl, uncertain whether to refuse or not, but before he could make up his mind Mandy caught it from his hands.

"Oh, Ma!" she exclaimed in a horrified tone.

"What's the matter?" exclaimed her mother. "A little cream won't hurt."

But Mandy set the bowl at the far end of the table and passed another to Cameron, who accepted it with resolute determination and continued his breakfast.

But Perkins, followed by Webster and Tim, rose from the table and passed out into the yard, whence his voice could be heard in explosions of laughter. Cameron in the meantime was making heroic attempts to cover up the sound by loud-voiced conversation with Haley, and, rendered desperate by the exigencies of the situation, went so far as to venture a word of praise to Mrs. Haley upon the excellence and abundance of her cooking.

"She ain't got no chance," said her husband. "She's got too much to do and it's awful hard to get help. Of course, there's Mandy."

"Of course, there's Mandy," echoed his wife. "I guess you'd just better say, 'There's Mandy.' She's the whole thing is Mandy. What I'd do without her goodness only knows."

But Mandy was no longer present to enjoy her

mother's enconiums. Her voice could be heard in the yard making fierce response to Perkins' jesting remarks. As Cameron was passing out from the kitchen he heard her bitter declaration: "I don't care, it was real mean of you, and I'll pay you for it yet, Mr. Perkins—before a stranger, too." Mandy's voice suggested tears.

"Oh, pshaw, Mandy!" remonstrated Perkins, "it was all a joke, and who cares for him anyway, unless it's yourself?"

But Mandy, catching sight of Cameron, fled with fiery face behind the kitchen, leaving Perkins gazing after her with an apologetic grin upon his countenance.

"She's rather hot under the collar," he confided to Cameron, "but she needn't get so, I didn't mean nothin'."

Cameron ignored him. He was conscious mainly of a resolute determination that at all costs he must not yield to his almost uncontrollable desire to wipe off the apologetic smile with a well directed blow. Mr. Denman's parting advice was in his mind and he was devoting all his powers to the business of adjusting himself to his present environment. But to his fastidious nature the experiences of the morning made it somewhat doubtful if he should be able to carry out the policy of adjustment to the extreme of schooling himself to bear with equal mind the daily contact with the dirt and disorder which held so large a place in the domestic economy of the Haley household. One thing he was firmly resolved upon, he would henceforth perform his toilet in his own room, and thereby save himself the horror of the family roller towel and the family comb.

Breakfast over, the men stood waiting orders for the day.

"We'll have to crowd them turnips through, Tim," said his father, who seemed to avoid as far as possible giving direct orders to his men. "Next week we'll have to git at the hay." So to the turnip field they went.

It is one of the many limitations of a city-bred boy that he knows nothing of the life history and the culture of the things that grow upon a farm. Apples and potatoes he recognises when they appear as articles of diet upon the table; oats and wheat he vaguely associates in some mysterious and remote way with porridge and bread, but whether potatoes grow on trees or oats in pods he has no certain knowledge. Blessed is the country boy for many reasons, but for none more than this, that the world of living and growing things, animate and inanimate, is one which he has explored and which he intimately knows; and blessed is the city boy for whom his wise parents provide means of acquaintance with this wonder workshop of old mother Nature, God's own open country.

Turnip-hoeing is an art, a fine art, demanding all the talents of high genius, a true eye, a sure hand, a sensitive conscience, industry, courage, endurance, and pride in achievement. These and other gifts are necessary to high success. Not to every man is it given to become a turnip-hoer in the truest sense of that word. The art is achieved only after long and patient devotion, and, indeed, many never attain high excellence. Of course, therefore, there are grades of artists in this as in other departments. There are turnip-hoers and turnip-hoers, just as there are painters and painters. It was Tim's ambition to be the first turnip-hoer of his district, and toward this end he had striven both last season and this with a devotion that deserved, if it did not achieve, success. Quietly he had been patterning himself upon that master artist, Perkins, who for some years had easily held the championship for the district. Keenly Tim

had been observing Perkins' excellencies and also his
defects; secretly he had been developing a style of his
own, and, all unnoted, he had tested his speed by that of
Perkins by adopting the method of lazily loafing along
and then catching up by a few minutes of whirlwind
work. Tim felt in his soul the day of battle could not
be delayed past this season; indeed, it might come any
day. The very thought of it made his slight body quiver
and his heart beat so quickly as almost to choke him.

To the turnip field hied Haley's men, Perkins and
Webster leading the way, Tim and Cameron bringing
up the rear.

"You promised to show me how to do it, Tim," said
Cameron. "Remember I shall be very slow."

"Oh, shucks!" replied Tim, "turnip-hoeing is as easy
as rollin' off a log if yeh know how to do it."

"Exactly!" cried Cameron, "but that is what I don't.
You might give me some pointers."

"Well, you must be able to hit what yeh aim at."

"Ah! that means a good eye and steady hand," said
Cameron. "Well, I can do billiards some and golf.
What else?"

"Well, you mustn't be too careful, slash right in and
don't give a rip."

"Ah! nerve, eh!" said Cameron. "Well, I have done
some Rugby in my day—I know something of that.
What else? This sounds good."

"Then you've got to leave only one turnip in one place
and not a weed; and you mustn't leave any blanks. Dad
gets hot over that."

"Indeed, one turnip in each place and not a weed,"
echoed Cameron. "Say! this business grows interesting. No blanks! Anything else?" he demanded.

"No, I guess not, only if yeh ever git into a race ye've

got to keep goin' after you're clear tuckered out and never let on. You see the other chap may be feelin' worse than you."

"By Jove, Tim! you're a born general!" exclaimed Cameron. "You will go some distance if you keep on in that line. Now as to racing let me venture a word, for I have done a little in my time. Don't spurt too soon."

"Eh!" said Tim, all eagerness.

"Don't get into your racing stride too early in the day, especially if you are up against a stronger man. Wait till you know you can stay till the end and then put your best licks in at the finish."

Tim pondered.

"By Jimminy! you're right," he cried, a glad light in his eye, and a touch of colour in his pale cheek, and Cameron knew he was studying war.

The turnip field, let it be said for the enlightening of the benighted and unfortunate city-bred folk, is laid out in a series of drills, a drill being a long ridge of earth some six inches in height, some eight inches broad on the top and twelve at the base. Upon each drill the seed has been sown in one continuous line from end to end of the field. When this seed has grown each drill will discover a line of delicate green, this line being nothing less than a compact growth of young turnip plants with weeds more or less thickly interspersed. The operation of hoeing consists in the eliminating of the weeds and the superfluous turnip plants in order that single plants, free from weeds, may be left some eight inches apart in unbroken line, extending the whole length of the drill. The artistic hoer, however, is not content with this. His artistic soul demands not only that single plants should stand in unbroken row from end to end along the drill top, but that the drill itself should be pared down on each side to the likeness of a house roof with a perfectly even ridge.

"Ever hoe turnips?" enquired Perkins.

"Never," said Cameron, "and I am afraid I won't make much of a fist at it."

"Well, you've come to a good place to learn, eh, Tim! We'll show him, won't we?"

Tim made no reply, but simply handed Cameron a hoe and picked up his own.

"Now, show me, Tim," said Cameron in a low voice, as Perkins and Webster set off on their drills.

"This is how you do it," replied Tim. "Click-click," forward and back went Tim's sharp shining instrument, leaving a single plant standing shyly alone where .had boldly bunched a score or more a moment before. "Click-click-click," and the flat-topped drill stood free of weeds and superfluous turnip plants and trimmed to its proper roof-like appearance.

"I say!" exclaimed Cameron, "this is high art. I shall never reach your class, though, Tim."

"Oh, shucks!" said Tim, "slash in, don't be afraid." Cameron slashed in. "Click-click," "Click-click-click," when lo! a long blank space of drill looked up reproachfully at him.

"Oh, Tim! look at this mess," he said in disgust.

"Never mind!" said Tim, "let her rip. Better stick one in though. Blanks look bad at the *end* of the drill." So saying, he made a hole in Cameron's drill and with his hoe dug up a bunch of plants from another drill and patted them firmly into place, and, weeding out the unnecessary plants, left a single turnip in its proper place.

"Oh, come, that isn't so bad," said Cameron. "We can always fill up the blanks."

"Yes, but it takes time," replied Tim, evidently with

the racing fever in his blood.   Patiently Tim schooled his pupil throughout the forenoon, and before the dinner hour had come Cameron was making what to Tim appeared satisfactory progress.   It was greatly in Cameron's favor that he possessed a trained and true eye and a steady hand and that he was quick in all his movements.

"You're doin' splendid," cried Tim, full of admiration.

"I say, Scotty !" said Perkins, coming up and casting a critical eye along Cameron's last drill, "you're going to make a turnip-hoer all right."

"I've got a good teacher, you see," cried Cameron.

"You bet you have," said Perkins.   "I taught Tim myself, and in two or three years he'll be almost as good as I am, eh, Tim !"

"Huh !" grunted Tim, contemptuously, but let it go at that.

"Perhaps you think you're that now, eh, Tim?" said Perkins, seizing the boy by the back of the neck and rubbing his hand over his hair in a manner perfectly maddening.   "Don't you get too perky, young feller, or I'll hang your shirt on the fence before the day's done."

Tim wriggled out of his grasp and kept silent.   He was not yet ready with his challenge.   All through the afternoon he stayed behind with Cameron, allowing the other two to help them out at the end of each drill, but as the day wore on there was less and less need of assistance for Cameron, for he was making rapid progress with his work and Tim was able to do, not only his own drill, but almost half of Cameron's as well.   By supper time Cameron was thoroughly done out.   Never had a day seemed so long, never had he known that he possessed so many muscles in his back.   The continuous stooping and the steady click-click of the hoe, together with the unceasing strain of hand and eye, and all this under the hot burning rays of a June sun, so exhausted his vitality that when the cow bell rang for supper it seemed to him a sound more delightful than the strains of a Richter orchestra in a Beethoven symphony.

On the way back to the field after supper Cameron observed that Tim was in a state of suppressed excitement and it dawned upon him that the hour of his challenge of Perkins' supremacy as a turnip-hoer was at hand.

"I say, Tim, boy!" he said earnestly, "listen to me. You are going to get after Perkins this evening, eh?"

"How did you know?" said Tim, in surprise.

"Never mind! Now listen to me; I have raced myself some and I have trained men to race. Are you not too tired with your day's work?"

"Tired! Not a bit," said the gallant little soul scornfully.

"Well, all right. It's nice and cool and you can't hurt yourself much. Now, how many drills do you do after supper as a rule?"

"Down and up twice," said Tim.

"How many drills can you do at your top speed, your very top speed, remember?"

"About two drills, I guess," replied Tim, after a moment's thought.

"Now, listen to me!" said Cameron impressively. "Go quietly for two and a half drills, then let yourself out and go your best. And, listen! I have been watching you this afternoon. You have easily done once and a half what Perkins has done and you are going to lick him out of his boots."

Tim gulped a moment or two, looked at his friend

with glistening eyes, but said not a word. For the first two and a half drills Cameron exerted to the highest degree his conversational powers with the two-fold purpose of holding back Perkins and Webster and also of so occupying Tim's mind that he might forget for a time the approaching conflict, the strain of waiting for which he knew would be exhausting for the lad. But when the middle of the second last drill had been reached, Tim began unconsciously to quicken his speed.

"I say, Tim," called Cameron, "come here! Am I getting these spaces too wide?" Tim came over to his side. "Now, Tim," said Cameron, in a low voice, "wait a little longer; you can never wear him out. Your only chance is in speed. Wait till the last drill."

But Tim was not to be held back. Back he went to his place and with a rush brought his drill up even with Webster, passed him, and in a few moments like a whirlwind passed Perkins and took the lead.

"Hello, Timmy! where are you going?" asked Perkins, in surprise.

"Home," said Tim proudly, "and I'll tell 'em you're comin'."

"All right, Timmy, my son!" replied Perkins with a laugh, "tell them you won't need no hot bath; I'm after you."

"Click-click," "Click-click-click" was Tim's only answer. It was a distinct challenge, and, while not openly breaking into racing speed, Perkins accepted it.

For some minutes Webster quickened his pace in an attempt to follow the leaders, but soon gave it up and fell back to help Cameron up with his drill, remarking, "I ain't no blamed fool. I ain't going to bust myself for any man. *They're* racing, not me."

"Will Tim win?" enquired Cameron.

"Naw! Not this year! Why, Perkins is the best man in the whole country at turnips. He took the Agricultural Society's prize two years ago."

"I believe Tim will beat him," said Cameron confidently, with his eyes upon the two in front.

"Beat nothing!" said Webster. "You just wait a bit, Perkins isn't letting himself out yet."

In a short time Tim finished his drill some distance ahead, and then, though it was quitting time, without a pause he swung into the next.

"Hello, Timmy!" cried Perkins good-naturedly, "going to work all night, eh? Well, I'll just take a whirl out of you," and for the first time he frankly threw himself into his racing gait.

"Good boy, Tim!" called out Cameron, as Tim bore down upon them, still in the lead and going like a small steam engine. "You're all right and going easy. Don't worry!"

But Perkins, putting on a great spurt, drew up within a hoe-handle length of Tim and there held his place.

"All right, Tim, my boy, you can hold him," cried Cameron, as the racers came down upon him.

"He can, eh?" replied Perkins. "I'll show him and you," and with an accession of speed he drew up on a level with Tim.

"Ah, ha! Timmy, my boy! we've got you where we want you, I guess," he exulted, and, with a whoop and still increasing his speed, he drew past the boy.

But Cameron, who was narrowly observing the combatants and their work, called out again:

"Don't worry, Tim, you're doing nice clean work and doing it easily." The inference was obvious, and Perkins, who had been slashing wildly and leaving many blanks and weeds behind him where neither blanks nor weeds should be, steadied down somewhat, and, taking more pains with his work, began to lose ground, while Tim, whose work was without flaw, moved again to the front place. There remained half a drill to be done and the issue was still uncertain. With half the length of a hoe handle between them the two clicked along at a furious pace. Tim's hat had fallen off. His face showed white and his breath was coming fast, but there was no slackening of speed, and the cleanness and ease with which he was doing his work showed that there was still some reserve in him. They were approaching the last quarter when, with a yell, Perkins threw himself again with a wild recklessness into his work, and again he gained upon Tim and passed him.

"Steady, Tim!" cried Cameron, who, with Webster, had given up their own work, it being, as the latter remarked, "quitting time anyway," and were following up the racers. "Don't spoil your work, Tim!" continued Cameron, "don't worry."

His words caught the boy at a critical moment, for Perkins' yell and his fresh exhibition of speed had shaken the lad's nerve. But Cameron's voice steadied him, and, quickly responding, Tim settled down again into his old style, while Perkins was still in the lead, but slashing wildly.

"Fine work, Tim," said Cameron quietly, "and you can do better yet." For a few paces he walked behind the boy, steadying him now and then with a quiet word, then, recognising that the crisis of the struggle was at hand, and believing that the boy had still some reserve of speed and strength, he began to call on him.

"Come on, Tim! Quicker, quicker; come on, boy, you can do better!" His words, and his tone more than his words, were like a spur to the boy. From some secret source of supply he called up an unsuspected reserve of strength and speed and, still keeping up his clean cutting finished style, foot by foot he drew away from Perkins, who followed in the rear, slashing more wildly than ever. The race was practically won. Tim was well in the lead, and apparently gaining speed with every click of his hoe.

"Here, you fellers, what are yeh hashin' them turnips for?" It was Haley's voice, who, unperceived, had come into the field. Tim's reply was a letting out of his last ounce of strength in a perfect fury of endeavour.

"There—ain't—no—hashin'—on this—drill—Dad!" he panted.

The sudden demand for careful work, however, at once lowered Perkins' rate of speed. He fell rapidly behind and, after a few moments of further struggle, threw down his hoe with a whoop and called out, "Quitting time, I guess," and, striding after Tim, he caught him by the arms and swung him round clear off the ground.

"Here, let me go!" gasped the boy, kicking, squirming, and trying to strike his antagonist with his hoe.

"Let the boy go!" said Cameron. The tone in his voice arrested Perkins' attention.

"What's your business?" he cried, with an oath, dropping the boy and turning fiercely upon Cameron.

"Oh, nothing very much, except that Tim's my candidate in this race and he mustn't be interfered with," replied Cameron in a voice still quiet and with a pleasant smile.

Perkins was white and panting; in a moment more he would have hurled himself at the man who stood smiling quietly in his face. At this critical moment Haley interposed.

"What's the row, boys?" he enquired, recognising that something serious was on.

"We have been having a little excitement, Sir, in the form of a race," replied Cameron, "and I've been backing Tim."

"Looks as if you've got him wound up so's he can't stop," replied Haley, pointing to the boy, who was still going at racing pace and was just finishing his drill. "Oh, well, a boy's a boy and you've got to humour him now and then," continued Haley, making conversation with diplomatic skill. Then turning to Perkins, as if dismissing a trivial subject, he added, "Looks to me as if that hay in the lower meadow is pretty nigh fit to cut. Guess we'd better not wait till next week. You best start Tim on that with the mower in the mornin'." Then, taking a survey of the heavens, he added, "Looks as if it might be a spell of good weather." His diplomacy was successful and the moment of danger was past. Meantime Cameron had sauntered to the end of the drill where Tim stood leaning quietly on his hoe.

"Tim, you are a turnip-hoer!" he said, with warm admiration in his tone, "and what's more, Tim, you're a sport. I'd like to handle you in something big. You will make a man yet."

Tim's whole face flushed a warm red under the coat of freckles. For a time he stood silently contemplating the turnips, then with difficulty he found his voice.

"It was you done it," he said, choking over his words. "I was beat there and was just quittin' when you came along and spoke. My!" he continued, with a sharp intake of his breath, "I was awful near quittin'," and then, looking straight into Cameron's eyes, "It was you done it, and—I—won't forget." His voice choked again, but, reading his eyes, Cameron knew that he had gained one of life's greatest treasures, a boy's adoring gratitude.

"This has been a great day, Tim," said Cameron. "I have learned to hoe turnips, and," putting his hand on the boy's shoulder, "I believe I have made a friend." Again the hot blood surged into Tim's face. He stood voiceless, but he needed no words. Cameron knew well the passionate emotion that thrilled his soul and shook the slight body, trembling under his hand. For Tim, too, it had been a notable day. He had achieved the greatest ambition of his life in beating the best turnip-hoer on the line, and he, too, had found what to a boy is a priceless treasure, a man upon whom he could lavish the hero worship of his soul.

CHAPTER IV

A RAINY DAY

IT was haying time. Over the fields of yellowing fall wheat and barley, of grey timothy and purple clover, the heat shimmered in dancing waves. Everywhere the growing crops were drinking in the light and heat with eager thirst, for the call of the harvest was ringing through the land. The air was sweet with scents of the hay fields, and the whole country side was humming with the sound of the mowers. It was the crowning time of the year; toward this season all the life of the farm moved steadily the whole year long; the next two months or three would bring to the farmer the fruit of long days of toil and waiting. Every minute of these harvest days, from the early grey dawn, when Mandy called the cows in for the milking, till the long shadows from the orchard lay quite across the wide barley field, when Tim, handling his team with careless pride, drove in the last load for the day, every minute was packed full of life and action. But though busy were the days and full of hard and at times back-breaking and nerve-straining work, what of it? The colour, the rush, the eager race with the flying hours, the sense of triumph, the promise of wealth, the certainty of comfort, all these helped to carry off the heaviest toil with a swing and vim that banished aches from the body and weariness from the soul.

To Cameron, all unskilled as he was, the days brought many an hour of strenuous toil, but every day his muscles were knitting more firmly, his hands were hardening, and his mastery of himself growing more complete.

In haying there is no large place for skill. This operation, unlike that of turnip-hoeing, demands chiefly strength, quickness, and endurance, and especially endurance. To stand all day in the hay field under the burning sun with its rays leaping back from the superheated ground, and roll up the windrows into huge bundles and toss them on to the wagon, or to run up a long line of cocks and heave them fork-handle high to the top of a load, calls for something of skill, but mainly for strength of arm and back. But skill had its place, and once more it was Tim who stood close to Cameron and showed him all the tricks of pitching hay. It was Tim who showed him how to stand with his back to the wagon so as to get the load properly poised with the least expenditure of strength; it was Tim who taught him the cunning trick of using his thigh as a fulcrum in getting his load up, rather than doing it by "main strength and awkwardness"; it was Tim who demonstrated the method of lifting half a cock by running the end of the fork handle into the ground so that the whole earth might aid in the hoisting of the load. Of course in all this Cameron's intelligence and quickness stood him in the place of long experience, and before the first day's hauling was done he was able to keep his wagon going.

But with all the stimulus of the harvest movement and colour, Cameron found himself growing weary of the life on the Haley farm. It was not the long days, and to none on the farm were the days longer than to Cameron, who had taken upon himself the duty of supplying the kitchen with wood and water, no small business, either at the beginning or at the end of a long day's work; it was not the heavy toil; it was chiefly the continuous contact with the dirt and disorder of his environment that wore his body down and his spirit raw. No

matter with how keen a hunger did he approach the
dinner table, the disgusting filth everywhere apparent
would cause his gorge to rise and, followed by the cheerful gibes of Perkins, he would retire often with his
strength unrecruited and his hunger unappeased, and,
though he gradually achieved a certain skill in picking
his way through a meal, selecting such articles of food
as could be less affected than others by the unsavoury
surroundings, the want of appetising and nourishing
food told disastrously upon his strength. His sleep,
too, was broken and disturbed by the necessity of shar-
ing a bed with Webster. He had never been accustomed
to "doubling up," and under the most favourable circumstances the experience would not have been conducive
to sound sleep, but Webster's manner of life was not
such as to render him an altogether desirable bed-fellow.
For, while the majority of farm lads in the neighbourhood made at least semi-weekly pilgrimages to the "dam"
for a swim, Webster felt no necessity laid upon him for
such an expenditure of energy after a hard and sweaty
day in the field. His ideas of hygiene were of the most
elementary nature; hence it was his nightly custom,
when released from the toils of the day, to proceed upstairs to his room and, slipping his braces from his shoulders, allow his nether garments to drop to the floor and,
without further preparation, roll into bed. Of the
effeminacy of a night robe Webster knew nothing except by somewhat hazy rumour. Once under the patch-
work quilt he was safe for the night, for, heaving himself
into the middle of the bed, he sank into solid and stertorous slumber, from which all Cameron's prods and kicks
failed to arouse him till the grey dawn once more summoned him to life, whereupon, resuming the aforesaid
nether garments, he was once more simply, but in his

opinion quite sufficiently, equipped for his place among
men. Many nights did it happen that the stertorous
melody of Webster's all too odourous slumbers drove
Cameron to find a bed upon the floor. Once again Tim
was his friend, for it was to Tim that Cameron owed the
blissful experience of a night in the hay loft upon the
newly harvested hay. There, buried in its fragrant
depths and drawing deep breaths of the clean unbreathed
air that swept in through the great open barn doors,
Cameron experienced a joy hitherto undreamed of in
association with the very commonplace exercise of sleep.
After his first night in the hay mow, which he shared
with Tim, he awoke refreshed in body and with a new
courage in his heart.

"By Jove, Tim! That's the finest thing I ever had in
the way of sleep. Now if we only had a tub."

"Tub! What for?"

"A dip, my boy, a splash."

"To wash in?" enquired Tim, wondering at the exuberance of his friend's desires. "I'll get a tub," he added,
and, running to the house, returned with wash tub and
towel.

"Tim, my boy, you're a jewel!" exclaimed Cameron.

From the stable cistern they filled the vessel full and
first Cameron and, after persuasion and with rather
dubious delight, Tim tasted the joy of a morning tub.
Henceforth life became distinctly more endurable to
Cameron.

But, more than all the other irritating elements in
his environment put together, Cameron chafed under
the unceasing rasp of Perkins' wit, clever, if somewhat
crude and cumbrous. Perkins had never forgotten nor
forgiven his defeat at the turnip-hoeing, which he at-
tributed chiefly to Cameron. His gibes at Cameron's

awkwardness in the various operations on the farm, his readiness to seize every opportunity for ridicule, his skill at creating awkward situations, all these sensibly increased the wear on Cameron's spirit. All these, however, Cameron felt he could put up with without endangering his self-control, but when Perkins, with vulgar innuendo, chaffed the farmer's daughter upon her infatuation for the "young Scotty," as he invariably designated Cameron, or when he rallied Cameron upon his supposed triumph in the matter of Mandy's youthful affections, then Cameron raged and with difficulty kept his hands from his cheerful and ever smiling tormentor. It did not help matters much that apparently Mandy took no offense at Perkins' insinuations; indeed, it gradually dawned upon Cameron that what to him would seem a vulgar impertinence might to this uncultured girl appear no more than a harmless pleasantry. At all costs he was resolved that under no circumstances would he allow his self-control to be broken through. He would finish out his term with the farmer without any violent outbreak. It was quite possible that Perkins and others would take him for a chicken-hearted fool, but all the same he would maintain this attitude of resolute self-control to the very end. After all, what mattered the silly gibes of an ignorant boor? And when his term was done he would abandon the farm life forever. It took but little calculation to make quite clear that there was not much to hope for in the way of advancement from farming in this part of Canada. Even Perkins, who received the very highest wage in that neighbourhood, made no more than $300 a year; and, with land at sixty to seventy-five dollars per acre, it seemed to him that he would be an old man before he could become the owner of a farm. He was heart sick

of the pettiness and sordidness of the farm life, whose
horizon seemed to be that of the hundred acres or so that
comprised it. Therefore he resolved that to the great
West he would go, that great wonderful West with its
vast spaces and its vast possibilities of achievement.
The rumour of it filled the country side. Meantime for
two months longer he would endure.

A rainy day brought relief. Oh, the blessed Sabbath
of a rainy day, when the wheels stop and silence falls
in the fields; and the tired harvest hands recline at
ease upon the new cut and sweet smelling hay on the
barn floor, and through the wide open doors look out
upon the falling rain that roars upon the shingles, pours
down in cataracts from the eaves and washes clean the
air that wanders in, laden with those subtle scents that
old mother earth releases only when the rain falls. Oh,
happy rainy days in harvest time when, undisturbed by
conscience, the weary toilers stretch and slumber and
wake to lark and chaff in careless ease the long hours
through!

In the Haleys' barn they were all gathered, gazing
lazily and with undisturbed content at the steady down-
pour that indicated an all-day rest. Even Haley, upon
whose crops the rain was teeming down, was enjoying
the rest from the toil, for most of the hay that had been
cut was already in cock or in the barn. Besides, Haley
worked as hard as the best of them and welcomed a
day's rest. So let it rain!

While they lay upon the hay on the barn floor, with
tired muscles all relaxed, drinking in the fragrant airs
that stole in from the rain-washed skies outside, in the
slackening of the rain two neighbours dropped in, big
"Mack" Murray and his brother Danny, for a "crack"
about things in general and especially to discuss the

Dominion Day picnic which was coming off at the end of the following week. This picnic was to be something out of the ordinary, for, in addition to the usual feasting and frolicking, there was advertised an athletic contest of a superior order, the prizes in which were sufficiently attractive to draw, not only local athletes, but even some of the best from the neighbouring city. A crack runner was expected and perhaps even McGee, the big policeman of the London City force, a hammer thrower of fame, might be present.

"Let him come, eh, Mack?" said Perkins. "I guess we ain't afraid of no city bug beating you with the hammer."

"Oh! I'm no thrower," said Mack modestly. "I just take the thing up and give it a fling. I haven't got the trick of it at all."

"Have you practised much?" said Cameron, whose heart warmed at the accent that might have been transplanted that very day from his own North country.

"Never at all, except now and then at the blacksmith's shop on a rainy day," replied Mack. "Have you done anything at it?"

"Oh, I have seen a good deal of it at the games in the north of Scotland," replied Cameron.

"Man! I wish we had a hammer and you could show me the trick of it," said Mack fervently, "for they will be looking to me to throw and I do not wish to be beaten just too easily."

"There's a big mason's hammer," said Tim, "in the tool house, I think."

"Get it, Tim, then," said Mack eagerly, "and we will have a little practise at it, for throw I must, and I have no wish to bring discredit on my country, for it will be a big day. They will be coming from all over. The

Band of the Seventh is coming out and Piper Sutherland from Zorra will be there."

"A piper!" echoed Cameron. "Is there much pipe playing in this country?"

"Indeed, you may say that!" said Mack, "and good pipers they are too, they tell me. Piper Sutherland, I think, was of the old Forty-twa. Are you a piper, perhaps?" continued Mack.

"Oh, I play a little," said Cameron. "I have a set in the house."

"God bless my soul!" cried Mack, "and we never knew it. Tell Danny where they are and he will fetch them out. Go, Danny!"

"Never mind, I will get them myself," said Cameron, trying to conceal his eagerness, for he had long been itching for a chance to play and his fingers were now tingling for the chanter.

It was an occasion of great delight, not only to big Mack and his brother Danny and the others, but to Cameron himself. Up and down the floor he marched, making the rafters of the big barn ring with the ancient martial airs of Scotland and then, dropping into a lighter strain, he set their feet a-rapping with reels and strathspeys.

"Man, yon's great playing!" cried Mack with fervent enthusiasm to the company who had gathered to the summons of the pipes from the house and from the high road, "and think of him keeping them in his chest all this time! And what else can you do?" went on Mack, with the enthusiasm of a discoverer. "You have been in the big games, too, I warrant you."

Cameron confessed to some experience of these thrilling events.

"Bless my soul! We will put you against the big

folk from the city. Come and show us the hammer," said Mack, leading the way out of the barn, for the rain had ceased, with a big mason's hammer in his hand. It needed but a single throw to make it quite clear to Cameron that Mack was greatly in need of coaching. As he said himself he "just took up the thing and gave it a fling." A mighty fling, too, it proved to be.

"Twenty-eight paces!" cried Cameron, and then, to make sure, stepped it back again. "Yes," he said, "twenty-eight paces, nearly twenty-nine. Great Cæsar! Mack, if you only had the Braemar swing you would be a famous thrower."

"Och, now, you are just joking me!" said Mack modestly.

"You can add twenty feet easily to your throw if you get the swing," asserted Cameron. "Look here, now, get this swing," and Cameron demonstrated in his best style the famous Braemar swing.

"Thirty-two paces!" said Mack in amazement after he had measured the throw. "Man alive! you can beat McGee, let alone myself."

"Now, Mack, get the throw," said Cameron, with enthusiasm. "You will be a great thrower." But try though he might Mack failed to get the swing.

"Man, come over to-night and bring your pipes. Danny will fetch out his fiddle and we will have a bit of a frolic, and," he added, as if in an afterthought, "I have a big hammer yonder, the regulation size. We might have a throw or so."

"Thanks, I will be sure to come," said Cameron eagerly.

"Come, all of you," said Mack, "and you too, Mandy. We will clear out the barn floor and have a regular hoe-down."

"Oh, pshaw!" giggled Mandy, tossing her head. "I can't dance."

"Oh, come along and watch me, then," said Mack, in good humour, who, with all his two hundred pounds, was lightfooted as a girl.

The Murrays' new big bank barn was considered the finest in the country and the new floor was still quite smooth and eminently suited to a "hoe-down." Before the darkness had fallen, however, Mack drew Cameron, with Danny, Perkins, and a few of the neighbours who had dropped in, out to the lane and, giving him a big hammer, "Try that," he said, with some doubt in his tone.

Cameron took the hammer.

"This is the right thing. The weight of it will make more difference to me, however, than to you, Mack."

"Oh, I'm not so sure," said Mack. "Show us how you do it."

The first throw Cameron took easily.

"Twenty-nine paces!" cried Mack, after stepping it off. "Man! that's a great throw, and you do it easy."

"Not much of a throw," laughed Cameron. "Try it yourself."

Ignoring the swing, Mack tried the throw in his own style and hurled the hammer two paces beyond Cameron's throw.

"You did that with your arms only," said Cameron. "Now you must put legs and shoulders into it."

"Let's see you beat that throw yourself," laughed Perkins, who was by no means pleased with the sudden distinction that had come to the "Scotty."

Cameron took the hammer and, with the easy slow grace of the Braemar swing, made his throw.

"Hooray!" yelled Danny, who was doing the measuring. "You got it yon time for sure. Three paces to the good. You'll have to put your back into it, Mack, I guess."

Once more Mack seized the hammer. Then Cameron took Mack in hand and, over and over again, coached him in the poise and swing.

"Now try it, and think of your legs and back. Let the hammer take care of itself. Now, nice and easy and slow, not far this time."

Again and again Mack practised the swing.

"You're getting it!" cried Cameron enthusiastically, "but you are trying too hard. Forget the distance this time and think only of the easy slow swing. Let your muscles go slack." So he coached his pupil.

At length, after many attempts, Mack succeeded in delivering his hammer according to instructions.

"Man! you are right!" he exclaimed. "That's the trick of it and it is as smooth as oil."

"Keep it up, Mack," said Cameron, "and always easy."

Over and over again he put the big man through the swing till he began to catch the notion of the rhythmic, harmonious coöperation of the various muscles in legs and shoulders and arms so necessary to the highest result.

"You've got the swing, Mack," at length said Cameron. "Now then, this time let yourself go. Don't try your best, but let yourself out. Easy, now, easy. Get it first in your mind."

For a moment Mack stood pondering. He was "getting it in his mind." Then, with a long swing, easy and slow, he gave the great hammer a mighty heave. With a shout the company crowded about.

"Thirty-three, thirty-four, thirty-five, thirty-six, thirty-seven! Hooray! bully for you, Mack. You are the lad!"

"Get the line on it," said Mack quietly. The measuring line showed one hundred and eleven and a half feet. The boys crowded round him, exclaiming, cheering, patting him on the back. Mack received the congratulations in silence, then, turning to Cameron, said very earnestly:

"Man! yon's as easy as eating butter. You have done me a good turn to-day."

"Oh, that's nothing, Mack," said Cameron, who was more pleased than any of them. "You got the swing perfectly that time. You can put twenty feet to that throw. One hundred and eleven feet! Why, I can beat that myself."

"Man alive! Do you tell me now!" said Mack in amazement, running his eyes over Cameron's lean muscular body.

"I have done it often when I was in shape."

"Oh, rats!" said Perkins with a laugh. "Where was that?"

Cameron flushed a deep red, then turned pale, but kept silent.

"I believe you, my boy," said Mack with emphasis and facing sharply upon Perkins, "and if ever I do a big throw I will owe it to you."

"Oh, come off!" said Perkins, again laughing scornfully. "There are others that know the swing besides Scotty here. What you have got you owe to no one but yourself, Mack."

"If I beat the man McGee next week," said Mack quietly, "it will be from what I learned to-night, and I know what I am saying. Man! it's a lucky thing we found you. But that will do for just now. Come along to the barn. Hooray for the pipes and the lassies! They are worth all the hammers in the world!" And, putting his arm through Cameron's, he led the way to the barn, followed by the others.

"If Scotty could only hoe turnips and tie wheat as well as he can play the pipes and throw the hammer," said Perkins to the others as they followed in the rear, "I guess he'd soon have us all leaning against the fence to dry."

"He will, too, some day," said Tim, whose indignation at Perkins overcame the shyness which usually kept him silent in the presence of older men.

"Hello, Timmy! What are you chipping in for?" said Perkins, reaching for the boy's coat collar. "He thinks this Scotty is the whole works, and he is great too—at showing people how to do things."

"I hear he showed Tim how to hoe turnips," said one of the boys slyly. The laugh that followed showed that the story of Tim's triumph over the champion had gone abroad.

"Oh, rot!" said Perkins angrily. "Tim's got a little too perky because I let him get ahead of me one night in a drill of turnips."

"Yeh done yer best, didn't he, Webster?" cried Tim with indignation.

"Well, he certainly was making some pretty big gashes in them drills," said Webster slowly.

"Oh, get out!" replied Perkins. "Though all the same Tim's quite a turnip-hoer," he conceded. "Hello! There's quite a crowd in the barn, Danny. I wish I had my store clothes on."

At this a girl came running to meet them.

"Come on, Danny! Tune up. I can hardly keep my heels on my boots."

"Oh, you'll not be wanting my little fiddle after you have heard Cameron on the pipes, Isa."

"Never you fear that, Danny," replied Isa, catching him by the arm and hurrying him onward.

"Wait a minute. I want you to meet Mr. Cameron," said Danny.

"Come away, then," replied Isa. "I am dying to get done with it and get the fiddle going."

But Cameron was in the meantime engaged, for Mack was busy introducing him to a bevy of girls who stood at one corner of the barn floor.

"My! but he's a braw lad!" said Isa gayly, as she watched Cameron making his bows.

"Yes, he is that," replied Danny with enthusiastic admiration, "and a hammer-thrower, too, he is."

"What! yon stripling?"

"You may say it. He can beat Mack there."

"Mack!" cried Isa, with scorn. "It's just big lies you are telling me."

"Indeed, he has beaten Mack's best throw many a time."

"And how do you know?" exclaimed Isa.

"He said so himself."

"Ah ha!" said Isa scornfully. "He is good at blowing his own horn whatever, and I don't believe he can beat Mack—and I don't like him a bit," she continued, her dark eyes flashing and the red colour glowing in her full round cheek.

"Come, Isa!" cried Mack, catching sight of her in the dim light. "Come here, I want Mr. Cameron to meet you."

"How do you do?" said the girl, giving Cameron her hand and glancing saucily into his face. "I hear you are a piper and a hammer-thrower and altogether a wonderful man."

"A wonderfully lucky man, to have the pleasure of meeting you," said Cameron, glancing boldly back at her.

"And I am sure you can dance the fling," continued Isa. "All the Highlanders do."

"Not all," said Cameron. "But with certain partners all Highlanders would love to try."

"Oh aye," with a soft Highland accent that warmed Cameron's blood. "I see you have the tongue. Come away, Danny, now, strike up, or I will go on without you." And the girl kilted her skirts and began a reel, and as Mack's eyes followed her every step there was no mistaking their expression. To Mack there was only one girl in the barn, or in all the world for that matter, and that was the leal-hearted, light-footed, black-eyed Isa MacKenzie. Bonnie she was, and that she well knew, the belle of the whole township, driving the men to distraction and for all that holding the love of her own sex as well. But her heart was still her own, or at least she thought it was, for all big Mack Murray's open and simple-hearted adoration, and she was ready for a frolic with any man who could give her word for word or dance with her the Highland reel.

With the courtesy of a true gentleman, Danny led off with his fiddle till they had all got thoroughly into the spirit and swing of the frolic, and then, putting his instrument back into its bag, he declared that they were all tired of it and were waiting for the pipes.

"Not a bit of it!" cried Isa. "But we will give you a rest, Danny, and besides I want to dance a reel with you myself—though Mr. Cameron is not bad," she added, with a little bow to Cameron, with whom she had just finished a reel.

Readily enough Cameron tuned his pipes, for he was

aching to get at them and only too glad to furnish music for the gay company of kindly hearted folk who were giving him his first evening's pleasure since he had left the Cuagh Oir.

From reel to schottische and from schottische to reel, foursome and eightsome, they kept him playing, ever asking for more, till the gloaming passed into moonlight and still they were not done. The respite came through Mandy, who, solid in weight and heavy of foot, had laboured through the reels as often as she could get a partner, and at other times had sat gazing in rapt devotion upon the piper.

"Whoop her up again, Scotty!" cried Perkins, when Cameron paused at the end of a reel.

"Don't you do it!" said Mandy sharply, her deep voice booming through the barn. "He's just tired of it, and I'm tired looking at him."

There was a shout of laughter which covered poor Mandy with wrathful confusion.

"Good for you, Mandy," cried Perkins with a great guffaw. "You want some music now, don't you? So do I. Come on, Danny."

"No, I don't," snapped Mandy, who could understand neither the previous laugh nor that which greeted Perkins' sally.

"Allan," she said, sticking a little over the name, "is tired out, and besides it's time we were going home."

"That's right, take him home, Mandy, and put the little dear to bed," said Perkins.

"You needn't be so smart, Joe Perkins," said Mandy angrily. "Anyway I'm going home. I've got to be up early."

"Me too, Mandy," said Cameron, packing up his pipes, for his sympathy had been roused for the girl who was championing him so bravely. "I have had a great night and I have played you all to death; but you will forgive me. I was lonely for the chanter. I have not touched it since I left home."

There was a universal cry of protest as they gathered about him.

"Indeed, Mr. Cameron, you have given us all a rare treat," cried Isa, coming close to him, "and I only wish you could pipe and dance at the same time."

"That's so!" cried Mack, "but what's the matter with the fiddle, Isa? Come, Danny, strike up. Let them have a reel together."

Cameron glanced at Mandy, who was standing impatiently waiting. Perkins caught the glance.

"Oh, please let him stay, Mandy," he pleaded.

"He can stay if he likes," sniffed Mandy scornfully. "I got no string on him; but I'm goin' home. Good-night, everybody."

"Good-night, Mandy," called Perkins. "Tell them we're comin'."

"Just a moment, Mandy!" said Cameron, "and I'm with you. Another time I hope to do a reel with you, Miss MacKenzie," he said, bidding her good-night, "and I hope it will be soon."

"Remember, then," cried Isa, warmly shaking hands with him. "I will keep you to your promise at the picnic."

"Fine!" said Cameron, and with easy grace he made his farewells and set off after Mandy, who by this time was some distance down the lane.

"You needn't come for me," she said, throwing her voice at him over her shoulder.

"What a splendid night we have had!" said Cameron, ignoring her wrath. "And what awfully nice people."

Mandy grunted and in silence continued her way down the lane, picking her steps between the muddy spots and pools left by the rain.

After some minutes Cameron, who was truly sorry for the girl, ventured to resume the conversation.

"Didn't you enjoy the evening, Mandy?"

"No, I didn't!" she replied shortly. "I can't dance and they all know it."

"Why don't you learn, Mandy? You could dance if you practised."

"I can't. I ain't like the other girls. I'm too clumsy."

"Not a bit of it," said Cameron. "I've watched you stepping about the house and you are not a bit clumsy. If you only practised a bit you would soon pick up the schottische."

"Oh, you're just saying that because you know I'm mad," said Mandy, slightly mollified.

"Not at all. I firmly believe it. I saw you try a schottische to-night with Perkins and—"

"Oh, shucks!" said Mandy. "He don't give me no show. He gets mad when I tramp on him."

"All you want is practise, Mandy," replied Cameron.

"Oh, I ain't got no one to show me," said Mandy. "Perkins he won't be bothered, and—and—there's no one else," she added shyly.

"Why, I—I would show you," replied Cameron, every instinct of chivalry demanding that he should play up to her lead, "if I had any opportunity."

"When?" said Mandy simply.

"When?" echoed Cameron, taken aback. "Why, the first chance we get."

As he spoke the word they reached the new bridge that crossed the deep ditch that separated the lane from the high road.

"Here's a good place right here on this bridge," said Mandy with a giggle.

"But we have no music," stammered Cameron, aghast at the prospect of a dancing lesson by moonlight upon the public highway.

"Oh, pshaw!" said Mandy. "We don't need music. You can just count. I seen Isa showin' Mack once and they didn't have no music. But," she added, regarding Cameron with suspicion, "if you don't want to—"

"Oh, I shall be glad to, but wouldn't the porch be better?" he replied in desperation.

"The porch! That's so," assented Mandy eagerly. "Let's hurry before the rest come home." So saying, she set off at a great pace, followed by Cameron ruefully wondering to what extent the lesson in the Terpsichorean art might be expected to go.

As soon as the porch was reached Mandy cried—

"Now let's at the thing. I'm going to learn that schottische if it costs a leg."

Without stopping to enquire whose leg might be in peril, Cameron proceeded with his lesson, and he had not gone through many paces till he began to recognise the magnitude of the task laid upon him. The girl's sense of time was accurate enough, but she was undeniably awkward and clumsy in her movements and there was an almost total absence of coördination of muscle and brain. She had, however, suffered too long and too keenly from her inability to join with the others in the dance to fail to make the best of her opportunity to relieve herself of this serious disability.

So, with fierce industry she poised, counted and hopped, according to Cameron's instructions and example, with never a sign of weariness, but alas with little indication of progress.

"Oh, shucks! I can't do it!" she cried at length, paus-ing in despair. "I think we could do it better together. That's the way Mack and Isa do it. I've seen them at it for an hour."

Cameron's heart sank within him. He had caught an exchange of glances between the two young people mentioned and he could quite understand how a lesson in the intricacies of the Highland schottische might very well be extended over an hour to their mutual sat-isfaction, but he shrank with a feeling of dismay, if not disgust, from a like experience with the girl before him.

He was on the point of abruptly postponing the lesson when his eye fell upon her face as she stood in the moon-light which streamed in through the open door. Was it the mystic alchemy of the moon on her face, or was it the glowing passion in her wonderful eyes that trans-figured the coarse features? A sudden pity for the girl rose in Cameron's heart and he said gently, "We will try it together, Mandy."

He took her hand, put his arm about her waist, but, as he drew her towards him, with a startled look in her eyes she shrank back saying hurriedly:

"I guess I won't bother you any more to-night. You've been awfully good to me. You're tired."

"Not a bit, Mandy, come along," replied Cameron briskly.

At that moment a shadow fell upon the square of moonlight on the floor. Mandy started back with a cry.

"My! you scairt me. We were—Allan—Mr. Cam-eron was learnin' me the Highland schottische." Her face and her voice were full of fear.

It was Perkins. White, silent, and rigid, he stood regarding them, for minutes, it seemed, then turned away.

"Let's finish," said Cameron quietly.

"Oh! no, no!" said Mandy in a low voice. "He's awful mad! I'm scairt to death! He'll do something! Oh! dear, dear! He's awful when he gets mad."

"Nonsense!" said Cameron. "He can't hurt you."

"No, but you!"

"Oh, don't worry about me. He won't hurt me."

Cameron's tone arrested the girl's attention.

"But promise me—promise me!" she cried, "that you won't touch him." She clutched his arm in a fierce grip.

"Certainly I won't touch him," said Cameron easily, "if he behaves himself." But in his heart he was conscious of a fierce desire that Perkins would give him the opportunity to wipe out a part at least of the accumulated burden of insult he had been forced to bear during the last three weeks.

"Oh!" wailed Mandy, wringing her hands. "I know you're going to fight him. I don't want you to! Do you hear me?" she cried, suddenly gripping Cameron again by the arm and shaking him. "I don't want you to! Promise me you won't!" She was in a transport of fear.

"Oh, this is nonsense, Mandy," said Cameron, laughing at her. "There won't be any fight. I'll run away."

"All right," replied the girl quietly, releasing his arm. "Remember you promised." She turned from him.

"Good night, Mandy. We will finish our lesson another time, eh?" he said cheerfully.

"Good night," replied Mandy, dully, and passed through the kitchen and into the house.

Cameron watched her go, then poured for himself a glass of milk from a pitcher that always stood upon the table for any who might be returning home late at night, and drank it slowly, pondering the situation the while.

"What a confounded mess it is!" he said to himself. "I feel like cutting the whole thing. By Jove! That girl is getting on my nerves! And that infernal bounder! She seems to— Poor girl! I wonder if he has got any hold on her. It would be the greatest satisfaction in the world to teach *him* a few things too. But I have made up my mind that I am not going to end up my time here with any row, and I'll stick to that; unless—" and, with a tingling in his fingers, he passed out into the moonlight.

As he stepped out from the door a dark mass hurled itself at him, a hand clutched at his throat, missed as he swiftly dodged back, and carried away his collar. It was Perkins, his face distorted, his white teeth showing in a snarl as of a furious beast. Again with a beast-like growl he sprang, and again Cameron avoided him; while Perkins, missing his clutch, stumbled over a block of wood and went crashing head first among a pile of pots and pans and, still unable to recover himself and wildly grasping whatever chanced to be within reach, fell upon the board that stood against the corner of the porch to direct the rain into the tub; but the unstable board slid slowly down and allowed the unfortunate Perkins to come sitting in the tub full of water.

"Very neatly done, Perkins!" cried Cameron, whose anger at the furious attack was suddenly transformed into an ecstasy of delight at seeing the plight of his enemy.

Like a cat Perkins was on his feet and, without a single moment's pause, came on again in silent fury. By an evil chance there lay in his path the splitting axe, gleaming in the moonlight. Uttering a low choking cry, as of joy, he seized the axe and sprang towards his foe. Quicker than thought Cameron picked up a heavy arm chair that stood near the porch to use it as a shield against the impending attack.

"Are you mad, Perkins?" he cried, catching the terrific blow that came crashing down, upon the chair.

Then, filled with indignant rage at the murderous attack upon him, and suddenly comprehending the desperate nature of the situation, he sprang at his antagonist, thrusting the remnants of the chair in his face and, following hard and fast upon him, pushed him backward and still backward till, tripping once more, he fell supine among the pots and pans. Seizing the axe that had dropped from his enemy's hand, Cameron hurled it far beyond the wood pile and then stood waiting, a cold and deadly rage possessing him.

"Come on, you dog!" he said through his shut teeth. "You have been needing this for some time and now you'll get it."

"What is it, Joe?"

Cameron quickly turned and saw behind him Mandy, her face blanched, her eyes wide, and her voice faint with terror.

"Oh, nothing much," said Cameron, struggling to recover himself. "Perkins stumbled over the tub among the pots and pans there. He made a great row, too," he continued with a laugh, striving to get his voice under control.

"What is it, Joe?" repeated Mandy, approaching Perkins. But Perkins stood leaning against the corner of the porch in a kind of dazed silence.

"You've been fighting," she said, turning upon Cameron.

"Not at all," said Cameron lightly, "but, if you must

know, Perkins went stumbling among these pots and pans and finally sat down in the tub; and naturally he is mad."

"Is that true, Joe?" said Mandy, moving slowly nearer him.

"Oh, shut up, Mandy! I'm all wet, that's all, and I'm going to bed."

His voice was faint as though he were speaking with an effort.

"You go into the house," he said to the girl. "I've got something to say to Cameron here."

"You are quarreling."

"Oh, give us a rest, Mandy, and get out! No, there's no quarreling, but I want to have a talk with Cameron about something. Go on, now!"

For a few moments she hesitated, looking from one to the other.

"It's all right, Mandy," said Cameron quietly. "You needn't be afraid, there won't be any trouble."

For a moment more she stood, then quietly turned away.

"Wait!" said Perkins to Cameron, and followed Mandy into the house. For some minutes Cameron stood waiting.

"Now, you murderous brute!" he said, when Perkins reappeared. "Come down to the barn where no girl can interfere." He turned towards the barn.

"Hold on!" said Perkins, breathing heavily. "Not to-night. I want to say something. She's waiting to see me go upstairs."

Cameron came back.

"What have you got to say, you cur?" he asked in a voice filled with a cold and deliberate contempt.

"Don't you call no names," replied Perkins. "It ain't

no use." His voice was low, trembling, but gravely earnest. "Say, I might have killed you to-night." His breath was still coming in quick short gasps.

"You tried your best, you dog!" said Cameron.

"Don't you call no names," panted Perkins again. "I might—a—killed yeh. I'm mighty—glad—I didn't." He spoke like a man who had had a great deliverance. "But don't yeh," here his teeth snapped like a dog's, "don't yeh ever go foolin' with that girl again. Don't yeh—ever—do it. I seen yeh huggin' her in there and I tell yeh—I tell yeh—," his breath began to come in sobs, "I won't stand it—I'll kill yeh, sure as God's in heaven."

"Are you mad?" said Cameron, scanning narrowly the white distorted face.

"Mad? Yes, I guess so—I dunno—but don't yeh do it, that's all. She's mine! Mine! D'yeh hear?"

He stepped forward and thrust his snarling face into Cameron's.

"No, I ain't goin' to touch yeh," as Cameron stepped back into a posture of defense, "not to-night. Some day, perhaps." Here again his teeth came together with a snap. "But I'm not going to have you or any other man cutting in on me with that girl. D'yeh hear me?" and he lifted a trembling forefinger and thrust it almost into Cameron's face.

Cameron stood regarding him in silent and contemptuous amazement. Neither of them saw a dark form standing back out of the moonlight, inside the door. At last Cameron spoke.

"Now what the deuce does all this mean?" he said slowly. "Is this girl by any unhappy chance engaged to you?"

"Yes, she is—or was as good as, till you came; but you

listen to me. As God hears me up there"—he raised his shaking hand and pointed up to the moonlit sky, and then went on, chewing on his words like a dog on a bone—"I'll cut the heart out of your body if I catch you monkeying round that girl again. You've got to get out of here! Everything was all right till you came sneaking in. You've got to get out! You've got to get out! D'yeh hear me? You've got to get out!"

His voice was rising, mad rage was seizing him again, his fingers were opening and shutting like a man in a death agony.

Cameron glanced towards the door.

"I'm done," said Perkins, noting the glance. "That's my last word. You'd better quit this job." His voice again took on an imploring tone. "You'd better go or something will sure happen to you. Nobody will miss you much, except perhaps Mandy." His ghastly face twisted into a snarling smile, his eyes appeared glazed in the moonlight, his voice was husky—the man seemed truly insane.

Cameron stood observing him quietly when he had ceased speaking.

"Are you finished? Then hear me. First, in regard to this girl, she doesn't want me and I don't want her, but make up your mind, I promise you to do all I can to prevent her falling into the hands of a brute like you. Then as to leaving this place, I shall go just when it suits me, no sooner."

"All right," said Perkins, his voice low and trembling. "All right, mind I warned you! Mind I warned you! But if you go foolin' with that girl, I'll kill yeh, so help me God."

These words he uttered with the solemnity of an oath and turned towards the porch. A dark figure flitted across the kitchen and disappeared into the house. Cameron walked slowly towards the barn.

"He's mad. He's clean daffy, but none the less dangerous," he said to himself. "What a rotten mess all this is!" he added in disgust. "By Jove! The whole thing isn't worth while."

But as he thought of Mandy's frightened face and imploring eyes and the brutal murderous face of the man who claimed her as his own, he said between his teeth:

"No, I won't quit now. I'll see this thing through, whatever it costs," and with this resolve he set himself to the business of getting to sleep; in which, after many attempts, he was at length successful.

CHAPTER V

HOW THEY SAVED THE DAY

THERE never was such a Dominion Day for weather since the first Dominion Day was born. Of this "Fatty" Freeman was fully assured. Fatty Freeman was a young man for whose opinion older men were accustomed to wait. His person more than justified his praenomen, for Mr. Harper Freeman, Jr., was undeniably fat. "Fat, but fine and frisky," was ever his own comment upon the descriptive adjective by which his friends distinguished him. And fine and frisky he was; fine in his appreciation of good eating, fine in his judgment of good cattle and fine in his estimate of men; frisky, too, and utterly irrepressible. "Harp's just like a young pup," his own father, the Reverend Harper Freeman, the old Methodist minister of the Maplehill circuit, used to say. "If Harp had a tail he would never do anything but play with it." On this, however, it is difficult to hold any well based opinion. Ebullient in his spirits, he radiated cheeriness wherever he went and was at the bottom of most of the practical jokes that kept the village of Maplehill in a state of ferment; yet if any man thought to turn a sharp corner in business with Mr. Harper Freeman, Jr., he invariably found that frisky individual waiting for him round the corner with a cheery smile of welcome, shrewd and disconcerting. It was this cheery shrewdness of his that made him the most successful cattle buyer in the county and at the same time secretary of the Middlesex Caledonian Society. As secretary of this society he was made chiefly responsible for the success of the Dominion

Day picnic and, as with everything that he took hold of, Fatty toiled at the business of preparation for this picnic with conscientious zeal, giving to it all his spare hours and many of his working hours for the three months preceding.

It was due solely to his efforts that so many distinguished county magnates appeared eager to lend their patronage. It needed but a little persuasion to secure the enthusiastic support of the Honourable J. J. Patterson, M.P.P., and, incidentally, the handsome challenge cup for hammer-throwing, for the honourable member of Parliament was a full-blooded Highlander himself and an ardent supporter of "the games." But only Fatty Freeman's finesse could have extracted from Dr. Kane, the Opposition candidate for Provincial Parliamentary honours, the cup for the hundred yards race, and other cups from other individuals more or less deeply interested in Dominion, Provincial, and Municipal politics. The prize list secured, it needed only a skillful manipulation of the local press and a judicious but persistent personal correspondence to swell the ranks of the competitors in the various events, and thus ensure a monster attendance of the people from the neighbouring townships and from the city near by.

The weather being assured, Fatty's anxieties were mostly allayed, for he had on the file in his office acceptance letters from the distinguished men who were to cast the spell of their oratory over the assembled multitude, as also from the big men in the athletic world who had entered for the various events in the programme of sports. It was a master stroke of diplomacy that resulted in the securing for the hammer-throwing contest the redoubtable and famous Duncan Ross of Zorra, who had at first disdained the bait of the Maplehill

Dominion Day picnic, but in some mysterious way had at length been hooked and landed. For Duncan was a notable man and held the championship of the Zorras; and indeed in all Ontario he was second only to the world-famous Rory Maclennan of Glengarry, who had been to Braemar itself and was beaten there only by a fluke. How he came to agree to be present at the Maplehill picnic "Black Duncan" could not quite understand, but had he compared notes with McGee, the champion of the London police force and of various towns and cities of the western peninsula, he would doubtless have received some enlightenment. To the skill of the same master hand was due the appearance upon the racing list of the Dominion Day picnic of such distinguished names as Cahill of London, Fullerton of Woodstock, and especially of Eugene La Belle of nowhere in particular, who held the provincial championship for skating and was a runner of provincial fame.

In the racing Fatty was particularly interested because his young brother Wilbur, of whom he was uncommonly proud, a handsome lad, swift and graceful as a deer, was to make his first essay for more than local honours.

The lists for the other events were equally well filled and every detail of the arrangements for the day had passed under the secretary's personal review. The feeding of the multitude was in charge of the Methodist Ladies' Aid, an energetic and exceptionally businesslike organization, which fully expected to make sufficient profit from the enterprise to clear off the debt from their church at Maplehill, an achievement greatly desired not only by the ladies themselves but by their minister, the Reverend Harper Freeman, now in the third year of his incumbency. The music was to be furnished by the Band of the Seventh from London and by no less a distinguished personage than Piper Sutherland himself from Zorra, former Pipe Major of "The old Forty-twa." The discovery of another piper in Cameron brought joy to the secretary's heart, who only regretted that an earlier discovery had not rendered possible a pipe competition.

Early in the afternoon the crowds began to gather to MacBurney's woods, a beautiful maple grove lying midway between the Haleys' farm and Maplehill village, about two miles distant from each. The grove of noble maple trees overlooking a grassy meadow provided an ideal spot for picnicking, furnishing as it did both shade from the sun and a fine open space with firm footing for the contestants in the games. High over a noble maple in the centre of the grassy meadow floated the Red Ensign of the Empire, which, with the Canadian coat of arms on the fly, by common usage had become the national flag of Canada. From the great trees the swings were hung, and under their noble spreading boughs were placed the tables, and the platform for the speech making and the dancing, while at the base of the encircling hills surrounding the grassy meadow, hard by the grove another platform was placed, from which distinguished visitors might view with ease and comfort the contests upon the campus immediately adjacent.

Through the fence, let down for the purpose, the people drove in from the high road. They came in top buggies and in lumber wagons, in democrats and in "three seated rigs," while from the city came a "four-in-hand" with McGee, Cahill, and their backers, as well as other carriages filled with good citizens of London drawn thither by the promise of a day's sport of more than usual excellence or by the lure of a day in the woods and fields of God's open country. A specially fine carriage and pair, owned and driven by the honourable member of Parliament himself, conveyed Piper Sutherland, with colours streaming and pipes playing, to the picnic grounds. Warmly was the old piper welcomed, not only by the frisky cheery secretary, but by many old friends, and by none more warmly than by the Reverend Alexander Munro, the douce old bachelor Presbyterian minister of Maplehill, a great lover of the pipes and a special friend of Piper Sutherland. But the welcome was hardly over when once more the sound of the pipes was heard far up the side line.

"Surely that will be Gunn," said Mr. Munro.

Sutherland listened for a minute or two.

"No, it iss not Gunn. Iss Ross coming? No, yon iss not Ross. That will be a stranger," he continued, turning to the secretary, but the secretary remained silent, enjoying the old man's surprise and perplexity.

"Man, that iss not so bad piping! Not so bad at all! Who iss it?" he added with some impatience, turning upon the secretary again.

"Oh, that's Haley's team and I guess that's his hired man, a young fellow just out from Scotland," replied the secretary indifferently. "I am no great judge of the pipes myself, but he strikes me as a crackajack and I shouldn't be surprised if he would make you all sit up."

But the old piper's ear was closed to his words and open only to the strains of music ever drawing nearer.

"Aye, yon's a piper!" he said at length with emphasis. "Yon's a piper!"

"I only wish I had discovered him in time for a competition," said Fatty regretfully.

"Aye," said Sutherland. "Yon's a piper worth playing against."

And very brave and gallant young Cameron looked as Tim swung his team through the fence and up to the platform under the trees where the great ones of the people were standing in groups. They were all there, Patterson the M.P.P., and Dr. Kane the Opposition candidate, Reeve Robertson, for ten years the Municipal head of his county, Inspector Grant, a little man with a massive head and a luminous eye, Patterson's understudy and generally regarded as his successor in Provincial politics, the Reverend Harper Freeman, Methodist minister, tall and lank, with shrewd kindly face and a twinkling eye, the Reverend Alexander Munro, the Presbyterian minister, solid and sedate, slow to take fire but when kindled a very furnace for heat. These, with their various wives and daughters, such as had them, and many others less notable but no less important, constituted a sort of informal reception committee under Fatty Freeman's general direction and management. And here and there and everywhere crowds of young men and maidens, conspicuous among the latter Isa MacKenzie and her special friends, made merry with each other, as brave and gallant a company of sturdy sun-browned youths and bonnie wholesome lassies as any land or age could ever show.

"Look at them!" cried the Reverend Harper Freeman, waving his hand toward the kaleidoscopic gathering. "There's your Dominion Day oration for you, Mr. Patterson."

"Most of it done in brown, too," chuckled his son, Harper Freeman, Jr.

"Yes, and set in jewels and gold," replied his father.

"You hold over me, Dad!" cried his son. "Here!" he called to Cameron, who was standing aloof from the others. "Come and meet a brother Scot and a brother piper, Mr. Sutherland from Zorra, though to your ignorant Scottish ear that means nothing, but to every intelligent Canadian, Zorra stands for all that's finest in brain and brawn in Canada."

"And it takes both to play the pipes, eh, Sutherland?" said the M.P.P.

"Oh aye, but mostly wind," said the piper.

"Just like politics, eh, Mr. Patterson?" said the Reverend Harper Freeman.

"Yes, or like preaching," replied the M.P.P.

"One on you, Dad!" said the irrepressible Fatty.

Meantime Sutherland was warmly complimenting Cameron on his playing.

"You haf been well taught," he said.

"No one taught me," said Cameron. "But we had a famous old piper at home in our Glen, Macpherson was his name."

"Macpherson! Did he effer play at the Braemar gathering?"

"Yes, but Maclennan beat him."

"Maclennan! I haf heard him." The tone was quite sufficient to classify the unhappy Maclennan. "And I haf heard Macpherson too. Yon iss a player. None of the fal-de-rals of your modern players, but grand and mighty."

"I agree with you entirely," replied Cameron, his heart warming at the praise of his old friend of the Glen Cuagh Oir. "But," he added, "Maclennan is a great player too."

"A great player? Yes and no. He has the fingers and the notes, but he iss not the beeg man. It iss the

soul that breathes through the chanter. The soul!"
Here he gripped Cameron by the arm. "Man! it iss
like praying. A beeg man will neffer show himself in
small things, but when he will be in communion with
his Maker or when he will be pouring out his soul in
a pibroch then the beegness of the man will be manifest.
Aye," continued the piper, warming to his theme and
encouraged by the eager sympathy of his listener, "and
not only the beegness but the quality of the soul. A
mean man can play the pipes, but he can neffer be a
piper. It iss only a beeg man and a fine man and, I
will venture to say, a good man, and there are not many
men can be pipers."

"Aye, Mr. Sutherland," broke in the Reverend Alexander Munro, "what you say is true, but it is true not
only of piping. It is true surely of anything great
enough to express the deepest emotions of the soul. A
man is never at his best in anything till he is expressing
his noblest self."

"For instance in preaching, eh!" said Dr. Kane.

"Aye, in preaching or in political oratory," replied
the minister.

At this, however, the old piper shook his head doubtfully.

"You do not agree with Mr. Munro in that?" said the
M.P.P.

"No," replied Sutherland, "speaking iss one thing,
piping iss another."

"And that is no lie, and a mighty good thing too it
is," said Dr. Kane flippantly.

"It iss no lie," replied the old piper with dignity.
"And if you knew much about either of them you would
say it deeferently."

"Why, what is the difference, Mr. Sutherland?" said

Dr. Kane, anxious to appease the old man. "They both are means of expressing the emotions of the soul, you say."

"The deeference! The deeference iss it? The deeference iss here, that the pipes will neffer lie."

There was a shout of laughter.

"One for you, Kane!" cried the Reverend Harper Freeman. "And," he continued when the laughing had ceased, "we will have to take our share too, Mr. Munro."

But the hour for beginning the programme had arrived and the secretary climbed to the platform to announce the events for the day.

"Ladies and gentlemen!" he cried, in a high, clear, penetrating voice, "the speech of welcome will be delivered toward the close of the day by the president of the Middlesex Caledonian Society, the Honourable J. J. Patterson, M.P.P. My duty is the very simple one of announcing the order of events on the programme and of expressing on behalf of the Middlesex Caledonian Society the earnest hope that you all may enjoy the day, and that each event on the programme will prove more interesting than the last. The programme is long and varied and I must ask your assistance to put it through on schedule time. First there are the athletic competitions. I shall endeavour to assist Dr. Kane and the judges in running these through without unnecessary and annoying delays. Then will follow piping, dancing, and feasting in their proper order, after which will come the presentation of prizes and speeches from our distinguished visitors. On the platform over yonder there are places for the speakers, the officials, and the guests of the society, but such is the very excellent character of the ground that all can be accommodated with grand stand seats. One disappointment, and one only, I must announce, the Band of the Seventh, London, cannot be with us to-day."

"But we will never miss them," interpolated the Reverend Alexander Munro with solemn emphasis.

"Exactly so!" continued Fatty when the laugh had subsided. "And now let's all go in for a good old time picnic, 'where even the farmers cease from grumbling and the preachers take a rest.' Now take your places, ladies and gentlemen, for the grand parade is about to begin."

The programme opened with the one hundred yard flat race. For this race there were four entries, Cahill from London, Fullerton from Woodstock, La Belle from nowhere in particular, and Wilbur Freeman from Maplehill. But Wilbur was nowhere to be seen. The secretary came breathless to the platform.

"Where's Wilbur?" he asked his father.

"Wilbur? Surely he is in the crowd, or in the tent perhaps."

At the tent the secretary found his brother nursing a twisted ankle, heart-sick with disappointment. Early in the day he had injured his foot in an attempt to fasten a swing upon a tree. Every minute since that time he had spent in rubbing and manipulating the injured member, but all to no purpose. While the pain was not great, a race was out of the question. The secretary was greatly disturbed and as nearly wrathful as ever he allowed himself to become. He was set on his brother making a good showing in this race; moreover, without Wilbur there would be no competitor to uphold the honour of Maplehill in this contest and this would deprive it of much of its interest.

"What the dickens were you climbing trees for?" he began impatiently, but a glance at his young brother's pale and woe-stricken face changed his wrath to pity. "Never mind, old chap," he said, "better luck next time, and you will be fitter too."

Back he ran to the platform, for he must report the dismal news to his mother, whose chief interest in the programme for the day lay in this race in which her latest born was to win his spurs. The cheery secretary was nearly desperate. It was an ominous beginning for the day's sports. What should he do? He confided his woe to Mack and Cameron, who were standing close by the platform.

"It will play the very mischief with the programme. It will spoil the whole day, for Wilbur was the sole Maplehill representative in the three races; besides, I believe the youngster would have shown up well."

"He would that!" cried Mack heartily. "He was a bird. But is there no one else from the Hill that could enter?"

"No, no one with a chance of winning, and no fellow likes to go in simply to be beaten."

"What difference?" said Cameron. "It's all in a day's sport."

"That's so," said Mack. "If I could run myself I would enter. I wonder if Danny would—"

"Danny!" said the secretary shortly. "You know better than that. Danny's too shy to appear before this crowd even if he were dead sure of winning."

"Say, it is too bad!" continued Mack, as the magnitude of the calamity grew upon him. "Surely we can find some one to make an appearance. What about yourself, Cameron? Did you ever race?"

"Some," said Cameron. "I raced last year at the Athole Games."

Fatty threw himself upon him.

"Cameron, you are my man! Do you want to save your country, and perhaps my life, certainly my reputation? Get out of those frills," touching his kilt, "and I'll get a suit from one of the jumpers for you. Go! Bless your soul, anything you want that's mine you can have! Only hustle for dear life's sake! Go! Go! Go! Take him away, Mack. We'll get something else on!"

Fatty actually pushed Cameron clear away from the platform and after him big Mack.

"There seems to be no help for it," said Cameron, as they went to the tent together.

"It's awful good of you," replied Mack, "but you can see how hard Fatty takes it, though it is not a bit fair to you."

"Oh, nobody knows me here," said Cameron, "and I don't mind being a victim."

But as Mack saw him get into his jersey and shorts he began to wonder a bit.

"Man, it would be great if you should beat yon Frenchman!" he exclaimed.

"Frenchman?"

"Yes! La Belle. He is that stuck on himself; he thinks he is a winner before he starts."

"It's a good way to think, Mack. Now let us get down into the woods and have a bit of a practise in the 'get away.' How do they start here? With a pistol?"

"No," replied Mack. "We are not so swell. The starter gives the word this way, 'All set? Go!'"

"All right, Mack, you give me the word sharp. I am out of practise and I must get the idea into my head."

"You are great on the idea, I see," replied Mack.

"Right you are, and it is just the same with the hammer, Mack."

"Aye, I have found that out."

For twenty minutes or so Cameron practised his start and at every attempt Mack's confidence grew, so that when he brought his man back to the platform he announced to a group of the girls standing near, "Don't say anything, but I have the winner right here for you."

"Why, Mr. Cameron," cried Isa, "what a wonder you are! What else can you do? You are a piper, a dancer, a hammer-thrower, and now a runner."

"Jack-of-all-trades," laughed Perkins, who, with Mandy, was standing near.

"Yes, but you can't say 'Master of none,'" replied Isa sharply.

"Better wait," said Cameron. "I have entered this race only to save Mr. Freeman from collapse."

"Collapse? Fatty? He couldn't," said Isa with emphasis.

"Lass, I do not know," said Mack gravely. "He looked more hollow than ever I have seen him before."

"Well, we'll all cheer for you, Mr. Cameron, anyway," cried Isa. "Won't we, girls? Oh, if wishes were wings!"

"Wings?" said Mandy, with a puzzled air. "What for? This is a *race.*"

"Didn't you never see a hen run, Mandy?" laughed Perkins.

"Yes, I have, but I tell you Mr. Cameron ain't no hen," replied Mandy angrily. "And more! He's going to win."

"Say, Mandy, that is the talk," said Mack, when the laugh had passed. "Did you hear yon?" he added to Cameron.

Cameron nodded.

"It is a good omen," he said. "I am going to do my best."

"And, by Jingo! if you only had a chance," said Mack, "I believe you would lick them all."

At this Fatty bustled up.

"All ready, eh? Cameron, I shall owe you something for this. La Belle kicked like a steer against your entering at the last minute. It is against the rules, you know. But he's given in."

Fatty did not explain that he had intimated to La Belle that there was no need for anxiety as far as the "chap from the old country" was concerned; he was there merely to fill up.

But if La Belle's fears were allayed by the secretary's disparaging description of the latest competitor, they sprang full grown into life again when he saw Cameron "all set" for the start, and more especially so when he heard his protest against the Frenchman's method in the "get away."

"I want you to notice," he said firmly to Dr. Kane, who was acting as starter, "that this man gets away *with* the word 'Go' and not *after* it. It is an old trick, but long ago played out."

Then the Frenchman fell into a rage.

"Eet ees no treeck!" sputtered La Belle. "Eet ees too queeck for him."

"All right!" said Dr. Kane. "You are to start after the word 'Go.' Remember! Sorry we have no pistol."

Once more the competitors crouched over the scratch.

"All set? Go!"

Like the releasing of a whirlwind the four runners spring from the scratch, La Belle, whose specialty is his "get away," in front, Fullerton and Cameron in second place, Cahill a close third. A blanket would cover them all. A tumult of cheers from the friends of the various runners follows them along their brief course.

"Who is it? Who is it?" cries Mandy breathlessly, clutching Mack by the arm.

"Cameron, I swear!" roars Mack, pushing his way through the crowd to the judges.

"No! No! La Belle! La Belle!" cried the Frenchman's backers from the city. The judges are apparently in dispute.

"I swear it is Cameron!" roars Mack again in their ears, his eyes aflame and his face alight with a fierce and triumphant joy. "It is Cameron I am telling you!"

"Oh, get out, you big bluffer!" cries a thin-faced man, pressing close upon the judges. "It is La Belle by a mile!"

"By a mile, is it?" shouts Mack. "Then go and hunt your man!" and with a swift motion his big hand falls upon the thin face and sweeps it clear out of view, the man bearing it coming to his feet in a white fury some paces away. A second look at Mack, however, calms his rage, and from a distance he continues leaping and yelling "La Belle! La Belle!"

After a few moments' consultation the result is announced.

"A tie for the first place between La Belle and Cameron! Time eleven seconds! The tie will be run off in a few minutes."

In a tumult of triumph big Mack shoulders Cameron through the crowd and carries him off to the dressing tent, where he spends the next ten minutes rubbing his man's legs and chanting his glory.

"Who is this Cameron?" enquired the M.P.P., leaning over the platform railing.

Quick came the answer from the bevy of girls throng-
ing past the platform.

"Cameron? He's our man!" It was Mandy's voice,
bold and strong.

"Your man?" said the M.P.P., laughing down into
the coarse flushed face.

"Yes, *our* man!" cried Isa MacKenzie back at him.
"And a winner, you may be sure."

"Ah, happy man!" exclaimed the M.P.P. "Who
would not win with such backers? Why, I would win
myself, Miss Isa, were you to back me so. But who is
Cameron?" he continued to the Methodist minister at
his side.

"He is Haley's hired man, I believe, and that first
girl is Haley's daughter."

"Poor thing!" echoed Mrs. Freeman, a kindly smile
on her motherly face. "But she has a good heart has
poor Mandy."

"But why 'poor'?" enquired the M.P.P.

"Oh, well," answered Mrs. Freeman with hesitation,
"you see she is so very plain—and—well, not like other
girls. But she is a good worker and has a kind heart."

Once more the runners face the starter, La Belle gay,
alert, confident; Cameron silent, pale, and grim.

"All set? Go!" La Belle is away ere the word is
spoken. The bell, however, brings him back, wrathful
and less confident.

Once more they stand crouching over the scratch.
Once more the word releases them like shafts from the
bow. A beautiful start, La Belle again in the lead, but
Cameron hard at his heels and evidently with something
to spare. Thus for fifty yards, sixty, yes, sixty-five.

"La Belle! La Belle! He wins! He wins!" yell his
backers frantically, the thin-faced man dancing madly

near the finishing tape. Twenty yards to go and still
La Belle is in the lead. High above the shouting rises
Mack's roar.

"Now, Cameron! For the life of you!"

It was as if his voice had touched a spring somewhere
in Cameron's anatomy. A great leap brings him even
with La Belle. Another, another, and still another, and
he breasts the tape a winner by a yard, time ten and
three fifths seconds. The Maplehill folk go mad, and
madder than all Isa and her company of girl friends.

"I got—one—bad—start—me! He—pull—me back!"
panted La Belle to his backers who were holding him up.

"Who pulled you back?" indignantly cried the thin-
faced man, looking for blood.

"That *sacré* startair!"

"You ran a fine race, La Belle!" said Cameron, coming up.

"*Non! Peste!* I mak heem in ten and one feeft,"
replied the disgusted La Belle.

"I have made it in ten," said Cameron quietly.

"Aha!" exclaimed La Belle. "You are one black
horse, eh? So! I race no more to-day!"

"Then no more do I!" said Cameron firmly. "Why,
La Belle, you will beat me in the next race sure. I have
no wind."

Under pressure La Belle changed his mind, and well
for him he did; for in the two hundred and twenty
yards and in the quarter mile Cameron's lack of condition told against him, so that in the one he ran second
to La Belle and in the other third to La Belle and
Fullerton.

The Maplehill folk were gloriously satisfied, and Fatty
in an ecstasy of delight radiated good cheer everywhere.
Throughout the various contests the interest continued

to deepen, the secretary, with able generalship, reserving the hammer-throwing as the most thrilling event to the last place. For, more than anything in the world, men, and especially women, love strong men and love to see them in conflict. For that fatal love cruel wars have been waged, lands have been desolated, kingdoms have fallen. There was the promise of a very pretty fight indeed between the three entered for the hammer-throwing contest, two of them experienced in this warfare and bearing high honours, the third new to the game and unskilled, but loved for his modest courage and for the simple, gentle heart he carried in his great body. He could not win, of course, for McGee, the champion of the city police force, had many scalps at his girdle, and Duncan Ross, "Black Duncan," the pride of the Zorras, the unconquered hero of something less than a hundred fights—who could hope to win from him? But all the more for this the people loved big Mack and wished him well. So down the sloping sides of the encircling hills the crowds pressed thick, and on the platform the great men leaned over the rail, while they lifted their ladies to places of vantage upon the chairs beside them.

"Oh, I cannot see a bit!" cried Isa MacKenzie, vainly pressing upon the crowding men who, stolidly unaware of all but what was doing in front of them, effectually shut off her view.

"And you want to see?" said the M.P.P., looking down at her.

"Oh, so much!" she cried.

"Come up here, then!" and, giving her a hand, he lifted her, smiling and blushing, to a place on the platform whence she with absorbing interest followed the movements of big Mack, and incidentally of the

others in as far as they might bear any relation to those
of her hero.

And now they were drawing for place.

"Aha! Mack is going to throw first!" said the Reverend Alexander Munro. "That is a pity."

"It's a shame!" cried Isa, with flashing eyes. "Why
don't they put one of those older—ah—?"

"Stagers?" suggested the M.P.P.

"Duffers," concluded Isa.

"The lot determines the place, Miss Isa," said Mr.
Freeman, with a smile at her. "But the best man will
win."

"Oh, I am not so sure of that!" cried the girl in a
distressed voice. "Mack might get nervous."

"Nervous?" laughed the M.P.P. "That giant?"

"Yes, indeed, I have seen him that nervous—" said
Isa, and stopped abruptly.

"Ah! That is quite possible," replied the M.P.P. with
a quizzical smile.

"And there is young Cameron yonder. He is not
going to throw, is he?" enquired Mr. Munro.

"He is coaching Mack," explained Isa, "and fine he
is at it. Oh, there! He is going to throw! Oh, if he
only gets the swing! Oh! Oh! Oh! He has got it
fine!"

A storm of cheers followed Mack's throw, then a deep
silence while the judges took the measurement.

"One hundred and twenty-one feet!"

"One hundred and twenty-one!" echoed a hundred
voices in amazement.

"One hundred and twenty-one! It is a lie!" cried
McGee with an oath, striding out to personally super-
vise the measuring.

"One hundred and twenty-one!" said Duncan Ross,

shaking his head doubtfully, but he was too much of a gentleman to do other than wait for the judges' decision.

"One hundred and twenty-one feet and two inches," was the final verdict, and from the crowd there rose a roar that rolled like thunder around the hills.

"It's a fluke, and so it is!" said McGee with another oath.

"Give me your hand, lad," said Duncan Ross, evidently much roused. "It iss a noble throw whateffer, and worthy of beeg Rory himself. I haf done better, howeffer, but indeed I may not to-day."

It was indeed a great throw, and one immediate result was that there was no holding back in the contest, no playing 'possum. Mack's throw was there to be beaten, and neither McGee nor even Black Duncan could afford to throw away a single chance. For hammer-throwing is an art requiring not only strength but skill as well, and not only strength and skill but something else most difficult to secure. With the strength and the skill there must go a rhythmic and perfect coördination of all the muscles in the body, with exactly the proper contracting and relaxing of each at exactly the proper moment of time, and this perfect coördination is a result rarely achieved even by the greatest throwers, but when achieved, and with the man's full strength behind it, his record throw is the result.

Meantime Cameron was hovering about his man in an ecstasy of delight.

"Oh, Mack, old man!" he said. "You got the swing perfectly. It was a dream. And if you had put your full strength into it you would have made a world record. Why, man, you could add ten feet to it!"

"It is a fluke!" said McGee again, as he took his place.

"Make one like it, then, my lad," said Black Duncan with a grim smile.

But this McGee failed to do, for his throw measured ninety-seven feet.

"A very fair throw, McGee," said Black Duncan. "But not your best, and nothing but the best will do the day appearingly."

With that Black Duncan took place for his throw. One—twice—thrice he swung the great hammer about his head, then sent it whirling into the air. Again a mighty shout announced a great throw and again a dead silence waited for the measurement.

"One hundred and fourteen feet!"

"Aha!" said Black Duncan, and stepped back apparently well satisfied.

It was again Mack's turn.

"You have the privilege of allowing your first throw to stand," said Dr. Kane.

"Best let it stand, lad, till it iss beat," advised Black Duncan kindly. "It iss a noble throw."

"He can do better, though," said Cameron.

"Very well, very well!" said Duncan. "Let him try."

But Mack's success had keyed him up to the highest pitch. Every nerve was tingling, every muscle taut. His first throw he had taken without strain, being mainly anxious, under Cameron's coaching, to get the swing, but under the excitement incident to the contest he had put more strength into the throw than appeared either to himself or to his coach. Now, however, with nerves and muscles taut, he was eager to increase his distance, too eager it seemed, for his second throw measured only eighty-nine feet.

A silence fell upon his friends and Cameron began to chide him.

"You went right back to your old style, Mack. There wasn't the sign of a swing."

"I will get it yet, or bust!" said big Mack between his teeth.

McGee's second throw went one hundred and seventeen feet. A cheer arose from his backers, for it was a great throw and within five feet of his record. Undoubtedly McGee was in great form and he might well be expected to measure up to his best to-day.

Black Duncan's second throw measured one hundred and nineteen feet seven, which was fifteen feet short of his record and showed him to be climbing steadily upward.

Once more the turn came to Mack, and once more, with almost savage eagerness, he seized the hammer preparatory to his throw.

"Now, Mack, for heaven's sake go easy!" said Cameron. "Take your swing easy and slow."

But Mack heeded him not. "I can beat it!" he muttered between his shut teeth, "and I will." So, with every nerve taut and every muscle strained to its limit, he made his third attempt. It was in vain. The measure showed ninety-seven feet six. A suppressed groan rose from the Maplehill folk.

"A grand throw, lad, for a beginner," said Black Duncan.

The excitement now became intense. By his first throw of one hundred and twenty-one feet two, Mack remained still the winner. But McGee had only four feet to gain and Black Duncan less than two to equal him. The little secretary went skipping about aglow with satisfaction and delight. The day was already famous in the history of Canadian athletics.

Again McGee took place for his throw, his third

and last. The crowd gathered in as near as they dared. But McGee had done his best for that day, and his final throw measured only one hundred and five feet.

There remained yet but a single chance to wrest from Mack Murray the prize for that day, but that chance lay in the hands of Duncan Ross, the cool and experienced champion of many a hard-fought fight. Again Black Duncan took the hammer. It was his last throw. He had still fifteen feet to go to reach his own record, and he had often beaten the throw that challenged him to-day, but, on the other hand, he had passed through many a contest where his throw had fallen short of the one he must now beat to win. A hush fell upon the people as Black Duncan took his place. Once— twice—and, with ever increasing speed, thrice he swung the great hammer, then high and far it hurtled through the air.

"Jerusalem!" cried Mack. "What a fling!"

"Too high," muttered Black Duncan. "You have got it, lad, you have got it, and you well deserve it."

"Tut-tut, nonsense!" said Mack impatiently. "Wait you a minute."

Silent and expectant the crowd awaited the result. Twice over the judges measured the throw, then announced "One hundred and twenty-one feet." Mack had won by two inches.

A great roar rose from the crowd, round Mack they surged like a flood, eager to grip his hands and eager to carry him off shoulder high. But he threw them off as a rock throws back the incoming tide and made for Duncan Ross, who stood, calm and pale, and with hand outstretched, waiting him. It was a new experience for Black Duncan, and a bitter, to be second in a contest.

Only once in many years had he been forced to lower his colours, and to be beaten by a raw and unknown youth added to the humiliation of his defeat. But Duncan Ross had in his veins the blood of a long line of Highland gentlemen who knew how to take defeat with a smile.

"I congratulate you, Mack Murray," he said in a firm, clear voice. "Your fame will be through Canada to-morrow, and well you deserve it."

But Mack caught the outstretched hand in both of his and, leaning toward Black Duncan, he roared at him above the din.

"Mr. Ross, Mr. Ross, it is no win! Listen to me!" he panted. "What are two inches in a hundred and twenty feet? A stretching of the tape will do it. No, no! Listen to me! You must listen to me as you are a man! I will not have it! You can beat me easily in the throw! At best it is a tie and nothing else will I have to-day. At least let us throw again!" he pleaded. But to this Ross would not listen for a moment.

"The lad has made his win," he said to the judges, "and his win he must have."

But Mack declared that nothing under heaven would make him change his mind. Finally the judges, too, agreed that in view of the possibility of a mistake in measuring with the tape, it would be only right and fair to count the result a tie. Black Duncan listened respectfully to the judges' decision.

"You are asking me a good deal, Mack," he said at length, "but you are a gallant lad and I am an older man and—"

"Aye! And a better!" shouted Mack.

"And so I will agree."

Once more the field was cleared. And now there fell

upon the crowding people a hush as if they stood in the presence of death itself.

"Ladies and gentlemen!" said the M.P.P. "Do you realise that you are looking upon a truly great contest, a contest great enough to be of national, yes, of international, importance?"

"You bet your sweet life!" cried the irrepressible Fatty. "We're going some. 'What's the matter with our Mack?'" he shouted.

"'He's—all—right!'" came back the chant from the surrounding hills in hundreds of voices.

"And what's the matter with Duncan Ross?" cried Mack, waving a hand above his head.

Again the assurance of perfect rightness came back in a mighty roar from the hills. But it was hushed into immediate silence, a silence breathless and overwhelming, for Black Duncan had taken once more his place with the hammer in his hand.

"Oh, I do wish they would hurry!" gasped Isa, her hands pressed hard upon her heart.

"My heart is rather weak, too," said the M.P.P. "I fear I cannot last much longer. Ah! There he goes, thank God!"

"Amen!" fervently responds little Mrs. Freeman, who, in the intensity of her excitement, is standing on a chair holding tight by her husband's coat collar.

Not a sound breaks the silence as Black Duncan takes his swing. It is a crucial moment in his career. Only by one man in Canada has he ever been beaten, and with the powers of his antagonist all untried and unknown, for anyone could see that Mack has not yet thrown his best, he may be called upon to surrender within the next few minutes the proud position he has held so long in the athletic world. But there is not a sign of excitement in his face. With great care, and with almost painful deliberation, he balances the hammer for a moment or two, then once—twice—and, with a tremendous quickening of speed,—thrice—he swings, and his throw is made. A great throw it is, anyone can see, and one that beats the winner. In hushed and strained silence the people await the result.

"One hundred and twenty-one feet nine."

Then rises the roar that has been held pent up during the last few nerve-racking minutes.

"It iss a good enough throw," said Black Duncan with a quiet smile, "but there iss more in me yet. Now, lad, do your best and there will be no hard feeling with thiss man whateffer happens."

Black Duncan's accent and idioms reveal the intense excitement that lies behind his quiet face.

Mack takes the hammer.

"I will not beat it, you may be sure," he says. "But I will just take a fling at it anyway."

"Now, Mack," says Cameron, "for the sake of all you love forget the distance and show them the Braemar swing. Easy and slow."

But Mack waves him aside and stands pondering. He is "getting the idea."

"Man, do you see him?" whispers his brother Danny, who stands near to Cameron. "I believe he has got it."

Cameron nods his head. Mack wears an impressive air of confidence and strength.

"It will be a great throw," says Cameron to Danny.

"Easy and slow" Mack poises the great hammer in his hand, swinging it gently backward and forward as if it had been a boy's toy, the great muscles in arms and back rippling up and down in firm full waves under his white skin, for he is now stripped to the waist for this throw.

Suddenly, as if at command, the muscles seem to spring to their places, tense, alert. "Easy." Yes, truly, but by no means "slow." "Easy," the great hammer swings about his head in whirling circles, swift and ever swifter. Once—and twice—the great muscles in back and arms and back and legs knotted in bunches—thrice!

"Ah-h-h!" A long, wailing, horrible sound, half moan, half cry, breaks from the people. Mack has missed his direction, and the great hammer, weighted with the potentialities of death, is describing a parabola high over the heads of the crowding, shrieking, scattering people.

"Oh, my God! My God! Oh, my God! My God!" With his hands covering his eyes the big man is swaying from side to side like a mighty tree before a tempest. Cameron and Ross both spring to him. On the hillsides men stand rigid, pale, shaking; women shriek and faint. One ghastly moment of suspense, and then a horrid sickening thud; one more agonising second of silence, and then from a score of throats rises a cry:

"It's all right! All right! No one hurt!"

From five hundred throats breaks a weird unearthly mingling of strange sounds; cheers and cries, shouts and sobs, prayers and oaths. In the midst of it all Mack sinks to his knees, with hands outstretched to heaven.

"Great God, I thank Thee! I thank Thee!" he cries brokenly, the tears streaming down his ghastly face. Then, falling forward upon his hands, he steadies himself while great sobs come heaving from his mighty chest. Cameron and Ross, still upholding him, through the crowd a man comes pushing his way, hurling men and women right and left.

"Back, people! And be still." It is the minister, Alexander Munro. "Be still! It is a great deliverance that God has wrought! Peace, woman! God is near! Let us pray."

Instantly all noises are hushed, hats come off, and all up the sloping hills men and women fall to their knees, or remain standing with heads bowed, while the minister, upright beside the kneeling man, spreads his hands towards heaven and prays in a voice steady, strong, thrilling:

"Almighty God, great and wonderful in Thy ways, merciful and gracious in Thy providence, Thou hast wrought a great deliverance before our eyes this day. All power is in Thy hands. All forces move at Thy command. Thine hand it is that guided this dread hammer harmless to its own place, saving the people from death. It is ever thus, Father, for Thou art Love. We lift to Thee our hearts' praise. May we walk softly before Thee this day and alway. Amen!"

"Amen! Amen!" On every hand and up the hillsides rises the fervent solemn attestation.

"Rise, Mr. Murray!" says the minister in a loud and solemn voice, giving Mack his hand. "God has been gracious to you this day. See that you do not forget."

"He has that! He has that!" sobs Mack. "And God forgive me if I ever forget." And, suddenly pushing from him the many hands stretched out towards him, he stumbles his way through the crowd, led off by his two friends towards the tent.

"Hold on there a minute! Let us get this measurement first." It was the matter-of-fact, cheery voice of

Fatty Freeman. "If I am not mistaken we have a great throw to measure."

"Quite right, Mr. Freeman," said the minister. "Let us get the measurement and let not the day be spoiled."

"Here, you people, don't stand there gawking like a lot of dotty chumps!" cried the secretary, striving to whip them out of the mood of horror into which they had fallen. "Get a move on! Give the judges a chance! What is it, doctor?"

The judges were consulting. At length the decision was announced.

"One hundred and twenty-nine seven."

"Hooray!" yelled Fatty, flinging his straw hat high. "One hundred and twenty-nine seven! It is a world throw! Why don't you yell, you people? Don't you know that you have a world-beater among you? Yell! Yell!"

"Three cheers for Mack Murray!" called out the Reverend Harper Freeman from the platform, swinging his great black beaver hat over his head.

It was what the people wanted. Again, and again, and yet again the crowd exhausted its pent-up emotions in frantic cheers. The clouds of gloom were rolled back, the sun was shining bright again, and with fresh zest the people turned to the enjoyment of the rest of the programme.

"Thank you, Sir!" said Fatty amid the uproar, gripping the hand of Mr. Munro. "You have saved the day for us. We were all going to smash, but you pulled us out."

Meantime in the tent Duncan Ross was discoursing to his friends.

"Man, Mack! Yon's a mighty throw! Do you know it iss within five feet of my own record and within ten of Big Rory's? Then," he said solemnly, "you are in the world's first class to-day, my boy, and you are just beginning."

"I have just quit!" said Mack.

"Whist, lad! Thiss iss not the day for saying anything about it. We will wait a wee and to-day we will just be thankful." And with that they turned to other things.

They were still in the dressing tent when the secretary thrust his cheery face under the flap.

"I say, boys! Are you ready? Cameron, we want you on the pipes."

"Harp!" said Mack. "I am going home. I am quite useless."

"And me, too," said Cameron. "I shall go with you, Mack."

"What?" cried Fatty in consternation. "Look here, boys! Is this a square deal? God knows I am nearly all in myself. I've had enough to keep this thing from going to pieces. Don't you go back on me now!"

"That is so!" said Mack slowly. "Cameron, you must stay. You are needed. I will spoil things more by staying than by going. I would be forever seeing that hammer crushing down—" He covered his face with his hands and shuddered.

"All right, Mack! I will stay," said Cameron. "But what about you?"

"Oh," said Black Duncan, "Mack and I will walk about and have a smoke for a little."

"Thanks, boys, you are the stuff!" said Fatty fervently. "Once more you have saved the day. Come then, Cameron! Get your pipes. Old Sutherland is waiting for you."

But before he set off Mack called Cameron to him.

"You will see Isa," he said, "and tell her why I could not stay. And you will take her home." His face was still pallid, his voice unsteady.

"I will take care of her, Mack, never fear. But could you not remain? It might help you."

But Mack only shook his head. His fervent Highland soul had too recently passed through the valley of death and its shadows were still upon him.

Four hours later Fatty looked in upon Mack at his own home. He found him sitting in the moonlight in the open door of the big new barn, with his new-made friend, Duncan Ross, at one door post and old Piper Sutherland at the other, while up and down the floor in the shadow within Cameror marched, droning the wild melody of the "Maccrimmon Lament." Mournful and weird it sounded through the gloom, but upon the hearts of these Highlanders it fell like a soothing balm. With a wave of his hand Mack indicated a seat, which Fatty took without a word. Irrepressible though he was, he had all the instincts of a true gentleman. He knew it was the time for silence, and silent he stood till the Lament had run through its "doubling" and its "trebling," ending with the simple stately movement of its original theme. To Fatty it was a mere mad and unmelodious noise, but, reading the faces of the three men before him in the moonlight, he had sense enough to recognise his own limitations.

At length the Lament was finished and Cameron came forward into the light.

"Ah! That iss good for the soul," said old piper Sutherland. "Do you know what your pipes have been saying to me in yon Lament?

'Yea, though I walk through Death's dark vale,
Yet will I fear none ill;
For Thou art with me, and Thy rod
And staff me comfort still.'

And we have been in the valley thiss day."

Mack rose to his feet.

"I could not have said it myself, but, as true as death, that is the word for me."

"Well," said Fatty, rising briskly, "I guess you are all right, Mack. I confess I was a bit anxious about you, but—"

"There is no need," said Mack gravely. "I can sleep now."

"Good-night, then," replied Fatty, turning to go. "Cameron, I owe you a whole lot. I won't forget it." He set his hat upon the back of his head, sticking his hands into his pockets and surveying the group before him. "Say! You Highlanders are a great bunch. I do not pretend to understand you, but I want to say that between you you have saved the day." And with that the cheery, frisky, irrepressible, but kindly little man faded into the moonlight and was gone.

For the fourth time the day had been saved.

CHAPTER VI

A SABBATH DAY IN LATE AUGUST

IT was a Sabbath day in late August, and in no month of the year does a Sabbath day so chime with the time. For the Sabbath day is a day for rest and holy thought, and the late August is the rest time of the year, when the woods and fields are all asleep in a slumberous blue haze; the sacred time, too, for in late August old Mother Earth is breathing her holiest aspirations heavenward, having made offering of her best in the full fruitage of the year. Hence a Sabbath day in late August chimes marvellously well with the time.

And this particular Sabbath day was perfect of its kind, a dreamy, drowsy day, a day when genial suns and hazy cool airs mingle in excellent harmony, and the tired worker, freed from his week's toil, basks and stretches, yawns and revels in rest under the orchard trees; unless, indeed, he goes to morning church. And to morning church Cameron went as a rule, but to-day, owing to a dull ache in his head and a general sense of languor pervading his limbs, he had chosen instead, as likely to be more healing to his aching head and his languid limbs, the genial sun, tempered with cool and lazy airs under the orchard trees. And hence he lay watching the democrat down the lane driven off to church by Perkins, with Mandy beside him in the front seat, the seat of authority and of activity, and Mr. Haley alone in the back seat, the seat of honour and of retirement. Mrs. Haley was too overborne by the heat and rush of the busy week to adventure the heat and dust of the road, and to sustain the somewhat strenuous discourse of the Reverend Harper Freeman, to whose flock the Haleys belonged. This, however, was not Mrs. Haley's invariable custom. In the cooler weather it was her habit to drive on a Sunday morning to church, sitting in the back seat beside her husband, with Tim and Mandy occupying the front seat beside the hired man, but during the heat and hurry of the harvest time she would take advantage of the quietness of the house and of the two or three hours' respite from the burden of household duties to make up arrears of sleep accumulated during the preceding week, salving her conscience, for she had a conscience in the matter, with a promise that she might go in the evening when it was cooler and when she was more rested. This promise, however, having served its turn, was never fulfilled, for by the evening the wheels of household toil began once more to turn, and Mrs. Haley found it easier to worship vicariously, sending Mandy and Tim to the evening service. And to this service the young people were by no means loath to go, for it was held on fair evenings in MacBurney's woods, two miles away by the road, one mile by the path through the woods. On occasion Perkins would hitch up in the single buggy Dexter, the fiery young colt, too fiery for any other to drive, and, as a special attention to his employer's daughter, would drive her to the service. But since the coming of Cameron, Mandy had allowed this custom to fall into disuse, at first somewhat to Perkins' relief, for the colt was restless and fretted against the tie rein; and, besides, Perkins was not as yet quite prepared to acknowledge any special relationship between himself and the young lady in question before the assembled congregation, preferring to regard himself and to be regarded by others as a free lance. Later, however, as Mandy's preference for a walk through the woods became more marked, Perkins, much to his disgust, found himself reduced to the attitude of a suppliant, urging the superior attraction of a swift drive behind Dexter as against a weary walk to the service. Mandy, however, with the directness of her simple nature, had no compunction in frankly maintaining her preference for a walk with Tim and Cameron through the woods; indeed, more than once she allowed Perkins to drive off with his fiery colt, alone in his glory.

But this Sabbath morning, as Cameron lay under the orchard trees, he was firmly resolved that he would give the whole day to the nursing of the ache in his head and the painful languor in his body. And so lying he allowed his mind to wander uncontrolled over the happenings of the past months, troubled by a lazy consciousness of a sore spot somewhere in his life. Gradually there grew into clearness the realisation of the cause of this sore spot.

"What is the matter with Perkins?" he asked of Tim, who had declined to go to church, and who had strolled into the orchard to be near his friend.

"What is the matter with Perkins?" Cameron asked a second time, for Tim was apparently too much engaged with a late harvest apple to answer.

"How?" said the boy at length.

"He is so infernally grumpy with me."

"Grumpy? He's sore, I guess."

"Sore?"

"You bet! Ever since I beat him in the turnips that day."

"Ever since *you* beat him?" asked Cameron in amazement. "Why should he be sore against me?"

"He knows it was you done it," said Tim.

"Nonsense, Tim! Besides, Perkins isn't a baby. He surely doesn't hold that against me."

"Huh, huh," said Tim, "everybody's pokin' fun at him, and he hates that, and ever since the picnic, too, he hates you."

"But why in the world?"

"Oh, shucks!" said Tim, impatient at Cameron's density. "I guess you know all right."

"Know? Not I!"

"Git out!"

"Honor bright, Tim," replied Cameron, sitting up. "Now, honestly, tell me, Tim, why in the world Perkins should hate me."

"You put his nose out of joint, I guess," said Tim with a grin.

"Oh, rot, Tim! How?"

"Every how," said Tim, proceeding to elaborate. "First when you came here you were no good—I mean—" Tim checked himself hastily.

"I know what you mean, Tim. Go on. You are quite right. I couldn't do anything on the farm."

"Now," continued Tim, "you can do anything jist as good as him—except bindin', of course. He's a terror at bindin', but at pitchin' and shockin' and loadin' you're jist as good."

"But, Tim, that's all nonsense. Perkins isn't such a fool as to hate me because I can keep up my end."

"He don't like you," said Tim stubbornly.

"But why? Why in the name of common sense?"

"Well," said Tim, summing up the situation, "before you come he used to be the hull thing. Now he's got to play second fiddle."

But Cameron remained unenlightened.

"Oh, pshaw!" continued Tim, making further concessions to his friend's stupidity. "At the dances, at the raisin's, runnin', jumpin'—everythin'—Perkins used to be the King Bee. Now—" Tim's silence furnished an impressive close to the contrast. "Why! They all think you are just fine!" said Tim, with a sudden burst of confidence.

"They?"

"All the boys. Yes, and the girls, too," said Tim, allowing his solemn face the unusual luxury of a smile.

"The girls?"

"Aw, yeh know well enough—the Murray girls, and the MacKenzies, and the hull lot of them. And then—and then—there's Mandy, too." Here Tim shot a keen glance at his friend, who now sat leaning against the trunk of an apple tree with his eyes closed.

"Now, Tim, you are a shrewd little chap"—here Cameron sat upright—"but how do you know about the girls, and what is this you say about Mandy? Mandy is good to me—very kind and all that, but—"

"She used to like Perkins pretty well," said Tim, with a kind of hesitating shyness.

"And Perkins?"

"Oh, he thought he jist owned her. Guess he ain't so sure now," added Tim. "I guess you've changed Mandy all right."

It was the one thing Cameron hated to hear, but he made light of it.

"Oh, nonsense!" he exclaimed. "But if I did I would be mighty glad of it. Mandy is too good for a man like Perkins. Why, he isn't safe."

"He's a terror," replied Tim seriously. "They are all scairt of him. He's a terror to fight. Why, at MacKenzie's raisin' last year he jist went round foamin' like an old boar and nobody dast say a word to him.

Even Mack Murray was scairt to touch him. When he gets like that he ain't afraid of nothin' and he's awful quick and strong."

Tim proceeded to enlarge upon this theme, which apparently fascinated him, with tales of Perkins' prowess in rough-and-tumble fighting. But Cameron had lost interest and was lying down again with his eyes closed.

"Well," he said, when Tim had finished his recital, "if he is that kind of a man Mandy should have nothing to do with him."

But Tim was troubled.

"Dad likes him," he said gloomily. "He is a good hand. And ma likes him, too. He taffies her up."

"And Mandy?" enquired Cameron.

"I don't know," said Tim, still more gloomy. "I guess he kind of makes her. I'd—I'd jist like to take a lump out of him." Tim's eyes blazed into a sudden fire. "He runs things on this farm altogether too much."

"Buck up then, Tim, and beat him," said Cameron, dismissing the subject. "And now I must have some sleep. I have got an awful head on."

Tim was quick enough to understand the hint, but still he hovered about.

"Say, I'm awful sorry," he said. "Can't I git somethin'? You didn't eat no breakfast."

"Oh, all I want is sleep, Tim. I will be all right to-morrow," replied Cameron, touched by the tone of sympathy in Tim's voice. "You are a fine little chap. Trot along and let me sleep."

But no sleep came to Cameron, partly because of the hammer knocking in his head, but chiefly because of the thoughts set going by Tim. Cameron was not abnormally egotistical, but he was delightedly aware of

the new place he held in the community ever since the
now famous Dominion Day picnic, and, now that the
harvest rush had somewhat slackened, social engage-
ments had begun to crowd upon him.   Dances and
frolics, coon hunts and raisings were becoming the vogue
throughout the community, and no social function was
complete without the presence of Cameron.   But this
sudden popularity had its embarrassments, and among
them, and threatening to become annoying, was the
hostility of Perkins, veiled as yet, but none the less real.
Moreover, behind Perkins stood a band of young fellows of whom he was the recognised leader and over
whom his ability in the various arts and crafts of the
farm, his physical prowess in sports, his gay, cheery
manner, and, it must be said, the reputation he bore for
a certain fierce brute courage in rough-and-tumble fighting, gave him a sort of ascendency.

But Perkins' attitude towards him did not after all
cause Cameron much concern.   There was another and
more annoying cause of embarrassment, and that was
Mandy.   Tim's words kept reiterating themselves in his
brain, "You've changed Mandy all right."   Over this
declaration of Tim's, Cameron proceeded to argue with
himself.   He sat bolt upright that he might face himself on the matter.

"Now, then," he said to himself, "let's have this thing
out."

"Most willingly.   This girl was on the way to engage-
ment to this young man Perkins.   You come on the
scene.   Everything is changed."

"Well!   What of it?   It's a mighty good thing for
her."

"But you are the cause of it."

"The occasion, rather."

"No, the cause. You have attracted her to you."

"I can't help that. Besides, it is a mere passing whim. She'll get over all that." And Cameron laughed scornfully in his own face.

"Do you know that? And how do you know it? Tim thinks differently."

"Oh, confound it all! I see that I shall have to get out of here."

"A wise decision truly, and the sooner the better. Do you propose to go at once?"

"At once? Well, I should like to spend the winter here. I have made a number of friends and life is beginning to be pleasant."

"Exactly! It suits your convenience, but how about Mandy?"

"Oh, rubbish! Must I be governed by the fancies of that silly girl? Besides, the whole thing is absurdly ridiculous."

"But facts are stubborn, and anyone can see that the girl is—"

"Hang it all! I'll go at the end of the month."

"Very well. And in the leavetaking—?"

"What?"

"It is pleasant to be appreciated and to carry away with one memories, I will not say tender, but appreciative."

"I can't act like a boor. I must be decent to the girl. Besides, she isn't altogether a fool."

"No, but very crude, very primitive, very passionate, and therefore very defenseless."

"All right, I shall simply shake hands and go."

So, with the consequent sense of relief that high resolve always brings, Cameron lay down again and fell into slumber and dreams of home.

From these dreams of home Mandy recalled him with a summons to dinner. As his eye, still filled with the vision of his dreams, fell upon her in all the gorgeous splendour of her Sunday dress, he was conscious of a strong sense of repulsion. How coarse, how crude, how vulgar she appeared, how horribly out of keeping with those scenes through which he had just been wandering in his dreams.

"I want no dinner, Mandy," he said shortly. "I have a bad head and I am not hungry."

"No dinner?" That a man should not want dinner was to Mandy quite inexplicable, unless, indeed, he were ill.

"Are you sick?" she cried in quick alarm.

"No, I have a headache. It will pass away," said Cameron, turning over on his side. Still Mandy lingered.

"Let me bring you a nice piece of pie and a cup of tea."

Cameron shuddered.

"No," he said, "bring me nothing. I merely wish to sleep."

But Mandy refused to be driven away.

"Say, I'm awful sorry. I know you're sick."

"Nonsense!" said Cameron, impatiently, waiting for her to be gone. Still Mandy hesitated.

"I'm awful sorry," she said again, and her voice, deep, tender, full-toned, revealed her emotion.

Cameron turned impatiently towards her.

"Look here, Mandy! There's nothing wrong with me. I only want a little sleep. I shall be all right to-morrow."

But Mandy's fears were not to be allayed.

"Say," she cried, "you look awful bad."

"Oh, get out, Mandy! Go and get your dinner. Don't mind me." Cameron's tone was decidedly cross.

Without further remonstrance Mandy turned silently away, but before she turned Cameron caught the gleam of tears in the great blue eyes. A swift compunction seized him.

"I say, Mandy, I don't want to be rude, but—"

"Rude?" cried the girl. "You? You couldn't be. You are always good—to me—and—I—don't—know—" Here her voice broke.

"Oh, come, Mandy, get away to dinner. You are a good girl. Now leave me alone."

The kindness in his voice quite broke down Mandy's all too slight control. She turned away, audibly sniffling, with her apron to her eyes, leaving Cameron in a state of wrathful perplexity.

"Oh, confound it all!" he groaned to himself. "This is a rotten go. By Jove! This means the West for me. The West! After all, that's the place. Here there is no chance anyway. Why did I not go sooner?"

He rose from the grass, shivering with a sudden chill, went to his bed in the hay mow, and, covering himself with Tim's blankets and his own, fell again into sleep. Here, late in the afternoon, Tim found him and called him to supper.

With Mandy's watchful eye upon him he went through the form of eating, but Mandy was not to be deceived.

"You ain't eatin' nothin'," she said reproachfully as he rose from the table.

"Enough for a man who is doing nothing," replied Cameron. "What I want is exercise. I think I shall take a walk."

"Going to church?" she enquired, an eager light springing into her eye.

"To church? I hadn't thought of it," replied Cameron, but, catching the gleam of a smile on Perkins' face and noting the utterly woebegone expression on Mandy's, he added, "Well, I might as well walk to church as any place else. You are going, Tim?"

"Huh huh!" replied Tim.

"I am going to hitch up Deck, Mandy," said Perkins.

"Oh, I'm goin' to walk!" said Mandy, emphatically.

"All right!" said Perkins. "Guess I'll walk too with the crowd."

"Don't mind me," said Mandy.

"I don't," laughed Perkins, "you bet! Nor anybody else."

"And that's no lie!" sniffed Mandy, with a toss of her head.

"Better drive to church, Mandy," suggested her mother. "You know you're jist tired out and it will be late when you get started."

"Tired? Late?" cried Mandy, with alacrity. "I'll be through them dishes in a jiffy and be ready in no time. I like the walk through the woods."

"Depends on the company," laughed Perkins again. "So do I. Guess we'll all go together."

True to her promise, Mandy was ready within half an hour. Cameron shuddered as he beheld the bewildering variety of colour in her attire and the still more bewildering arrangement of hat and hair.

"You're good and gay, Mandy," said Perkins. "What's the killing?"

Mandy made no reply save by a disdainful flirt of her skirts as she set off down the lane, followed by Perkins, Cameron and Tim bringing up the rear.

The lane was a grassy sward, cut with two wagon-wheel tracks, and with a picturesque snake fence on either side. Beyond the fences lay the fields, some of them with stubble raked clean, the next year's clover showing green above the yellow, some with the grain standing still in the shock, and some with the crop, the late oats for instance, still uncut, but ready for the reaper. The turnip field was splendidly and luxuriantly green with never a sign of the brown earth. The hay meadow, too, was green and purple with the second growth of clover.

So down the lane and between the shorn fields, yellow and green, between the clover fields and the turnips, they walked in silence, for the spell of the Sabbath evening lay upon the sunny fields, barred with the shadows from the trees that grew along the fence lines everywhere. At the "slashing" the wagon ruts faded out and the road narrowed to a single cow path, winding its way between stumps and round log piles, half hidden by a luxuriant growth of foxglove and fireweed and asters, and everywhere the glorious goldenrod. Then through the bars the path led into the woods, a noble remnant of the beech and elm and maple forest from which the farm had been cut some sixty years before. Cool and shadowy they stood, and shot through with bright shafts of gold from the westering sun, full of mysterious silence except for the twittering of the sleepy birds or for the remonstrant call of the sentinel crow from his watch tower on the dead top of a great elm. Deeper into the shade the path ran until in the gloom it faded almost out of sight.

Soothed by the cool shade, Cameron loitered along the path, pausing to learn of Tim the names of plants and trees as he went.

"Ain't yeh never comin'?" called Mandy from the gloom far in front.

"What's all the rush?" replied Tim, impatiently, who loved nothing better than a quiet walk with Cameron through the woods.

"Rush? We'll be late, and I hate walkin' up before the hull crowd. Come on!" cried his sister in impatient tone.

"All right, Mandy, we're nearly through the woods. I begin to see the clearing yonder," said Cameron, pointing to where the light was beginning to show through the tree tops before them.

But they were late enough, and Mandy was glad of the cover of the opening hymn to allow her to find her way to a group of her girl friends, the males of the party taking shelter with a neighbouring group of their own sex near by.

Upon the sloping sides of the grassy hills and under the beech and maple trees, the vanguard of the retreating woods, sat the congregation, facing the preacher, who stood on the grassy level below. Behind them was the solid wall of thick woods, over them the spreading boughs, and far above the trees the blue summer sky, all the bluer for the little white clouds that sailed serene like ships upon a sea. At their feet lay the open country, checkered by the snake fences into fields of yellow, green, and brown, and rolling away to meet the woods at the horizon.

The Sabbath rest filled the sweet air, breathed from the shady woods, rested upon the checkered fields, and lifted with the hymn to the blue heaven above. A stately cathedral it was, this place of worship, filled with the incense of flowers and fields, arched by the high dome of heaven, and lighted by the glory of the setting sun.

Relieved by the walk for a time from the ache in his

head, Cameron surrendered himself to the mysterious influences of the place and the hour. He let his eyes wander over the fields below him to the far horizon, and beyond—beyond the woods, beyond the intervening leagues of land and sea—and was again gazing upon the sunlit loveliness of the Cuagh Oir. The Glen was abrim with golden light this summer evening, the purple was on the hills and the little loch gleamed sapphire at the bottom.

The preacher was reading his text.

"Unto one he gave five talents, to another two, to another one, to every man according to his several ability, and straightway took his journey," and so on to the end of that marvellously wise tale, wise with the wisdom of God, confirmed by the wisdom of human experience.

The Reverend Harper Freeman's voice could hardly, even by courtesy, be called musical; in fact, it was harsh and strident; but this evening the hills, and the trees, and the wide open spaces, Nature's mighty modulator, subdued the harshness, so that the voice rolled up to the people clear, full, and sonorous. Nor was the preacher possessed of great learning nor endued with the gift of eloquence. He had, however, a shrewd knowledge of his people and of their ways and of their needs, and he had a kindly heart, and, more than all, he had the preacher's gift, the divine capacity for taking fire.

For a time his words fell unheeded upon Cameron's outer ear.

"To every man his own endowments, some great, some small, but, mark you, no man left quite poverty-stricken. God gives every man his chance. No man can look God in the face, not one of you here can say that you have had no chance."

Cameron's vagrant mind, suddenly recalled, responded with a quick assent. Opportunity? Endowment? Yes, surely. His mind flashed back over the years of his education at the Academy and the University, long lazy years. How little he had made of them! Others had turned them into the gold of success. He wondered how old Dunn was getting on, and Linklater, and little Martin. How far away seemed those days, and yet only some four or five months separated him from them.

"One was a failure, a dead, flat failure," continued the preacher. "Not so much a wicked man, no murderer, no drunkard, no gambler, but a miserable failure. Poor fellow! At the end of life a wretched bankrupt, losing even his original endowment. How would you like to come home after ten, twenty, thirty years of experiment with life and confess to your father that you were dead broke and no good?"

Again Cameron's mind came back from its wandering with a start. Go back to his father a failure! He drew his lip down hard over his teeth. Not while he lived! And yet, what was there in prospect for him? His whole soul revolted against the dreary monotony and the narrowness of his present life, and yet, what other path lay open? Cameron went straying in fancy over the past, or in excursions into the future, while, parallel with his rambling, the sermon continued to make its way through its various heads and particulars.

"Why?" The voice of the preacher rose clear, dominant, arresting. "Why did he fail so abjectly, so meanly, so despicably? For there is no excuse for a failure. Listen! No man *need* fail. A man who is a failure is a mean, selfish, lazy chump." Mr. Freeman was colloquial, if anything. "Some men pity him. I don't. I have no use for him, and he is the one thing in all the world that God himself has no use for."

Again Cameron's mind was jerked back as a runaway horse by a rein. So far his life had been a failure. Was there then no excuse for failure? What of his upbringing, his education, his environment? He had been indulging the habit during these last weeks of shifting responsibility from himself for what he had become.

"What was the cause of this young man's failure?" reiterated the preacher. The preacher had a wholesome belief in the value of reiteration. He had a habit of rubbing in his points. "He blamed the boss. Listen to his impudence! 'I knew thee to be a hard man.' He blamed his own temperament and disposition. 'I was afraid.' But the boss brings him up sharp and short. 'Quit lying!' he said. 'I'll tell you what's wrong with you. You've got a mean heart, you ain't honest, and you're too lazy to live. Here, take that money from him and give it to the man that can do most with it, and take this useless loafer out of my sight.' And served him right, too, say I, impudent, lazy liar."

Cameron found his mind rising in wrathful defense of the unhappy wretched failure in the story. But the preacher was utterly relentless and proceeded to enlarge upon the character of the unhappy wretch.

"Impudent! The way to tell an impudent man is to let him talk. Now listen to this man cheek the boss! 'I knew you,' he said. 'You skin everybody in sight.' I have always noticed," remarked the preacher, with a twinkle in his eye, "that the hired man who can't keep up his end is the kind that cheeks the boss. And so it is with life. Why, some men would cheek Almighty God. They turn right round and face the other way when God is explaining things to them, when He is persuading them, when He is trying to help them. Then they glance back over their shoulders and say, 'Aw, gwan! I know better than you.' Think of the impudence of them! That's what many a man does with God. With *God,* mind you! *God!* Your Father in heaven, your Brother, your Saviour, God as you know him in the Man of Galilee, the Man you always see with the sick and the outcast and the broken-hearted. It is this God that owns you and all you've got—be honest and say so. You must begin by getting right with God."

"God!" Once more Cameron went wandering back into the far away days of childhood. God was very near then, and very friendly. How well he remembered when his mother had tucked him in at night and had kissed him and had put out the light. He never felt alone and afraid, for she left him, so she said, with God. It was God who took his mother's place, near to his bedside. In those days God seemed very near and very kind. He remembered his mother's look one day when he declared to her that he could hear God breathing just beside him in the dark. How remote God seemed to-day and how shadowy, and, yes, he had to confess it, unfriendly. He heard no more of the sermon. With a curious ache in his heart he allowed his mind to dwell amid those happy, happy memories when his mother and God were the nearest and dearest to him of all he knew. It may have been the ache in his head or the oppressive languor that seemed to possess his body, but throughout the prayer that followed the sermon he was conscious chiefly of a great longing for his mother's touch upon his head, and with that a longing for his boyhood's sense of the friendly God in his heart.

And so as the preacher led them up to God in prayer,

Cameron bowed his head with the others, thankful that he could still believe that, though clouds and darkness might be about Him, God was not beyond the reach of the soul's cry nor quite unmoved by human need. And for the first time for years he sent forth as a little child his cry of need, "God help me! God help me!"

CHAPTER VII

THE CHIVAREE

THERE was still light enough to see. The last hymn was announced. Cameron was conscious of a deep, poignant emotion. He glanced swiftly about him. The eyes of all were upon the preacher's face while he read in slow sonorous tones the words of the old Methodist hymn:

> "Come, Thou Fount of every blessing!
> Tune my heart to sing Thy grace;"

all except the group of young men of whom Perkins was the centre, who, by means of the saccharine medium known as conversation lozenges, were seeking to divert the attention of the band of young girls sitting before them. Among these sat Mandy. As his eye rested upon the billowy outlines of her figure, struggling with the limitations of her white blouse, tricked out with pink ribbons, he was conscious of a wave of mingled pity and disgust. Dull, stupid, and vulgar she looked. It was at her that Perkins was flipping his conversation lozenges. One fell upon her hymn book. With a start she glanced about. Not an eye except Cameron's was turned her way. With a smile and a blush that burned deep under the dull tan of her neck and cheek she took the lozenge, read its inscription, burning a deeper red. The words which she had read she took as Cameron's. She turned her eyes full upon his face. The light of tremulous joy in their lovely depths startled and thrilled him. A snicker from the group of young men behind roused in him a deep indignation. They were taking their coarse fun out of this simple-minded girl. Cameron's furious glance at them appeared only to increase their amusement. It did not lessen Cameron's embarrassment and rage that now and then during the reading of the hymn Mandy's eyes were turned upon him as if with new understanding. Enraged with himself, and more with the group of hoodlums behind him, Cameron stood for the closing hymn with his arms folded across his breast. At the second verse a hand touched his arm. It was Mandy offering him her book. Once more a snicker from the group of delighted observers behind him stirred his indignation on behalf of this awkward and untutored girl. He forced himself to listen to the words of the third verse, which rose clear and sonorous in the preacher's voice:

> "Here I raise my Ebenezer,
> Hither by Thy help I'm come;
> And I hope, by Thy good pleasure,
> Safely to arrive at home."

The serene assurance of the old Methodist hymn rose triumphant in the singing, an assurance born of an experience of past conflict ending in triumph. That note of high and serene confidence conjured up with a flash of memory his mother's face. That was her characteristic, a serene, undismayed courage. In the darkest hours that steady flame of courage never died down.

But once more he was recalled to the service of the hour by a voice, rich, full, low, yet of wonderful power, singing the old words. It took him a moment or two to discover that it was Mandy singing beside him. Her face was turned from him and upwards towards the trees above her, through the network of whose leaves the stars were beginning to shine. Amazed, enthralled, he listened to the flowing melody of her voice. It was like the song of a brook running deep in the forest shade, full toned yet soft, quiet yet thrilling. She seemed to have forgotten her surroundings. Her soul was holding converse with the Eternal. He lost sight of the coarse and fleshly habiliments in the glimpse he caught of the soul that lived within, pure, it seemed to him, tender, and good. His heart went out to the girl in a new pity. Before the hymn was done she turned her face towards him, and, whether it was the magic of her voice, or the glorious splendour of her eyes, or the mystic touch of the fast darkening night, her face seemed to have lost much of its coarseness and all of its stupidity.

As the congregation dispersed, Cameron, in silence, and with the spell of her voice still upon him, walked quietly beside Mandy towards the gap in the fence leading to the high road. Behind him came Perkins with his group of friends, chaffing with each other and with the girls walking in front of them. As Cameron was stepping over the rails where the fence had been let down, one of the young men following stumbled heavily against him, nearly throwing him down, and before he could recover himself Perkins had taken his place by Mandy's side and seized her arm. There was a general laugh at what was considered a perfectly fair and not unusual piece of jockeying in the squiring of young damsels. The proper procedure in such a case was that the discomfited cavalier should bide his time and serve a like turn upon his rival, the young lady meanwhile maintaining an attitude purely passive. But Mandy was not so minded. Releasing herself from Perkins' grasp, she turned upon the group of young men following, exclaiming angrily, "You ought to be ashamed of yourself, Sam Sailor!" Then, moving to Cameron's side, she said in a clear, distinct voice:

"Mr. Cameron, would you please take my book for me?"

"Come on, boys!" said Perkins, with his never failing laugh. "I guess we're not in this."

"Take your medicine, Perkins," laughed one of his friends.

"Yes, I'll take it all right," replied Perkins. But the laugh could not conceal the shake of passion in his voice. "It will work, too, you bet!"

So saying, he strode off into the gathering gloom followed by his friends.

"Come along, Mr. Cameron," said Mandy with a silly giggle. "I guess we don't need them fellows. They can't fool us, can they?"

Her manner, her speech, her laugh rudely dissipated all Cameron's new feeling towards her. The whole episode filled him only with disgust and annoyance.

"Come, then," he said, almost roughly. "We shall need to hurry, for there is a storm coming up."

Mandy glanced at the gathering clouds.

"My goodness!" she cried; "it's comin' up fast. My! I hate to git my clothes wet." And off she set at a rapid pace, keeping abreast of her companion and making gay but elephantine attempts at sprightly conversation. Before Cameron's unsympathetic silence, however, all her sprightly attempts came to abject failure.

"What's the matter with you?" at length she asked. "Don't you want to see me home?"

"What?" said Cameron, abruptly, for his thoughts were far away. "Oh, nonsense! Of course! Why not? But we shall certainly be caught in the storm. Let us hurry. Here, let me take your arm."

His manner was brusque, almost rude.

"Oh, I guess I can get along," replied Mandy, catching off her hat and gathering up her skirt over her shoulders, "but we'll have to hustle, for I'd hate to have you get wet." Her imperturbable good humour and her solicitude for him rebuked Cameron for his abruptness.

"I hope you will not get wet," he said.

"Oh, don't you worry about me. I ain't salt nor sugar, but I forgot all about your bein' sick." And with laboured breath poor Mandy hurried through the growing darkness with Cameron keeping close by her side. "We won't be long now," she panted, as they turned from the side line towards their own gate.

As if in reply to her words there sounded from behind the fence and close to their side a long loud howl. Cameron gave a start.

"Great Cæsar! What dog is that?" he exclaimed.

"Oh," said Mandy coolly, "guess it's MacKenzie's Carlo."

Immediately there rose from the fence on the other side an answering howl, followed by a full chorus of howls and yelps mingled with a bawling of calves and the ringing of cow bells, as if a dozen curs or more were in full cry after a herd of cattle. Cameron stood still in bewildered amazement.

"What the deuce are they at?" he cried, peering through the darkness.

"Huh!" grunted Mandy. "Them's curs all right, but they ain't much dog. You wait till I see them fellows. They'll pay for this, you bet!"

"Do you mean to say these are not dogs?" cried Cameron, speaking in her ear, so great was the din.

"Dogs?" answered Mandy with indignant scorn. "Naw! Just or'nary curs! Come along," she cried, catching his arm, "let's hurry."

"Here!" he cried, suddenly wrenching himself free, "I am going to see into this."

"No, no!" cried Mandy, gripping his arm once more with her strong hands. "They will hurt you. Come on! We're just home. You can see them again. No, I won't let you go."

In vain he struggled. Her strong hands held him fast. Suddenly there was a succession of short, sharp barks. Immediately dead silence fell. Not a sound could be heard, not a shape seen.

"Come out into the open, you cowardly curs!" shouted Cameron. "Come on! One, two, three at a time, if you dare!"

But silence answered him.

"Come," said Mandy in a low voice, "let's hurry. It's goin' to rain. Come on! Come along!"

Cameron stood irresolute. Then arose out of the black darkness a long quavering cat call. With a sudden dash Cameron sprang towards the fence. Instantly there was a sound of running feet through the plowed field on the other side, then silence.

"Come back, you cowards!" raged Cameron. "Isn't there a man among you?"

For answer a clod came hurtling through the dark and struck with a thud upon the fence. Immediately, as if at a signal, there fell about Cameron a perfect hail of clods and even stones.

"Oh! Oh!" shrieked Mandy, rushing towards him and throwing herself between him and the falling missiles. "Come away! Come away! They'll just kill you."

For answer Cameron put his arms about her and drew her behind him, shielding her as best he could with his body.

"Do you want to kill a woman?" he called aloud.

At once the hail of clods ceased and, raging as he was, Mandy dragged him homeward. At the door of the house he made to turn back.

"Not much, you don't," said Mandy, stoutly, "or I go with you."

"Oh, all right," said Cameron, "let them go. They are only a lot of curs, anyway."

For a few minutes they stood and talked in the kitchen, Cameron making light of the incident and making strenuous efforts to dissemble the rage that filled his soul. After a few minutes conversation Cameron announced his intention of going to bed, while Mandy passed upstairs. He left the house and stole down the lane toward the road. The throbbing pain in his head was forgotten in the blind rage that possessed him. He had only one longing, to stand within striking distance of the cowardly curs, only one fear, that they should escape him. Swiftly, silently, he stole down the lane, every nerve, every muscle tense as a steel spring. His throat was hot, his eyes so dazzled that he could scarcely see; his breath came in quick gasps; his hands were trembling as with a nervous chill. The storm had partially blown away. It had become so light that he could dimly discern a number of figures at the entrance to the lane. Having his quarry in sight, Cameron crouched in the fence corner, holding hard by the rail till he should become master of himself. He could hear their explosions of suppressed laughter. It was some minutes before he had himself in hand, then with a swift silent run he stood among them. So busy were they in recounting the various incidents in the recent "chivaree," that before they were aware Cameron was upon them. At his approach the circle broke and scattered, some flying to the fence. But Perkins with some others stood their ground.

"Hello, Cameron!" drawled Perkins. "Did you see our cows? I thought I heard some of them down the line."

For answer Cameron launched himself at him like a bolt from a bow. There was a single sharp crack and Perkins was literally lifted clear off his feet and hurled back upon the road, where he lay still. Fiercely Cameron faced round to the next man, but he gave back quickly. A third sprang to throw himself upon Cameron, but once more Cameron's hand shot forward and his assailant was hurled back heavily into the arms of his friends. Before Cameron could strike again a young giant, known as Sam Sailor, flung his arms about him, crying—

"Tut-tut, young fellow, this won't do, you know. Can't you take a bit of fun?"

For answer Cameron clinched him savagely, gripping him by the throat and planting two heavy blows upon his ribs.

"Here—boys," gasped the young fellow, "he's—chokin'—the—life—out—of me."

From all sides they threw themselves upon him and, striking, kicking, fighting furiously, Cameron went down under the struggling mass, his hand still gripping the throat it had seized.

"Say! He's a regular bull-dog," cried one. "Git hold of his legs and yank him off," which, with shouts and laughter, they proceeded to do and piled themselves upon him, chanting the refrain—"More beef! More beef!"

A few minutes more of frantic struggling and a wild agonised scream rose from beneath the mass of men.

"Git off, boys! Git off!" roared the young giant. "I'm afraid he's hurt."

Flinging them off on either side, he stood up and waited for their victim to rise. But Cameron lay on his face, moaning and writhing, on the ground.

"Say, boys," said Sam, kneeling down beside him, "I'm afraid he's hurted bad."

In his writhing Cameron lifted one leg. It toppled over to one side.

"Jumpin' Jeremiah!" said Sam in an awed voice. "His leg's broke! What in Sam Hill can we do?"

As he spoke there was a sound of running feet, coming down the lane. The moon, shining through the breaking clouds, revealed a figure with floating garments rapidly approaching.

"My cats!" cried Sam in a terrified voice. "It's Mandy."

Like leaves before a sudden gust of wind the group scattered and only Sam was left.

"What—what are you doin'?" panted Mandy. "Where is he? Oh, is that him?" She flung herself down in the dust beside Cameron and turned him over. His face was white, his eyes glazed. He looked like death. "Oh! Oh!" she moaned. "Have they killed you? Have they killed you?" She gathered his head upon her knees, moaning like a wounded animal.

"Good Lord, Mandy, don't go on like that!" cried Sam in a horrified voice. "It's only his leg broke."

Mandy laid his head gently down, then sprang to her feet.

"Only his leg broke? Who done it? Who done it, tell me? Who done it?" she panted, her voice rising with her gasping breath. "What coward done it? Was it you, Sam Sailor?"

"Guess we're all in it," said Sam stupidly. "It was jist a bit of fun, Mandy."

For answer she swung her heavy hand hard upon Sam's face.

"Say, Mandy! Hold hard!" cried Sam, surprise and the weight of the blow almost knocking him off his feet.

"You cowardly brute!" she gasped. "Get out of my sight. Oh, what shall we do?" She dropped on her knees and took Cameron's head once more in her arms. "What shall we do?"

"Guess we'll have to git him in somewheres," said Sam. "How can we carry him though? If we had some kind of a stretcher?"

"Wait! I know," cried Mandy, flying off up the lane. Before many minutes had passed she had returned, breathing hard.

"It's—the—milkhouse—door," she said. "I—guess that'll—do."

"That'll do all right, Mandy. Now I wish some of them fellers would come."

Sam pulled off his coat and made of it a pillow, then stood up looking for help. His eye fell upon the prostrate and senseless form of Perkins.

"Say, what'll we do with him?" he said, pointing to the silent figure.

"Who is it?" enquired Mandy. "What's the matter?"

"It's Perkins," replied Sam. "He hit him a terrible crack."

"Perkins!" said Mandy with scorn. "Let him lie, the dog. Come on, take his head."

"You can't do it, Mandy, no use trying. You can't do it."

"Come on, I tell you," she said fiercely. "Quit your

jawin'. He may be dyin' for all I know. I'd carry him alone if it wasn't for his broken leg." Slowly, painfully they carried him to the house and to the front door.

"Wait a minute!" said Mandy. "I'll have to git things fixed a bit. We mustn't wake mother. It would scare her to death."

She passed quickly into the house and soon Sam saw a light pass from room to room. In a few moments Mandy reappeared at the front door.

"Quick!" whispered Sam. "He's comin' to."

"Oh, thank goodness!" cried Mandy. "Let's git him in before he wakes."

Once more they lifted their burden and with infinite difficulty and much painful manoeuvering they got the injured man through the doors and upon the spare room bed.

"And now, Sam Sailor," cried Mandy, coming close to him, "you jist hitch up Deck and hustle for the doctor if ever you did in your life. Don't wait for nothin', but go! Go!" She fairly pushed him out of the door, running with him towards the stable. "Oh, Sam, hurry!" she pleaded, "for if this man should die I will never be the like again." Her face was white, her eyes glowing like great stars; her voice was soft and tremulous with tears.

Sam stood for a moment gazing as if upon a vision.

"What are you lookin' at?" she cried, stamping her foot and pushing him away.

"Jumpin' Jeremiah!" muttered Sam, as he ran towards the stable. "Is that Mandy Haley? Guess we don't know much about her."

His nimble fingers soon had Dexter hitched to the buggy and speeding down the lane at a pace sufficiently rapid to suit the high spirit of even that fiery young colt.

At the high road he came upon his friends, some of whom were working with Perkins, others conversing in awed and hurried undertones.

"Hello, Sam!" they called. "Hold up!"

"I'm in a hurry, boys, don't stop me. I'm scared to death. And you better git home. She'll be down on you again."

"How is he?" cried a voice.

"Don't know. I'm goin' for the doctor, and the sooner we git that doctor the better for everybody around." And Sam disappeared in a whirl of dust.

"Say! Who would a thought it?" he mused. "That Mandy Haley? She's a terror. And them eyes! Oh, git on, Deck, what you monkeyin' about? Wonder if she's gone on that young feller? I guess she is all right! Say, wasn't that a clout he handed Perkins. And didn't she give me one. But them eyes! Mandy Haley! By the jumpin' Jeremiah! And the way she looks at a feller! Here, Deck, what you foolin' about? Gwan now, or you'll git into trouble."

Deck, who had been indulging himself in a series of leaps and plunges, shying at even the most familiar objects by the road side, settled down at length to a businesslike trot which brought him to the doctor's door in about fifteen minutes from the Haleys' gate. But to Sam's dismay the doctor had gone to Cramm's Mill, six or seven miles away, and would not be back till the morning. Sam was in a quandary. There was another doctor at Brookfield, five miles further on, but there was a possibility that he also might be out.

"Say, there ain't no use goin' back without a doctor. She'd—she'd—Jumpin' Jeremiah! What would she do?

Say, Deck, you've got to git down to business. We're goin' to the city. There are doctors there thick as hair on a dog. We'll try Dr. Turnbull. Say, it'll be great if we could git him! Deck, we'll do it! But you got to git up and dust."

And this Deck proceeded to do to such good purpose that in about an hour's time he stood before Dr. Turnbull's door in the city, somewhat wet, it is true, but with his fiery spirit still untamed.

Here again adverse fate met the unfortunate Sam.

"Doctor Turnbull's no at home," said the maid, smart with cap and apron, who opened the door.

"How long will he be gone?" enquired Sam, wondering what she had on her head, and why.

"There's no tellin'. An hour, or two hours, or three."

"Three hours?" echoed Sam. "Say, a feller might kick the bucket in that time."

The maid smiled an undisturbed smile.

"Bucket? What bucket, eh? What bucket are ye talkin' aboot?" she enquired.

"Say, you're smart, ain't yeh! But I got a young feller that's broke his leg and—"

"His leg?" said the maid indifferently. "Well, he's got another?"

"Yes, you bet he has, but one leg ain't much good without the other. How would you like to hop around on one leg? And he's hurt inside, too, his lights, I guess, and other things." Sam's anatomical knowledge was somewhat vague. "And besides, his girl's takin' on awful."

"Oh, is she indeed?" replied the maid, this item apparently being to her of the very slightest importance.

"Say, if you only saw her," said Sam.

"Pretty, I suppose," said the maid with a touch of scorn.

"Pretty? No, ugly as a hedge fence. But say, I wish she was here right now. She'd bring you to your—to time, you bet."

"Would she, now? I'd sort her." And the little maid's black eyes snapped.

"Say, what'll I do? Jist got to have a doctor."

"Ye'll no git him till to-morrow."

"To-morrow?"

"How far oot are ye?"

"Twelve miles."

"Twelve miles? Ye'll no get him a minute afore to-morrow noon."

"Say, that young feller'll croak, sure. Away from home too. No friends. All his folks in Scotland."

"Scotland, did ye say?" Something appeared to wake up in the little maid. "Look here, why don't ye get a doctor instead o' daunderin' your time here?"

"Git a doctor?" echoed Sam in vast surprise. "And ain't I tryin' to git a doctor? Where'll I git a doctor?"

"Go to the hospital, ye gawk, and ask for Dr. Turnbull, and tell him the young lad is a stranger and that his folk are in Scotland. Hoots, ye gomeril, be off noo, an' the puir lad wantin' ye. Come, I'll pit ye on yer way." The maid by her speech was obviously excited.

Sam glanced at the clock as he passed out. He had been away an hour and a half.

"Jumpin' Jeremiah! I've got to hurry. She'll take my head off."

"Of course ye have," said the maid sharply. "Go down two streets there, then take the first turn to your left and go straight on for half a dozen blocks or so.

Mind ye tell the doctor the lad's frae Scotland!" she cried to Sam as he drove off.

At the hospital Sam was fortunate enough to catch Dr. Turnbull in the hall with one or two others, just as they were about to pass into the consulting room. Such was Sam's desperate state of mind that he went straight up to the group.

"I want Dr. Turnbull," he said.

"There he is before you," replied a sharp-faced young doctor, pointing to a benevolent looking old gentleman.

"Dr. Turnbull, there's a young feller hurt dreadful out our way. His leg's broke. Guess he's hurt inside too. And he's a stranger. His folks are all in Scotland. Guess he's dyin', and I've got—I've got a horse and buggy at the door. I can git you out and back in a jiffy. Say, doctor, I'm all ready to start."

A smile passed over the faces of the group. But Dr. Turnbull had too long experience with desperate cases and with desperate men.

"My dear Sir," he replied, "I cannot go for some hours."

"Doctor, I want you now. I got to have somebody right now."

"A broken leg?" mused the doctor.

"Yes, and hurt inside."

"How did it happen?" said the doctor.

"Eh? I don't know exactly," replied Sam, taken somewhat aback. "Somethin' fell on him. But he needs you bad."

"I can't go, my man, but we'll find some one. What's his name did you say?"

"His name is Cameron, and he's from Scotland."

"Cameron?" said the sharp-faced young doctor. "What does he look like?"

"Look like?" said Sam in a perplexed voice. "Well, the girls all think he looks pretty good. He's dark complected and he's a mighty smart young feller. Great on jumpin' and runnin'. Say, he's a crackajack. Why, at the Dominion Day picnic! But you must a' heard about him. He's the chap, you know, that won the hundred yards. Plays the pipes and—"

"Plays the pipes?" cried Dr. Turnbull and the young doctor together.

"And his name's Cameron?" continued the young doctor. "I wonder now if—"

"I say, Martin," said Dr. Turnbull, "I think you had better go. The case may be urgent."

"Cameron!" cried Martin again. "I bet my hat it's— Here, wait till I get my coat. I'll be with you in a jerk. Have you got a good horse?"

"He's all right," said Sam. "He'll git you there in an hour."

"An hour? How far is it?"

"Twelve miles."

"Great heavens! Come, then, get a move on!"

And so it came that within an hour Cameron, opening his eyes, looked up into the face of his friend.

"Martin! By Jove!" he said, and closed his eyes again. "Martin!" he said again, looking upon the familiar face. "Say, old boy, is this a dream? I seem to be having lots of them."

"It's no dream, old chap, but what in the mischief is the matter? What does all this fever mean? Let's look at you."

A brief examination was enough to show the doctor that a broken leg was the least of Cameron's trouble. A hasty investigation of the resources of the farm house determined the doctor's course.

"This man has typhoid fever, a bad case too," he said to Mandy. "We will take him in to the hospital."

"The hospital?" cried Mandy fiercely. "Will **you**, then?"

"He will be a lot of trouble to you," said the doctor.

"Trouble? Trouble? What are you talkin' about?"

"We're awful busy, Mandy," interposed the mother, who had been roused from her bed.

"Oh, shucks, mother! Oh, don't send him away," she pleaded. "I can nurse him, just as easy." She paused, with quivering lips.

"It will be much better for the patient to be in the hospital. He will get constant and systematic care. He will be under my own observation every hour. I assure you it will be better for him," said the doctor.

"Better for him?" echoed Mandy in a faint voice. "Well, let him go."

In less than an hour's time, such was Dr. Martin's energetic promptness, he had his patient comfortably placed in the democrat on an improvised stretcher and on his way to the city hospital.

And thus it came about that the problem of his leave-taking, which had vexed Cameron for so many days, was solved.

CHAPTER VIII

IN APPLE TIME

"A NOTHER basket of eggs, Mr. Cameron, and such delicious cream! I am deeply grieved to see you so nearly well."

"Grieved?"

"For you will be leaving us of course."

"Thanks, that is kind of you."

"And there will be an end to eggs and cream. Ah! You are a lucky man." And the trim, neat, bright-faced nurse shook her finger at him.

"So I have often remarked to myself these six weeks."

"A friend is a great discovery and by these same tokens you have found one."

"Truly, they have been more than kind."

"This makes the twelfth visit in six weeks," said the nurse. "In busy harvest and threshing time, too. Do you know what that means?"

"To a certain extent. It is awfully good of them."

"But she is shy, shy—and I think she is afraid of *you.* Her chief interest appears to be in the kitchen, which she has never failed to visit."

The blood slowly rose in Cameron's face, from which the summer tan had all been bleached by his six weeks' fight with fever, but he made no reply to the brisk, sharp-eyed, sharp-minded little nurse.

"And I know she is dying to see you, and, indeed," she chuckled, "it might do you good. She is truly wonderful." And again the nurse laughed. "Don't you think you could bear a visit?" The smile broadened upon her face.

But unaware she had touched a sensitive spot in her patient, his Highland pride.

"I shall be more than pleased to have an opportunity to thank Miss Haley for her great kindness," he replied with dignity.

"All right," replied the nurse. "I shall bring her in. Now don't excite yourself. That fever is not so far away. And only a few minutes. When we farmers go calling—I am a farmer, remember, and know them well —when we go calling we take our knitting and spend the afternoon."

In a few moments she returned with Mandy. The difference between the stout, red-faced, coarse-featured, obtrusively healthy country girl, heavy of foot and hand, slow of speech and awkward of manner, and the neat, quick, deft-fingered, bright-faced nurse was so marked that Cameron could hardly control the wave of pity that swept through his heart, for he could see that even Mandy herself was vividly aware of the contrast. In vain Cameron tried to put her at her ease. She simply sat and stared, now at the walls, now at the floor, refusing for a time to utter more than monosyllables, punctuated with giggles.

"I want to thank you for the eggs and cream. They are fine," said Cameron heartily.

"Oh, pshaw, that's nothin'! Lots more where they come from," replied Mandy with a giggle.

"But it's a long way for you to drive; and in the busy time too."

"Oh, we had to come in anyway for things," replied Mandy, making light of her service.

"You are all well?"

"Oh, pretty middlin'. Ma ain't right smart. She's too much to do, and that's the truth."

"And the boys?" Cameron hesitated to be more specific.

"Oh, there's nothin' eatin' them. I don't bother with them much." Mandy was desperately twisting her white cotton gloves.

At this point the nurse, with a final warning to the patient not to talk too much and not to excite himself, left the room. In a moment Mandy's whole manner changed.

"Say!" she cried in a hurried voice; "Perkins is left."

"Left?"

"I couldn't jist stand him after—after—that night. Dad wanted him to stay, but I couldn't jist stand him, and so he quit."

"Quit?"

"I jist hate him since—since—that night. When I think of what he done I could kill him. My, I was glad to see him lyin' there in the dust!" Mandy's words came hot and fast. "They might 'a killed you." For the first time in the interview she looked fairly into Cameron's eyes. "My, you do look awful!" she said, with difficulty commanding her voice.

"Nonsense, Mandy! You see, it wasn't my leg that hurt me. It was the fever that pulled me down."

"Oh, I'll never forget that night!" cried Mandy, struggling to keep her lips from quivering.

"Nor will I ever forget what you did for me that night, Mandy. Sam told me all about it. I shall always be your friend."

For a moment longer she held him with her eyes. Then her face grew suddenly pale and, with voice and hands trembling, she said:

"I must go. Good-by."

He took her great red hand in his long thin fingers.

"Good-by, Mandy, and thank you."

"My!" she said, looking down at the fingers she held in her hand. "Your hands is awful thin. Are you sure goin' to git better?"

"Of course I am, and I am coming out to see you before I go."

She sat down quickly, still holding his hand, as if he had struck her a heavy blow.

"Before you go? Where?" Her voice was hardly above a whisper; her face was white, her lips beyond her control.

"Out West to seek my fortune." His voice was jaunty and he feigned not to see her distress. "I shall be walking in a couple of weeks or so, eh, nurse?"

"A couple of weeks?" replied the nurse, who had just entered. "Yes, if you are good."

Mandy hastily rose.

"But if you are not," continued the nurse severely, "it may be months. Stay, Miss Haley, I am going to bring Mr. Cameron his afternoon tea and you can have some with him. Indeed, you look quite done up. I am sure all that work you have been telling me about is too much for you."

Her kindly tones broke the last shred of Mandy's self-control. She sank into her chair, covered her face with her great red hands and burst into tempestuous weeping. Cameron sat up quickly.

"What in the name of goodness is wrong, Mandy?"

"Lie down at once, Mr. Cameron!" said the nurse sternly. "Hush, hush, Miss Haley! You ought to be ashamed of yourself! Don't you know that you are hurting him?"

She could have chosen no better word. In an instant

Mandy was on her feet, mopping off her face and choking down her sobs.

"Ain't I a fool?" she cried angrily. "A blamed fool. Well, I won't bother you any longer. Guess I'll go now. Good-by all." Without another look at Cameron she was gone.

Cameron lay back upon his pillows, white and nerveless.

"Now can you tell me," he panted, "what's up?"

"Search me!" said the nurse gaily, "but I forbid you to speak a single word for half an hour. Here, drink this right off! Now, not a word! What will Dr. Martin say? Not a word! Yes, I shall see her safely off the place. Quiet now!" She kept up a continuous stream of sprightly chatter to cover her own anxiety and to turn the current of her patient's thoughts. By the time she had reached the entrance hall, however, Mandy had vanished.

"Great silly goose!" said the indignant nurse. "I'd see myself far enough before I'd give myself away like that. Little fool! He'll have a temperature sure and I will catch it. Bah! These girls! Next time she sees him it will not be here. I hope the doctor will just give me an hour to get him quiet again."

But in this hope she was disappointed, for upon her return to her patient she found Dr. Martin in the room. His face was grave.

"What's up, nurse? What is the meaning of this rotten pulse? What has he been having to eat?"

"Well, Dr. Martin, I may as well confess my sins," replied the nurse, "for there is no use trying to deceive you anyway. Mr. Cameron has had a visitor and she has excited him."

"Ah!" said the doctor in a relieved tone. "A visitor!

A lady visitor! A charming, sympathetic, interested, and interesting visitor."

"Exactly!" said the nurse with a giggle.

"It was Miss Haley, Martin," said Cameron gravely.

The doctor looked puzzled.

"The daughter of the farmer with whom I was working," explained Cameron.

"Ah, I remember her," said the doctor. "And a deuce of a time I had with her, too, getting you away from her, if I remember aright. I trust there is nothing seriously wrong in that quarter?" said Martin with unusual gravity.

"Oh, quit it, Martin!" said Cameron impatiently. "Don't rag. She's an awful decent sort. Her looks are not the best of her."

"Ah! I am relieved to hear that," said the doctor earnestly.

"She is very kind, indeed," said the nurse. "For these six weeks she has fed us up with eggs and cream so that both my patient and myself have fared sumptuously every day. Indeed, if it should continue much longer I shall have to ask an additional allowance for a new uniform. I have promised that Mr. Cameron shall visit the farm within two weeks if he behaves well."

"Exactly!" replied the doctor. "In two weeks if he is good. The only question that troubles me is—is it quite safe? You see in his present weak condition his susceptibility is decidedly emphasised, his resisting power is low, and who knows what might happen, especially if she should insist? I shall not soon forget the look in her eye when she dared me to lay a finger upon his person."

"Oh, cut it out, Martin!" said Cameron. "You make

me weary." He lay back on his pillow and closed his eyes.

The nurse threw a signal to the doctor.

"All right, old man, we must stop this chaff. Buck up and in two weeks we will let you go where you like. I have something in mind for you, but we won't speak of it to-day."

The harvest was safely stored. The yellow stubble showed the fields at rest, but the vivid green of the new fall wheat proclaimed the astounding and familiar fact that once more Nature had begun her ancient perennial miracle. For in those fields of vivid green the harvest of the coming year was already on the way. On these green fields the snowy mantle would lie soft and protecting all the long winter through and when the spring suns would shine again the fall wheat would be a month or more on the way towards maturity.

Somehow the country looked more rested, fresher, cleaner to Cameron than when he had last looked upon it in late August. The rain had washed the dust from the earth's face and from the green sward that bordered the grey ribbon of the high road that led out from the city. The pastures and the hay meadows and the turnip fields were all in their freshest green, and beyond the fields the forest stood glorious in all its autumn splendour, the ash trees bright yellow, the oaks rich brown, and the maples all the colours of the rainbow. In the orchard—ah, the wonder and the joy of it! even the bare and bony limbs of the apple trees only helped to reveal the sumptuous wealth of their luscious fruit. For it was apple time in the land! The evanescent harvest apples were long since gone, the snows were past their best, the pippins were mellowing under the sharp persuasion of the nippy, frosty nights and the brave gallantry of the sunny days. In this ancient warfare between the frosty nights and the gallant sunny days the apples ripened rapidly; and well that they should, for the warfare could not be for long. Already in the early morning hours the vanguard of winter's fierce hosts was to be seen flaunting its hoary banners even in the very face of the gallant sun so bravely making stand against it. But it was the time of the year in which men felt it good to be alive, for there was in the air that tang that gives speed to the blood, spring to the muscle, edge to the appetite, courage to the soul, and zest to life—the apple time of the year.

It was in apple time that Cameron came back to the farm. Under compulsion of Mandy, Haley had found it necessary to drive into the city for some things for the "women folk" and, being in the city, he had called for Cameron and had brought him out. Under compulsion, not at all because Haley was indifferent to the prospect of a visit from his former hired man, not alone because the fall plowing was pressing and the threshing gang was in the neighbourhood, but chiefly because, through the channel of Dr. Martin, the little nurse, and Mandy, it had come to be known in the Haley household and in the country side that the hired man was a "great swell in the old country," and Haley's sturdy independence shrank from anything that savoured of "suckin' round a swell," as he graphically put it. But Mandy scouted this idea and waited for the coming of the expected guest with no embarrassment from the knowledge that he had been in the old country "a great swell."

Hence when, through a crack beside the window blind, she saw him, a poor, pale shadow, descending wearily and painfully from the buggy, the great mother heart in the girl welled with pity. She could hardly forbear rushing out to carry him bodily in her strong arms to the spare room and lay him where she had once helped to lay him the night of the tragedy some eight weeks before. But in this matter she had learned her lesson. She remembered the little nurse and her indignant scorn of the lack of self-control she had shown on the occasion of her last visit to the hospital. So, instead of rushing forth, she clutched the curtains and forced herself to stand still, whispering to herself the while, "Oh, he will die sure! He will die sure!" But when she looked upon him seated comfortably in the kitchen with a steaming glass of ginger and whiskey, her mother's unfailing remedy for "anything wrong with the insides," she knew he would not die and her joy overflowed in boisterous welcome.

For five days they all, from Haley to Tim, gave him of their very best, seeking to hold him among them for the winter, for they had learned that his mind was set upon the West, till Cameron was ashamed, knowing that he must go.

The last afternoon they all spent in the orchard. The Gravensteins, in which species of apple Haley was a specialist, were being picked, and picked with the greatest care, Cameron plucking them from the limbs and dropping them into a basket held by Mandy below. It was one of those sunny days when, after weeks of chilly absence, summer comes again and makes the world glow with warmth and kindly life and quickens in the heart the blood's flow. Cameron was full of talk and fuller of laughter than his wont; indeed he was vexed to find himself struggling to maintain unbroken the flow of laughter and of talk. But in Mandy there was neither speech nor laughter, only a quiet dignity that disturbed and rebuked him.

The last tree of Gravensteins was picked and then there came the time of parting. Cameron, with a man's selfish desire for some token of a woman's adoration, even although he well knew that he could make no return, lingered in the farewell, hoping for some sign in the plain quiet face and the wonderful eyes with their new mystery that when he had gone he would not be forgotten; but though the lips quivered pitifully and the heavy face grew drawn and old and the eyes glowed with a deeper fire, the words, when they came, came quietly and the eyes looked steadily upon him, except that for one brief moment a fire leaped in them and quickly died down. But when the buggy, with Tim driving, had passed down the lane, behind the curtain of the spare room the girl stood looking through the crack beside the blind, with both hands pressed upon her bosom, her breath coming in sobs, her blue lips murmuring brokenly, "Good-by, good-by! Oh, why did you come at all? But, oh, I'm glad you came! God help me, I'm glad you came!" Then, when the buggy had turned down the side lane and out of sight, she knelt beside the bed and kissed, again and again, with tender, reverent kisses, the pillow where his head had lain.

BOOK THREE

CHAPTER I

THE CAMP BY THE GAP

ON the foot-hills' side of The Gap, on a grassy plain bounded on three sides by the Bow River and on the other by ragged hills and broken timber, stood Surveyor McIvor's camp, three white tents, seeming wondrously insignificant in the shadow of the mighty Rockies, but cosy enough. For on this April day the sun was riding high in the heavens in all his new spring glory, where a few days ago and for many months past the storm king with relentless rigour had raged, searching with pitiless fury these rock-ribbed hills and threatening these white tents and their dwellers with dire destruction. But threaten though he might and pin them though he did beneath their frail canvas covers, he could not make that gang beat retreat. McIvor was of the kind that takes no back trail. In the late fall he had set out to run the line through The Gap, and after many wanderings through the coulees of the foot-hills and after many vain attempts, he had finally made choice of his route and had brought his men, burnt black with chinook and frost and sun, hither to The Gap's mouth. Every chain length in those weary marches was a battle ground, every pillar, every picket stood a monument of victory. McIvor's advance through the foot-hill country to The Gap had been one unbroken succession of fierce fights with Nature's most terrifying forces, a triumphal march of heroes who bore on their faces and on their bodies the scars and laurels of the campaign. But to McIvor and his gang it was all in the day's work.

To Cameron the winter had brought an experience of

a life hitherto undreamed of, but never even in its wildest blizzards did he cherish anything but gratitude to his friend Martin, who had got him attached to McIvor's survey party. For McIvor was a man to "tie to," as Martin said, and to Cameron he was a continual cause of wonder and admiration. He was a big man, with a big man's quiet strength, patient, fearless of men and things, reverent toward Nature's forces, which it was his life's business to know, to measure, to control, and, if need be, to fight, careful of his men, whether amid the perils of the march, or amid the more deadly perils of trading post and railway construction camp. Cameron never could forget the thrill of admiration that swept his soul one night in Taylor's billiard and gambling "joint" down at the post where the Elbow joins the Bow, when McIvor, without bluff or bluster, took his chainman and his French-Canadian cook, the latter frothing mad with "Jamaica Ginger" and "Pain-killer," out of the hands of the gang of bad men from across the line who had marked them as lambs for the fleecing. It was not the courage of his big chief so much that had filled Cameron with amazed respect and admiration as the calm indifference to every consideration but that of getting his men out of harm's way, and the cool-headed directness of the method he employed.

"Come along, boys," McIvor had said, gripping them by their coat collars. "I don't pay you good money for this sort of thing." And so saying he had lifted them clear from their seats, upsetting the table, ignoring utterly the roaring oaths of the discomfited gamblers. What would have been the result none could say, for one of the gamblers had whipped out his gun and with sulphurous oaths was conducting a vigourous demonstration behind the unconscious back of McIvor, when there strolled into the room and through the crowd of men scattering to cover, a tall slim youngster in the red jacket and pill-box cap of that world-famous body of military guardians of law and order, the North West Mounted Police. Not while he lived would Cameron forget the scene that followed. With an air of lazy nonchalance the youngster strode quietly up to the desperado flourishing his gun and asked in a tone that indicated curiosity more than anything else, "What are you doing with that thing?"

"I'll show yeh!" roared the man in his face, continuing to pour forth a torrent of oaths.

"Put it down there!" said the youngster in a smooth and silky voice, pointing to a table near by. "You don't need that in this country."

The man paused in his demonstration and for a moment or two stood in amazed silence. The audacity of the youngster appeared to paralyse his powers of speech and action.

"Put it down there, my man. Do you hear?" The voice was still smooth, but through the silky tones there ran a fibre of steel. Still the desperado stood gazing at him. "Quick, do you hear?" There was a sudden sharp ring of imperious, of overwhelming authority, and, to the amazement of the crowd of men who stood breathless and silent about, there followed one of those phenomena which experts in psychology delight to explain, but which no man can understand. Without a word the gambler slowly laid upon the table his gun, upon whose handle were many notches, the tally of human lives it had accounted for in the hands of this same desperado.

"What is this for?" continued the young man, gently touching the belt of cartridges. "Take it off!"

The belt found its place beside the gun.

"Now, listen!" gravely continued the youngster. "I give you twenty-four hours to leave this post, and if after twenty-four hours you are found here it will be bad for you. Get out!"

The man, still silent, slunk out from the room. Irresistible authority seemed to go with the word that sent him forth, and rightly so, for behind that word lay the full weight of Great Britain's mighty empire. It was Cameron's first experience of the North West Mounted Police, that famous corps of frontier riders who for more than a quarter of a century have ridden the marches of Great Britain's territories in the far northwest land, keeping intact the Pax Britannica amid the wild turmoil of pioneer days. To the North West Mounted Police and to the pioneer missionary it is due that Canada has never had within her borders what is known as a "wild and wicked West." It was doubtless owing to the presence of that slim youngster in his scarlet jacket and pill-box cap that McIvor got his men safely away without a hole in his back and that his gang were quietly finishing their morning meal this shining April day, in their camp by the Bow River in the shadow of the big white peaks that guard The Gap.

Breakfast over, McIvor heaved his great form to the perpendicular.

"How is the foot, Cameron?" he asked, filling his pipe preparatory to the march.

"Just about fit," replied Cameron.

"Better take another day," replied the chief. "You can get up wood and get supper ready. Benoit will be glad enough to go out and take your place for another day on the line."

"Sure ting," cried Benoit, the jolly French-Canadian

cook. "Good for my healt. He's tak off my front porsch here." And the cook patted affectionately the little round paunch that marred the symmetry of his figure.

"You ought to get Cameron to swap jobs with you, Benny," said one of the axemen. "You would be a dandy in about another month."

Benoit let his eye run critically over the line of his person.

"Bon! Dat's true, for sure. In tree, four mont I mak de beeg spark on de girl, me."

"You bet, Benny!" cried the axeman. "You'll break 'em all up."

"Sure ting!" cried Benny, catching up a coal for his pipe. "By by, Cameron. *Au revoir.* I go for tak some more slice from my porsch."

"Good-bye, Benny," cried Cameron. "It is your last chance, for to-morrow I give you back your job. I don't want any 'front porsch' on me."

"Ho! ho!" laughed Benny scornfully, as he turned to hurry after his chief. "Dat's not moch front porsch on you. Dat's one rail fence—clabbord."

And indeed Benoit was right, for there was no "porsch" or sign of one on Cameron's lean and muscular frame. The daily battle with winter's fierce frosts and blizzards, the strenuous toil, the hard food had done their work on him. Strong, firm-knit, clean and sound, hard and fit, he had come through his first Canadian winter. No man in the camp, not even the chief himself, could "bush" him in a day's work. He had gained enormously in strength lately, and though the lines of his frame still ran to angles, he had gained in weight as well. Never in the days of his finest training was he as fit to get the best out of himself as now. An injured foot had held him in camp for a week, but the injury was now almost completely repaired and the week's change of work only served to replenish his store of snap and vim.

An hour or two sufficed to put the camp in the perfect order that he knew Benoit would consider ideal and to get all in readiness for the evening meal when the gang should return. He had the day before him and what a day it was! Cameron lay upon a buffalo skin in front of the cook-tent, content with all the world and for the moment with himself. Six months ago he had engaged as an axeman in the surveyors' gang at $30 per month and "found," being regarded more in the light of a supernumerary and more or less of a burden than anything else. Now he was drawing double the wage as rodman, and, of all the gang, stood second to none in McIvor's regard. In this new venture he had come nearer to making good than ever before in his life. So in full content with himself he allowed his eyes to roam over the brown grassy plain that sloped to the Bow in front, and over the Bow to the successive lines of hills, rounded except where the black rocks broke jagged through the turf, and upward over the rounded hills to the grey sides of the mighty masses of the mountains, and still upward to where the white peaks lost themselves in the shining blue of the sky. Behind him a coulee ran back between hills to a line of timber, and beyond the timber more hills and more valleys, and ever growing higher and deeper till they ran into the bases of the great Rockies.

As Cameron lay thus luxuriating upon his buffalo skin and lazily watching the hills across the river through the curling wreaths that gracefully and fragrantly rose from his briar root, there broke from the line of timber two jumping deer, buck and doe, the latter slow-footed because heavy with young. Behind them in

hot pursuit came a pack of yelping coyotes. The doe
was evidently hard pressed. The buck was running
easily, but gallantly refusing to abandon his mate to her
cowardly foes. Straight for the icy river they made,
plunged in, and, making the crossing, were safe from
their pursuing enemy. Cameron, intent upon fresh meat,
ran for McIvor's Winchester, but ere he could buckle
round him a cartridge belt and throw on his hunting
jacket the deer had disappeared over the rounded top
of the nearest hill. Up the coulee he ran to the timber
and there waited, but there was no sign of his game.
Cautiously he made his way through the timber and
dropped into the next valley circling westward towards
the mountains. The deer, however, had completely vanished. Turning back upon his tracks, he once more
pierced the thin line of timber, when just across the
coulee, some three hundred yards away, on the sky line,
head up and sniffing the wind, stood the buck in clear
view. Taking hurried aim Cameron fired. The buck
dropped as if dead. Marking the spot, Cameron hurried
forward, but to his surprise found only a trail of blood.
  "He's badly hit though," he said to himself. "I must
get the poor chap now at all costs." Swiftly he took up
the trail, but though the blood stains continued clear
and fresh he could get no sight of the wounded animal.
Hour after hour he kept up the chase, forgetful of everything but his determination to bring back his game to
camp. From the freshness of the stains he knew that
the buck could not be far ahead and from the footprints
it was clear that the animal was going on three legs.
  "The beggar is hearing me and so keeps out of sight,"
said Cameron as he paused to listen. He resolved to
proceed more slowly and with greater caution, but
though he followed this plan for another half hour it

brought him no better success. The day was fast passing and he could not much longer continue his pursuit. He became conscious of pain in his injured foot. He sat down to rest and to review his situation. For the first time he observed that the bright sky of the morning had become overcast with a film of hazy cloud and that the temperature was rapidly falling. Prudence suggested that he should at once make his way back to camp, but with the instinct of the true hunter he was loath to abandon the poor wounded beast to its unhappy fate. He resolved to make one further attempt. Refreshed by his brief rest, but with an increasing sense of pain in his foot, he climbed the slight rising ground before him, cautiously pushed his way through some scrub, and there, within easy shot, stood the buck, with drooping head and evidently with strength nearly done. Cameron took careful aim—there must be no mistake this time—and fired. The buck leaped high in the air, dropped and lay still. The first shot had broken his leg, the second had pierced his heart.

Cameron hurried forward and proceeded to skin the animal. But soon he abandoned this operation. "We'll come and get him to-morrow," he muttered, "and he is better with his skin on. Meantime we'll have a steak, however." He hung a bit of skin from a pole to keep off the wolves and selected a choice cut for the supper. He worked hurriedly, for the sudden drop in the temperature was ominous of a serious disturbance in the weather, but before he had finished he was startled to observe a large snowflake lazily flutter to the ground beside him. He glanced towards the sky and found that the filmy clouds were rapidly assuming definite shape and that the sun had almost disappeared. Hurriedly he took his bearings and, calculating as best he could the direction of the camp, set off, well satisfied with the outcome of his expedition and filled with the pleasing anticipation of a venison supper for himself and the rest of the gang.

The country was for the most part open except for patches of timber here and there, and with a clear sky the difficulty of maintaining direction would have been but slight. With the sky overcast, however, this difficulty was sensibly increased. He had not kept an accurate reckoning of his course, but from the character of the ground he knew that he must be a considerable distance westward of the line of the camp. His training during the winter in holding a line of march helped him now to maintain his course steadily in one direction. The temperature was still dropping rapidly. Over the woods hung a dead stillness, except for the lonely call of an occasional crow or for the scream of the impudent whiskey-jack. But soon even these became silent. As he surmounted each hill top Cameron took his bearings afresh and anxiously scanned the sky for weather signs. In spite of himself there crept over him a sense of foreboding, which he impatiently tried to shake off.

"I can't be so very far from camp now," he said to himself, looking at his watch. "It is just four. There are three good hours till dark."

A little to the west of his line of march stood a high hill which appeared to dominate the surrounding country and on its top a lofty pine. "I'll just shin up that tree," said he. "I ought to get a sight of the Bow from the top." In a few minutes he had reached the top of the hill, but even in those minutes the atmosphere had thickened. "Jove, it's getting dark!" he exclaimed. "It can't be near sundown yet. Did I make a mistake in the time?" He looked at his watch again. It showed a quarter after four. "I must get a look at this country." Hurriedly he threw off his jacket and proceeded to climb the big pine, which, fortunately, was limbed to the ground. From the lofty top his eye could sweep the country for many miles around. Over the great peaks of the Rockies to the west dark masses of black cloud shot with purple and liver-coloured bars hung like a pall. To the north a line of clear light was still visible, but over the foot-hills towards east and south there lay almost invisible a shimmering haze, soft and translucent, and above the haze a heavy curtain, while over the immediate landscape there shone a strange weird light, through which there floated down to earth large white snowflakes. Not a breath of air moved across the face of the hills, but still as the dead they lay in solemn oppressive silence. Far to the north Cameron caught the gleam of water.

"That must be the Bow," he said to himself. "I am miles too far toward the mountains. I don't like the look of that haze and that cloud bank. There is a blizzard on the move if this winter's experience teaches me anything."

He had once been caught in a blizzard, but on that occasion he was with McIvor. He was conscious now of a little clutch at his heart as he remembered that desperate struggle for breath, for life it seemed to him, behind McIvor's broad back. The country was full of stories of men being overwhelmed by the choking, drifting whirl of snow. He knew how swift at times the on-fall of the blizzard could be, how long the storm could last, how appalling the cold could become. What should he do? He must think and act swiftly. That gleaming water near which his camp lay was, at the very best going, two hours distant. The blizzard might strike at any moment and once it struck all hope of advance would be cut off. He resolved to seek the best cover available and wait till the storm should pass. He had his deer meat with him and matches. Could he but make shelter he doubted not but he could weather the storm. Swiftly he swept the landscape for a spot to camp. Half a mile away he spied a little coulee where several valleys appeared to lose themselves in thick underbrush. He resolved to make for that spot. Hurriedly he slipped down the tree, donned belt and jacket and, picking up gun and venison, set off at a run for the spot he had selected. A puff of wind touched his cheek. He glanced up and about him. The flakes of snow were no longer floating gently down, but were slanting in long straight lines across the landscape. His heart took a quicker beat.

"It is coming, sure enough," he said to himself between his teeth, "and a bad one too at that." He quickened his pace to racing speed. Down the hill, across the valley and up the next slope he ran without pause, but as he reached the top of the slope a sound arrested him, a deep, muffled, hissing roar, and mingled with it the beating of a thousand wings. Beyond the top of the next hill there hung from sky to earth the curtain, thick, black, portentous, and swiftly making approach, devouring the landscape as it came and filling his ears with its muffled, hissing roar.

In the coulee beyond that hill was the spot he had marked for his shelter. It was still some three hundred yards away. Could he beat that roaring, hissing, portentous cloud mass? It was extremely doubtful. Down the hill he ran, slipping, skating, pitching, till he struck the bottom, then up the opposite slope he struggled, straining every nerve and muscle. He glanced upward towards the top of the hill. Merciful heaven! There it was, that portentous cloud mass, roaring down upon him. Could he ever make that top? He ran a few steps further, then, dropping his gun, he clutched a small poplar and hung fast. A driving, blinding, choking, whirling mass of whiteness hurled itself at him, buffeting him heavily, filling eyes, ears, nose, and mouth, clutching at his arms and legs and body with a thousand impalpable insistent claws. For a moment or two he lost all sense of direction, all thought of advance. One instinct only he obeyed—to hold on for dear life to the swaying quivering poplar. The icy cold struck him to the heart, his bare fingers were fast freeezing. A few moments he hung, hoping for a lull in the fury of the blizzard, but lull there was none, only that choking, blinding, terrifying Thing that clutched and tore at him. His heart sank within him. This, then, was to be the end of him. A vision of his own body, stark and stiff, lying under a mound of drifting snow, swiftly passed before his mind. He threw it off wrathfully. "Not yet! Not just yet!" he shouted in defiance into the face of the howling storm.

Through the tumult and confusion of his thoughts one idea dominated—he must make the hill-top. Sliding his hands down the trunk of the little poplar he once more found his rifle and, laying it in the hollow of his arm, he hugged it close to his side, shoved his freezing hands into his pockets and, leaning hard against the driving blizzard, set off towards the hill-top. A few paces he made, then turning around leaned back upon the solid massive force of the wind till he could get breath. Again a few steps upward and again a rest against the wind. His courage began to come back.

"Aha!" he shouted at the storm. "Not yet! Not.

yet!" Gradually, and with growing courage, he fought his way to the top. At length he stood upon the storm-swept summit. "I say," he cried, heartening himself with his speech, "this is so much to the good anyway. Now for the coulee." But exactly where did it lie? Absolutely nothing could he see before him but this blinding, choking mass of whirling snow. He tried to recall the direction in relation to the hill as he had taken it from the top of the tree. How long ago that seemed! Was it minutes or hours? Downward and towards the left lay the coulee. He could hardly fail to strike it. Plunging headlong into the blizzard, he fought his way once more, step by step.

"It was jolly well like a scrimmage," he said grimly to the storm which began in his imagination to assume a kind of monstrous and savage personality. It heartened him much to remember his sensations in many a desperate struggle against the straining steaming mass of muscle and bone in the old fierce football fights. He recalled, too, a word of his old captain, "Never say die! The next minute may be better."

"Never say die!" he cried aloud in the face of his enemy. "But I wish to heaven I could get up some of that heat just now. This cold is going to be the death of me."

As he spoke he bumped into a small bushy spruce tree. "Hello! Here you are, eh!" he cried, determined to be cheerful. "Glad to meet you. Hope there are lots more of you." His hope was realised! A few more steps and he found himself in the heart of a spruce thicket.

"Thank God!" he exclaimed. Then again—"Yes, thank God it is!" It steadied his heart not a little to remember the picture in his mother's Bible that had so often stirred his youthful imagination of One standing in the fishing boat and bidding the storm be still. In the spruce thicket he stood some moments to regain his breath and strength.

"Now what next?" he asked himself. Although the thicket broke the force of the wind, something must be done, and quickly. Night was coming on and that meant an even intenser cold. His hands were numb. His hunting jacket was but slight protection against the driving wind and the bitter cold. If he could only light a fire! A difficult business in this tumultuous whirlwind and snow. He had learned something of this art, however, from his winter's experience. He began breaking from the spruce trees the dead dry twigs. Oh for some birch bark! Like a forgotten dream it came to him that from the tree top he had seen above the spruce thicket the tops of some white birch trees purpling under the touch of spring.

"Let's see! Those birches must be further to my left," he said, recalling their position. Painfully he forced his way through the scrubby underbrush. His foot struck hard against an obstruction that nearly threw him to the ground. It was a jutting rock. Peering through the white mass before his eyes, he could make out a great black, looming mass. Eagerly he pushed forward. It was a towering slab of rock. Following it round on the lee side, he suddenly halted with a shout of grateful triumph. A great section had fallen out of the rock, forming a little cave, storm-proof and dry.

"Thank God once more!" he said, and this time with even deeper reverence. "Now for a fire. If I could only get some birch bark."

He placed his rifle in a corner of the cave and went out on his hunt. "By Jove, I must hurry, or my hands will be gone sure." Looking upwards in the shelter of the rock through the driving snow he saw the bare tops of trees. "Birch, too, as I am alive!" he cried, and plunging through the bushes came upon a clump of white birches.

With fingers that could hardly hold the curling bark he gathered a few bunches and hurried back to the cave. Again he went forth and gathered from the standing trees an armful of dead dry limbs. "Good!" he cried aloud in triumph. "We're not beaten yet. Now for the fire and supper." He drew forth his steel matchbox with numb and shaking fingers, opened it and stood stricken dumb. There were only three matches in the box. Unreasoning terror seized him. Three chances for life! He chose a match, struck it, but in his numb and nerveless fingers the match snapped near the head. With a new terror seizing him he took a second match and struck it. The match flared, sputtering. Eagerly he thrust the birch bark at it; too eagerly, alas, for the bark rubbed out the tiny flame. He had one match left! One hope of life! He closed his matchbox. His hands were trembling with the cold and more with nervous fear that shook him in every limb. He could not bring himself to make the last attempt. Up and down the cave and out and in he stamped, beating his hands to bring back the blood and fighting hard to get back his nerve.

"This is all rotten funk!" he cried aloud, raging at himself. "I shall not be beaten."

Summoning all his powers, he once more pulled out his matchbox, rubbed his birch bark fine and, kneeling down, placed it between his knees under the shelter of his hunting jacket. Kneeling there with the matchbox in his hand, there fell upon his spirit a great calm. "Oh,

God!" he said quietly and with the conviction in his soul that there was One listening, "help me now." He opened the matchbox, took out the match, struck it carefully and laid it among the birch bark. For one heart-racking moment it flickered unsteadily, then, catching a resinous fibre of the bark, it flared up, shot out a tiny tongue to one of the heavier bunches, caught hold, sputtered, smoked, burst into flame. With the prayer still going in his heart, "God help me now," Cameron fed the flame with bits of bark and tiny twigs, adding more and more till the fire began to leap, dance, and snap, and at length gaining strength it roared its triumph over the grim terror so recently threatened.

For the present at least the blizzard was beaten.

"Now God be thanked for that," said Cameron. "For it was past my doing."

CHAPTER II

ON THE WINGS OF THE STORM

SHIVERING and hungry and fighting with sleep, Cameron stamped up and down his cave, making now and then excursions into the storm to replenish his fire. On sharpened sticks slices of venison were cooking for his supper. Outside the storm raged with greater violence than ever and into the cave the bitter cold penetrated, effectually neutralizing the warmth of the little fire, for the wood was hard to get and a larger fire he could not afford.

He looked at his watch and was amazed to find it only five o'clock. How long could he maintain this fight? His heart sank at the prospect of the long night before him. He sat down upon the rock close beside his cooking venison and in a few moments was fast asleep.

He awoke with a start and found that the fire had crept along a jutting branch and had reached his fingers. He sprang to his feet. The fire lay in smouldering embers, for the sticks were mere brushwood. A terrible fear seized him. His life depended upon the maintaining of this fire. Carefully he assembled the embers and nursed them into bright flame. At all costs he must keep awake. A further excursion into the woods for fuel thoroughly roused him from his sleep. Soon his fire was blazing brightly again.

Consulting his watch, he found that he must have slept half an hour. He determined that in order to keep himself awake and to provide against the growing cold he would lay in a stock of firewood, and so he began a systematic search for fallen trees that he might drag to his shelter.

As he was setting forth upon his search he became aware of a new sound mingling with the roaring of the storm about him, a soft, pounding, rhythmic sound. With every nerve strained he listened. It was like the beating of hoofs. He ran out into the storm and, holding his hands to his ears, bent forward to listen. Faintly over the roaring of the blizzard, and rising and falling with it, there came the sound of singing.

"Am I mad?" he said to himself, beating his head with his hands. He rushed into the cave, threw upon the fire all the brushwood he had gathered, until it sprang up into a great glare, lighting up the cave and its surroundings. Then he rushed forth once more to the turn of the rock. The singing could now be plainly heard.

"Three cheers for the red, white— Get on there, you variously coloured and multitudinously cursed brutes!— Three cheers for the red— Hie there, look out, Little Thunder! They are off to the left."

"Hello!" yelled Cameron at the top of his voice. "Hello, there!"

"Whoa!" yelled a voice sharply. The sound of hoof beats ceased and only the roaring of the blizzard could be heard.

"Hello!" cried Cameron again. "Who are you?" But only the gale answered him.

Again and again he called, but no voice replied. Once more he rushed into the cave, seized his rifle and fired a shot into the air.

"Crack-crack," two bullets spat against the rock over his head.

"Hold on there, you fool!" yelled Cameron, dodging

back behind the rock. "What are you shooting at? Hello there!" Still there was no reply.

Long he waited till, desperate with anxiety lest his unknown visitors should abandon him, he ran forward once more beyond the ledge of the rock, shouting, "Hello! Hello! Don't shoot! I'm coming out to you."

At the turn of the rocky ledge he paused, concentrating his powers to catch some sound other than the dull boom and hiss of the blizzard. Suddenly at his side something moved.

"Put up your hands, quick!"

A dark shape, with arm thrust straight before it, loomed through the drift of snow.

"Oh, I say—" began Cameron.

"Quick!" said the voice, with a terrible oath, "or I drop you where you stand."

"All right!" said Cameron, lifting up his hands with his rifle high above his head. "But hurry up! I can't stand this long. I am nearly frozen as it is."

The man came forward, still covering him with his pistol. He ran his free hand over Cameron's person.

"How many of you?" he asked, in a voice sharp and crisp.

"I am all alone. But hurry up! I am about all in."

"Lead on to your fire!" said the stranger. "But if you want to live, no monkey work. I've got you lined."

Cameron led the way to the fire. The stranger threw a swift glance around the cave, then, with eyes still holding Cameron, he whistled shrilly on his fingers. Almost immediately, it seemed to Cameron, there came into the light another man who proved to be an Indian, short, heavily built, with a face hideously ugly and rendered more repulsive by the small, red-rimmed, blood-shot eyes that seemed to Cameron to peer like gimlets into his very soul.

At a word of command the Indian possessed himself of Cameron's rifle and stood at the entrance.

"Now," said the stranger, "talk quick. Who are you? How did you come here? Quick and to the point."

"I am a surveyor," said Cameron briefly. "McIvor's gang. I was left at camp to cook, saw a deer, wounded it, followed it up, lost my way, the storm caught me, but, thank God, I found this cave, and with my last match lit the fire. I was trying to cook my venison when I heard you coming."

The grey-brown eyes of the stranger never left Cameron's face while he was speaking.

"You're a liar!" he said with cold insolence when Cameron had finished his tale. "You look to me like a blank blank horse thief or whiskey trader."

Faint as he was with cold and hunger, the deliberate insolence of the man stirred Cameron to sudden rage. The blood flooded his pale face.

"You coward!" he cried in a choking voice, gathering himself to spring at the man's throat.

But the stranger only laughed and, stepping backward, spoke a word to the Indian behind him. Before he could move Cameron found himself covered by the rifle with the malignant eye of the Indian behind it.

"Hold on, Little Thunder, drop it!" said the stranger with a slight laugh.

Reluctantly the rifle came down.

"All right, Mr. Surveyor," said the stranger with a good-natured laugh. "Pardon my abruptness. I was merely testing you. One cannot be too careful in these parts nowadays when the woods are full of horse thieves and whiskey runners. Oh, come on," he continued, glancing at Cameron's face, "I apologise. So you're lost, eh? Hungry too? Well, so am I, and though I was not going to feed just yet we may as well grub together. Bring the cattle into shelter here," he said to Little Thunder. "They will stand right enough. And get busy with the grub."

The Indian grunted a remonstrance.

"Oh, that's all right," replied the stranger. "Hand it over." He took Cameron's rifle from the Indian and set it in the corner. "Now get a move on! We have no time to waste."

So saying he hurried out himself into the storm. In a few minutes Cameron could hear the blows of an axe, and soon the stranger appeared with a load of dry wood with which he built up a blazing fire. He was followed shortly by the Indian, who from a sack drew out bacon, hardtack, and tea, and, with cooking utensils produced from another sack, speedily prepared supper.

"Pile in," said the stranger to Cameron, passing him the pan in which the bacon and venison had been fried. "Pass the tea, Little Thunder. No time to waste. We've got to hustle."

Cameron was only too eager to obey these orders, and in the generous warmth of the big fire and under the stimulus of the boiling tea his strength and nerve began to come back to him.

For some minutes he was too intent on satisfying his ravenous hunger to indulge in conversation with his host, but as his hunger became appeased he began to give his attention to the man who had so mysteriously blown in upon him out of the blizzard. There was something fascinating about the lean, clean-cut face with its firm lines about the mouth and chin and its deep-set brown-grey eyes that glittered like steel or shone like limpid pools of light according to the mood of the man. They were extraordinary eyes. Cameron remembered them like dagger points behind the pistol and then like kindly lights in a dark window when he had smiled. Just now as he sat eating with eager haste the eyes were staring forward into the fire out of deep sockets, with a far-away, reminiscent, kindly look in them. The lumberman's heavy skin-lined jacket and the overalls tucked into boots could not hide the athletic lines of the lithe muscular figure. Cameron looked at his hands with their long, sinewy fingers. "The hands of a gentleman," thought he. "What is his history? And where does he come from?"

"London's my home," said the stranger, answering Cameron's mental queries. "Name, Raven—Richard Colebrooke Raven—Dick for short; rancher, horse and cattle trader; East Kootenay; at present running in a stock of goods and horses; and caught like yourself in this beastly blizzard."

"My name's Cameron, and I'm from Edinburgh a year ago," replied Cameron briefly.

"Edinburgh? Knew it ten years ago. Quiet old town, quaint folk. Never know what they are thinking about you."

Cameron smiled. How well he remembered the calm, detached, critical but uncurious gaze with which the dwellers of the modern Athens were wont to regard mere outsiders.

"I know," he said. "I came from the North myself."

The stranger had apparently forgotten him and was gazing steadily into the fire. Suddenly, with extraordinary energy, he sprang from the ground where he had been sitting.

"Now," he cried, *"en avant!"*

"Where to?" asked Cameron, rising to his feet.

"East Kootenay, all the way, and hustle's the word."

"Not me," said Cameron. "I must get back to my camp. If you will kindly leave me some grub and some matches I shall be all right and very much obliged. McIvor will be searching for me to-morrow."

"Ha!" burst forth the stranger in vehement expletive. "Searching for you, heh?" He stood for a few moments in deep thought, then spoke to the Indian a few words in his own language. That individual, with a fierce glance towards Cameron, grunted a gruff reply.

"No, no," said Raven, also glancing at Cameron. Again the Indian spoke, this time with insistent fierceness. "No! no! you cold-blooded devil," replied the trader. "No! But," he added with emphasis, "we will take him with us. Pack! Here, bring in coat, mitts, socks, Little Thunder. And move quick, do you hear?" His voice rang out in imperious command.

Little Thunder, growling though he might, no longer delayed, but dived into the storm and in a few moments returned bearing a bag from which he drew the articles of clothing desired.

"But I am not going with you," said Cameron firmly. "I cannot desert my chief this way. It would give him no end of trouble. Leave me some matches and, if you can spare it, a little grub, and I shall do finely."

"Get these things on," replied Raven, "and quit talking. Don't be a fool! We simply can't leave you behind. If you only knew the alternative, you'd—"

Cameron glanced at the Indian. The eager fierce look on that hideous face startled him.

"We will send you back all safe in a few days," continued the trader with a smile. "Come, don't delay! March is the word."

"I won't go!" said Cameron resolutely. "I'll stay where I am."

"All right, you fool!" replied Raven with a savage oath. "Take your medicine then."

He nodded to the Indian. With a swift gleam of joy in his red-rimmed eyes the Indian reached swiftly for Cameron's rifle.

"No, too much noise," said Raven, coolly finishing the packing.

A swift flash of a knife in the firelight, and the Indian hurled himself upon the unsuspecting Cameron. But quick as was the attack Cameron was quicker. Gripping the Indian's uplifted wrist with his left hand, he brought his right with terrific force upon the point of his assailant's chin. The Indian spun round like a top and pitched out into the dark.

"Neatly done!" cried the trader with a great oath and a laugh. "Hold on, Little Thunder!" he continued, as the Indian reappeared, knife in hand. "He'll come now. Quiet, you beast! Ah-h-h! Would you?" He seized by the throat and wrist the Indian, who, frothing with rage and snarling like a wild animal, was struggling to reach Cameron again. "Down, you dog! Do you hear me?"

With a twist of his arms he brought the Indian to his knees and held him as he might a child. Quite suddenly the Indian grew still.

"Good!" said Raven. "Now, no more of this. Pack up."

Without a further word or glance at Cameron, Little Thunder gathered up the stuff and vanished.

"Now," continued the trader, "you perhaps see that

it would be wise for you to come along without further delay."

"All right," said Cameron, trembling with indignant rage, "but remember, you'll pay for this."

The trader smiled kindly upon him.

"Better get these things on," he said, pointing to the articles of clothing upon the cave floor. "The blizzard is gathering force and we have still some hours to ride. But," he continued, stepping close to Cameron and looking him in the eyes, "there must be no more nonsense. You can see my man is somewhat short in temper; and indeed mine is rather brittle at times."

For a single instant a smile curled the firm lips and half closed the steely eyes of the speaker, and, noting the smile and the steely gleam in the grey-brown eyes, Cameron hastily decided that he would no longer resist.

Warmed and fed and protected against the blizzard, but with his heart full of indignant wrath, Cameron found himself riding on a wretched cayuse before the trader whose horse could but dimly be seen through the storm, but which from his antics appeared to be possessed of a thousand demons.

"Steady, Nighthawk, old boy! We'll get 'em moving after a bit," said his master, soothing the kicking beast. "Aha, that was just a shade violent," he remonstrated, as the horse with a scream rushed open mouthed at a blundering pony and sent him scuttling forward in wild terror after the bunch already disappearing down the trail, following Little Thunder upon his broncho.

The blizzard was now in their back and, though its force was thereby greatly lessened, the black night was still thick with whirling snow and the cold grew more intense every moment. Cameron could hardly see his pony's ears, but, loping easily along the levels, scrambling wildly up the hills, and slithering recklessly down the slopes, the little brute followed without pause the cavalcade in front. How they kept the trail Cameron could not imagine, but, with the instinct of their breed, the ponies never faltered. Far before in the black blinding storm could be heard the voice of Little Thunder, rising and falling in a kind of singing chant, a chant which Cameron was afterwards to know right well.

> "Kai-yai, hai-yah! Hai! Hai!! Hai!!!
> Kai-yai, hai-yah! Hai! Hai!! Hai!!!"

Behind him came the trader, riding easily his demon-spirited broncho, and singing in full baritone the patriotic ode dear to Britishers the world over:

> "Three cheers for the red, white and blue!
> Three cheers for the red, white and blue!
> The army and navy for ever,
> Three cheers for the red, white and blue!"

As Cameron went pounding along through the howling blizzard, half asleep upon his loping, scrambling, slithering pony, with the "Kai-yai, hai-yah" of Little Thunder wailing down the storm from before him and the martial notes of the trader behind him demanding cheers for Her Majesty's naval and military forces, he seemed to himself to be in the grip of some ghastly nightmare which, try as he might, he was unable to shake off.

The ghastly unreality of the nightmare was dispelled by the sudden halt of the bunch of ponies in front.

"All off!" cried the trader, riding forward upon his broncho, which, apparently quite untired by the long night ride, danced forward through the bunch gaily biting and slashing as he went. "All off! Get them into the 'bunk-house' there, Little Thunder. Come along, Mr. Cameron, we have reached our camp. Take off the bridle and blanket and let your pony go."

Cameron did as he was told, and guided by the sound of the trader's voice made his way to a low log building which turned out to be the deserted "grub-house" of an old lumber camp.

"Come along," cried the trader heartily. "Welcome to Fifty Mile Camp. Its accommodation is somewhat limited, but we can at least offer you a bunk, grub, and fire, and these on a night like this are not to be despised." He fumbled around in the dark for a few moments and found and lit a candle stuck in an empty bottle. "There," he cried in a tone of genial hospitality and with a kindly smile, "get a fire on here and make yourself at home. Nighthawk demands my attention for the present. Don't look so glum, old boy," he added, slapping Cameron gaily on the back. "The worst is over." So saying, he disappeared into the blizzard, singing at the top of his voice in the cheeriest possible tones:

> "The army and navy for ever,
> Three cheers for the red, white and blue!"

and leaving Cameron sorely perplexed as to what manner of man this might be, who one moment could smile with all the malevolence of a fiend and again could welcome him with all the generous and genial hospitality he might show to a loved and long-lost friend.

CHAPTER III

THE STONIES

THE icy cold woke Cameron as the grey light came in through the dirty windows and the cracks between the logs of the grub-house. Already Little Thunder was awake and busy with the fire in the cracked and rusty stove. Cameron lay still and watched. Silently, swiftly the Indian moved about his work till the fire began to roar and the pot of snow on the top to melt. Then the trader awoke. With a single movement he was out upon the floor.

"All hands awake!" he shouted. "Aha, Mr. Cameron! Good sleep, eh? Slept like a bear myself. Now grub, and off! Still blowing, eh? Well, so much the better. There is a spot thirty miles on where we will be snug enough. How's breakfast, Little Thunder? This is our only chance to-day, so don't spare the grub."

Cameron made but slight reply. He was stiff and sore with the cold and the long ride of the day before. This, however, he minded but little. If he could only guess what lay before him. He was torn between anxiety and indignation. He could hardly make himself believe that he was alive and in his waking senses. Twenty-four hours ago he was breakfasting with McIvor and his gang in the camp by The Bow; now he was twenty or thirty miles away in the heart of the mountains and practically a prisoner in the hands of as blood-thirsty a looking Indian as he had ever seen, and a man who remained to him an inexplicable mystery. Who and what was this man? He scanned his face in the growing light. Strength, daring, alertness, yes, and kindliness, he read in the handsome, brown, lean face of this stranger, lit by its grey-brown hazel eyes and set off with brown wavy hair which the absence of a cap now for the first time revealed.

"He looks all right," Cameron said to himself. And yet when he recalled the smile that had curled these thin lips and half closed these hazel eyes in the cave the night before, and when he thought of that murderous attack of his Indian companion, he found it difficult wholly to trust the man who was at once his rescuer and his captor.

In the days of the early eighties there were weird stories floating about through the Western country of outlaw Indian traders whose chief stock for barter was a concoction which passed for whiskey, but the ingredients of which were principally high wines and tobacco juice, with a little molasses to sweeten it and a touch of blue stone to give it bite. Men of reckless daring were these traders, resourceful and relentless. For a bottle of their "hell-fire fluid" they would buy a buffalo hide, a pack of beaver skins, or a cayuse from an Indian without hesitation or remorse. With a keg or two of their deadly brew they would approach a tribe and strip it bare of a year's catch of furs.

In the fierce fights that often followed, the Indian, poorly armed and half dead with the poison he had drunk, would come off second best and many a wretched native was left to burn and blister upon the plains or among the coulees at the foothills to mark the trail of the whiskey runners.

In British territory all this style of barter was of course unlawful. The giving, selling, or trading of any sort of intoxicant to the Indians was absolutely prohibited. But it was a land of vast and mighty spaces, and everywhere were hiding places where armies could be safely disposed, and therefore there was small chance for the enforcement of the laws of the Dominion. There was little risk to the whiskey runners; and, indeed, however great the risk, the immense profits of their trade would have made them willing to take it.

Hence all through the Western plains the whiskey runners had their way to the degradation and demoralization of the unhappy natives and to the rapid decimation of their numbers. Horse thieves, too, and cattle "rustlers" operating on both sides of "the line" added to the general confusion and lawlessness that prevailed and rendered the lives and property of the few pioneer settlers insecure.

It was to deal with this situation that the Dominion Government organised and despatched the North West Mounted Police to Western Canada. Immediately upon the advent of this famous corps matters began to improve. The open ravages of the whiskey runners ceased and these daring outlaws were forced to carry on their fiendish business by midnight marches and through the secret trails and coulees of the foothills. The profits of the trade, however, were still great enough to tempt the more reckless and daring of these men. Cattle rustling and horse stealing still continued, but on a much smaller scale. To the whole country the advent of the police proved an incalculable blessing. But to the Indian tribes especially was this the case. The natives soon learned to regard the police officers as their friends. In them they found protection from the unscrupulous traders who had hitherto cheated them without mercy or conscience, as well as from the whiskey runners through whose devilish activities their people had suffered irreparable loss.

The administration of the law by the officers of the police with firm and patient justice put an end also to the frequent and bloody wars that had prevailed previously between the various tribes, till, by these wild and savage people the red coat came to be regarded with mingled awe and confidence, a terror to evil-doers and a protection to those that did well.

To which class did this man belong? This Cameron was utterly unable to decide.

With this problem vexing his mind he ate his breakfast in almost complete silence, making only monosyllabic replies to the trader's cheerful attempts at conversation.

Suddenly, with disconcerting accuracy, the trader seemed to read his mind.

"Now, Mr. Cameron," he said, pulling out his pipe, "we will have a smoke and a chat. Fill up." He passed Cameron his little bag of tobacco. "Last night things were somewhat strained," he continued. "Frankly, I confess, I took you at first for a whiskey runner and a horse thief, and having suffered from these gentlemen considerably I was taking no chances."

"Why force me to go with you, then?" asked Cameron angrily.

"Why? For your good. There is less danger both to you—and to me—with you under my eye," replied the trader with a smile.

"Yet your man would have murdered me?"

"Well, you see Little Thunder is one of the Blood Tribe and rather swift with his knife at times, I confess. Besides, his family has suffered at the hands of the whiskey runners. He is a chief and he owes it to these devils that he is out of a job just now. You may imagine he is somewhat touchy on the point of whiskey traders. "

"It was you set him on me," said Cameron, still wrathful.

"No, no," said the trader, laughing quietly. "That was merely to startle you out of your, pardon me, unreasonable obstinacy. You must believe me it was the only thing possible that you should accompany us, for if you were a whiskey runner then it was better for us that you should be under guard, and if you were a surveyor it was better for you that you should be in our care. Why, man, this storm may go for three days, and you would be stiff long before anyone could find you. No, no, I confess our measures may have seemed somewhat—ah—abrupt, but, believe me, they were necessary, and in a day or two you will acknowledge that I am in the right of it. Meantime let's trust each other, and there is my hand on it, Cameron."

There was no resisting the frank smile, the open manner of the man, and Cameron took the offered hand with a lighter heart than he had known for the last twelve hours.

"Now, then, that's settled," cried the trader, springing to his feet. "Cameron, you can pack this stuff together while Little Thunder and I dig out our bunch of horses. They will be half frozen and it will be hard to knock any life into them."

It was half an hour before Cameron had his packs ready, and, there being no sign of the trader, he put on his heavy coat, mitts, and cap and fought his way through the blizzard, which was still raging in full force, to the bunk-house, a log building about thirty feet long and half as wide, in which were huddled the horses and

ponies to the number of about twenty. Eight of the
ponies carried pack saddles, and so busy were Raven
and the Indian with the somewhat delicate operation
of assembling the packs that he was close upon them
before they were aware. Boxes and bags were strewn
about in orderly disorder, and on one side were several
small kegs. As Cameron drew near the Indian, who
was the first to notice him, gave a grunt.

"What the blank blank are you doing here?" cried
Raven with a string of oaths, flinging a buffalo robe
over the kegs. "My word! You startled me," he added
with a short laugh. "I haven't got used to you yet.
All right, Little Thunder, get these boxes together.
Bring that grey cayuse here, Cameron, the one with
the rope on near the door."

This was easier said than done, for the half-broken
brute snorted and plunged till Cameron, taking a turn
of the rope round his nose, forced him up through the
trembling, crowding bunch.

"Good!" said the trader. "You are all right. You
didn't learn to rope a cayuse in Edinburgh, I guess.
Here's his saddle. Cinch it on."

While Cameron was engaged in carrying out these
orders Little Thunder and the trader were busy roping
boxes and kegs into pack loads with a skill and dexterity that could only be the result of long practice.

"Now, then, Cameron, we'll load some of this
molasses on your pony."

So saying, Raven picked up one of the kegs.

"Hello, Little Thunder, this keg's leaking. It's lost
the plug, as I'm a sinner."

Sure enough, from a small auger hole golden syrup
was streaming over the edge of the keg.

"I am certain I put that plug in yesterday," said

Raven. "Must have been knocked out last night. Fortunately it stood right end up or we should have lost the whole keg."

While he was speaking he was shaping a small stick into a small plug, which he drove tight into the keg.

"That will fix it," he said. "Now then, put these boxes on the other side. That will do. Take your pony toward the door and tie him there. Little Thunder and I will load the rest and bring them up."

In a very short time all the remaining goods were packed into neat loads and lashed upon the pack ponies in such a careful manner that neither box nor keg could be seen outside the cover of blankets and buffalo skins.

"Now then," cried Raven. "Boots and saddles! We will give you a better mount to-day," he continued, selecting a stout built sorrel pony. "There you are! And a dandy he is, sure-footed as a goat and easy as a cradle. Now then, Nighthawk, we shall just clear out this bunch."

As he spoke he whipped the blanket off his horse. Cameron could not forbear an exclamation of wonder and admiration as his eyes fell upon Raven's horse. And not without reason, for Nighthawk was as near perfection as anything in horse flesh of his size could be. His coal-black satin skin, his fine flat legs, small delicate head, sloping hips, round and well ribbed barrel, all showed his breed. Rolling up the blanket, Raven strapped it to his saddle and, flinging himself astride his horse, gave a yell that galvanised the wretched, shivering, dispirited bunch into immediate life and activity.

"Get out the packers there, Little Thunder. Hurry up! Don't be all day. Cameron, fall behind with me."

Little Thunder seized the leading line of the first packer, leaped astride his own pony, and pushed out into the storm. But the rest of the animals held back and refused to face the blizzard. The traditions of the cayuse are unheroic in the matter of blizzards and are all in favor of turning tail to every storm that blows. But Nighthawk soon overcame their reluctance, whether traditional or otherwise. With a fury nothing less than demoniacal he fell upon the animals next him and inspired them with such terror that, plunging forward, they carried the bunch crowding through the door. It was no small achievement to turn some twenty shivering, balky, stubborn cayuses and bronchos out of their shelter and swing them through the mazes of the old lumber camp into the trail again. But with Little Thunder breaking the trail and chanting his encouraging refrain in front and the trader and his demoniac stallion dynamically bringing up the rear, this achievement was effected without the straying of a single animal. Raven was in great spirits, singing, shouting, and occasionally sending Nighthawk open-mouthed in a fierce charge upon the laggards hustling the long straggling line onwards through the whirling drifts without pause or falter. Occasionally he dropped back beside Cameron, who brought up the rear, bringing a word of encouragement or approval.

"How do they ever keep the trail?" asked Cameron on one of these occasions.

"Little Thunder does the trick. He is the greatest tracker in this country, unless it is his cayuse, which has a nose like a bloodhound and will keep the trail through three feet of snow. The rest of the bunch follow. They are afraid to do anything else in a blizzard like this."

So hour after hour, upward along mountainsides, for by this time they were far into the Rockies, and down again through thick standing forests in the valleys, across ravines and roaring torrents which the warm weather of the previous days had released from the glaciers, and over benches of open country, where the grass lay buried deep beneath the snow, they pounded along. The clouds of snow ever whirling about Cameron's head and in front of his eyes hid the distant landscape and engulfed the head of the cavalcade before him. Without initiative and without volition, but in a dreamy haze, he sat his pony to which he entrusted his life and fortune and waited for the will of his mysterious companion to develope.

About mid-day Nighthawk danced back out of the storm ahead and dropped in beside Cameron's pony.

"A chinook coming," said Raven. "Getting warmer, don't you notice?"

"No, I didn't notice, but now that you call attention to it I do feel a little more comfortable," replied Cameron.

"Sure thing. Rain in an hour."

"An hour? In six perhaps."

"In less than an hour," replied Raven, "the chinook will be here. We're riding into it. It blows down through the pass before us and it will lick up this snow in no time. You'll see the grass all about you before three hours are passed."

The event proved the truth of Raven's prediction. With incredible rapidity the temperature continued to rise. In half an hour Cameron discarded his mitts and unbuttoned his skin-lined jacket. The wind dropped to a gentle breeze, swinging more and more into the southwest, and before the hour was gone the sun was shining fitfully again and the snow had changed into a drizzling rain.

The extraordinary suddenness of these atmospheric changes only increased the sense of phantasmic unreality with which Cameron had been struggling during the past thirty-six hours. As the afternoon wore on the air became sensibly warmer. The moisture rose in steaming clouds from the mountainsides, the snow ran everywhere in gurgling rivulets, the rivulets became streams, the streams rivers, and the mountain torrents which they had easily forded earlier in the day threatened to sweep them away.

The trader's spirits appeared to rise with the temperature. He was in high glee. It was as if he had escaped some imminent peril.

"We will make it all right!" he shouted to Little Thunder as they paused for a few moments in a grassy glade. "Can we make the Forks before dark?"

Little Thunder's grunt might mean anything, but to the trader it expressed doubt.

"On then!" he shouted. "We must make these brutes get a move on. They'll feed when we camp."

So saying he hurled his horse upon the straggling bunch of ponies that were eagerly snatching mouthfuls of grass from which the chinook had already melted the snow. Mercilessly and savagely the trader, with whip and voice and charging stallion, hustled the wretched animals into the trail once more. And through the long afternoon, with unceasing and brutal ferocity, he belabored the faltering, stumbling, half-starved creatures, till from sheer exhaustion they were like to fall upon the trail. It was a weary business and disgusting, but the demon spirit of Nighthawk seemed to have passed into his master, and with an insistence that knew no mercy together they battered that wretched bunch up and down the long slopes till at length the merciful night fell upon the straggling, stumbling cavalcade and made a rapid pace impossible.

At the head of a long slope Little Thunder came to an abrupt halt, rode to the rear and grunted something to his chief.

"What?" cried Raven in a startled voice. "Stonies! Where?"

Little Thunder pointed.

"Did they see you?" This insult Little Thunder disdained to notice. "Good!" replied Raven. "Stay here, Cameron, we will take a look at them."

In a very few minutes he returned, an eager tone in his voice, an eager gleam in his eyes.

"Stonies!" he exclaimed. "And a big camp. On their way back from their winter's trapping. Old Macdougall himself in charge, I think. Do you know him?"

"I have heard of him," said Cameron, and his tone indicated his reverence for the aged pioneer Methodist missionary who had accomplished such marvels during his long years of service with his Indian flock and had gained such a wonderful control over them.

"Yes, he is all right," replied Raven, answering his tone. "He is a shrewd old boy, though. Looks mighty close after the trading end. Well, we will perhaps do a little trade ourselves. But we won't disturb the old man," he continued, as if to himself. "Come and take a look at them."

Little Thunder had halted at a spot where the trail forked. One part led to the right down the long slope of the mountain, the other to the left, gradually climbing toward the top. The Stonies had come by the right hand trail and were now camped off the trail on a little sheltered bench further down the side of the mountain and surrounded by a scattering group of tall pines. Through the misty night their camp fires burned cheerily, lighting up their lodges. Around the fires could be seen groups of men squatted on the ground and here and there among the lodges the squaws were busy, evidently preparing the evening meal. At one side of the camp could be distinguished a number of tethered ponies and near them others quietly grazing.

But though the camp lay only a few hundred yards away and on a lower level, not a sound came up from it to Cameron's ears except the occasional bark of a dog. The Indians are a silent people and move noiselessly through Nature's solitudes as if in reverence for her sacred mysteries.

"We won't disturb them," said Raven in a low tone. "We will slip past quietly."

"They come from Morleyville, don't they?" enquired Cameron.

"Yes."

"Why not visit the camp?" exclaimed Cameron eagerly. "I am sure Mr. Macdougall would be glad to see us. And why could not I go back with him? My camp is right on the trail to Morleyville."

Raven stood silent, evidently perplexed.

"Well," he replied hesitatingly, "we shall see later. Meantime let's get into camp ourselves. And no noise, please." His voice was low and stern.

Silently, and as swiftly as was consistent with silence, Little Thunder led his band of pack horses along the upper trail, the trader and Cameron bringing up the rear with the other ponies. For about half a mile they proceeded in this direction, then, turning sharply to the right, they cut across through the straggling woods, and so came upon the lower trail, beyond the encampment of the Stonies and well out of sight of it.

"We camp here," said Raven briefly. "But remember, no noise."

"What about visiting their camp?" enquired Cameron.

"There is no immediate hurry."

He spoke a few words to Little Thunder in Indian.

"Little Thunder thinks they may be Blackfeet. We can't be too careful. Now let's get grub."

Cameron made no reply. The trader's hesitating manner awakened all his former suspicions. He was firmly convinced the Indians were Stonies and he resolved that come what might he would make his escape to their camp.

Without unloading their packs they built their fire upon a large flat rock and there, crouching about it, for the mists were chilly, they had their supper.

In undertones Raven and Little Thunder conversed in the Indian speech. The gay careless air of the trader had given place to one of keen, purposeful determination. There was evidently serious business on foot. Immediately after supper Little Thunder vanished into the mist.

"We may as well make ourselves comfortable," said Raven, pulling a couple of buffalo skins from a pack and giving one to Cameron. "Little Thunder is gone to reconnoiter." He threw some sticks upon the fire. "Better go to sleep," he suggested. "We shall probably visit the camp in the morning if they should prove to be Stonies."

Cameron made no reply, but, lying down upon his buffalo skin, pretended to sleep, though with the firm resolve to keep awake. But he had passed through an exhausting day and before many minutes had passed he fell into a doze.

From this he awoke with a start, his ears filled with the sound of singing. Beyond the fire lay Raven upon his face, apparently sound asleep. The singing came from the direction of the Indian camp. Noiselessly he rose and stole up the trail to a point from which the camp was plainly visible. A wonderful scene lay before his eyes. A great fire burned in the centre of the camp and round the fire the whole band of Indians was gathered with their squaws in the background. In the centre of the circle stood a tall man with a venerable beard, apparently reading. After he had read the sound of singing once more rose upon the night air.

"Stonies, all right," said Cameron exultantly to himself. "And at evening prayers, too, by Jove."

He remembered hearing McIvor tell how the Stonies never went on a hunting expedition without their hymn books and never closed a day without their evening worship. The voices were high-pitched and thin, but from that distance they floated up soft and sweet. He could clearly distinguish the music of the old Methodist hymn, the words of which were quite familiar to him:

> "There is a fountain filled with blood
> Drawn from Immanuel's veins;
> And sinners plunged beneath that flood,
> Lose all their guilty stains."

Over and over again, with strange wild cadences of their own invention, the worshippers wailed forth the refrain,

> "Lose all their guilty stains."

Then, all kneeling, they went to prayer. Over all, the misty moon struggling through the broken clouds cast a pale and ghostly light. It was, to Cameron with his old-world religious conventions and traditions, a weirdly fascinating but intensely impressive scene. Afar beyond the valley, appeared in dim outline the great mountains, with their heads thrust up into the sky. Nearer at their bases gathered the pines, at first in solid gloomy masses, then, as they approached, in straggling groups, and at last singly, like tall sentinels on guard. On the grassy glade, surrounded by the sentinel pines, the circle of dusky worshippers, kneeling about their camp fire, lifted their faces heavenward and their hearts Godward in prayer, and as upon those dusky faces the firelight fell in fitful gleams, so upon their hearts, dark with the superstitions of a hundred generations, there fell the gleams of the torch held high by the hands of their dauntless ambassador of the blessed Gospel of the Grace of God.

With mingled feelings of reverence and of pity Cameron stood gazing down upon this scene, resolved more than ever to attach himself to this camp whose days closed with evening prayer.

"Impressive scene!" said a mocking voice in his ear.

Cameron started. A sudden feeling of repulsion seized him.

"Yes," he said gravely, "an impressive scene, in my eyes at least, and I should not wonder if in the eyes of God as well."

"Who knows?" said Raven gruffly, as they both turned back to the fire.

CHAPTER IV

THE DULL RED STAIN

THE minutes passed slowly. The scene in the camp of the Stonies that he had just witnessed drove all sleep from Cameron. He was firmly resolved that at the first opportunity he would make his break for liberty; for he was now fully aware that though not confessedly he was none the less really a prisoner.

As he lay intently thinking, forming and discarding plans of escape, two Indians, followed by Little Thunder, walked quietly within the circle of the firelight and with a nod and a grunt towards Raven sat down by the fire. Raven passed his tobacco bag, which, without a word, they accepted; and, filling their pipes, they gravely began to smoke.

"White Cloud," grunted Little Thunder, waving his hand to the first Indian. "Big Chief. Him," pointing to the second Indian, "White Cloud brother."

"My brothers had good hunting this year," said Raven.

The Indians grunted for reply.

"Your packs are heavy?"

Another grunt made answer.

"We have much goods," continued Raven. "But the time is short. Come and see."

Raven led them out into the dark towards the pack horse, Little Thunder remaining by the fire. From the darkness Cameron could hear Raven's voice in low tones and the Indians' guttural replies mingled with unusual laughter.

When they returned the change in their appearance was plainly visible. Their eyes were gleaming with an unnatural excitement, their grave and dignified demeanour had given place to an eager, almost childish excitement. Cameron did not need the whiff that came to him from their breath to explain the cause of this sudden change. The signs were to him only too familiar.

"My brothers will need to hurry," said Raven. "We move when the moon is high."

"Good!" replied White Cloud. "Go, quick." He waved his hand toward the dark. "Come." He brought it back again. "Heap quick." Without further word they vanished, silent as the shadows that swallowed them up.

"Now, then, Cameron, we have big business on foot. Up and give us a hand. Little Thunder, take the bunch down the trail a couple of miles and come back."

Selecting one of the pack ponies, he tied it to a pine tree and the others he hurried off with Little Thunder down the trail.

"Going to do some trading, are you?" enquired Cameron.

"Yes, if the price is right, though I'm not too keen," replied Raven, throwing himself down beside the fire.

"What are you after? Furs?"

"Yes, furs mostly. Anything they have to offer."

"What do you give in exchange?"

Raven threw him a sharp glance, but Cameron's face was turned toward the fire.

"Oh, various articles. Wearing apparel, tobacco, finery. Molasses too. They are very fond of molasses."

"Molasses?" echoed Cameron, with a touch of scorn. "It was not molasses they had to-night. Why did you give them whiskey?" he asked boldly.

Raven started. His eyes narrowed to two piercing points.

"Why? That's my business, my friend. I keep a flask to treat my guests occasionally. Have you any objection?"

"It is against the law, I understand, and mighty bad for the Indians."

"Against the law?" echoed Raven in childlike surprise. "You don't tell me!"

"So the Mounted Police declare," said Cameron, turning his eyes upon Raven's face.

"The Mounted Police!" exclaimed Raven, pouring forth a flood of oaths. "That! for the Mounted Police!" he said, snapping his fingers.

"But," replied Cameron, "I understood you very especially to object to the operations of the whiskey runners?"

"Whiskey runners? Who's speaking of whiskey runners? I'm talking of the approved method of treating our friends in this country, and if the police should interfere between me and my friends they would be carrying things a little too far. But all the same," he continued, hastily checking himself, "the police are all right. They put down a lot of lawlessness in this country. But I may as well say to you here, Mr. Cameron," he continued, "that there are certain things it is best not to see, or, having seen, to speedily forget." As he spoke these words his eyes narrowed again to two grey points that seemed to bore right through to Cameron's brain.

"This man is a very devil," thought Cameron to himself. "I was a fool not to see it before." But to the trader he said, "There are some things I would rather not see and some things I cannot forget."

Before another hour had passed the Stonies reappeared, this time on ponies. The trader made no move to meet them. He sat quietly smoking by the fire. Silently the Indians approached the fire and threw down a pack of furs.

"Huh!" said White Cloud. "Good! Ver good!" He opened his pack and spread out upon the rock with impressive deliberation its contents. And good they were, even to Cameron's uncultured eye. Wolf skins and bear, cinnamon and black, beaver, fox, and mink, as well as some magnificent specimens of mountain goat and sheep. "Good! Good! Big—fine—heap good!" White Cloud continued to exclaim as he displayed his collection.

Raven turned them over carelessly, feeling the furs, examining and weighing the pelts. Then going to the pack horse he returned and spread out upon the rock beside the furs the goods which he proposed to offer in exchange. And a pitiful display it was, gaudy calicoes and flimsy flannels, the brilliance of whose colour was only equalled by the shoddiness of the material, cheap domestic blankets, half wool half cotton, prepared especially for the Indian trade. These, with beads and buttons, trinkets, whole strings of brass rings, rolls of tobacco, bags of shot and powder, pot metal knives, and other articles, all bearing the stamp of glittering fraud, constituted his stock for barter. The Indians made strenuous efforts to maintain an air of dignified indifference, but the glitter in their eyes betrayed their eagerness. White Cloud picked up a goat skin, heavy with its deep silky fur and with its rich splendour covered over the glittering mass of Raven's cheap and tawdry stuff.

"Good trade," said White Cloud. "Him," pointing to

the skin, "and," turning it back, "him," laying his hand upon the goods beneath.

Raven smiled carelessly, pulled out a flask from his pocket, took a drink and passed it to the others. Desperately struggling to suppress his eagerness and to maintain his dignified bearing, White Cloud seized the flask and, drinking long and deep, passed it to his brother.

"Have a drink, Cameron," said Raven, as he received his flask again.

"No!" said Cameron shortly. "And I would suggest to your friends that they complete the trade before they drink much more."

"My friend here says this is no good," said Raven to the Indians, tapping the flask with his finger. "He says no more drink."

White Cloud shot a keen enquiring glance at Cameron, but he made no reply other than to stretch out his hand for Raven's flask again. Before many minutes the efficacy of Raven's methods of barter began to be apparent. The Indians lost their grave and dignified demeanour. They became curious, eager, garrulous, and demonstrative. With childish glee they began examining more closely Raven's supply of goods, trying on the rings, draping themselves in the gaudy calicoes and flannels. At length Raven rolled up his articles of barter and set them upon one side.

"How much?" he said.

White Cloud selected the goat skin, laid upon it some half dozen beaver and mink, and a couple of foxes, and rolling them up in a pile laid them beside Raven's bundle.

The trader smiled and shook his head. "No good. No good." So saying he took from his pack another flask and laid it upon his pile.

Instantly the Indian increased his pile by a bear skin, a grey wolf, and a mountain goat. Then, without waiting for Raven's words, he reached for the flask.

"No, not yet," said Raven quietly, laying his hand down upon the flask.

The Indian with gleaming eyes threw on the pile some additional skins.

"Good!" said Raven, surrendering the flask.

Swiftly the Indian caught it up and, seizing the cork in his teeth, bit it off close to the neck of the flask. Snatching his knife from his pocket with almost frantic energy, he proceeded to dig out the imbedded cork.

"Here," said Raven, taking the flask from him. "Let me have it." From his pocket he took a knife containing a corkscrew and with this he drew the cork and handed the flask back to the Indian.

With shameless, bestial haste the Indian placed the bottle to his lips and after a long pull passed it to his waiting brother.

At this point Raven rose as if to close the negotiations and took out his own flask for a final drink, but found it empty.

"Aha!" he exclaimed, turning the empty flask upside down. At once the Indian passed him his flask. Raven, however, waved him aside and, going to his pack, drew out a tin oil can which would contain about a gallon. From this with great deliberation he filled his flask.

"Huh!" exclaimed the Indian, pointing to the can. "How much?"

Raven shook his head. "No sell. For me," he answered, tapping himself on the breast.

"How much?" said the Indian fiercely.

Still Raven declined to sell.

Swiftly the Indian gathered up the remaining half of his pack of furs and, throwing them savagely at Raven's feet, seized the can.

Still Raven refused to let it go.

At this point the soft padding of a loping pony was heard coming up the trail and in a few minutes Little Thunder silently took his place in the circle about the fire. Cameron's heart sank within him, for now it seemed as if his chance of escape had slipped from him.

Raven spoke a few rapid words to Little Thunder, who entered into conversation with the Stonies. At length White Cloud drew from his coat a black fox skin. In spite of himself Raven uttered a slight exclamation. It was indeed a superb pelt. With savage hate in every line of his face and in every movement of his body, the Indian flung the skin upon the pile of furs and without a "By your leave" seized the can and passed it to his brother.

At this point Raven, with a sudden display of reckless generosity, placed his own flask upon the Indian's pile of goods.

"Ask them if they want molasses," said Raven to Little Thunder.

"No," grunted the Indian contemptuously, preparing to depart.

"Ask them, Little Thunder."

Immediately as Little Thunder began to speak the contemptuous attitude of the Stonies gave place to one of keen interest and desire. After some further talk Little Thunder went to the pack-pony, returned bearing a small keg and set it on the rock beside Raven's pile of furs. Hastily the Stonies consulted together, White Cloud apparently reluctant, the brother recklessly eager to close the deal. Finally with a gesture

White Cloud put an end to the conversation, stepped out hastily into the dark and returned leading his pony into the light. Cutting asunder the lashings with his knife, he released a bundle of furs and threw it down at Raven's feet.

"Same ting. Good!" he said.

But Raven would not look at the bundle and proceeded to pack up the spoils of his barter. Earnestly the Stonies appealed to Little Thunder, but in vain. Angrily they remonstrated, but still without result. At length Little Thunder pointed to the pony and without hesitation White Cloud placed the bridle rein in his hands.

Cameron could contain himself no longer. Suddenly rising from his place he strode to the side of the Indians and cried, "Don't do it! Don't be such fools! This no good," he said, kicking the keg. "What would Mr. Macdougall say? Come! I go with you. Take back these furs."

He stepped forward to seize the second pack. Swiftly Little Thunder leaped before him, knife in hand, and crouched to spring. The Stonies had no doubt as to his meaning. Their hearts were filled with black rage against the unscrupulous trader, but their insane thirst for the "fire-water" swept from their minds every other consideration but that of determination to gratify this mad lust. Unconsciously they ranged themselves beside Cameron, their hands going to their belts. Quietly Raven spoke a few rapid words to Little Thunder, who, slowly putting up his knife, made a brief but vigourous harangue to the Stonies, the result of which was seen in the doubtful glances which they cast upon Cameron from time to time.

"Come on!" cried Cameron again, laying his hand

upon the nearest Indian. "Let's go to your camp. Take your furs. He is a thief, a robber, a bad man. All that," sweeping his hand towards Raven's goods, "no good. This," kicking the keg, "bad. Kill you."

These words they could not entirely understand, but his gestures were sufficiently eloquent and significant. There was an ugly gleam in Raven's eyes and an ugly curl to his thin lips, but he only smiled.

"Come," he said, waving his hand toward the furs, "take them away. Tell them we don't want to trade, Little Thunder." He pulled out his flask, slowly took a drink, and passed it to Little Thunder, who greedily followed his example. "Tell them we don't want to trade at all," insisted Raven.

Little Thunder volubly explained the trader's wishes.

"Good-bye," said Raven, offering his hand to White Cloud. "Good friends," he added, once more passing him his flask.

"Don't!" said Cameron, laying his hand again upon the Indian's arm. For a single instant White Cloud paused.

"Huh!" grunted Little Thunder in contempt. "Big chief scared."

Quickly the Stony shook off Cameron's hand, seized the flask and, putting it to his lips, drained it dry.

"Come," said Cameron to the other Stony. "Come with me."

Raven uttered a warning word to Little Thunder. The Indians stood for some moments uncertain, their heads bowed upon their breasts. Then White Cloud, throwing back his head and looking Cameron full in the face, said —"Good man. Good man. Me no go."

"Then I go alone," cried Cameron, springing off into the darkness.

As he turned his foot caught the pile of wood brought for the fire. He tripped and stumbled almost to the ground. Before he could recover himself Little Thunder, swift as a wildcat, leaped upon his back with his ever-ready knife in his upraised hand, but before he could strike, Cameron had turned himself and throwing the Indian off had struggled to his feet.

"Hold there!" cried Raven with a terrible oath, flinging himself upon the struggling pair.

A moment or two the Stonies hesitated, then they too seized Cameron and between them all they bore him fighting to the ground.

"Keep back! Keep back!" cried Raven in a terrible voice to Little Thunder, who, knife in hand, was dancing round, seeking an opportunity to strike. "Will you lie still, or shall I knock your head in?" said Raven to Cameron through his clenched teeth, with one hand on his throat and the other poising a revolver over his head. Cameron gave up the struggle.

"Speak and quick!" cried Raven, his face working with passion, his voice thick and husky, his breath coming in quick gasps from the fury that possessed him.

"All right," said Cameron. "Let me up. You have beaten me this time."

Raven sprang to his feet.

"Let him up!" he said. "Now, then, Cameron, give me your word you won't try to escape."

"No, I will not! I'll see you hanged first," said Cameron.

Raven deliberately drew his pistol and said slowly:

"I have saved your life twice already, but the time is past for any more trifling. Now you've got to take it."

At this Little Thunder spoke a word, pointing toward the camp of the Stonies. Raven hesitated, then with an oath he strode toward Cameron and thrusting his pistol in his face said in tones of cold and concentrated rage:

"Listen to me, you fool! Your life is hanging by a hair trigger that goes off with a feather touch. I give you one more chance. Move hand or foot and the bullet in this gun will pass neatly through your eye. So help me God Almighty!"

He spoke to Little Thunder, still keeping Cameron covered with his gun. The Indian slipped quietly behind Cameron and swiftly threw a line over his shoulders and, drawing it tight, bound his arms to his side. Again and again he repeated this operation till Cameron stood swathed in the coils of the rope like a mummy, inwardly raging, not so much at his captor, but at himself and his stupid bungling of his break for liberty. His helpless and absurd appearance seemed to restore Raven's good humour.

"Now, then," he said, turning to the Stonies and resuming his careless air, "we will finish our little business. Sit down, Mr. Cameron," he continued, with a pleasant smile. "It may be less dignified, but it is much more comfortable."

Once more he took out his flask and passed it round, forgetting to take it back from his Indian visitors, who continued to drink from it in turn.

"Listen," he said. "I give you all you see here for your furs and a pony to pack them. That is my last word. Quick, yes or no? Tell them no more trifling, Little Thunder. The moon is high. We start in ten minutes."

There was no further haggling. The Indians seemed to recognise that the time for that was past. After a brief consultation they grunted their acceptance and proceeded to pack up their goods, but with no good will.

More vividly than any in the company they realised the immensity of the fraud that was being perpetrated upon them. They were being robbed of their whole winter's kill and that of some of their friends as well, but they were helpless in the grip of their mad passion for the trader's fire-water. Disgusted with themselves and filled with black rage against the man who had so pitilessly stripped them bare of the profits of a year's toil and privation, how gladly would they have put their knives into his back, but they knew his sort by only too bitter experience and they knew that at his hands they need expect no pity.

"Here," cried Raven, observing their black looks. "A present for my brothers." He handed them each a roll of tobacco. "And a present for their squaws," adding a scarlet blanket apiece to their pack.

Without a word of thanks they took the gifts and, loading their stuff upon their remaining pony, disappeared down the trail.

"Now, Little Thunder, let's get out of this, for once their old man finds out he will be hot foot on our trail."

With furious haste they fell to their packing. Cameron stood aghast at the amazing swiftness and dexterity with which the packs were roped and loaded. When all was complete the trader turned to Cameron in gay good humour.

"Now, Mr. Cameron, will you go passenger or freight?" Cameron made no reply. "In other words, shall we pack you on your pony or will you ride like a gentleman, giving me your word not to attempt to escape? Time presses, so answer quick! Give me twenty-four hours. Give me your word for twenty-four hours, after which you can go when you like."

"I agree," said Cameron shortly.

"Cut him loose, Little Thunder." Little Thunder hesitated. "Quick, you fool! Cut him loose. I know a gentleman when I see him. He is tied tighter than with ropes."

"It is a great pity," he continued, addressing Cameron in a pleasant conversational tone as they rode down the trail together, "that you should have made an ass of yourself for those brutes. Bah! What odds? Old Macdougall or some one else would get their stuff sooner or later. Why not I? Come, cheer up. You are jolly well out of it, for, God knows, you may live to look death in the face many a time, but never while you live will you be so near touching the old sport as you were a few minutes ago. Why I have interfered to save you these three times blessed if I know! Many a man's bones have been picked by the coyotes in these hills for a fraction of the provocation you have given me, not to speak of Little Thunder, who is properly thirsting for your blood. But take advice from me," here he leaned over towards Cameron and touched him on the shoulder, while his voice took a sterner tone, "don't venture on any further liberties with him."

Suddenly Cameron's rage blazed forth.

"Now perhaps you will listen to me," he said in a voice thrilling with passion. "First of all, keep your hands off me. As for your comrade and partner in crime, I fear him no more than I would a dog and like a dog I shall treat him if he dares to attack me again. As for you, you are a coward and a cad. You have me at a disadvantage. But put down your guns and fight me on equal terms, and I will make you beg for your life!"

There was a gleam of amused admiration in Raven's eyes.

"By Jove! It would be a pretty fight, I do believe, and one I should greatly enjoy. At present, however, time is pressing and therefore that pleasure we must postpone. Meantime I promise you that when it comes it will be on equal terms."

"I ask no more," said Cameron.

There was no further conversation, for Raven appeared intent on putting as large a space as possible between himself and the camp of the Stonies. The discovery of the fraud he knew would be inevitable and he knew, too, that George Macdougall was not the man to allow his flock to be fleeced with impunity.

So before the grey light of morning began to steal over the mountaintops Raven, with his bunch of ponies and his loot, was many miles forward on his journey. But the endurance even of bronchos and cayuses has its limit, and their desperate condition from hunger and fatigue rendered food and rest imperative.

The sun was fully up when Raven ordered a halt, and in a sunny valley, deep with grass, unsaddling the wearied animals, he turned them loose to feed and rest. Apparently careless of danger and highly contented with their night's achievement, he and his Indian partner abandoned themselves to sleep. Cameron, too, though his indignation and chagrin prevented sleep for a time, was finally forced to yield to the genial influences of the warm sun and the languid airs of the spring day, and, firmly resolving to keep awake, he fell into dreamless slumber.

The sun was riding high noon when he was awakened by a hand upon his arm. It was Raven.

"Hush!" he said. "Not a word. Mount and quick!"

Looking about Cameron observed that the pack horses were ready loaded and Raven standing by his broncho ready to mount. Little Thunder was nowhere to be seen.

"What's up?" said Cameron.

For answer Raven pointed up the long sloping trail down which they had come. There three horsemen could be seen riding hard, but still distant more than half a mile.

"Saw them three miles away, luckily enough," said Raven.

"Where's Little Thunder?" enquired Cameron.

"Oh, rounding up the bunch," answered Raven carelessly, waving his hand toward the valley. "Those men are coming some," he added, swinging into his saddle.

As he spoke a rifle shot shattered the stillness of the valley. The first of the riders threw up his hands, clutched wildly at the vacant air and pitched headlong out of the saddle. "Good God! What's that?" gasped Cameron. The other two wheeled in their course. Before they could turn a second shot rang out and another of the riders fell upon his horse's neck, clung there for a moment, then gently slid to the ground. The third, throwing himself over the side of his pony, rode back for dear life.

A third and a fourth shot were heard, but the fleeing rider escaped unhurt.

"What does that mean?" again asked Cameron, weak and sick with horror.

"Mount!" yelled Raven with a terrible oath and flourishing a revolver in his hand. "Mount quick!" His face was pale, his eyes burned with a fierce glare, while his voice rang with the blast of a bugle.

"Lead those pack horses down that trail!" he yelled, thrusting the line into Cameron's hand. "Quick, I tell you!"

"Crack-crack!" Twice a bullet sang savagely past Cameron's ears.

"Quicker!" shouted Raven, circling round the bunch of ponies with wild cries and oaths like a man gone mad. Again and again the revolver spat wickedly and here and there a pony plunged recklessly forward, nicked in the ear by one of those venomous singing pellets. Helpless to defend himself and expecting every moment to feel the sting of a bullet somewhere in his body, Cameron hurried his pony with all his might down the trail, dragging the pack animals after him. In huddled confusion the terrified brutes followed after him in a mad rush, for hard upon their rear, like a beast devil-possessed, Nighthawk pressed, biting, kicking, squealing, to the accompaniment of his rider's oaths and yells and pistol shots. Down the long sloping trail to the very end of the valley the mad rush continued. There the ascent checked the fury of the speed and forced a quieter pace. But through the afternoon there was no weakening of the pressure from the rear till the evening shadows and the frequent falling of the worn-out beasts forced a slackening of the pace and finally a halt.

Sick with horror and loathing, Cameron dismounted and unsaddled his broncho. He had hardly finished this operation when Little Thunder rode up upon a strange pony, leading a beautiful white broncho behind. Cameron could not repress an exclamation of disgust as the Indian drew near him.

"Beautiful beast that," said Raven carelessly, pointing to the white pony.

Cameron turned his eyes upon the pony and stood transfixed with horror.

"My God!" he exclaimed. "Look at that!" Across the beautiful white shoulders and reaching down clear to the fetlock there ran a broad stain, dull red and horrible. Then through his teeth, hard clenched together, these words came forth: "Some day, by God's help, I shall wipe out that stain."

The trader shrugged his shoulders carelessly, but made no reply.

CHAPTER V

SERGEANT CRISP

THE horror of the day followed Cameron through the night and awoke with him next morning. Every time his eyes found the Indian his teeth came together in a grinding rage as he repeated his vow, "Some day I shall bring you to justice. So help me God!"

Against Raven somehow he could not maintain the same heat of rage. That he was a party to the murder of the Stonies there was little reason to doubt, but as all next day they lay in the sunny glade resting the ponies, or went loping easily along the winding trails making ever towards the Southwest, the trader's cheerful face, his endless tales, and his invincible good humour stole from Cameron's heart, in spite of his firm resolve, the fierceness of his wrath. But the resolve was none the less resolute that one day he would bring this man to justice.

As they journeyed on, the woods became more open and the trees larger. Mid-day found them resting by a little lake, from which a stream flowed into the upper reaches of the Columbia River.

"We shall make the Crow's Nest trail by to-morrow night," said Raven, "where we shall part; not to your very great sorrow, I fancy, either."

The evening before Cameron would have said, "No, but to my great joy," and it vexed him that he could not bring himself to say so to-day with any great show of sincerity. There was a charm about this man that he could not resist.

"And yet," continued Raven, allowing his eyes to

rest dreamily upon the lake, "in other circumstances I might have found in you an excellent friend, and a most rare and valuable find that is."

"That it is!" agreed Cameron, thinking of his old football captain, "but one cannot make friends with a—"

"It is an ugly word, I know," said Raven. "But, after all, what is a bunch of furs more or less to those Indians?"

"Furs?" exclaimed Cameron in horror. "What are the lives of these men?"

"Oh," replied Raven carelessly, "these Indians are always getting killed one way or another. It is all in the day's work with them. They pick each other off without query or qualm. Besides, Little Thunder has a grudge of very old standing against the Stonies, whom he heartily despises, and he doubtless enjoys considerable satisfaction from the thought that he has partially paid it. It will be his turn next, like as not, for they won't let this thing sleep. Or perhaps mine!" he added after a pause. "The man is doubtless on the trail at this present minute who will finally get me."

"Then why expose yourself to such a fate?" said Cameron. "Surely in this country a man can live an honest life and prosper."

"Honest life? I doubt it! What is an honest life? Does any Indian trader lead an honest life? Do the Hudson Bay traders, or I. G. Baker's people, or any of them do the honest thing by the Indian they trade with? In the long run it is a question of the police. What escapes the police is honest. The crime, after all, is in getting caught."

"Oh, that is too old!" said Cameron. "You know you are talking rot."

"Quite right! It is rot," assented Raven. "The whole

business is rot. 'Vanity of vanities, saith the preacher.' Oh, I know the Book, you see. I was not born a—a—an outlaw." The grey-brown eyes had in them a wistful look. "Bah!" he exclaimed, springing to his feet and shaking himself. "The sight of your Edinburgh face and the sound of your Edinburgh speech and your old country ways and manners have got on my recollection works, and I believe that accounts for you being alive to-day, old man."

He whistled to his horse. Nighthawk came trotting and whinneying to him.

"I have one friend in the world, old boy," he said, throwing his arm over the black, glossy neck and searching his pocket for a biscuit. "And even you," he added bitterly, "I fear do not love me for naught."

Saddling his horse, he mounted and calling Little Thunder to him said:

"Take the bunch on as far as the Big Canyon and wait there for me. I am going back a bit. It is better to be sure than sorry. Cameron, your best route lies with us. Your twenty-four hours' parole is already up. To-morrow, perhaps to-night, I shall put you on the Macleod trail. You are a free man, but don't try to make any breaks when I am gone. My friend here is extremely prompt with his weapons. Farewell! Get a move on, Little Thunder! Cameron will bring up the rear."

He added some further words in the Indian tongue, his voice taking a stern tone. Little Thunder grunted a surly and unwilling acquiescence, and, waving his hand to Cameron, the trader wheeled his horse up the trail.

In spite of himself Cameron could not forbear a feeling of pity and admiration as he watched the lithe, upright figure swaying up the trail, his every movement in unison with that of the beautiful demon he bestrode. But with all his pity and admiration he was none the less resolved that he would do what in him lay to bring these two to justice.

"This ugly devil at least shall swing!" he said to himself as he turned his eyes upon Little Thunder getting his pack ponies out upon the trail. This accomplished, the Indian, pointing onward, said gruffly,

"You go in front—me back."

"Not much!" cried Cameron. "You heard the orders from your chief. You go in front. I bring up the rear. I do not know the trail."

"Huh! Trail good," grunted Little Thunder, the red-rimmed eyes gleaming malevolently. "You go front —me back." He waved his hand impatiently toward the trail. Following the direction of his hand, Cameron's eyes fell upon the stock of his own rifle protruding from a pack upon one of the ponies. For a moment the protruding stock held his eyes fascinated.

"Huh!" said the Indian, noting Cameron's glance, and slipping off his pony. In an instant both men were racing for the pack and approaching each other at a sharp angle. Arrived at striking distance, the Indian leaped at Cameron, with his knife, as was his wont, ready to strike.

The appearance of the Indian springing at him seemed to set some of the grey matter in Cameron's brain moving along old tracks. Like a flash he dropped to his knees in an old football tackle, caught the Indian by the legs and tossed him high over his shoulders, then, springing to his feet, he jerked the rifle free from the pack and stood waiting for Little Thunder's attack.

But the Indian lay without sound or motion. Cameron used his opportunity to look for his cartridge belt, which, after a few minutes' anxious search, he discovered in the pack. He buckled the belt about him, made sure his Winchester held a shell, and stood waiting.

That he should be waiting thus with the deliberate purpose of shooting down a fellow human being filled him with a sense of unreality. But the events of the last forty-eight hours had created an entirely new environment, and with extraordinary facility his mind had adjusted itself to this environment, and though two days before he would have shrunk in horror from the possibility of taking a human life, he knew as he stood there that at the first sign of attack he should shoot the Indian down like a wild beast.

Slowly Little Thunder raised himself to a sitting posture and looked about in dazed surprise. As his mind regained its normal condition there deepened in his eyes a look of cunning hatred. With difficulty he rose to his feet and stood facing Cameron. Cameron waited quietly, watching his every move.

"You go in front!" at length commanded Cameron. "And no nonsense, mind you," he added, tapping his rifle, "or I shoot quick."

The Indian might not have understood all Cameron's words, but he was in no doubt as to his meaning. It was characteristic of his race that he should know when he was beaten and stoically accept defeat for the time being. Without further word or look he led off his pack ponies, while Cameron took his place at the rear.

But progress was slow. Little Thunder was either incapable of rapid motion or sullenly indifferent to any necessity for it. Besides, there was no demoniacal dynamic forcing the beasts on from the rear. They had not been more than three hours on the trail when

Cameron heard behind him the thundering of hoofs. Glancing over his shoulder, he saw coming down upon him Raven, riding as if pursued by a thousand demons. The condition of his horse showed that the race had been long and hard; his black satin skin was dripping as if he had come through a river, his eyes were bloodshot and starting from his head, his mouth was wide open and from it in large clots the foam had fallen upon his neck and chest.

Past Cameron and down upon Little Thunder Raven rushed like a whirlwind, yelling with wild oaths the while,

"Get on! Get on! What are you loafing about here for?"

A few vehement directions to the Indian and he came thundering back upon Cameron.

"What have you been doing?" he cried with an oath. "Why are you not miles on? Get on! Move! Move!! Move!!!" At every yell he hurled his frenzied broncho upon the ponies which brought up the rear, and in a few minutes had the whole cavalcade madly careering down the sloping trail. Wilder and wilder grew the pace. Turning a sharp corner round a jutting rock a pack pony stumbled and went crashing fifty feet to the rock below. "On! On!" yelled Raven, emptying his gun into the struggling animal as he passed. More and more difficult became the road until at length it was impossible to keep up the pace.

"We cannot make it! We cannot make it!" muttered Raven with bitter oaths. "Oh, the cursed fools! Another two miles would do it!"

At length they came to a spot where the trail touched a level bench.

"Halt!" yelled the trader, as he galloped to the head

of the column. A few minutes he spent in rapid and fierce consultation with Little Thunder and then came raging back. "We are going to get this bunch down into the valley there," he shouted, pointing to the thick timber at the bottom. "I do not expect your help, but I ask you to remain where you are for the present. And let me assure you this is no moment for trifling."

With extraordinary skill and rapidity Little Thunder managed to lead first the pack ponies and then the others, one by one, at intervals, off the trail as they went onward, taking infinite pains to cover their tracks at the various points of departure. While this was being done the trader stood shouting directions and giving assistance with a fury of energy that seemed to communicate itself to the very beasts. But the work was one of great difficulty and took many minutes to accomplish.

"Half an hour more, just half an hour! Fifteen minutes!" he kept muttering. "Just a short fifteen minutes and all would be well."

As the last pony disappeared into the woods Raven turned to Cameron and with a smile said quietly,

"There, that's done. Now you are free. Here we part. This is your trail. It will take you to Macleod. I am sorry, however, that owing to a change in circumstances for which I am not responsible I must ask you for that rifle." With the swiftness of a flash of light he whipped his gun into Cameron's face. "Don't move!" he said, still smiling. "This gun of mine never fails. Quick, don't look round. Yes, those hoof beats are our friends the police. Quick! It is your life or mine. I'd hate to kill you, Cameron. I give you one chance more."

There was no help for it, and Cameron, with his heart filled with futile fury, surrendered his rifle.

"Now ride in front of me a little way. They have just seen us, but they don't know that we are aware of their presence. Ride! Ride! A little faster!" Nighthawk rushed upon Cameron's lagging pony. "There, that's better."

A shout fell upon their ears.

"Go right along!" said Raven quietly. "Only a few minutes longer, then we part. I have greatly enjoyed your company."

Another shout.

"Aha!" said Raven, glancing round. "It is, I verily believe it is my old friend Sergeant Crisp. Only two of them, by Jove! If we had only known we need not have hurried."

Another shout, followed by a bullet that sang over their heads.

"Ah, this is interesting—too interesting by half! Well, here goes for you, sergeant!" He wheeled as he spoke. Turning swiftly in his saddle, Cameron saw him raise his rifle.

"Hold up, you devil!" he shouted, throwing his pony across the black broncho's track.

The rifle rang out, the police horse staggered, swayed, and pitched to the earth, bringing his rider down with him.

"Ah, Cameron, that was awkward of you," said Raven gently. "However, it is perhaps as well. Good-bye, old man. Tell the sergeant not to follow. Trails hereabout are dangerous and good police sergeants are scarce. Again farewell." He swung his broncho off the trail and, waving his hand, with a smile, disappeared into the thick underbrush.

"Hold up your hands!" shouted the police officer, who had struggled upright and was now swaying on his feet and covering Cameron with his carbine.

"Hurry! Hurry!" cried Cameron, springing from his pony and waving his hands wildly in the air. "Come on. You'll get him yet."

"Stand where you are and hold up your hands!" cried the sergeant.

Cameron obeyed, shouting meanwhile wrathfully, "Oh, come on, you bally fool! You are losing him. Come on, I tell you!"

"Keep your hands up or I shoot!" cried the sergeant sternly.

"All right," said Cameron, holding his hands high, "but for God's sake hurry up!" He ran towards the sergeant as he spoke, with his hands still above his head.

"Halt!" shouted the sergeant, as Cameron came near. "Constable Burke, arrest that man!"

"Oh, come, get it over," cried Cameron in a fury of passion. "Arrest me, of course, but if you want to catch that chap you'll have to hurry. He cannot be far away."

"Ah, indeed, my man," said the sergeant pleasantly. "He is not far away?"

"No, he's a murderer and a thief and you can catch him if you hurry."

"Ah! Very good, very good! Constable Burke, tie this man up to your saddle and we'll take a look round. How many might there be in your gang?" enquired the sergeant. "Tell the truth now. It will be the better for you."

"One," said Cameron impatiently. "A chap calling himself Raven."

"Raven, eh?" exclaimed Sergeant Crisp with a new interest. "Raven, by Jove!"

"Yes, and an Indian. Little Thunder he called him."

"Little Thunder! Jove, what a find!" exclaimed the sergeant.

"Yes," continued Cameron eagerly. "Raven is just ahead in the woods there alone and the Indian is further back with a bunch of ponies down in the river bottom."

"Oh, indeed! Very interesting! And so Raven is all alone in the scrub there, waiting doubtless to give himself up," said Sergeant Crisp with fine sarcasm. "Well, we are not yet on to your game, young man, but we will not just play up to that lead yet a while."

In vain Cameron raged and pleaded and stormed and swore, telling his story in incoherent snatches, to the intense amusement of Sergeant Crisp and his companion. At length Cameron desisted, swallowing his rage as best he could.

"Now then, we shall move on. The pass is not more than an hour away. We will put this young man in safe keeping and return for Mr. Raven and his interesting friend." For a moment he stood looking down upon his horse. "Poor old chap!" he said. "We have gone many a mile together on Her Majesty's errands. If I have done my duty as faithfully as you have done yours I need not fear my record. Take his saddle and bridle off, Burke. We've got one of the gang. Some day we shall come up with Mr. Raven himself."

"Yes," said Cameron with passionate bitterness. "And that might be to-day if you had only listened to me. Why, man," he shouted with reviving rage, "we three could take him even yet!"

"Ah!" said Sergeant Crisp, "so we could."

"You had him in your hands to-day," said Cameron, "but like a fool you let him go. But some day, so help me God, I shall bring these murderers to justice."

"Ah!" said Sergeant Crisp again. "Good! Very good indeed! Now, my man, march!"

CHAPTER VI

A DAY IN THE MACLEOD BARRACKS

"WHAT'S this, Sergeant Crisp?" The Commissioner, a tall, slight, and soldier-like man, keen-eyed and brisk of speech, rapped out his words like a man intent on business.

"One of a whiskey gang, Sir. Dick Raven's, I suspect."

"And the charge?"

"Whiskey trading, theft, and murder."

The Commissioner's face grew grave.

"Murder? Where did you find him?"

"Kootenay trail, Sir. Got wind of him at Calgary, followed up the clue past Morleyville, then along the Kootenay trail. A blizzard came on and we feared we had lost them. We fell in with a band of Stony Indians, found that the band had been robbed and two of their number murdered."

"Two murdered?" The Commissioner's voice was stern.

"Yes, Sir. Shot down in cold blood. We have the testimony of an eye witness. We followed the trail and came upon two of them. My horse was shot. One of them escaped; this man we captured."

The Commissioner sat pondering. Then with disconcerting swiftness he turned upon the prisoner.

"Your name?"

"Cameron, Sir."

"Where from?"

"I was working in McIvor's survey camp near Morleyville. I went out shooting, lost my way in a blizzard, was captured by a man who called himself Raven—"

"Wait!" said the Commissioner sharply. "Bring me that file!"

The orderly brought a file from which the Commissioner selected a letter. His keen eyes rapidly scanned the contents and then ran over the prisoner from head to foot. Thereupon, without a moment's hesitation, he said curtly:

"Release the prisoner!"

"But, Sir—" began Sergeant Crisp, with an expression of utter bewilderment and disgust upon his face.

"Release the prisoner!" repeated the Commissioner sharply. "Mr. Cameron, I deeply regret this mistake. Under the circumstances it could hardly have been avoided. You were in bad company, you see. I am greatly pleased that my men have been of service to you. We shall continue to do all we can for you. In the meantime I am very pleased to have the pleasure of meeting you." He passed the letter to Sergeant Crisp. "I have information about you from Morleyville, you see. Now tell us all about it."

It took Cameron some moments to recover his wits, so dumbfounded was he at the sudden change in his condition.

"Well, Sir," he began, "I hardly know what to say."

"Sit down, sit down, Mr. Cameron. Take your time," said the Commissioner. "We are somewhat hurried these days, but you must have had some trying experiences."

Then Cameron proceeded with his tale. The Commissioner listened with keen attention, now and then arresting him with a question or a comment. When

Cameron came to tell of the murder of the Stonies his voice shook with passion.

"We will get that Indian some day," said the Commissioner, "never fear. What is his name?"

"Little Thunder, Raven called him. And I would like to take a hand in that too, Sir," said Cameron eagerly.

"You would, eh?" said the Commissioner with a sharp look at him. "Well, we'll see. Little Thunder," he repeated to himself. "Bring that Record Book!"

The orderly laid a large canvas-covered book before him.

"Little Thunder, eh?" he repeated, turning the leaves of the book. "Oh, yes, I thought so! Blood Indian— formerly Chief—supplanted by Red Crow—got into trouble with whiskey traders. Yes, I remember. He is at his old tricks. This time, however, he has gone too far. We will get him. Go on, Mr. Cameron!"

When Cameron had concluded his story the Commissioner said to the orderly sharply:

"Send me Inspector Dickson!"

In a few moments Inspector Dickson appeared, a tall, slight man, with a gentle face and kindly blue eyes.

"Inspector Dickson, how are we for men? Can you spare two or three to round up a gang of whiskey traders and to run down a murderer? We are on the track of Raven's bunch, I believe."

"We are very short-handed at present, Sir. This half-breed trouble in the north is keeping our Indians all very restless. We must keep in touch with them."

"Yes, yes, I know. By the way, how are the Bloods just now?"

"They are better, Sir, but the Blackfeet are restless and uneasy. There are a lot of runners from the east among them."

"How is old Crowfoot behaving?"

"Crowfoot himself is apparently all right so far, but of course no man can tell what Crowfoot is thinking."

"That's right enough," replied the Commissioner.

"By the way, Sir, it was Crowfoot's son that got into that trouble last night with that Macleod man. The old Chief is in town, too, in fact is outside just now and quite worked up over the arrest."

"Well, we will settle this Crowfoot business in a few minutes. Now, about this Raven gang. You cannot go yourself with a couple of men? He is an exceedingly clever rascal."

The Inspector enumerated the cases immediately pressing.

"Well then, at the earliest possible moment we must get after this gang. Keep this in mind, Inspector Dickson. That Indian I consider an extremely dangerous man. He is sure to be mixed up with this half-breed trouble. He has very considerable influence with a large section of the Bloods. I shouldn't be surprised if we should find him on their reserve before very long. Now then, bring in young Crowfoot!"

The Inspector saluted and retired, followed by Sergeant Crisp, whose face had not yet regained its normal expression.

"Mr. Cameron," said the Commissioner, "if you care to remain with me for the morning I shall be glad to have you. The administration of justice by the police may prove interesting to you. Later on we shall discuss your return to your camp."

Cameron expressed his delight at being permitted to

remain in the court room, not only that he might observe the police methods of administering justice, but especially that he might see something of the great Blackfeet Chief, Crowfoot, of whom he had heard much since his arrival in the West.

In a few minutes Inspector Dickson returned, followed by a constable leading a young Indian, handcuffed. With these entered Jerry, the famous halfbreed interpreter, and last of all the father of the prisoner, old Crowfoot, tall, straight, stately. One swift searching glance the old Chief flung round the room, and then, acknowledging the Commissioner's salute with a slight wave of the hand and a grunt, and declining the seat offered him, he stood back against the wall and there viewed the proceedings with an air of haughty defiance.

The Commissioner lost no time in preliminaries. The charge was read and explained to the prisoner. The constable made his statement. The young Indian had got into an altercation with a citizen of Macleod, and on being hard pressed had pulled the pistol which was laid upon the desk. There was no defense. The interpreter, however, explained, after conversation with the prisoner, that drink was the cause. At this point the old Chief's face swiftly changed. Defiance gave place to disgust, grief, and rage.

The Commissioner, after carefully eliciting all the facts, gave the prisoner an opportunity to make a statement. This being declined, the Commissioner proceeded gravely to point out the serious nature of the offense, to emphasize the sacredness of human life and declare the determination of the government to protect all Her Majesty's subjects, no matter what their race or the colour of their skin. He then went on to point out the serious danger which the young man had so narrowly escaped.

"Why, man," exclaimed the Commissioner, "you might have committed murder."

Here the young fellow said something to the interpreter. There was a flicker of a smile on the half-breed's face.

"He say dat pistol he no good. He can't shoot. He not loaded."

The Commissioner's face never changed a line. He gravely turned the pistol over in his hand, and truly enough the rusty weapon appeared to be quite innocuous except to the shooter.

"This is an extremely dangerous weapon. Why, it might have killed yourself—if it had been loaded. We cannot allow this sort of thing. However, since it was not loaded we shall make the sentence light. I sentence you to one month's confinement."

The interpreter explained the sentence to the young Indian, who received the explanation without the movement of a muscle or the flicker of an eyelid. The constable touched him on the shoulder and said, "Come!"

Before he could move old Crowfoot with two strides stood before the constable, and waving him aside with a gesture of indescribable dignity, took his son in his arms and kissed him on either cheek. Then, stepping back, he addressed him in a voice grave, solemn, and vibrant with emotion. Jerry interpreted to the Court.

"I have observed the big Chief. This is good medicine. It is good that wrong should suffer. All good men are against wickedness. My son, you have done foolishly. You have darkened my eyes. You have covered my face before my people. They will ask—where is your son? My voice will be silent. My face will be covered with shame. I shall be like a dog kicked from the lodge. My son, I told you to go only to the store. I warned you against bad men and bad places. Your ears were closed, you were wiser than your father. Now we both must suffer, you here shut up from the light of the sky, I in my darkened lodge. But," he continued, turning swiftly upon the Commissioner, "I ask my father why these bad men who sell whiskey to the poor Indian are not shut up with my son. My son is young. He is like the hare in the woods. He falls easily into the trap. Why are not these bad men removed?" The old Chief's face trembled with indignant appeal.

"They shall be!" said the Commissioner, smiting the desk with his fist. "This very day!"

"It is good!" continued the old Chief with great dignity. Then, turning again to his son, he said, and his voice was full of grave tenderness:

"Now, go to your punishment. The hours will be none too long if they bring you wisdom." Again he kissed his son on both cheeks and, without a look at any other, stalked haughtily from the room.

"Inspector Dickson," sharply commanded the Commissioner, "find out the man that sold that whiskey and arrest him at once!"

Cameron was profoundly impressed with the whole scene. He began to realise as never before the tremendous responsibilities that lay upon those charged with the administration of justice in this country. He began to understand, too, the secret of the extraordinary hold that the Police had upon the Indian tribes and how it came that so small a force could maintain the "Pax Britannica" over three hundred thousand square miles of unsettled country, the home of hundreds of wild adventurers and of thousands of savage Indians, utterly strange to any rule or law except that of their own sweet will.

"This police business is a big affair," he ventured to say to the Commissioner when the court room was cleared. "You practically run the country."

"Well," said the Commissioner modestly, "we do something to keep the country from going to the devil. We see that every man gets a fair show."

"It is great work!" exclaimed Cameron.

"Yes, I suppose it is," replied the Commissioner. "We don't talk about it, of course. Indeed, we don't think of it. But," he continued, "that blue book there could tell a story that would make the old Empire not too ashamed of the men who 'ride the line' and patrol the ranges in this far outpost." He opened the big canvas-bound book as he spoke and turned the pages over. "Look at that for a page," he said, and Cameron glanced over the entries. What a tale they told!

"Fire-fighting!"

"Yes," said the Commissioner, "that saved a settler's wife and child—a prairie fire. The house was lost, but the constable pulled them out and got rather badly burned in the business."

Cameron's finger ran down the page.

"Sick man transported to Post."

"That," commented the Superintendent, "was a journey of over two hundred miles by dog sleighs in winter. Saved the man's life."

And so the record ran. "Cattle thieves arrested." "Whiskey smugglers captured." "Stolen horses recovered." "Insane man brought to Post."

"That was rather a tough case," said the Commissioner. "Meant a journey of some eight hundred miles with a man, a powerful man too, raving mad."

"How many of your men on that journey?" enquired Cameron.

"Oh, just one. The fellow got away twice, but was recaptured and finally landed. Got better too. But the constable was all broken up for weeks afterwards."

"Man, that was great!" exclaimed Cameron. "What a pity it should not be known."

"Oh," said the Commissioner lightly, "it's all in the day's duty."

The words thrilled Cameron to the heart. "All in the day's duty!" The sheer heroism of it, the dauntless facing of Nature's grimmest terrors, the steady patience, the uncalculated sacrifice, the thought of all that lay behind these simple words held him silent for many minutes as he kept turning over the leaves.

As he sat thus turning the leaves and allowing his eye to fall upon those simple but eloquent entries, a loud and strident voice was heard outside.

"Waal, I tell yuh, I want to see him right naow. I ain't come two hundred miles for nawthin'. I mean business, I do."

The orderly's voice was heard in reply

"I ain't got no time to wait. I want to see yer Chief of Police right naow."

Again the orderly's voice could be distinguished.

"In court, is he? Waal, you hurry up and tell him J. B. Cadwaller of Lone Pine, Montana, an American citizen, wants to see him right smart."

The orderly came in and saluted.

"A man to see you, Sir," he said. "An American."

"What business?"

"Horse-stealing case, Sir."

"Show him in!"

In a moment the orderly returned, followed by, not one, but three American citizens.

"Good-day, Jedge! My name's J. B. Cadwaller, Lone Pine, Montana. I—"

"Take your hat off in the court!" said the orderly sharply.

Mr. Cadwaller slowly surveyed the orderly with an expression of interested curiosity in his eyes, removing his hat as he did so.

"Say, you're pretty swift, ain't yuh? You might give a feller a show to git in his interductions," said Mr. Cadwaller. "I was jes goin' to interdooce to you, Jedge, these gentlemen from my own State, District Attorney Hiram S. Sligh and Mr. Rufus Raimes, rancher."

The Commissioner duly acknowledged the introduction, standing to receive the strangers with due courtesy.

"Now, Jedge, I want to see yer Chief of Police. I've got a case for him."

"I have the honor to be the Commissioner. What can I do for you?"

"Waal, Jedge, we don't want to waste no time, neither yours nor ours. The fact is some of yer blank blank Indians have been rustlin' hosses from us fer some time back. We don't mind a cayuse now and then, but when it comes to a hull bunch of vallable hosses there's where we kick and we ain't goin' to stand fer it. And we want them hosses re-stored. And what's more, we want them blank blank copper snakes strung up."

"How many horses have you lost?"

"How many? Jeerupiter! Thirty or forty fer all I know; they've been rustlin' 'em for a year back."

"Why didn't you report before?"

"Why we thought we'd git 'em ourselves, and if we had we wouldn't 'a troubled yuh—and I guess they wouldn't 'a troubled us much longer. But they are so slick—so blank slick!"

"Mr. Cadwaller, we don't allow any profanity in this court room," said the Commissioner in a quiet voice.

"Eh? Who's givin' yuh profanity? I don't mean no profanity. I'm talkin' about them blank blank—"

"Stop, Mr. Cadwaller!" said the Commissioner. "We must end this interview if you cannot make your statements without profanity. This is Her Majesty's Court of Justice and we cannot tolerate any unbecoming language."

"Waal, I'll be—!"

"Pardon me, Mr. Commissioner," said Mr. Hiram S. Sligh, interruping his friend and client. "Perhaps I may make a statement. We've lost some twenty or thirty horses."

"Thirty-one" interjected Mr. Raimes quietly.

"Thirty-one!" burst in Mr. Cadwaller indignantly. "That's only one little bunch."

"And," continued Mr. Sligh, "we have traced them right up to the Blood reserve. More than that, Mr. Raimes has seen the horses in the possession of the Indians and we want your assistance in recovering our property."

"Yes, by gum!" exclaimed Mr. Cadwaller. "And we want them—eh—eh—consarned redskin thieves strung up."

"You say you have seen the stolen horses on the Blood reserve, Mr. Raimes?" enquired the Commissioner.

Mr. Raimes, who was industriously chewing a quid of tobacco, ejected, with a fine sense of propriety and with great skill and accuracy, a stream of tobacco juice out of the door before he answered.

"I seen 'em."

"When did you lose your horses?"

Mr. Raimes considered the matter for some moments, chewing energetically the while, then, having delivered himself with the same delicacy and skill as before of his surplus tobacco juice, made laconic reply:

"Seventeen, no, eighteen days ago."

"Did you follow the trail immediately yourselves?"

"No, Jim Eberts."

"Jim Eberts?"

"Foreman," said Mr. Raimes, who seemed to regard conversation in the light of an interference with the more important business in which he was industriously engaged.

"But you saw the horses yourself on the Blood reserve?"

"Followed up and seen 'em."

"How long since you saw them there, Mr. Raimes?"

"Two days."

"You are quite sure about the horses?"

"Sure."

"Call Inspector Dickson!" ordered the Commissioner. Inspector Dickson appeared and saluted.

"We have information that a party of Blood Indians have stolen a band of horses from these gentlemen from Montana and that these horses are now on the Blood reserve. Take a couple of men and investigate, and if you find the horses bring them back."

"Couple of men!" ejaculated Mr. Cadwaller breathlessly. "A couple of hundred, you mean, General!"

"What for?"

"Why, to sur—raound them—there—Indians." The regulations of the court room considerably hampered Mr. Cadwaller's fluency of speech.

"It is not necessary at all, Mr. Cadwaller. Besides, we have only some eighty men all told at this post. Our whole force in the territories is less than five hundred men."

"Five hundred men! You mean for this State, General—Alberta?"

"No, Sir. For all Western Canada. All west of Manitoba."

"How much territory do you cover?" enquired the astonished Mr. Cadwaller.

"We regularly patrol some three hundred thousand square miles, besides taking an occasional expedition into the far north."

"And how many Indians?"

"About the same number as you have, I imagine, in Montana and Dakota. In Alberta, about nine thousand."

"And less than five hundred police! Say, General, I take off my hat. Ten thousand Indians! By the holy poker! And five hundred police! How in Cain do you keep down the devils?"

"We don't try to keep them down. We try to take care of them."

"Guess you've hit it," said Mr. Raimes, dexterously squirting out of the door.

"Jeerupiter! Say, General, some day they'll massacree yuh sure!" said Mr. Cadwaller, a note of anxiety in his voice.

"Oh, no, they are a very good lot on the whole."

"Good! We've got a lot of good Indians too, but they're all under graound. Five hundred men! Jee-

rupiter! Say, Sligh, how many soldiers does Uncle
Sam have on this job?"

"Well, I can't say altogether, but in Montana and
Dakota I happen to know we have about four thousand
regulars.

"Say, figger that out, will yuh?" continued Mr. Cadwaller. "Allowed four times the territory, about the
same number of Indians and about one-eighth the number of police. Say, General, I take off my hat again.
Put it there! You Canucks have got the trick sure!"

"Easier to care for 'em than kill 'em, I guess," said
Mr. Raimes casually.

"But, say, General," continued Mr. Cadwaller, "you
ain't goin' to send for them hosses with no three men?"

"I'm afraid we cannot spare any more."

"Jeerupiter, General!" exclaimed Mr. Cadwaller. "I'll
wait outside the reserve till this picnic's over. Say,
General, let's have twenty-five men at least."

"What do you say, Inspector Dickson? Will two men
be sufficient?"

"We'll try, Sir," replied the Inspector.

"How soon can you be ready?"

"In a quarter of an hour."

"Jeerupiter!" muttered Mr. Cadwaller to himseli, as
he followed the Inspector out of the room.

"I say, Commissioner, will you let me in on this
thing?" said Cameron.

"Do you mean that you want to join the force?" enquired the Commissioner, letting his eye run approv-
ingly up and down Cameron's figure.

"There is McIvor, Sir—" began Cameron.

"Oh, I could fix that all right," replied the Commissioner. "We want men, and we want men like you. We
have no vacancy among the officers, but you could en-

list as a constable and there is always opportunity to advance."

"It is a great service!" exclaimed Cameron. "I'd like awfully to join."

"Very well," said the Commissioner promptly, "we will take you. You are physically sound, wind, limb, eye-sight, and so forth?"

"As far as I know, perfectly fit," replied Cameron.

Once more Inspector Dickson was summoned.

"Inspector Dickson, Mr. Cameron wishes to join the force. We will have his application taken and filled in later, and we will waive examination for the present. Will you administer the oath?"

"Cameron, stand up!" commanded the Inspector sharply.

With a little thrill at his heart Cameron stood up, took the Bible in his hand and repeated after the Inspector the words of the oath,

"I, Allan Cameron, solemnly swear that I will faithfully, diligently, and impartially execute and perform the duties required of me as a member of the North West Mounted Police Force, and will well and truly obey and perform all lawful orders and instructions which I shall receive as such, without fear, favour, or affection of or toward any person. So help me, God."

"Now then, Cameron, I congratulate you upon your new profession. The Inspector will see about your outfit and later you will receive instructions as to your duties. Meantime, take him along with you, Inspector, and get those horses."

It was a somewhat irregular mode of procedure, but men were sorely needed at the Macleod post and the Commissioner had an eye that took in not only the lines of a man's figure but the qualities of his soul.

"That chap will make good, or I am greatly mistaken," he said to the Inspector as Cameron went off with the orderly to select his uniform.

"Well set up chap," said the Inspector. "We'll try him out to-night."

"Come now, don't kill him. Remember, other men have something else in them besides whalebone and steel, if you have not."

In half an hour the Inspector, Sergeant Crisp and Cameron, with the three American citizens, were on their way to the Blood reserve.

Cameron had been given a horse from the stable.

All afternoon and late into the evening they rode, then camped and were early upon the trail the following morning. Cameron was half dead with the fatigue from his experiences of the past week, but he would have died rather than have hinted at weariness. He was not a little comforted to notice that Sergeant Crisp, too, was showing signs of distress, while District Attorney Sligh was evidently in the last stages of exhaustion. Even the steel and whalebone combination that constituted the frame of the Inspector appeared to show some slight signs of wear; but all feeling of weariness vanished when the Inspector, who was in the lead, halted at the edge of a wide sweeping valley and, pointing far ahead, said, "The Blood reserve. Their camp lies just beyond that bluff."

"Say, Inspector, hold up!" cried Mr. Cadwaller as the Inspector set off again. "Ain't yuh goin' to sneak up on 'em like?"

"Sneak up on them? No, of course not," said the Inspector curtly. "We shall ride right in."

"Say, Raimes," said Mr. Cadwaller, "a hole would be a blame nice thing to find just now."

"Do you think there will be any trouble?" enquired Mr. Hiram Sligh of Sergeant Crisp.

"Trouble? Perhaps so," replied Crisp, as if to him it were a matter of perfect indifference.

"We'll never git them hosses," said Raimes. "But we've got to stay with the chief, I guess."

And so they followed Inspector Dickson down into the valley, where in the distance could be seen a number of horses and cattle grazing. They had not ridden far along the valley bottom when Mr. Cadwaller spurred up upon the Inspector and called out excitedly,

"I say, Inspector, them's our hosses right there. Say, let's run 'em off."

"Can you pick them out?" enquired the Inspector, turning in his saddle.

"Every last one!" said Raimes.

"Very well, cut them out and get them into a bunch," said the Inspector. "I see there are some Indians herding them apparently. Pay no attention to them, but go right along with your work."

"There's one of 'em off to give tongue!" cried Mr. Cadwaller excitedly. "Bring him down, Inspector! Bring him down! Quick! Here, let me have your rifle!" Hurriedly he snatched at the Inspector's carbine.

"Stop!" cried the Inspector in sharp command. "Now, attention! We are on a somewhat delicate business. A mistake might bring disaster. I am in command of this party and I must have absolute and prompt obedience. Mr. Cadwaller, it will be at your peril that you make any such move again. Let no man draw a gun until ordered by me! Now, then, cut out those horses and bunch them together!"

"Jeerupiter! He's a hull brigade himself," said Mr.

Cadwaller in an undertone, dropping back beside Mr. Sligh. "Waal, here goes for the bunch."

But though both Mr. Cadwaller and Mr. Raimes, as well as Sergeant Crisp and the Inspector, were expert cattle men, it took some little time and very considerable manœuvering to get the stolen horses bunched together and separated from the rest of the animals grazing in the valley, and by the time this was accomplished Indian riders had appeared on every side, gradually closing in upon the party. It was clearly impossible to drive off the bunch through that gradually narrowing cordon of mounted Indians without trouble.

"Now, what's to be done?" said Mr. Cadwaller, nervously addressing the Inspector.

"Forward!" cried the Inspector in a loud voice. "Towards the corral ahead there!"

This movement nonplussed the Indians and in silence they fell in behind the party who, going before, finally succeeded in driving the bunch of horses into the corral.

"Sergeant Crisp, you and Constable Cameron remain here on guard. I shall go and find the Chief. Here," he continued, addressing a young Indian brave who had ridden up quite close to the gate of the corral, "lead me to your Chief, Red Crow!"

The absence alike of all hesitation or fear, and of all bluster in his tone and bearing, apparently impressed the young brave, for he wheeled his pony and set off immediately at a gallop, followed by the Inspector at a more moderate pace.

Quickly the Indians gathered about the corral and the group at its gate. With every passing minute their numbers increased, and as their numbers increased so did the violence of their demonstration. The three

Americans were placed next the corral, Sergeant Crisp and Cameron being between them and the excited Indians. Cameron had seen Indians before about the trading posts. A shy, suspicious, and subdued lot of creatures they had seemed to him. But these were men of another breed, with their lean, lithe, muscular figures, their clean, copper skins, their wild fierce eyes, their haughty bearing. Those others were poor beggars seeking permission to exist; these were men, proud, fearless, and free.

"Jove, what a team one could pick out of the bunch!" said Cameron to himself, as his eye fell upon the clean bare limbs and observed their graceful motions. But to the Americans they were a hateful and fearsome sight. Indians with them were never anything but a menace to be held in check, or a nuisance to be got rid of.

Louder and louder grew the yells and wilder the gesticulations as the savages worked themselves up into a fury. Suddenly, through the yelling, careering, gesticulating crowd of Indians a young brave came tearing at full gallop and, thrusting his pony close up to the Sergeant's, stuck his face into the officer's and uttered a terrific war whoop. Not a line of the Sergeant's face nor a muscle of his body moved except that the near spur slightly touched his horse's flank and the fingers tightened almost imperceptibly upon the bridle rein. Like a flash of light the Sergeant's horse wheeled and with a fierce squeal let fly two wicked heels hard upon the pony's ribs. In sheer terror and surprise the little beast bolted, throwing his rider over his neck and finally to the ground. Immediately a shout of jeering laughter rose from the crowd, who greatly enjoyed their comrade's discomfiture. Except that the Sergeant's face wore a look of pleased surprise, he simply maintained his attitude of calm indifference. No other Indian, however, appeared ready to repeat the performance of the young brave.

At length the Inspector appeared, followed by the Chief, Red Crow.

"Tell your people to go away!" said the Inspector as they reached the corral. "They are making too much noise."

Red Crow addressed his braves at some length.

"Open the corral," ordered the Inspector, "and get those horses out on the trail."

For a few moments there was silence. Then, as the Indians perceived the purpose of the police, on every side there rose wild yells of protest and from every side a rush was made toward the corral. But Sergeant Crisp kept his horse on the move in a series of kicks and plunges that had the effect of keeping clear a wide circle about the corral gate.

"Touch your horse with the spur and hold him up tight," he said quietly to Cameron.

Cameron did so and at once his horse became seemingly as unmanageable as the Sergeant's, plunging, biting, kicking. The Indian ponies could not be induced to approach. The uproar, however, only increased. Guns began to go off, bullets could be heard whistling overhead. Red Crow's voice apparently could make no impression upon the maddened crowd of Indians. A minor Chief, White Horse by name, having whirled in behind the Sergeant, seized hold of Mr. Cadwaller's bridle and began to threaten him with excited gesticulations. Mr. Cadwaller drew his gun.

"Let go that line, you blank blank redskin!" he roared, flourishing his revolver.

In a moment, with a single plunge, the Inspector was at his side and, flinging off the Indian, shouted:

"Put up that gun, Mr. Cadwaller! Quick!" Mr. Cadwaller hesitated. "Sergeant Crisp, arrest that man!" The Inspector's voice rang out like a trumpet. His gun covered Mr. Cadwaller.

"Give me that gun!" said the Sergeant.

Mr. Cadwaller handed over his gun.

"Let him go," said the Inspector to Sergeant Crisp. "He will probably behave."

The Indians had gathered close about the group. White Horse, in the centre, was talking fast and furious and pointing to Mr. Cadwaller.

"Get the bunch off, Sergeant!" said the Inspector quietly. "I will hold them here for a few minutes."

Quietly the Sergeant backed out of the circle, leaving the Inspector and Mr. Cadwaller with White Horse and Red Crow in the midst of the crowding, yelling Indians.

"White Horse say this man steal Bull Back's horses last fall!" shouted Red Crow in the Inspector's ear.

"Too much noise here," said the Inspector, moving toward the Indian camp and away from the corral and drawing the crowd with him. "Tell your people to be quiet, Red Crow. I thought you were the Chief."

Stung by the taunt, Red Crow raised his rifle and fired into the air. Then, standing high in his stirrups, he held up his hand and called out a number of names. Instantly ten men rode to his side. Again Red Crow spoke. The ten men rode out again among the crowd. Immediately the shouting ceased.

"Good!" said the Inspector. "I see my brother is strong. Now, where is Bull Back?"

The Chief called out a name. There was no response.

"Bull Back not here," he said.

"Then listen, my brother," said the Inspector earnestly. "This man," pointing to Mr. Cadwaller, "waits with me at the Fort two days to meet White Horse, Bull Back, and any Indians who know about this man; and what is right will be done. I have spoken. Farewell!" He gave his hand to Chief Red Crow. "My brother knows," he added, "the Police do not lie."

So saying, he wheeled his horse and, with Mr. Cadwaller before him, rode off after the others of the party, who had by this time gone some distance up the trail.

For a few moments hesitation held the crowd, then with a loud cry White Horse galloped up and again seized Mr. Cadwaller's bridle. Instantly the Inspector covered him with his gun.

"Hold up your hands quick!" he said.

The Indian dropped the bridle rein. The Inspector handed his gun to Mr. Cadwaller.

"Don't shoot till I speak or I shoot you!" he said sternly. Mr. Cadwaller took the gun and covered the Indian. In a twinkling White Horse found himself with handcuffs on his wrists and his bridle line attached to the horn of the Inspector's saddle.

"Now give me that gun, Mr. Cadwaller, and here take your own—but wait for the word.   Forward!"

He had not gone a pace till he was surrounded by a score of angry and determined Indians with levelled rifles. For the first time the Inspector hesitated. Through the line of levelled rifles Chief Red Crow rode up and in a grave but determined voice said:

"My brother is wrong. White Horse, chief. My young men not let him go."

"Good!" said the Inspector, promptly making up his mind. "I let him go now. In two days I come again and get him. The Police never lie."

So saying, he released White Horse and without further word, and disregarding the angry looks and levelled rifles, rode slowly off after his party. On the edge of the crowd he met Sergeant Crisp.

"Thought I'd better come back, Sir. It looked rather ugly for a minute," said the Sergeant.

"Ride on," said the Inspector. "We will get our man to-morrow. Steady, Mr. Cadwaller, not too fast." The Inspector slowed his horse down to a walk, which he gradually increased to an easy lope and so brought up with Cameron and the others.

Through the long evening they pressed forward till they came to the Kootenay River, having crossed which they ventured to camp for the night.

After supper the Inspector announced his intention of riding on to the Fort for reinforcements, and gave his instructions to the Sergeant.

"Sergeant Crisp," he said, "you will make an early start and bring in the bunch to-morrow morning. Mr. Cadwaller, you remember you are to remain at the Fort two days so that the charges brought by White Horse may be investigated."

"What?" exclaimed Mr. Cadwaller. "Wait for them blank blank devils? Say, Inspector, you don't mean that?"

"You heard me promise the Indians," said the Inspector.

"Why, yes. Mighty smart, too! But say, you were jest joshing, weren't you?"

"No, Sir," replied the Inspector. "The Police never break a promise to white man or Indian."

Then Mr. Cadwaller cut loose for a few moments. He did not object to waiting any length of time to oblige a friend, but that he should delay his journey to answer the charges of an Indian, variously and picturesquely described, was to him an unthinkable proposition.

"Sergeant Crisp, you will see to this," said the Inspector quietly as he rode away.

Then Mr. Cadwaller began to laugh and continued laughing for several minutes.

"By the holy poker, Sligh!" at last he exclaimed. "It's a joke. It's a regular John Bull joke."

"Yes," said Mr. Sligh, while he cut a comfortable chew from his black plug. "Good joke, too, but not on John. I guess that's how five hundred police hold down —no, take care of—twenty thousand redskins."

And the latest recruit to Her Majesty's North West Mounted Police straightened up till he could feel the collar of his tunic catch him on the back of the neck and was conscious of a little thrill running up his spine as he remembered that he was a member of that same force.

CHAPTER VII

THE MAKING OF BRAVES

IT was to Cameron an extreme satisfaction to ride with some twenty of his comrades behind White Horse, who, handcuffed and with bridle reins tied to those of two troopers, and accompanied by Chief Red Crow, Bull Back, and others of their tribe, made ignominious and crestfallen entry into the Fort next day. It was hardly less of a satisfaction to see Mr. Cadwaller exercise himself considerably in making defence against the charges of Bull Back and his friends. The defence was successful, and the American citizens departed to Lone Pine, Montana, with their recovered horses and with a new and higher regard for both the executive and administrative excellence of Her Majesty's North West Mounted Police officers and men. Chief Red Crow, too, returned to his band with a chastened mind, it having been made clear to him that a chief who could not control his young braves was not the kind of a chief the Great White Mother desired to have in command of her Indian subjects. White Horse, also, after three months sojourn in the cooling solitude of the Police guard room, went back to his people a humbler and a wiser brave.

The horse-stealing, however, went merrily on and the summer of 1884 stands in the records of the Police as the most trying period of their history in the Northwest up to that date. The booming upon the eastern and southern boundaries of Western Canada of the incoming tide of humanity, hungry for land, awakened

ominous echoes in the little primitive settlements of
half-breed people and throughout the reservations of
the wild Indian tribes as well. Everywhere, without
warning and without explanation, the surveyors' flags
and posts made appearance. Wild rumours ran
through the land, till every fluttering flag became the
symbol of dispossession and every gleaming post an
emblem of tyrannous disregard of a people's rights. The
ancient aboriginal inhabitants of the western plains
and woods, too, had their grievances and their fears.
With phenomenal rapidity the buffalo had vanished
from the plains once black with their hundreds of thousands. With the buffalo vanished the Indians' chief
source of support, their food, their clothing, their
shelter, their chief article of barter. Bereft of these and
deprived at the same time of the supreme joy of existence, the chase, bitten with cold, starved with hunger,
fearful of the future, they offered fertile soil for the
seeds of rebellion. A government more than usually
obsessed with stupidity, as all governments become at
times, remained indifferent to appeals, deaf to remon-
strances, blind to danger signals, till through the remote
and isolated settlements of the vast west and among the
tribes of Indians, hunger-bitten and fearful for their
future, a spirit of unrest, of fear, of impatience of all
authority, spread like a secret plague from Prince
Albert to the Crow's Nest and from the Cypress Hills to
Edmonton. A violent recrudescence of whiskey-smuggling, horse-stealing, and cattle-rustling made the work
of administering the law throughout this vast territory
one of exceeding difficulty and one calling for prompti-
tude, wisdom, patience, and courage, of no ordinary
quality. Added to all this, the steady advance of the
railroad into the new country, with its huge construc-

tion camps, in whose wake followed the lawless hordes of whiskey smugglers, tinhorn gamblers, thugs, and harlots, very materially added to the dangers and difficulties of the situation for the Police.

For the first month after enlistment Cameron was kept in close touch with the Fort and spent his hours under the polishing hands of the drill sergeant. From five in the morning till ten at night the day's routine kept him on the grind. Hard work it was, but to Cameron a continuous delight. For the first time in his life he had a job that seemed worth a man's while, and one the mere routine of which delighted his soul. He loved his horse and loved to care for him, and, most of all, loved to ride him. Among his comrades he found congenial spirits, both among the officers and the men. Though discipline was strict, there was an utter absence of anything like a spirit of petty bullying which too often is found in military service; for in the first place the men were in very many cases the equals and sometimes the superiors of the officers both in culture and in breeding, and further, and very specially, the nature of the work was such as to cultivate the spirit of true comradeship. When officer and man ride side by side through rain and shine, through burning heat and frost "Forty below," when they eat out of the same pan and sleep in the same "dug-out," when they stand back to back in the midst of a horde of howling savages, rank comes to mean little and manhood much.

Between Inspector Dickson and Cameron a genuine friendship sprang up; and after his first month was in, Cameron often found himself the comrade of the Inspector in expeditions of special difficulty where there was a call for intelligence and nerve. The reports of these expeditions that stand upon the police record have

as little semblance of the deeds achieved as have stark
and grinning skeletons in the medical student's private
cupboard to the living moving bodies they once were.
The records of these deeds are the bare bones. The flesh
and blood, the life and colour are to be found only in the
memories of those who were concerned in their achievement.

But even in these bony records there are to be seen
frequent entries in which the names of Inspector Dickson
and Constable Cameron stand side by side. For the Inspector was a man upon whom the Commissioner and
the Superintendent delighted to load their more dangerous and delicate cases, and it was upon Cameron when
it was possible that the Inspector's choice for a comrade
fell.

It was such a case as this that held the Commissioner
and Superintendent Crawford in anxious consultation
far into a late September night. When the consultation
was over, Inspector Dickson was called in and the
result of this consultation laid before him.

"We have every reason to believe, as you well know,
Inspector Dickson," said the Commissioner, "that there
is a secret and wide-spread propagandum being carried
on among our Indians, especially among the Piegans,
Bloods, and Blackfeet, with the purpose of organizing
rebellion in connection with the half-breed discontent in
the territories to the east of us. Riel, you know, has
been back for some time and we believe his agents are
busy on every reservation at present. This outbreak of
horse-stealing and whiskey-smuggling in so many parts
of the country at the same time is a mere blind to a
more serious business, the hatching of a very wide conspiracy. We know that the Crees and the Assiniboines
are negotiating with the half-breeds. Big Bear, Beardy,

and Little Pine are keen for a fight.   There is some very powerful and secret influence at work among our Indians here.   We suspect that the ex-Chief of the Bloods, Little Thunder, is the head of this organization.   A very dangerous and very clever Indian he is, as you know.   We have a charge of murder against him already, and if we can arrest him and one or two others it would do much to break up the gang, or at least to hold in check their organization work.   We want you to get quietly after this business, visit all the reservations, obtain all information possible, and when you are ready, strike. You will be quite unhampered in your movements and the whole force will co-operate with you if necessary. We consider this an extremely critical time and we must be prepared.   Take a man with you.   Make your own choice."

"I expect we know the man the Inspector will choose," said Superintendent Crawford with a smile.

"Who is that?" asked the Commissioner.

"Constable Cameron, of course."

"Ah, yes, Cameron.   You remember I predicted he would make good.   He has certainly fulfilled my expectation."

"He is a good man," said the Inspector quietly.

"Oh come, Inspector, you know you consider him the best all-round man at this post," said the Superintendent.

"Well, you see, Sir, he is enthusiastic for the service, he works hard and likes his work."

"Right you are!" exclaimed the Superintendent.   "In the first place, he is the strongest man on the force, then he is a dead shot, a good man with a horse, and has developed an extraordinary gift in tracking, and besides he is perfectly straight."

"Is that right, Inspector?"

"Yes," said the Inspector very quietly, though his eyes were gleaming at the praise of his friend. "He is a good man, very keen, very reliable, and of course afraid of nothing."

The Superintendent laughed quietly.

"You want him then, I suppose?"

"Yes," said the Inspector, "if it could be managed."

"I don't know," said the Commissioner. "That reminds me." He took a letter from the file. "Read that," he said, "second page there. It is a private letter from Superintendent Strong at Calgary."

The Inspector took the letter and read at the place indicated—

"Another thing. The handling of these railroad construction gangs is no easy matter. We are pestered with whiskey-smugglers, gamblers, and prostitutes till we don't know which way to turn. As the work extends into the mountains and as the camps grow in numbers the difficulty of control is very greatly increased. I ought to have my force strengthened. Could you not immediately spare me at least eight or ten good men? I would like that chap Cameron, the man, you know, who caught the half-breed Louis in the Sarcee camp and carried him out on his horse's neck—a very fine bit of work. Inspector Dickson will tell you about him. I had it from him. Could you spare Cameron? I would recommend him at once as a sergeant."

The Inspector handed back the letter without comment.

"Well?" said the Commissioner.

"Cameron would do very well for the work," said the Inspector, "and he deserves promotion."

"What was that Sarcee business, Inspector?" enquired

the Commissioner. "That must have been when I was down east."

"Oh," said the Inspector, "it was a very fine thing indeed of Cameron. Louis 'the Breed' had been working the Bloods. We got on his track and headed him up in the Sarcee camp. He is rather a dangerous character and is related to the Sarcees. We expected trouble in his arrest. We rode in and found the Indians, to the number of a hundred and fifty or more, very considerably excited. They objected strenuously to the arrest of the half-breed. Constable Cameron and I were alone. We had left a party of men further back over the hill. The half-breed brought it upon himself. He was rash enough to make a sudden attack upon Cameron. That is where he made his mistake. Before he knew where he was Cameron slipped from his horse, caught him under the chin with a very nice left-hander that laid him neatly out, swung him on to his horse, and was out of the camp before the Indians knew what had happened."

"The Inspector does not tell you," said Superintendent Crawford, "how he stood off that bunch of Sarcees and held them where they were till Cameron was safe with his man over the hill. But it was a very clever bit of work, and, if I may say it, deserves recognition."

"I should like to give you Cameron if it were possible," said the Commissioner, "but this railroad business is one of great difficulty and Superintendent Strong is not the man to ask for assistance unless he is in pretty desperate straits. An unintelligent or reckless man would be worse than useless."

"How would it do," suggested the Superintendent, "to allow Cameron in the meantime to accompany the Inspector? Then later we might send him to Superintendent Strong."

Reporting this arrangement to Cameron a little later, the Inspector enquired:

"How would you like to have a turn in the mountains? You would find Superintendent Strong a fine officer."

"I desire no change in that regard," replied Cameron. "But, curiously enough, I have a letter this very mail that has a bearing upon this matter. Here it is. It is from an old college friend of mine, Dr. Martin."

The Inspector took the letter and read—

"I have got myself used up, too great devotion to scientific research; hence I am accepting an offer from the railroad people for work in the mountains. I leave in a week. Think of it! The muck and the ruck, the execrable grub and worse drink! I shall have to work my passage on hand cars and doubtless by tie pass. My hands will lose all their polish. However, there may be some fun and likely some good practice. I see they are blowing themselves up at a great rate. Then, too, there is the prospective joy of seeing you, of whom quite wonderful tales have floated east to us. I am told you are in direct line for the position of the High Chief Muck-a-muck of the Force. Look me up in Superintendent Strong's division. I believe he is the bulwark of the Empire in my district.

"A letter from the old burgh across the pond tells me your governor is far from well. Awfully sorry to hear it. It is rough on your sister, to whom, when you write, remember your humble servant.

"I am bringing out two nurses with me, both your devotees. Look out for squalls. If you get shot up see that you select a locality where the medical attendance and nursing are 'A 1.'"

"It would be awfully good to see the old boy," said

Cameron as he took the letter from the Inspector. "He is a decent chap and quite up-to-date in his profession."

"What about the nurses?" enquired the Inspector gravely.

"Oh, I don't know them. Never knew but one. A good bright little soul she was. Saw me through a typhoid trip. Little too clever sometimes," he added, remembering the day when she had taken her fun out of the slow-footed, slow-minded farmer's daughter.

"Well, said the Inspector, "we shall possibly come across them in our round-up. This is rather a big game, a very big game and one worth playing."

A bigger game it turned out than any of the players knew, bigger in its immediate sweep and in its nation-wide issues.

For three months they swept the plains, haunting the reservations at unexpected moments. But though they found not a few horses and cattle whose obliterated brands seemed to warrant confiscation, and though there were signs for the instructed eye of evil doings in many an Indian camp, yet there was nothing connected with the larger game upon which the Inspector of Police could lay his hand.

Among the Bloods there were frequent sun-dances where many braves were made and much firewater drunk with consequent blood-letting. Red Crow deprecated these occurrences, but confessed his powerlessness to prevent the flow of either firewater or of blood. A private conversation with the Inspector left with the Chief some food for thought, however, and resulted in the cropping of the mane of White Horse, of whose comings and goings the Inspector was insistently curious.

On the Blackfeet reservation they ran into a great pow-wow of chiefs from far and near, to which old

Crowfoot invited the representatives of the Great White Mother with impressive cordiality, an invitation, however, which the Inspector, such was his strenuous hunt for stolen horses, was forced regretfully to decline.

"Too smooth, old boy, too smooth!" was the Inspector's comment as they rode off. "There are doings there without doubt. Did you see the Cree and the Assiniboine?"

"I could not pick them out," said Cameron, "but I saw Louis the Breed."

"Ah, you did! He needs another term at the Police sanatarium."

They looked in upon the Sarcees and were relieved to find them frankly hostile. They had not forgotten the last visit of the Inspector and his friend.

"That's better," remarked the Inspector as they left the reservation. "Neither the hostile Indian nor the noisy Indian is dangerous. When he gets smooth and quiet watch him, like old Crowfoot. Sly old boy he is! But he will wait till he sees which way the cat jumps. He is no leader of lost causes."

At Morleyville they breathed a different atmosphere. They felt themselves to be among friends. The hand of the missionary here was upon the helm of government and the spirit of the missionary was the spirit of the tribe.

"Any trouble?" enquired the Inspector.

"We have a great many visitors these days," said the missionary. "And some of our young men don't like hunger, and the offer of a full feast makes sweet music in their ears."

"Any sun-dances?"

"No, no, the sun-dances are all past. Our people are no longer pagans."

"Good man!" was the Inspector's comment as they took up the trail again toward the mountains. "And with quite a sufficient amount of the wisdom of the serpent in his guileless heart. We need not watch the Stonies. Here's a spot at least where religion pays. And a mighty good thing for us just now," added the Inspector. "These Stonies in the old days were perfect devils for fighting. They are a mountain people and for generations kept the passes against all comers. But Macdougall has changed all that."

Leaving the reservation, they came upon the line of the railway.

"There lies my old trail," said Cameron. "And my last camp was only about two miles west of here."

"It was somewhere here that Raven fell in with you?"

"No, some ten miles off the line, down the old Kootenay trail."

"Aha!" said the Inspector. "It might not be a bad idea to beat up that same old trail. It is quite possible that we might fall in with your old friends."

"It would certainly be a great pleasure," replied Cameron, "to conduct Mr. Raven and his Indian friend over this same trail as they did me some nine months ago."

"We will take a chance on it," said the Inspector. "We lose time going back the other way."

Upon the site of McIvor's survey camp they found camped a large construction gang. Between the lines of tents, for the camp was ordered in streets like a city, they rode till they came to the headquarters of the Police, and enquired for the Superintendent. The Superintendent had gone up the line, the Sergeant informed them, following the larger construction gangs. The Sergeant and two men had some fifty miles of line

under patrol, with some ten camps of various kinds on
the line and in the woods, and in addition they had the
care of that double stream of humanity flowing in and
flowing out without ceasing day or night.

As the Inspector stepped inside the Police tent Cameron's attention was arrested by the sign "Hospital"
upon a large double-roofed tent set on a wooden floor
and guyed with more than ordinary care.

"Wonder if old Martin is anywhere about," he said to
himself as he rode across to the open door.

"Is Dr. Martin in?" he enquired of a Chinaman, who
appeared from a tent at the rear.

"Doc Matin go 'way 'long tlain."

"When will he come back?" demanded Cameron.

"Donno. See missy woman."

So saying, he disappeared into the tent while Cameron
waited.

"You wish to see the doctor? He has gone west. Oh!
Why, it—"

Cameron was off his horse, standing with his hat in
one hand, the other outstretched toward the speaker.

"Why! it cannot be!—it is—my patient." The little
nurse had his hand in both of hers. "Oh, you great big
monster soldier! Do you know how fine you look?"

"No," replied Cameron, "but I do know how perfectly
fine you look."

"Well, don't devour me. You look dangerous."

"I should truly love one little bite."

"Oh, Mr. Cameron, stop! You terrible man! Right
in the open street!" The little nurse's cheeks flamed
red as she quickly glanced about her. "What would Dr.
Martin say?"

"Dr. Martin!" Cameron laughed. "Besides, I couldn't
help it."

"Oh, I am so glad!"

"Thank you," said Cameron.

"I mean I am so glad to see you. They told us you would be coming to join us. And now they are gone. What a pity! They will be so disappointed."

"Who, pray, will be thus blighted?"

Oh, the doctor I mean, and—and"—here her eyes danced mischievously—"the other nurse, of course. But you will be going west?"

"No, south, to-day, and in a few minutes. Here comes the Inspector. May I present him?"

The little nurse's snapping eyes glowed with pleasure as they ran over the tall figure of the Inspector and rested upon his fine clean-cut face. The Inspector had just made his farewell to the Sergeant preparatory to an immediate departure, but it was a full half hour before they rose from the dainty tea table where the little nurse had made them afternoon tea from her own dainty tea set.

"It makes me think of home," said the Inspector with a sigh as he bent over the little nurse's hand in gratitude. "My first real afternoon tea in ten years."

"Poor man!" said the nurse. "Come again."

"Ah, if I could!"

"But *you* are coming?" said the little nurse to Cameron as he held her hand in farewell. "I heard the doctor say you were coming and we are quite wild with impatience over it."

Cameron looked at the Inspector.

"I had thought of keeping Cameron at Macleod," said the latter. "But now I can hardly have the heart to do so."

"Oh, you needn't look at me so," said the little nurse with a saucy toss of her head. "He wouldn't bother himself about me, but—but—there is another. No, I won't tell him." And she laughed gaily.

Cameron stood mystified.

"Another? There is old Martin of course, but there is no other?"

The little nurse laughed, this time scornfully.

"Old Martin indeed! He is making a shameless pretence of ignorance, Inspector Dickson."

"Disgraceful bluff I call it," cried the Inspector.

"Who can it be?" said Cameron. "I really don't know any nurse. Of course it can't be—Mandy—Miss Haley?" He laughed a loud laugh almost of derision as he made the suggestion.

"Ah, he's got it!" cried the nurse, clapping her hands. "As if he ever doubted."

"Good Heavens!" exclaimed Cameron. "You don't mean to tell me that Mandy—! What is poor Mandy doing here? Cooking?"

"Cooking indeed!" exclaimed the nurse. "Cooking indeed! Just let the men in this camp, from John here," indicating the Chinaman at the rear of the tent, "to the Sergeant yonder, hear you by the faintest tone indicate anything but adoration for Nurse Haley, and you will need the whole Police Force to deliver you from their fury."

"Good Heavens!" said Cameron in an undertone. "A nurse! With those hands!" He shuddered. "I mean, of course—you know—she's awfully good-hearted and all that, but as a nurse you know she is impossible."

The little nurse laughed long and joyously.

"Oh, this is fun! I wish Dr. Martin could hear you. You forget, Sir, that for a year and a half she has had the benefit of my example and tuition."

"Think of that, Cameron!" murmured the Inspector reproachfully. But Cameron only shook his head.

"Good-bye!" he said. "No, I don't think I pine for mountain scenery. Remember me to Martin and to Man —to Nurse Haley."

"Good-bye!" said the little nurse. "I have a good mind to tell them what you said. I may. Just wait, though. Some day you will very humbly beg my pardon for that slight upon my assistant."

"Slight? Believe me, I mean none. I would be an awful cad if I did. But—well, you know as well as I do that, good soul as Mandy is, she is in many ways impossible."

"Do I?" Again the joyous laugh pealed out. "Well, well, come back and see." And waving her hand she stood to watch them down the trail.

"Jolly little girl," said the Inspector, as they turned from the railway tote road down the coulee into the Kootenay trail. "But who is this other?"

"Oh," said Cameron impatiently, "I feel like a beastly cad. She's the daughter of the farmer where I spent a summer in Ontario, a good simple-hearted girl, but awfully—well—crude, you know. And yet—" Cameron's speech faded into silence, for his memory played a trick upon him, and again he was standing in the orchard on that sunny autumn day looking into a pair of wonderful eyes, and, remembering the eyes, he forgot his speech.

"Ah, yes," said the Inspector. "I understand."

"No, you don't," said Cameron almost rudely. "You would have to see her first. By Jove!" He broke into a laugh. "It is a joke with a vengeance," and relapsed into silence that lasted for some miles.

That night they slept in the old lumber camp, and the

afternoon of the second day found them skirting the Crow's Nest.

"We've had no luck this trip," growled the Inspector, for now they were facing toward home.

"Listen!" said Cameron, pulling up his horse sharply. Down the pass the faraway beat of a drum was heard. It was the steady throb of the tom-tom rising and falling with rhythmic regularity.

"Sun-dance," said the Inspector, as near to excitement as he generally allowed himself. "Piegans."

"Where?" said Cameron.

"In the sun-dance canyon," answered the Inspector. "I believe in my soul we shall see something now. Must be two miles off. Come on."

Though late in December the ground was still unfrozen and the new-made government trail gave soft footing to their horses. And so without fear of detection they loped briskly along till they began to hear rising above the throb of the tom-tom the weird chant of the Indian sun-dancers.

"They are right down in the canyon," said the Inspector. "I know the spot well. We can see them from the top. This is their most sacred place and there is doubtless something big going on."

They left the main trail and, dismounting, led their horses through the scrubby woods, which were thick enough to give them cover without impeding very materially their progress. Within a hundred yards of the top they tied their horses in the thicket and climbed the slight ascent. Crawling on hands and knees to the lip of the canyon, they looked down upon a scene seldom witnessed by the eyes of white men. The canyon was a long narrow valley, whose rocky sides, covered with underbrush, rose some sixty feet from a little plain about fifty yards wide. The little plain was filled with the Indian encampment. At one end a huge fire blazed. At the other, and some fifty yards away, the lodges were set in a semicircle, reaching from side to side of the canyon, and in front of the lodges were a mass of Indian warriors, squatting on their hunkers, beating time, some with tom-toms, others with their hands, to the weirdly monotonous chant, that rose and fell in response to the gesticulations of one who appeared to be their leader. In the centre of the plain stood a post and round this two circles of dancers leaped and swayed. In the outer circle the men, with clubs and rifles in their hands, recited with pantomimic gestures their glorious deeds in the war or in the chase. The inner circle presented a ghastly and horrid spectacle. It was composed of younger men, naked and painted, some of whom were held to the top of the post by long thongs of buffalo hide attached to skewers thrust through the muscles of the breast or back. Upon these thongs they swayed and threw themselves in frantic attempts to break free. With others the skewers were attached by thongs to buffalo skulls, stones or heavy blocks of wood, which, as they danced and leaped, tore at the bleeding flesh. Round and round the post the naked painted Indians leaped, lurching and swaying from side to side in their desperate efforts to drag themselves free from those tearing skewers, while round them from the dancing circle and from the mass of Indians squatted on the ground rose the weird, maddening, savage chant to the accompaniment of their beating hands and throbbing drums.

"This is a big dance," said the Inspector, subduing his voice to an undertone, though in the din there was little chance of his being heard. "See! many braves have been made already," he added, pointing to a place on one side of the fire where a number of forms could be seen, some lying flat, some rolling upon the earth, but all apparently more or less in a stupor.

Madder and madder grew the drums, higher and higher rose the chant. Now and then an older warrior from the squatting circle would fling his blanket aside and, waving his rifle high in the air, would join with loud cries and wild gesticulations the outer circle of dancers.

"It is a big thing this," said the Inspector again. "No squaws, you see, and all in war paint. They mean business. We must get closer."

Cameron gripped him by the arm.

"Look!" he said, pointing to a group of Indians standing at a little distance beyond the lodges. "Little Thunder and Raven!"

"Yes, by Jove!" said the Inspector. "And White Horse, and Louis the Breed and Rainy Cloud of the Blackfeet. A couple of Sarcee chaps, I see, too, some Piegans and Bloods; the rest are Crees and Assiniboines. The whole bunch are here. Jove, what a killing if we could get them! Let's work nearer. Who is that speaking to them?"

"That's Raven," said Cameron, "and I should like to get my hands on him."

"Steady now," said the Inspector. "We must make no mistake."

They worked along the top of the ravine, crawling through the bushes, till they were immediately over the little group of which Raven was the centre. Raven was still speaking, the half-breed interpreting to the Crees and the Assiniboines, and now and then, as the noise from the chanting, drumming Indians subsided, the policemen could catch a few words. After Raven had finished Little Thunder made reply, apparently in stren-

uous opposition. Again Raven spoke and again Little
Thunder made reply. The dispute waxed warm. Little
Thunder's former attitude towards Raven appeared to
be entirely changed. The old subservience was gone.
The Indian stood now as a Chief among his people and
as such was recognized in that company. He spoke with
a haughty pride of conscious strength and authority.
He was striving to bring Raven to his way of thinking.
At length Raven appeared to throw down his ultimatum.

"No!" he cried, and his voice rang up clear through
the din. "You are fools! You are like little partridges
trying to frighten the hunter. The Great White Mother
has soldiers like the leaves of the trees. I know, for I
have seen them. Do not listen to this man!" pointing to
Little Thunder. "Anger has made him mad. The Police
with their big guns will blow you to pieces like this." He
seized a bunch of dead leaves, ground them in his hands
and puffed the fragments in their faces.

The half-breed and Little Thunder were beside themselves with rage. Long and loud they harangued the
group about them. Only a little of their meaning could
the Inspector gather, but enough to let him know that
they were looking down upon a group of conspirators
and that plans for a widespread rebellion were being
laid before them.

Through the harangues of Little Thunder and Louis
the half-breed Raven stood calmly regarding them, his
hands on his hips. He knew well, as did the men watching from above, that all that stood between him and
death were those same two hands and the revolvers in
his belt, whose butts were snugly nosing up to his fingers.
Little Thunder had too often seen those fingers close and
do their deadly work while an eyelid might wink to
venture any hasty move.

"Is that all?" said Raven at last.

Little Thunder made one final appeal, working himself up into a fine frenzy of passion. Then Raven made reply.

"Listen to me!" he said. "It is all folly, mad folly! And besides," and here his voice rang out like a trumpet, "I am for the Queen, God bless her!" His figure straightened up, his hands dropped on the butts of his guns.

"By Jove!" exclaimed Cameron. "Isn't that great?"

"Very fine, indeed," said the Inspector softly. Both men's guns were lined upon the conspirators.

Then the half-breed spoke, shrugging his shoulders in contempt.

"Let heem go. Bah! No good." He spat upon the ground.

Raven stood as he was for a few moments, smiling.

"Good-bye, all," he said. *"Bon jour,* Louis. Let no man move! Let no man move! I never need to shoot at a man twice. Little Thunder knows. And don't follow!" he added. "I shall be waiting behind the rocks."

He slowly backed away from the group, turned in behind a sheltering rock, then swiftly began to climb the rocky sides of the canyon. The moment he was out of sight Little Thunder dodged in behind the ledges, found his rifle, and, making a wide détour, began to climb the side of the ravine at an angle which would cut off Raven's retreat. All this took place in full view of the two watchers above.

"Let's get that devil," said the Inspector. But Cameron was already gone. Swiftly along the lip of the canyon Cameron ran and worked his way down the side till he stood just over the sloping ledge upon which the Indian was crouched and waiting. Along this ledge came the unconscious Raven, softly whistling to himself his favourite air,

"Three cheers for the red, white and blue,"

There was no way of warning him. Three steps more and he would be within range. The Inspector raised his gun and drew a bead upon the crouching Indian.

"Wait!" whispered Cameron. "Don't shoot. It will bring them all down on us." Gathering himself together as he spoke, he vaulted clear over the edge of the rock and dropped fair upon the shoulders of the Indian below, knocking the breath completely out of him and bearing him flat to the rock. Like a flash Cameron's hand was on the Indian's throat so that he could make no outcry. A moment later Raven came in view. Swifter than light his guns were before his face and levelled at Cameron.

"Don't shoot!" said the Inspector quietly from above. "I have you covered."

Perilous as the situation was, Cameron was conscious only of the humourous side of it and burst into a laugh.

"Come here, Raven," he said, "and help me to tie up this fellow." Slowly Raven moved forward.

"Why, by all the gods! If it isn't our long-lost friend, Cameron," he said softly, putting up his guns. "All right, old man," he added, nodding up at the Inspector. "Now, what's all this? What? Little Thunder? So! Then I fancy I owe my life to you, Cameron."

Cameron pointed to Little Thunder's gun. Raven stood looking down upon the Indian, who was recovering his wind and his senses. His face suddenly darkened.

"You treacherous dog! Well, we are now nearly quits. Once you saved my life, now you would have taken it."

Meantime Cameron had handcuffed Little Thunder.

"Up!" he said, prodding him with his revolver. "And not a sound!"

Keeping within cover of the bushes, they scrambled up the ravine side. As they reached the top the Indian with a mighty wrench tore himself from Cameron's grip and plunged into the thicket. Before he had taken a second step, however, the Inspector was upon him like a tiger and bore him to the ground.

"Will you go quietly," said the Inspector, "or must we knock you on the head?" He raised his pistol over the Indian as he spoke.

"I go," grunted the Indian solemnly.

"Come, then," said the Inspector, "we'll give you one chance more. Where's your friend?" he added, looking about him. But Raven was gone.

"I am just as glad," said Cameron, remembering Raven's declaration of allegiance a few moments before. "He wasn't too bad a chap after all. We have this devil anyhow."

"Quick, now," said the Inspector. "We have not a moment to lose. This is an important capture. How the deuce we are to get him to the Fort I don't know."

Through the bushes they hurried their prisoner, threatening him with their guns. When they came to their horses they were amazed to find Little Thunder's pony beside their own and on the Inspector's saddle a slip of paper upon which in the fading light they found inscribed "One good turn deserves another. With Mr. Raven's compliments."

"By Jove, he's a trump!" said the Inspector. "I'd like to get him, but all the same—"

And so they rode off to the Fort.

CHAPTER VIII

NURSE HALEY

THE railway construction had reached the Beaver, and from Laggan westward the construction gangs were strewn along the line in straggling camps, straggling because, though the tents of the railway men were set in orderly precision, the crowds of camp-followers spread themselves hither and thither in disorderly confusion around the outskirts of the camp.

To Cameron, who for a month had been attached to Superintendent Strong's division, the life was full of movement and colour. The two constables and Sergeant Ferry found the duty of keeping order among the navvies, but more especially among the outlaw herd that lay in wait to fling themselves upon their monthly pay like wolves upon a kill, sufficiently arduous to fill to repletion the hours of the day and often of the night.

The hospital tent where the little nurse reigned supreme became to Cameron and to the Sergeant as well a place of refuge and relief. Nurse Haley was in charge further down the line.

The post had just come in and with it a letter for Constable Cameron. It was from Inspector Dickson.

"You will be interested to know," it ran, "that when I returned from Stand Off two days ago I found that Little Thunder, who had been waiting here for his hanging next month, had escaped. How, was a mystery to everybody; but when I learned that a stranger had been at the Fort and had called upon the Superintendent with a tale of horse-stealing, had asked to see Little Thunder

and identified him as undoubtedly the thief, and had left
that same day riding a particularly fine black broncho,
I made a guess that we had been honoured by a visit
from your friend Raven. That guess was confirmed as
correct by a little note which I found waiting me from
this same gentleman explaining Little Thunder's absence
as being due to Raven's unwillingness to see a man go to
the gallows who had once saved his life, but conveying
the assurance that the Indian was leaving the country for
good and would trouble us no more. The Superintendent, who seems to have been captured by your friend's
charm of manner, does not appear to be unduly worried
and holds the opinion that we are well rid of Little
Thunder. But I venture to hold a different opinion,
namely, that we shall yet hear from that Indian brave
before the winter is over.

"Things are quiet on the reservations—altogether too
quiet. The Indians are so exceptionally well behaved
that there is no excuse for arresting any suspects, so
White Horse, Rainy Cloud, those Piegan chaps, and the
rest of them are allowed to wander about at will. The
country is full of Indian and half-breed runners and
nightly pow-wows are the vogue everywhere. Old Crowfoot, I am convinced, is playing a deep game and is
simply waiting the fitting moment to strike.

"How is the little nurse? Present my duty to her and
to that other nurse over whom hangs so deep a mystery."

Cameron folded up his letter and imparted some of the
news to the Sergeant.

"That old Crowfoot is a deep one, sure enough," said
Sergeant Ferry. "It takes our Chief here to bring him
to time. Superintendent Strong has the distinction of
being the only man that ever tamed old Crowfoot. Have
you never heard of it? No? Well, of course, we don't

talk about these things. I was there though, and for cold iron nerve I never saw anything like it. It was a bad half-breed," continued Sergeant Ferry, who, when he found a congenial and safe companion, loved to spin a yarn—"a bad half-breed who had been arrested away down the line, jumped off the train and got away to the Blackfeet. The Commissioner happened to be in Calgary and asked the Superintendent himself to see about the capture of this desperado. So with a couple of us mounted and another driving a buckboard we made for Chief Crowfoot's encampment. It was a black night and raining a steady drizzle. We lay on the edge of the camp for a couple of hours in the rain and then at early dawn we rode in. It took the Superintendent about two minutes to locate Crowfoot's tent, and, leaving us outside, he walked straight in. There was our man, as large as life, in the place of honour beside old Crowfoot. The interpreter, who was scared to death, afterwards told me all about it.

" 'I want this man,' said the Superintendent, hardly waiting to say good-day to the old Chief .

"Crowfoot was right up and ready for a fight. The Superintendent, without ever letting go the half-breed's shoulder, set out the case. Meantime the Indians had gathered in hundreds about the tent outside, all armed, and wild for blood, you bet. I could hear the Superintendent making his statement. All at once he stopped and out he came with his man by the collar, old Crowfoot after him in a fury, but afraid to give the signal of attack. The Indians were keen to get at us, but the old Chief had his men in hand all right.

" 'Don't think you will not get justice,' said the Superintendent. 'You come yourself and see. Here's a pass for you on the railroad and for any three of your men.

But let me warn you that if one hair of my men is touched, it will be a bad day for you, Crowfoot, and for your band.'

"He bundled his man into the buckboard and sent him off. The Superintendent and I waited on horseback in parley with old Crowfoot till the buckboard was over the hill. Such a half hour I never expect to see again. I felt like a man standing over an open keg of gunpowder with a lighted match. Any moment a spark might fall, and then good-bye. And it is this same nerve of his that holds down these camps along this line. Here we are with twenty-five men from Laggan to Beaver keeping order among twenty-five hundred railroad navvies, not a bad lot, and twenty-five hundred others, the scum, the very devil's scum from across the line, and not a murder all these months. Whiskey, of course, but all under cover. I tell you, he's put the fear of death on all that tinhorn bunch that hang around these camps."

"There doesn't seem to be much trouble just now," remarked Cameron.

"Trouble? There may be the biggest kind of trouble any day. Some of these contractors are slow in their pay. They expect men to wait a month or two. That makes them mad and the tinhorn bunch keep stirring up trouble. Might be a strike any time, and then look out. But our Chief will be ready for them. He won't stand any nonsense, you bet."

At this point in the Sergeant's rambling yarn the door was flung open and a man called breathlessly, "Man killed!"

"How is that?" cried the Sergeant, springing to buckle on his belt.

"An accident—car ran away—down the dump."

"They are altogether too flip with those cars," growled the Sergeant. "Come on!"

They ran down the road and toward the railroad dump where they saw a crowd of men. The Sergeant, followed by Cameron, pushed his way through and found a number of navvies frantically tearing at a pile of jagged blocks of rock under which could be seen a human body. It took only a few minutes to remove the rocks and to discover lying there a young man, a mere lad, from whose mangled and bleeding body the life appeared to have fled.

As they stood about him, a huge giant of a man came tearing his way through the crowd, pushing men to right and left.

"Let me see him," he cried, dropping on his knees. "Oh Jack, lad, they have done for you this time."

As he spoke the boy opened his eyes, looked upon the face of his friend, smiled and lay still. Then the Sergeant took command.

"Is the doctor back, does anyone know?"

"No, he's up the line yet. He is coming in on number seven."

"Well, we must get this man to the hospital. Here, you," he said, touching a man on the arm, "run and tell the nurse we are bringing a wounded man."

They improvised a stretcher and laid the mangled form upon it, the blood streaming from wounds in his legs and trickling from his pallid lips.

"Here, two men are better than four. Cameron, you take the head, and you," pointing to Jack's friend, "take his feet. Steady now! I'll just go before. This is a ghastly sight."

At the door of the hospital tent the little nurse met them, pale, but ready for service.

"Oh, my poor boy!" she cried, as she saw the white face. "This way, Sergeant," she added, passing into a smaller tent at one side of the hospital. "Oh, Mr. Cameron, is that you? I am glad you are here."

"Has Nurse Haley come?" enquired the Sergeant.

"Yes, she came in last night, thank goodness. Here, on this table, Sergeant. Oh I wish the doctor were here! Now we must lift him on to this stretcher. Ah, here's Nurse Haley," she added in a relieved voice, and before Cameron was aware, a girl in a nurse's uniform stood by him and appeared quietly to take command.

"Here Sergeant," she said, "two men take his feet." She put her arms under the boy's shoulder and gently and with apparent ease, assisted by the others, lifted him to the table. "A little further—there. Now you are easier, aren't you?" she said, smiling down into the lad's face. Her voice was low and soft and full toned.

"Yes, thank you," said the boy, biting back his groans and with a pitiful attempt at a smile.

"You're fine now, Jack. You'll soon be fixed up now," said his friend.

"Yes Pete, I'm all right, I know."

"Oh, I wish the doctor were here!" groaned the little nurse.

"What about a hypo?" enquired Nurse Haley quietly.

"Yes, yes, give him one."

Cameron's eyes followed the firm, swift-moving fingers as they deftly gave the hypodermic.

"Now we must get this bleeding stopped," she said.

"Get them all out, Sergeant, please," said the little nurse. "One or two will do to help us. You stay, Mr. Cameron."

At the mention of his name Nurse Haley, who had

been busy preparing bandages, dropped them, turned, and for the first time looked Cameron in the face.

"Is it you?" she said softly, and gave him her hand, and, as more than once before, Cameron found himself suddenly forgetting all the world. He was looking into her eyes, blue, deep, wonderful.

It was only for a single moment that his eyes held hers, but to him it seemed as if he had been in some far away land. Without a single word of greeting he allowed her to withdraw her hand. Wonder, and something he could not understand, held him dumb.

For the next half hour he obeyed orders, moving as in a dream, assisting the nurses in their work; and in a dream he went away to his own quarters and thence out and over the dump and along the tote road that led through the straggling shacks and across the river into the forest beyond. But of neither river nor forest was he aware. Before his eyes there floated an illusive vision of masses of fluffy golden hair above a face of radiant purity, of deft fingers moving in swift and sure precision as they wound the white rolls of bandages round bloody and broken flesh, of two round capable arms whose lines suggested strength and beauty, of a firm knit, pliant body that moved with easy sinuous grace, of eyes—but ever at the eyes he paused, forgetting all else, till, recalling himself, he began again, striving to catch and hold that radiant, bewildering, illusive vision. That was a sufficiently maddening process, but to relate that vision of radiant efficient strength and grace to the one he carried of the farmer's daughter with her dun-coloured straggling hair, her muddy complexion, her stupid face, her clumsy, grimy hands and heavy feet, her sloppy figure, was quite impossible. After long and strenuous attempts he gave up the struggle.

"Mandy!" he exclaimed aloud to the forest trees. "That Mandy! What's gone wrong with my eyes, or am I clean off my head? I will go back," he said with sudden resolution, "and take another look."

Straight back he walked to the hospital, but at the door he paused. Why was he there? He had no excuse to offer and without excuse he felt he could not enter. He was acting like a fool. He turned away and once more sought his quarters, disgusted with himself that he should be disturbed by the thought of Mandy Haley or that it should cause him a moment's embarrassment to walk into her presence with or without excuse. determinedly he set himself to regain his one-time attitude of mind toward the girl. With little difficulty he recalled his sense of superiority, his kindly pity, his desire to protect her crude simplicity from those who might do her harm. With a vision of that Mandy before him, the drudge of the farm, the butt of Perkins' jokes, the object of pity for the neighbourhood, he could readily summon up all the feelings he had at one time considered it the correct and rather fine thing to cherish for her. But for this young nurse, so thoroughly furnished and fit, and so obviously able to care for herself, these feelings would not come. Indeed, it made him squirm to remember how in his farewell in the orchard he had held her hand in gentle pity for her foolish and all too evident infatuation for his exalted and superior self. His groan of self-disgust he hastily merged into a cough, for the Sergeant had his eyes upon him. Indeed, the Sergeant did not help his state of mind, for he persisted in executing a continuous fugue of ecstatic praise of Nurse Haley in various keys and tempos, her pluck, her cleverness, her skill, her patience, her jolly laugh, her voice, her eyes. To her eyes the Sergeant ever kept harking back as to the main motif of his fugue, till Cameron would have dearly loved to chuck him and his fugue out of doors.

He was saved from deeds of desperate violence by a voice at the door.

"Letta fo' Mis Camelon!"

"Hello, Cameron!" exclaimed the Sergeant, handing him the note. "You're in luck." There was no mistaking the jealousy in the Sergeant's voice.

"Oh, hang it!" said Cameron as he read the note.

"What's up?"

"Tea!"

"Who?" enquired the Sergeant eagerly.

"Me. I say, you go in my place."

The Sergeant swore at him frankly and earnestly.

"All right John," said Cameron rather ungraciously.

"You come?" enquired the Chinaman.

"Yes, I'll come."

"All lite!" said John, turning away with his message.

"Confound the thing!" growled Cameron.

"Oh come, you needn't put up any bluff with me, you know," said the Sergeant.

But Cameron made no reply. He felt he was not ready for the interview before him. He was distinctly conscious of a feeling of nervous embarrassment, which to a man of experience is disconcerting and annoying. He could not make up his mind as to the attitude which it would be wise and proper for him to assume toward —ah—Nurse Haley. Why not resume relations at the point at which they were broken off in the orchard that September afternoon a year and a half ago? Why not? Mandy was apparently greatly changed, greatly improved. Well, he was delighted at the improvement, and he would frankly let her see his pleasure and

approval. There was no need for embarrassment.
Pshaw! Embarrassment? He felt none.

And yet as he stood at the door of the nurses' tent
he was disquieted to find himself nervously wondering
what in thunder he should talk about. As it turned out
there was no cause for nervousness on this score. The
little nurse and the doctor—Nurse Haley being on duty
—kept the stream of talk rippling and sparkling in an
unbroken flow. Whenever a pause did occur they
began afresh with Cameron and his achievements, of
which they strove to make him talk. But they ever
returned to their own work among the sick and wounded
of the camps, and as often as they touched this theme
the pivot of their talk became Nurse Haley, till Cameron began to suspect design and became wrathful.
They were talking at him and were taking a rise out of
him. He would show them their error. He at once
became brilliant.

In the midst of his scintillation he abruptly paused
and sat listening. Through the tent walls came the
sound of singing, low-toned, rich, penetrating. He
had no need to ask about that voice. In silence they
looked at him and at each other.

> "We're going home, no more to roam,
>   No more to sin and sorrow,
>   No more to wear the brow of care,
>   We're going home to-morrow.
>
> "We're going home; we're going home;
>   We're going home to-morrow."

Softer and softer grew the music. At last the voice
fell silent. Then Nurse Haley appeared, radiant, fresh,
and sweet as a clover field with the morning dew upon
it, but with a light as of another world upon her face.

With the spell of her voice, of her eyes, of her radiant face upon him, Cameron's scintillation faded and snuffed out. He felt like a boy at his first party and enraged at himself for so feeling. How bright she was, how pure her face under the brown gold hair, how dainty the bloom upon her cheek, and that voice of hers, and the firm lithe body with curving lines of budding womanhood, grace in every curve and movement! The Mandy of old faded from his mind. Have I seen you before? And where? And how long ago? And what's happening to me? With these questions he vexed his soul while he strove to keep track of the conversation between the three.

A call from the other tent summoned Nurse Haley.

"Let me go instead," cried the little nurse eagerly. But, light-footed as a deer, Mandy was already gone.

When the tent flap had fallen behind her Cameron pushed back his plate, leaned forward upon the table and, looking the little nurse full in the face, said:

"Now, it's no use carrying this on. What have you done to her?" And the little nurse laughed her brightest and most joyous laugh.

"What has she done to us, you mean."

"No. Come now, take pity on a fellow. I left her—well—you know what. And now—how has this been accomplished?"

"Soul, my boy," said the doctor emphatically, "and the hairdresser and—"

But Cameron ignored him

"Can you tell me?" he said to the nurse.

"Well, as a nurse, is she quite impossible?"

"Oh, spare me," pleaded Cameron. "I acknowledge my sin and my folly is before me. But tell me, how was this miracle wrought?"

"What do you mean exactly? Specify."

"Oh, hang it! Well, beginning at the top, there's her hair."

"Her hair?"

"Yes."

"Then, her complexion—her grace of form—her style —her manner. Oh, confound it! Her hands—every-thing."

"Well," said the little nurse with deliberation, "let's begin at the top. Her hair? A hairdresser explains that. Her complexion? A little treatment, massage, with some help from the doctor. Her hands? Again treatment and release from brutalising work. Her figure? Well, you know, that depends, though we don't acknowledge it always, to a certain extent on—well— things—and how you put them on."

"Nurse," said the doctor gravely, "you're all off. The transformation is from within and is explained, as I have said, by one word—soul. The soul has been set free, has been allowed to break through. That is all. Why, my dear fellow," continued the doctor with rising enthusiasm, "when that girl came to us we were in despair; and for three months she kept us there, pur-suing us, hounding us with questions. Never saw any-thing like it. One telling was enough though. Her eyes were everywhere, her ears open to every hint, but it was her soul, like a bird imprisoned and beating for the open air. The explanation is, as I have said just now, soul—intense, flaming, unquenchable soul—and, I must say it, the dressmaker, the hairdresser, and the rest directed by our young friend here," pointing to the little nurse. "Why, she had us all on the job. We all became devotees of the Haley Cult."

"No," said the nurse, "it was herself."

"Isn't that what I have been telling you?" said the doctor impatiently. "Soul—soul—soul! A soul somehow on fire."

And with that Cameron had to be content.

Yes, a soul it was, at one time dormant and enwrapped within its coarse integument. Now, touched into life by some divine fire, it had through its own subtle power transformed that coarse integument into its own pure gold. What was that fire? What divine touch had kindled it? And, more important still, was that fire still aglow, or, having done its work, had it for lack of food flickered and died out? With these questions Cameron vexed himself for many days, nor found an answer.

CHAPTER IX

"CORPORAL" CAMERON

JACK GREEN did not die. Every morning for a fortnight Constable Cameron felt it to be his duty to make enquiry—the Sergeant, it may be added—performing the same duty with equal diligence in the afternoon, and every day the balance, which trembled evenly for some time between hope and fear, continued to dip more and more decidedly toward the former.

"He's going to live, I believe," said Dr. Martin one day. "And he owes it to the nurse." The doctor's devotion to and admiration for Nurse Haley began to appear to Cameron unnecessarily pronounced. "She simply would not let him go!" continued the doctor. "She nursed him, sang to him her old 'Come all ye' songs and Methodist hymns, she spun him barnyard yarns and orchard idyls, and always 'continued in our next,' till the chap simply couldn't croak for wanting to hear the next."

At times Cameron caught through the tent walls snatches of those songs and yarns and idyls, at times he caught momentary glimpses of the bright young girl who was pouring the vigour of her life into the lad fighting for his own, but these snatches and glimpses only exasperated him. There was no opportunity for any lengthened and undisturbed converse, for on the one hand the hospital service was exacting beyond the strength of doctor and nurses, and on the other there was serious trouble for Superintendent Strong and his men in the camps along the line, for a general strike had been declared in all the camps and no one knew at what minute it might flare up into a fierce riot.

It was indeed exasperating to Cameron. The relations between himself and Nurse Haley were unsatisfactory, entirely unsatisfactory. It was clearly his duty—indeed he owed it to her and to himself—to arrive at some understanding, to establish their relations upon a proper and reasonable basis. He was at very considerable pains to make it clear, not only to the Sergeant, but to the cheerful little nurse and to the doctor as well, that as her oldest friend in the country it was incumbent upon him to exercise a sort of kindly protectorate over Nurse Haley. In this it is to be feared he was only partially successful. The Sergeant was obviously and gloomily incredulous of the purity of his motives, the little nurse arched her eyebrows and smiled in a most annoying manner, while the doctor pendulated between good-humoured tolerance and mild sarcasm. It added not a little to Cameron's mental disquiet that he was quite unable to understand himself; indeed, through these days he was engaged in conducting a bit of psychological research, with his own mind as laboratory and his mental phenomena as the *materia* for his investigation. It was a most difficult and delicate study and one demanding both leisure and calm—and Cameron had neither. The brief minutes he could snatch from Her Majesty's service were necessarily given to his friends in the hospital and as to the philosophic calm necessary to research work, a glimpse through the door of Nurse Haley's golden head bending over a sick man's cot, a snatch of song in the deep mellow tones of her voice, a touch of her strong firm hand, a quiet steady look from her deep, deep eyes—any one of

these was sufficient to scatter all his philosophic deter-
minings to the winds and leave his soul a chaos of
confused emotions.

Small wonder, then, that twenty times a day he cursed
the luck that had transferred him from the compara-
tively peaceful environment of the Police Post at Fort
Macleod to the maddening whirl of conflicting desires
and duties attendant upon the Service in the railroad
construction camps. A letter from his friend Inspector
Dickson accentuated the contrast.

"Great doings, my boy," wrote the Inspector, evidently under the spell of overmastering excitement.
"We have Little Thunder again in the toils, this time
to stay, and we owe this capture to your friend Raven.
A week ago Mr. Raven coolly walked into the Fort and
asked for the Superintendent. I was down at stables
at the time. As he was coming out I ran into him and
immediately shouted 'Hands up!'

" 'Ah, Mr. Inspector,' said my gentleman, as cool as
ice, 'delighted to see you again.'

" 'Stand where you are!' I said, and knowing my man
and determined to take no chances, I ordered two constables to arrest him. At this the Superintendent appeared.

" 'Ah, Inspector,' he said, 'there is evidently some
mistake here.'

" 'There is no mistake, Superintendent,' I replied.
'I know this man. He is wanted on a serious charge.'

" 'Kindly step this way, Mr. Raven,' said the Superintendent, 'and you, Inspector. I have something of
importance to say to you.'

"And, by Jove, it was important. Little Thunder
had broken his pledge to Raven to quit the rebellion
business and had perfected a plan for a simultaneous

rising of Blackfeet, Bloods, Piegans, and Sarcees next month. Raven had stumbled upon this and had deliberately put himself in the power of the Police to bring this information. 'I am not quite prepared,' he said, 'to hand over this country to a lot of bally half-breeds and bloody savages.' Together the Superintendent and he had perfected a plan for the capture of the heads of the conspiracy.

"'As to that little matter of which you were thinking, Inspector Dickson,' said my Chief, 'I think if you remember, we have no definite charge laid against Mr. Raven, who has given us, by the way, very valuable information upon which we must immediately act. We are also to have Mr. Raven's assistance.'

"Well, we had a glorious hunt, and by Jove, that man Raven is a wonder. He brought us right to the bunch, walked in on them, cool and quiet, pulled two guns and held them till we all got in place. There will be no rebellion among these tribes this year, I am confident."

And though it does not appear in the records it is none the less true that to the influence of Missionary Macdougall among the Stonies and to the vigilance of the North West Mounted Police was it due that during the Rebellion of '85 Canada was spared the unspeakable horrors of an Indian war.

It was this letter that deepened the shadow upon Cameron's face and sharpened the edge on his voice as he looked in upon his hospital friends one bright winter morning.

"You are quite unbearable!" said the little nurse after she had listened to his grumbling for a few minutes. "And you are spoiling us all."

"Spoiling you all?"

"Yes, especially me, and—Nurse Haley."

"Nurse Haley?"

"Yes. You are disturbing her peace of mind."

"Disturbing her? Me?"

A certain satisfaction crept into Cameron's voice. Nothing is so calculated to restore the poise of the male mind as a consciousness of power to disturb the equilibrium of one of the imperious sex.

"And you must not do it!" continued the little nurse. "She has far too much to bear now."

"And haven't I been just telling you that?" said Cameron savagely. "She never gets off. Night and day she is on the job. I tell you, I won't—it should not be allowed." Cameron was conscious of a fine glow of fraternal interest in this young girl. "For instance, a day like this! Look at these white mountains, and that glorious sky, and this wonderful air, and not a breath of wind! What a day for a walk! It would do her—it would do you all a world of good."

"Wait!" cried the little nurse, who had been on duty all night. "I'll tell her what you say."

Apparently it took some telling, for it was a full precious quarter of an hour before they appeared again.

"There, now, you see the effect of your authority. She would not budge for me, but—well—there she is! Look at her!"

There was no need for this injunction. Cameron's eyes were already fastened upon her. And she was worth any man's while to look at in her tramping costume of toque and blanket coat. Tall, she looked, beside the little nurse, lithe and strong, her close-fitting Hudson Bay blanket coat revealing the swelling lines of her budding womanhood. The dainty white toque perched upon the masses of gold-brown hair accentuated the girlish freshness of her face. At the nurse's words she turned her eyes upon Cameron and upon her face, pale with long night watches, a faint red appeared. But her eyes were quiet and steady and kind; too quiet and too kind for Cameron, who was looking for other signals. There was no sign of disturbance in that face.

"Come on!" he said impatiently. "We have only one hour."

"Oh, what a glorious day!" cried Nurse Haley, drawing a deep breath and striding out like a man to keep pace with Cameron. "And how good of you to spare me the time!"

"I have been trying to get you alone for the last two weeks," said Cameron.

"Two weeks?"

"Yes, for a month! I wanted to talk to you."

"To talk with me? About what?"

"About—well—about everything—about yourself."

"Me?"

"Yes. I don't understand you. You have changed so tremendously."

"Oh," exclaimed the girl, "I am so glad you have noticed that! Have I changed much?"

"Much? I should say so! I find myself wondering if you are the Mandy I used to know at all."

"Oh," she exclaimed, "I am so glad! You see, I needed to change so much."

"But how has it happened?" exclaimed Cameron. "It is a miracle to me."

"How a miracle?"

For a few moments they walked on in silence, the tote road leading them into the forest. After a time the nurse said softly,

"It was you who began it."

"I?"

"Yes, you—and then the nurse. Oh, I can never repay her! The day that you left—that was a dreadful day. The world was all black. I could not have lived, I think, many days like that. I had to go into town and I couldn't help going to her. Oh, how good she was to me that day! how good! She understood, she understood at once. She made me come for a week to her, and then for altogether. That was the beginning; then I began to see how foolish I had been."

"Foolish?"

"Yes, wildly foolish! I was like a mad thing, but I did not know then, and I could not help it."

"Help what?"

"Oh, everything! But the nurse showed me—she showed me—"

"Showed you?"

"Showed me how to take care of myself—to take care of my body—of my dress—of my hair. Oh, I remember well," she said with a bright little laugh, "I remember that hair-dresser. Then the doctor came and gave me books and made me read and study—and then I began to see. Oh, it was like a fire—a burning fire within me. And the doctor was good to me, so very patient, till I began to love my profession; to love it at first for myself, and then for others. How good they all were to me those days!—the nurses in the hospital, the doctors, the students—everyone seemed to be kind; but above them all my own nurse here and my own doctor."

In hurried eager speech she poured forth her heart as if anxious to finish her tale—her voice, her eyes, her face all eloquent of the intense emotion that filled her soul.

"It is wonderful!" said Cameron.

"Yes," she replied, "wonderful indeed! And I wanted to see you and have you see me," she continued, still hurrying her speech, "for I could not bear that you should remember me as I was those dreadful days; and I am so glad that you—you—are pleased!" The appeal in her voice and in her eyes roused in Cameron an overwhelming tide of passion.

"Pleased!" he cried. "Pleased! Great Heavens, Mandy! You are wonderful! Don't you know that?"

"No," she said thoughtfully; "but," she drew a long breath, "I like to hear you say it. That is all I want. You see I owe it all to you." The face she turned to him so innocently happy might have been a child's.

"Mandy," cried Cameron, stopping short in his walk, "you—I—!" That frank childlike look in her eyes checked his hot words. But there was no need for words; his eyes spoke for his faltering lips. A look of fear leaped to her eyes, a flow of red blood to her cheeks; then she stood, white, trembling and silent.

"I am tired, I think," she said after a moment's silence, "we will go back."

"Yes, you are tired," said Cameron angrily. "You are tired to death. Mandy, you need some one to take care of you. I wish you would let me." They were now walking back toward the town.

"They are all good to me; they are all kind to me." Her voice was quiet and steady. She had gained control of herself again. "Why, even John the Chinaman," she added with a laugh, "spoils me. Oh, no harm can come to me—I have no fear!"

"But," said Cameron, "I—I want to take care of you, Mandy. I want the right to take care of you, always."

"I know, I know," she said kindly. "You are so good; you were always so good; but I need no one."

Cameron glanced at the lithe, strong, upright figure striding along beside him with easy grace; and the truth came to him in swift and painful revelation.

"You are right," he said as if to himself. "You need no one, and you don't need me."

"But," she cried eagerly, "it was good of you all the same."

"Good!" he said impatiently. "Good! Nonsense! I tell you, Mandy, I want you, I want you. Do you understand? I want to marry you."

"Oh, don't say that!" she cried, stopping short, her voice disturbed, but kindly, gentle and strong. "Don't say that," she repeated, "for, of course, that is impossible."

"Impossible!" he exclaimed angrily.

"Yes," she said, her voice still quiet and steady, "quite impossible. But I love you for saying it, oh—," she suddenly caught her breath. "Oh, I love you for saying it." Then pointing up the road she cried, "Look! Some one for you, I am sure." A horseman was galloping swiftly towards them.

"Oh hang it all!" said Cameron. "What the deuce does he want now?"

"We must talk this out again, Mandy," he said.

"No, no!" she cried, "never again. Please don't, ever again; I could not bear it. But I shall always remember, and—I am so glad." As she spoke, her hands, with her old motion, went to her heart.

"Oh the deuce take it!" said Cameron as the Sergeant flung his horse back on his heels at their side. "What does he want?"

"Constable Cameron," said the Sergeant in a voice

of sharp command, "there's a row on. Constable Scott has been very badly handled in trying to make an arrest. You are to report at once for duty."

"All right, Sir," said Cameron, "I shall return immediately."

The Sergeant wheeled and was gone.

"You must go!" cried Mandy, quick fear springing into her eyes.

"Yes," said Cameron, "at once. Come, I shall take you home."

"No, never mind me!" she cried. "Go! Go! I can take care of myself. I shall follow." Her voice rang out strong and clear; she was herself once more.

"You are the right sort, Mandy," cried Cameron, taking her hand. "Good bye!"

"Good bye!" she replied, her face suddenly pale and her lips beginning to quiver. "I shall always remember—I—shall—always be glad for—what you said today."

Cameron stood looking at her for a moment somewhat uncertainly, then,

"Good bye!" he said abruptly, and, turning, went at the double towards his quarters.

The strikers had indeed broken loose, supported by the ruffianly horde of camp followers who were egging them on to violence and destruction of property. At present they were wild with triumph over the fact that they had rescued one of their leaders, big Joe Coyle, from Constable Scott. It was an exceedingly dangerous situation, for the riot might easily spread from camp to camp. Bruised and bloody, Constable Scott reported to Superintendent Strong lying upon his sick bed.

"Sergeant," said the Superintendent, "take Constables Cameron and Scott, arrest that man at once and bring him here!"

In the village they found between eight hundred and a thousand men, many of them crazed with bad whiskey, some armed with knives and some with guns, and all ready for blood. Big Joe Coyle they found in the saloon. Pushing his way through, the Sergeant seized his man by the collar.

"Come along, I want you!" he said, dragging him to the open door.

"Shut that there door, Hep!" drawled a man with a goatee and a moustache dyed glossy black.

"All right, Bill!" shouted the man called Hep, springing to the door; but before he could make it Cameron had him by the collar.

"Hold on, Hep!" he said, "not so fast."

For answer Hep struck hard at him, and the crowd of men threw themselves at Cameron and between him and the door. Constable Scott, who also had his hand upon the prisoner, drew his revolver and looked towards the Sergeant who was struggling in the grasp of three or four ruffians.

"No!" shouted the Sergeant above the uproar. "Don't shoot—we have no orders! Let him go!"

"Go on!" he said savagely, giving his prisoner a final shake. "We will come back for you."

There was a loud chorus of derisive cheers. The crowd opened and allowed the Sergeant and constables to pass out. Taking his place at the saloon door with Constable Scott, the Sergeant sent Cameron to report and ask for further orders.

"Ask if we have orders to shoot," said the Sergeant.

Cameron found the Superintendent hardly able to lift his head and made his report.

"The saloon is filled with men who oppose the arrest, Sir. What are your orders?"

"My orders are, Bring that man here, and at once!"

"Have we instructions to shoot?"

"Shoot!" cried the Superintendent, lifting himself on his elbow. "Bring that man if you have to shoot every man in the saloon!"

"Very well, Sir, we will bring him," said Cameron, departing on a run.

At the door of the saloon he found the Sergeant and Constable white hot under the jeers and taunts of the half drunken gang gathered about them.

"What are the orders, Constable Cameron?" enquired the Sergeant in a loud voice.

"The orders are, Shoot every man in the saloon if necessary!" shouted Cameron.

"Revolvers!" commanded the Sergeant. "Constable Cameron, hold the door! Constable Scott, follow me!"

At the door stood the man named Hep, evidently keeping guard.

"Want in?" he said with a grin.

For answer, Cameron gripped his collar, with one fierce jerk lifted him clear out of the door to the platform, and then, putting his body into it, heaved him with a mighty swing far into the crowd below, bringing two or three men to the ground with the impact of his body.

"Come here, man!" cried Cameron again, seizing a second man who stood near the door and flinging him clear off the platform after the unlucky Hep.

Speedily the crowd about the door gave back, and before they were aware the Sergeant and Constable Scott appeared with big Joe Coyle between them.

"Take him!" said the Sergeant to Cameron.

Cameron seized him by the collar.

"Come here!" he said, and, clearing the platform in a spring, he brought his prisoner in a heap with him. "Get up!" he roared at him, jerking him to his feet as if he had been a child.

"Let him go!" shouted the man with the goatee, named Bill, rushing up.

"Take that, then," said Cameron, giving him a swift half-arm jab on the jaw, "and I'll come back for you again," he added, as the man fell back into the arms of his friends.

"Forward!" said the Sergeant, falling in with Constable Scott behind Cameron and facing the crowd with drawn revolvers. The swift fierceness of the attack seemed to paralyse the senses of the crowd.

"Come on, boys!" yelled the goatee man, bloody and savage with Cameron's blow. "Don't let the blank blank blank rattle you like a lot of blank blank chickens. Come on!"

At once rose a roar from eight hundred throats like nothing human in its sound, and the crowd began to press close upon the Police. But the revolvers had an ugly appearance to those in front looking into their little black throats.

"Aw, come on!" yelled a man half drunk, running with a lurch upon the Sergeant.

"Crack!" went the Sergeant's revolver, and the man dropped with a bullet through his shoulder.

"Next man," shouted the Sergeant, "I shall kill!"

The crowd gave back and gathered round the wounded man. A stream lay in the path of the Police, crossed by a little bridge.

"Hurry!" said the Sergeant, "let's make the bridge before they come again." But before they could make the bridge the crowd had recovered from their momentary panic and, with wild oaths and yells and brandishing knives and guns, came on with a rush, led by goatee Bill.

Already the prisoner was half way across the bridge, the Sergeant and the constable guarding the entrance, when above the din was heard a roar as of some animal enraged. Looking beyond the Police the crowd beheld a fearsome sight. It was the Superintendent himself, hatless, and with uniform in disarray, a sword in one hand, a revolver in the other. Across the bridge he came like a tornado and, standing at the entrance, roared,

"Listen to me, you dogs! The first man who sets foot on this bridge I shall shoot dead, so help me God!"

His towering form, his ferocious appearance and his well-known reputation for utter fearlessness made the crowd pause and, before they could make up their minds to attack that resolute little company headed by their dread commander, the prisoner was safe over the bridge and well up the hill toward the guard room. Half way up the hill the Superintendent met Cameron returning from the disposition of his prisoner.

"There's another man down there, Sir, needs looking after," he said.

"Better let them cool off, Cameron," said the Superintendent.

"I promised I'd go for him, Sir," said Cameron, his face all ablaze for battle.

"Then go for him," said the Superintendent. "Let a couple of you go along—but I am done—just now."

"We will see you up the hill, Sir," said the Sergeant.

"Come on, Scott!" said Cameron, setting off for the village once more.

The crowd had returned from the bridge and the leaders had already sought their favourite resort, the saloon. Straight to the door marched Cameron, followed by Scott. Close to the counter stood goatee Bill, loudly orating, and violently urging the breaking in of the guard room and the release of the prisoner.

"In my country," he yelled, "we'd have that feller out in about six minutes in spite of all the blank blank Police in this blank country. *They* ain't no good. They're scairt to death."

At this point Cameron walked in upon him and laid a compelling grip upon his collar. Instantly Bill reached for his gun, but Cameron, swiftly shifting his grip to his arm, wrenched him sharply about and struck him one blow on the ear. As if held by a hinge, the head fell over on one side and the man slithered to the floor.

"Out of the way!" shouted Cameron, dragging his man with him, but just as he reached the door a heavy glass came singing through the air and caught him on the head. For a moment he staggered, caught hold of the lintel and held himself steady.

"Here, Scott," he cried, "put the bracelets on him."

With revolver drawn Constable Scott sprang to his side.

"Come out!" he said to the goatee man, slipping the handcuffs over his wrists, while Cameron, still clinging to the lintel, was fighting back the faintness that was overpowering him. Seeing his plight, Hep sprang toward him, eager for revenge, but Cameron covering him with his gun held him in check and, with a supreme effort getting command of himself, again stepped towards Hep.

"Now, then," he said between his clenched teeth, "will you come?" So terrible were his voice and look that Hep's courage wilted.

"I'll come, Colonel, I'll come," he said quickly.

"Come then," said Cameron, reaching for him and bringing him forward with a savage jerk.

In three minutes from the time the attack was made both men, thoroughly subdued and handcuffed, were marched off in charge of the constables.

"Hurry, Scott," said Cameron in a low voice to his comrade. "I am nearly in."

With all possible speed they hustled their prisoners along over the bridge and up the hill. At the hospital door, as they passed, Dr. Martin appeared.

"Hello, Cameron!" he cried. "Got him, eh?" Great Cæsar, man, what's up?" he added as Cameron, turning his head, revealed a face and neck bathed in blood. "You are white as a ghost."

"Get me a drink, old chap. I am nearly in," said Cameron in a faint voice.

"Come into my tent here," said the doctor.

"Got to see these prisoners safe first," said Cameron, swaying on his feet.

"Come in, you idiot!" cried the doctor.

"Go in, Cameron," said Constable Scott. "I'll take care of 'em all right," he added, drawing his gun.

"No," said Cameron, still with his hand on goatee Bill's collar. "I'll see them safe first," saying which he swayed drunkenly about and, but for Bill's support, would have fallen.

"Go on!" said Bill good-naturedly. "Don't mind me, I'm good now."

"Come!" said the doctor, supporting him into the tent.

"Forward!" commanded Constable Scott, and marched his prisoners before him up the hill.

The wound on Cameron's head was a ghastly affair, full six inches long, and went to the bone.

"Rather ugly," said the doctor, feeling round the wound. "Nurse!" he called. "Nurse!" The little nurse came running in. "Some water and a sponge!"

There was a cry behind her—low, long, pitiful.

"Oh, what is this?" With a swift movement Nurse Haley was beside the doctor's bed. Cameron, who had been lying with his eyes closed and was ghastly white from loss of blood, opened his eyes and smiled up into the face above him.

"I feel fine—now," he said and closed his eyes again.

"Let me do that," said Nurse Haley with a kind of jealous fierceness, taking the sponge and basin from the little nurse.

Examination revealed nothing more serious, however, than a deep scalp wound and a slight concussion.

"He will be fit enough in a couple of days," said the doctor when the wound was dressed.

Then, pale and haggard as if with long watching, Nurse Haley went to her room there to fight out her lonely fight while Cameron slept.

The day passed in quiet, the little nurse on guard, and the doctor looking in every half hour upon his patient. As evening fell Cameron woke and demanded Nurse Haley. The doctor felt his pulse.

"Send her in!" he said and left the tent.

The rays of the sun setting far down the Pass shone through the walls and filled the tent with a soft radiance. Into this radiance she came, her face pale as of one who has come through conflict, and serene as of one who has conquered, pale and strong and alight, not with the radiance of the setting sun, but with light of a soul that has made the ancient sacrifice of self-effacing love.

"You want me?" she said, her voice low and sweet, but for all her brave serenity tremulous.

"Yes," said Cameron, holding out his arms. "I want you; I want *you*, Mandy."

"Oh," cried the girl, while her hands fluttered to her heart, "don't ask me to go through it again. I am so weak." She stood like a frightened bird poised for flight.

"Come," he said, "I want you."

"You want me? You said you wanted to take care of me," she breathed.

"I was a fool, Mandy; a conceited fool! Now I know what I want—I want—just *you*. Come." Again he lifted his arms.

"Oh, it cannot be," she breathed as if to herself. "Are you sure—sure? I could not bear it if you were not sure."

"Come, dear love," he cried, "with all my heart and soul and body I want you—I want only *you*."

For a single moment longer she stood, her soul searching his through her wonderful eyes. Then with a little sigh she sank into his arms.

"Oh, my darling," she whispered, wreathing her strong young arms around his neck and laying her cheek close to his, "my darling, I thought I had given you up, but how could I have done it?"

At the hospital door the doctor was on guard. A massive figure loomed in the doorway.

"Hello, Superintendent Strong, what on earth are you doing out of bed?"

"Where is he?" said the Superintendent abruptly.

"Who?"

"Corporal Cameron."

"*Corporal* Cameron? Constable Cameron is—"

"Corporal Cameron, I said. I have just had Constable Scott's report and felt I must see him at once."

"Come in, Superintendent! Sit down! I shall enquire if he is resting. Nurse! Nurse! Enquire if Corporal Cameron can be seen."

The little nurse tip-toed into the doctor's tent, lifted the curtain, took one glance and drew swiftly back. This is what her eyes looked upon. A girl's form kneeling by the bed, golden hair mingling with black upon the pillow, two strong arms holding her close and hers wreathed in answering embrace.

"Mr. Cameron I am afraid," she reported, "cannot be seen. He is—I think—he is—engaged."

"Ah!" said the doctor.

"Well," said the Superintendent, "just tell Corporal Cameron for me that I am particularly well pleased with his bearing to-day, and that I hope he will be very soon fit for duty."

"Certainly, Superintendent. Now let me help you up the hill."

"Never mind, here's the Sergeant. Good evening! Very fine thing! Very fine thing indeed! I see rapid promotion in his profession for that young man."

"Inspector, eh?" said the doctor.

"Yes, Sir, I should without hesitation recommend him and should be only too pleased to have him as Inspector in my command."

It was not, however, as Inspector that Corporal Cameron served under the gallant Superintendent, but in another equally honourable capacity did they ride away together one bright April morning a few weeks later, on duty for their Queen and country. But that is another story.

"That message ought to be delivered, nurse," said the doctor thoughtfully.

"But not at once," replied the nurse.

"It is important," urged the doctor.

"Yes, but—there are other things."

"Ah! Other things?"

"Yes, equally—pressing," said the nurse with an undeniably joyous laugh. The doctor looked at her a moment.

"Ah, nurse," he said in a shocked tone, "how often have I deprecated your tendency to—"

"I don't care one bit!" laughed the nurse saucily.

"The message ought to be delivered," insisted the doctor firmly as he moved toward the tent door.

"Well, deliver it then. But wait!" The little nurse ran in before him and called "Nu-u-u-r-s-e Ha-l-ey!"

"All right!" called Cameron from the inside. "Come in!"

"Go on then," said the little nurse to the doctor, "you wanted to."

"'A message from the Superintendent," said the doctor, lifting the curtain and passing in.

"Don't move, Mandy," said Cameron. "Never mind him."

"No, don't, I beg," said the doctor, ignoring what he saw. "A message, an urgent message for—Corporal Cameron!"

"*Corporal* Cameron?" echoed Nurse Haley.

"He distinctly said and repeated it—Corporal Cameron. And the Corporal is to report for duty as speedily as possible."

"He can't go," said Mandy, standing up very straight

with a light in her eyes that the doctor had not seen since that tragic night nearly two years before.

"Can't, eh?" said the doctor. "But the Superintendent says Corporal Cameron is—"

"Corporal Cameron can't go!"

"You—"

"Yes, I forbid it."

"The Corporal is—?"

"Yes," she said proudly, "the Corporal is mine."

"Then," said the doctor emphatically, "of all the lucky chaps it has been my fortune to meet, by all the gods the luckiest of them is this same Corporal Cameron!"

And Cameron, drawing down to him again the girl standing so straight and proud beside him, looked up at his friend and said:

"Yes, old chap, the luckiest man in all the world is that same Corporal Cameron."